DR. SEVIER

DR. SEVIER

BY
GEORGE W. CABLE

Charles Scribner's Sons
New York 〜〜〜 1911

TO MY FRIEND

MARION A. BAKER

CONTENTS.

4 CONTENTS.

DR. SEVIER.

CHAPTER I.

THE DOCTOR.

THE main road to wealth in New Orleans has long
been Carondelet street. There you see the most
alert faces; noses — it seems to one — with more and
sharper edge, and eyes smaller and brighter and with
less distance between them than one notices in other
streets. It is there that the stock and bond brokers
hurry to and fro and run together promiscuously — the
cunning and the simple, the headlong and the wary — at
the four clanging strokes of the Stock Exchange gong.
There rises the tall façade of the Cotton Exchange.
Looking in from the sidewalk as you pass, you see its
main hall, thronged but decorous, the quiet engine-room
of the surrounding city's most far-reaching occupation,
and at the hall's farther end you descry the "Future
Room," and hear the unearthly ramping and bellowing
of the bulls and bears. Up and down the street, on
either hand, are the ship-brokers and insurers, and in the
upper stories foreign consuls among a multitude of lawyers and notaries.

In 1856 this street was just assuming its present

character. The cotton merchants were making it their favorite place of commercial domicile. The open thoroughfare served in lieu of the present exchanges; men made fortunes standing on the curb-stone, and during bank hours the sidewalks were perpetually crowded with cotton factors, buyers, brokers, weighers, reweighers, classers, pickers, pressers, and samplers, and the air was laden with cotton quotations and prognostications.

Number 3½, second floor, front, was the office of Dr. Sevier. This office was convenient to everything. Immediately under its windows lay the sidewalks where congregated the men who, of all in New Orleans, could best afford to pay for being sick, and least desired to die. Canal street, the city's leading artery, was just below, at the near left-hand corner. Beyond it lay the older town, not yet impoverished in those days, — the French quarter. A single square and a half off at the right, and in plain view from the front windows, shone the dazzling white walls of the St. Charles Hotel, where the nabobs of the river plantations came and dwelt with their fair-handed wives in seasons of peculiar anticipation, when it is well to be near the highest medical skill. In the opposite direction a three minutes' quick drive around the upper corner and down Common street carried the Doctor to his ward in the great Charity Hospital, and to the school of medicine, where he filled the chair set apart to the holy ailments of maternity. Thus, as it were, he laid his left hand on the rich and his right on the poor; and he was not left-handed.

Not that his usual attitude was one of benediction. He stood straight up in his austere pure-mindedness, tall, slender, pale, sharp of voice, keen of glance, stern in judgment, aggressive in debate, and fixedly untender everywhere, except — but always except — in the sick chamber. His inner heart was all of flesh; but his demands for the rectitude of mankind pointed out like the muzzles of cannon through the embrasures of his virtues. To demolish evil! — that seemed the finest of aims; and even as a physician, that was, most likely, his motive until later years and a better self-knowledge had taught him that to do good was still finer and better. He waged war — against malady. To fight; to stifle; to cut down; to uproot; to overwhelm, — these were his springs of action. That their results were good proved that his sentiment of benevolence was strong and high; but it was well-nigh shut out of sight by that impatience of evil which is very fine and knightly in youngest manhood, but which we like to see give way to kindlier moods as the earlier heat of the blood begins to pass.

He changed in later years; this was in 1856. To " resist not evil" seemed to him then only a rather feeble sort of knavery. To face it in its nakedness, and to inveigh against it in high places and low, seemed the consummation of all manliness; and manliness was the key-note of his creed. There was no other necessity in this life.

" But a man must live," said one of his kindred, to whom, truth to tell, he had refused assistance.

" No, sir; that is just what he can't do. A man must die! So, while he lives, let him be a man!"

How inharmonious a setting, then, for Dr. Sevier, was 3½ Carondelet street! As he drove, each morning, down to that point, he had to pass through long, irregular files of fellow-beings thronging either sidewalk, — a sadly unchivalric grouping of men whose daily and yearly life was subordinated only and entirely to the getting of wealth, and whose every eager motion was a repetition of the sinister old maxim that " Time is money."

"It's a great deal more, sir; it's life!" the Doctor always retorted.

Among these groups, moreover, were many who were all too well famed for illegitimate fortune. Many occupations connected with the handling of cotton yielded big harvests in perquisites. At every jog of the Doctor's horse, men came to view whose riches were the outcome of semi-respectable larceny. It was a day of reckless operation; much of the commerce that came to New Orleans was simply, as one might say, beached in Carondelet street. The sight used to keep the long, thin, keen-eyed doctor in perpetual indignation.

"Look at the wreckers!" he would say.

It was breakfast at eight, indignation at nine, dyspepsia at ten.

So his setting was not merely inharmonious; it was damaging. He grew sore on the whole matter of money-getting.

"Yes, I have money. But I don't go after it. It comes to me, because I seek and render service for the service's sake. It will come to anybody else the same way; and why should it come any other way?"

He not only had a low regard for the motives of most seekers of wealth; he went further, and fell into much disbelief of poor men's needs. For instance, he looked upon a man's inability to find employment, or upon a poor fellow's run of bad luck, as upon the placarded woes of a hurdy-gurdy beggar.

"If he wants work he will find it. As for begging, it ought to be easier for any true man to starve than to beg."

The sentiment was ungentle, but it came from the bottom of his belief concerning himself, and a longing for moral greatness in all men.

"However," he would add, thrusting his hand into his pocket and bringing out his purse, "I'll help any man to make himself useful. And the sick — well, the sick, as a matter of course. Only I must know what I'm doing."

Have some of us known Want? To have known her — though to love her was impossible — is "a liberal education." The Doctor was learned; but this acquaintanceship, this education, he had never got. Hence his untenderness. Shall we condemn the fault? Yes. And the man? We have not the face. To be *just*, which he never knowingly failed to be, and at the same time to feel tenderly for the unworthy, to deal kindly with the erring, — it is a double grace that hangs not always in easy reach even of the tallest. The Doctor attained to it — but in later years; meantime, this story — which, I believe, had he ever been poor would never have been written.

CHAPTER II.

A YOUNG STRANGER.

IN 1856 New Orleans was in the midst of the darkest
ten years of her history. Yet she was full of new-comers
from all parts of the commercial world, — strangers seek
ing livelihood. The ravages of cholera and yellow-fever,
far from keeping them away, seemed actually to draw
them. In the three years 1853, '54, and '55, the ceme-
teries had received over thirty-five thousand dead; yet
here, in 1856, besides shiploads of European immigrants,
came hundreds of unacclimated youths, from all parts of
the United States, to fill the wide gaps which they
imagined had been made in the ranks of the great export-
ing city's clerking force.

Upon these pilgrims Dr. Sevier cast an eye full of
interest, and often of compassion hidden under outward
impatience. "Who wants to see," he would demand,
"men — *and women* — increasing the risks of this un-
certain life?" But he was also full of respect for them.
There was a certain nobility rightly attributable to emi-
gration itself in the abstract. It was the cutting loose
from friends and aid, — those sweet-named temptations, —
and the going forth into self-appointed exile and into dan
gers known and unknown, trusting to the help of one's
own right hand to exchange honest toil for honest bread
and raiment. His eyes kindled to see the goodly, broad,
red-cheeked fellows. Sometimes, though, he saw women,
and sometimes tender women, by their side; and that

sight touched the pathetic chord of his heart with a rude twangle that vexed him.

It was on a certain bright, cool morning early in October that, as he drove down Carondelet street toward his office, and one of those little white omnibuses of the old Apollo-street line, crowding in before his carriage, had compelled his driver to draw close in by the curbstone and slacken speed to a walk, his attention chanced to fall upon a young man of attractive appearance, glancing stranger-wise and eagerly at signs and entrances while he moved down the street. Twice, in the moment of the Doctor's enforced delay, he noticed the young stranger make inquiry of the street's more accustomed frequenters, and that in each case he was directed farther on. But, the way opened, the Doctor's horse switched his tail and was off, the stranger was left behind, and the next moment the Doctor stepped across the sidewalk and went up the stairs of Number 3½ to his office. Something told him — we are apt to fall into thought on a stairway — that the stranger was looking for a physician.

He had barely disposed of the three or four waiting messengers that arose from their chairs against the corridor wall, and was still reading the anxious lines left in various handwritings on his slate, when the young man entered. He was of fair height, slenderly built, with soft auburn hair, a little untrimmed, neat dress, and a diffident, yet expectant and courageous, face.

"Dr. Sevier?"

"Yes, sir."

"Doctor, my wife is very ill; can I get you to come at once and see her?"

"Who is her physician?"

"I have not called any; but we must have one now."

"I don't know about going at once. This is my hour

for being in the office. How far is it, and what's the trouble?"

"We are only three squares away, just here in Custom-house street." The speaker began to add a faltering enumeration of some very grave symptoms. The Doctor noticed that he was slightly deaf; he uttered his words as though he did not hear them.

"Yes," interrupted Dr. Sevier, speaking half to himself as he turned around to a standing case of cruel-looking silver-plated things on shelves; "that's a small part of the penalty women pay for the doubtful honor of being our mothers. I'll go. What is your number? But you had better drive back with me if you can." He drew back from the glass case, shut the door, and took his hat.

"Narcisse!"

On the side of the office nearest the corridor a door let into a hall-room that afforded merely good space for the furniture needed by a single accountant. The Doctor had other interests besides those of his profession, and, taking them altogether, found it necessary, or at least convenient, to employ continuously the services of a person to keep his accounts and collect his bills. Through the open door the book-keeper could be seen sitting on a high stool at a still higher desk, — a young man of handsome profile and well-knit form. At the call of his name he unwound his legs from the rounds of the stool and leaped into the Doctor's presence with a superlatively highbred bow.

"I shall be back in fifteen minutes," said the Doctor. "Come, Mr. ——,' and went out with the stranger.

Narcisse had intended to speak. He stood a moment, then lifted the last half inch of a cigarette to his lips, took a long, meditative inhalation, turned half round on his heel, dashed the remnant with fierce emphasis into a spittoon, ejected two long streams of smoke from his nostrils, and extending his fist toward the door by which the Doctor had gone out, said : —

"All right, ole hoss !" No, not that way. It is hard to give his pronunciation by letter. In the word "right" he substituted an a for the r, sounding it almost in the same instant with the i, yet distinct from it: All a-ight, ole hoss !"

Then he walked slowly back to his desk, with that feeling of relief which some men find in the renewal of a promissory note, twined his legs again among those of the stool, and, adding not a word, resumed his pen.

The Doctor's carriage was hurrying across Canal street.

"Dr. Sevier," said the physician's companion, "I don't know what your charges are" —

"The highest," said the Doctor, whose dyspepsia was gnawing him just then with fine energy. The curt reply struck fire upon the young man.

"I don't propose to drive a bargain, Dr. Sevier!" He flushed angrily after he had spoken, breathed with compressed lips, and winked savagely, with the sort of indignation that school-boys show to a harsh master.

The physician answered with better self-control.

"What do you propose?"

"I was going to propose — being a stranger to you, sir — to pay in advance." The announcement was made with a tremulous, but triumphant, *hauteur*, as though it must cover the physician with mortification. The speaker stretched out a rather long leg, and, drawing a pocket-book, produced a twenty-dollar piece.

The Doctor looked full in his face with impatient surprise, then turned his eyes away again as if he restrained himself, and said, in a subdued tone : —

" I would rather you had haggled about the price."

" I don't hear " — said the other, turning his ear.

The Doctor waved his hand : —

" Put that up, if you please."

The young stranger was disconcerted. He remained silent for a moment, wearing a look of impatient embarrassment. He still extended the piece, turning it over and over with his thumb-nail as it lay on his fingers.

" You don't know me, Doctor," he said. He got another cruel answer.

" We're getting acquainted," replied the physician.

The victim of the sarcasm bit his lip, and protested, by an unconscious, sidewise jerk of the chin : —

" I wish you'd " — and he turned the coin again.

The physician dropped an eagle's stare on the gold.

" I don't practise medicine on those principles."

" But, Doctor," insisted the other, appeasingly, " you can make an exception if you will. Reasons are better than rules, my old professor used to say. I am here without friends, or letters, or credentials of any sort ; this is the only recommendation I can offer."

" Don't recommend you at all ; anybody can do that."

The stranger breathed a sigh of overtasked patience, smiled with a baffled air, seemed once or twice about to speak, but doubtful what to say, and let his hand sink.

" Well, Doctor," — he rested his elbow on his knee, gave the piece one more turn over, and tried to draw the physician's eye by a look of boyish pleasantness, — " I'll not ask you to take pay in advance, but I will ask you to take care of this money for me. Suppose I should lose it, or have it stolen from me, or — Doctor, it would be a real comfort to me if you would."

" I can't help that. I shall treat your wife, and then send in my bill." The Doctor folded arms and appeared to give attention to his driver. But at the same time he asked : —

"Not subject to epilepsy, eh?"

"No, sir!" The indignant shortness of the retort drew no sign of attention from the Doctor; he was silently asking himself what this nonsense meant. Was it drink, or gambling, or a confidence game? Or was it only vanity, or a mistake of inexperience? He turned his head unexpectedly, and gave the stranger's facial lines a quick, thorough examination. It startled them from a look of troubled meditation. The physician as quickly turned way again.

"Doctor," began the other, but added no more.

The physician was silent. He turned the matter over once more in his mind. The proposal was absurdly unbusiness-like. That his part in it might look ungenerous was nothing; so his actions were right, he rather liked them to bear a hideous aspect: that was his war-paint. There was that in the stranger's attitude that agreed fairly with his own theories of living. A fear of debt, for instance if that was genuine it was good; and, beyond and better than that, a fear of money. He began to be more favorably impressed.

"Give it to me," he said, frowning; "mark you, this is your way," — he dropped the gold into his vest-pocket, — "it isn't mine."

The young man laughed with visible relief, and rubbed his knee with his somewhat too delicate hand. The Doctor examined him again with a milder glance.

"I suppose you think you've got the principles of life all right, don't you?"

"Yes, I do," replied the other, taking his turn at olding arms.

"H-m-m! I dare say you do. What you lack is the practice." The Doctor sealed his utterance with a nod.

The young man showed amusement; more, it may be, than he felt, and presently pointed out his lodging-place.

"Here, on this side; Number 40;" and they alighted.

CHAPTER III.

HIS WIFE.

IN former times the presence in New Orleans, during the cooler half of the year, of large numbers of mercantile men from all parts of the world, who did not accept the fever-plagued city as their permanent residence, made much business for the renters of furnished apartments. At the same time there was a class of persons whose residence was permanent, and to whom this letting of rooms fell by an easy and natural gravitation; and the most respectable and comfortable rented rooms of which the city could boast were those *chambres garnies* in Customhouse and Bienville streets, kept by worthy free or freed mulatto or quadroon women.

In 1856 the gala days of this half-caste people were quite over. Difference was made between virtue and vice, and the famous quadroon balls were shunned by those who aspired to respectability, whether their whiteness was nature or only toilet powder. Generations of domestic service under ladies of Gallic blood had brought many of them to a supreme pitch of excellence as housekeepers. In many cases money had been inherited; in other cases it had been saved up. That Latin feminine ability to hold an awkward position with impregnable serenity, and, like the yellow Mississippi, to give back no reflection from the overhanging sky, emphasized this superior fitness. That bright, womanly business ability that comes of the same blood added again to their excellence. Not to be home itself, nothing could be more like it than were the apartments let by Madame Cécile, or Madame Sophie, or Madame Athalie, or Madame Polyxène, or whatever the name might be.

It was in one of these houses, that presented its dull brick front directly upon the sidewalk of Custom-house street, with the unfailing little square sign of *Chambres à louer* (Rooms to let), dangling by a string from the overhanging balcony and twirling in the breeze, that the sick wife lay. A waiting slave-girl opened the door as the two men approached it, and both of them went directly upstairs and into a large, airy room. On a high, finely carved, and heavily hung mahogany bed, to which the remaining furniture corresponded in ancient style and massiveness, was stretched the form of a pale, sweet-faced little woman.

The proprietress of the house was sitting beside the bed,— a quadroon of good, kind face, forty-five years old or so, tall and broad. She rose and responded to the Doctor's silent bow with that pretty dignity of greeting which goes with all French blood, and remained standing. The invalid stirred.

The physician came forward to the bedside. The patient could not have been much over nineteen years of age. Her face was very pleasing; a trifle slender in outline; the brows somewhat square, not wide; the mouth small. She would not have been called beautiful, even in health, by those who lay stress on correctness of outlines. But she had one thing that to some is better. Whether it was in the dark blue eyes that were lifted to the Doctor's with a look which changed rapidly from inquiry to confidence, or in the fine, scarcely perceptible strands of pale-brown hair that played about her temples, he did not make out; but, for one cause

or another, her face was of that kind which almost
any one has seen once or twice, and no one has seen
often, — that seems to give out a soft, but veritable,
light.

She was very weak. Her eyes quickly dropped away
from his, and turned wearily, but peacefully, to those of
her husband.

The Doctor spoke to her. His greeting and gentle
inquiry were full of a soothing quality that was new to
the young man. His long fingers moved twice or thrice
softly across her brow, pushing back the thin, waving
strands, and then he sat down in a chair, continuing his
kind, direct questions. The answers were all bad.

He turned his glance to the quadroon; she understood
it; the patient was seriously ill. The nurse responded
with a quiet look of comprehension. At the same time
the Doctor disguised from the young strangers this inter
change of meanings by an audible question to the quadroon

"Have I ever met you before?"

"No, seh."

"What is your name?"

"Zénobie."

"Madame Zenobia," softly whispered the invalid,
turning her eyes, with a glimmer of feeble pleasantry,
first to the quadroon and then to her husband.

The physician smiled at her an instant, and then gave
a few concise directions to the quadroon. "Get me"—
thus and so.

The woman went and came. She was a superior nurse,
like so many of her race. So obvious, indeed, was this,
that when she gently pressed the young husband an inch
or two aside, and murmured that "de doctah" wanted him
to "go h-out," he left the room, although he knew the
physician had not so indicated.

By-and-by he returned, but only at her beckon, and remained at the bedside while Madame Zénobie led the Doctor into another room to write his prescription.

"Who are these people?" asked the physician, in an undertone, looking up at the quadroon, and pausing with the prescription half torn off.

She shrugged her large shoulders and smiled perplexedly.

"Mizzez — Reechin?" The tone was one of query rather than assertion. "Dey sesso," she added.

She might nurse the lady like a mother, but she was not going to be responsible for the genuineness of a stranger's name.

"Where are they from?"

"I dunno? — Some pless? — I nevva yeh dat nem biffo?"

She made a timid attempt at some word ending in "walk," and smiled, ready to accept possible ridicule.

"Milwaukee?" asked the Doctor.

She lifted her palm, smiled brightly, pushed him gently with the tip of one finger, and nodded. He had hit the nail on the head.

"What business is he in?"

The questioner arose.

She cast a sidelong glance at him with a slight enlargement of her eyes, and, compressing her lips, gave her head a little, decided shake. The young man was not employed.

"And has no money either, I suppose," said the physician, as they started again toward the sick-room.

She shrugged again and smiled; but it came to her mind that the Doctor might be considering his own interests, and she added, in a whisper: —

"Dey pay me."

She changed places with the husband, and the physician and he passed down the stairs together in silence.

"Well, Doctor?" said the young man, as he stood, prescription in hand, before the carriage-door.

"Well," responded the physician, "you should have called me sooner."

The look of agony that came into the stranger's face caused the Doctor instantly to repent his hard speech.

"You don't mean" — exclaimed the husband.

"No, no; I don't think it's too late. Get that prescription filled and give it to Mrs. —— "

"Richling," said the young man.

"Let her have perfect quiet," continued the Doctor. "I shall be back this evening."

And when he returned she had improved.

She was better again the next day, and the next; but on the fourth she was in a very critical state. She lay quite silent during the Doctor's visit, until he, thinking he read in her eyes a wish to say something to him alone, sent her husband and the quadroon out of the room on separate errands at the same moment. And immediately she exclaimed : —

"Doctor, save my life! You mustn't let me die! Save me, for my husband's sake! To lose all he's lost for me, and then to lose me too — save me, Doctor! save me!"

"I'm going to do it!" said he. "You shall get well!"

And what with his skill and her endurance it turned out so.

CHAPTER IV.

CONVALESCENCE AND ACQUAINTANCE.

A MAN'S clothing is his defence; but with a woman all dress is adornment. Nature decrees it; adornment is her instinctive delight. And, above all, the adorning of a bride; it brings out so charmingly the meaning of the thing. Therein centres the gay consent of all mankind and womankind to an innocent, sweet apostasy from the ranks of both. The value of living — which is loving; the sacredest wonders of life; all that is fairest and of best delight in thought, in feeling, yea, in substance, — all are apprehended under the floral crown and hymeneal veil. So, when at length one day Mrs. Richling said, "Madame Zénobie, don't you think I might sit up?" it would have been absurd to doubt the quadroon's willingness to assist her in dressing. True, here was neither wreath nor veil, but here was very young wifehood, and its re-attiring would be like a proclamation of victory over the malady that had striven to put two hearts asunder. Her willingness could hardly be doubted, though she smiled irresponsibly, and said : —

"If you thing"— She spread her eyes and elbows suddenly in the manner of a crab, with palms turned upward and thumbs outstretched — " Well ! " — and so dropped them.

" You don't want wait till de doctah comin'?" she asked.

" I don't think he's coming ; it's after his time."

" Yass? "

The woman was silent a moment, and then threw up
one hand again, with the forefinger lifted alertly forward.

" I make a lill fi' biffo."

She made a fire.   Then she helped the convalescent to
put on a few loose drapings.   She made no concealment
of the enjoyment it gave her, though her words were few,
and generally were answers to questions; and when at
length she brought from the wardrobe, pretending not to
notice her mistake, a loose and much too ample robe of
woollen and silken stuffs to go over all, she moved as
though she trod on holy ground, and distinctly felt, herself, the thrill with which the convalescent, her young
eyes beaming their assent, let her arms into the big
sleeves, and drew about her small form the soft folds of
her husband's morning-gown.

" He goin' to fine that droll," said the quadroon.

The wife's face confessed her pleasure.

" It's as much mine as his," she said.

" Is you mek dat? " asked the nurse, as she drew its
silken cord about the convalescent's waist.

" Yes.   Don't draw it tight; leave it loose — so; but
you can tie the knot tight.   That will do; there! "   She
smiled broadly.   " Don't tie me in as if you were tying
me in forever."

Madame Zénobie understood perfectly, and, smiling in
response, did tie it as if she were tying her in forever.

Half an hour or so later the quadroon, being — it may
have been by chance — at the street door, ushered in a
person who simply bowed in silence.

But as he put one foot on the stair he paused, and,
bending a severe gaze upon her, asked : —

" Why do you smile? "

She folded her hands limply on her bosom, and

drawing a cheek and shoulder toward each other, re
plied : —

"Nuttin'"—

The questioner's severity darkened.

"Why do you smile at nothing?"

She laid the tips of her fingers upon her ips to compose
them.

"You din come in you' carridge. She goin' to thing
'tis Miché Reechin." The smile forced its way through
her fingers. The visitor turned in quiet disdain and went
upstairs, she following.

At the top he let her pass. She led the way and,
softly pushing open the chamber-door, entered noiselessly, turned, and, as the other stepped across the
threshold, nestled her hands one on the other at her waist,
shrank inward with a sweet smile, and waved one palm toward the huge, blue-hung mahogany four-poster, — empty.

The visitor gave a slight double nod and moved on
across the carpet. Before a small coal fire, in a grate too
wide for it, stood a broad, cushioned rocking-chair, with
the corner of a pillow showing over its top. The visitor
went on around it. The girlish form lay in it, with
eyes closed, very still ; but his professional glance quickly
detected the false pretence of slumber. A slippered foot
was still slightly reached out beyond the bright colors of
the long gown, and toward the brazen edge of the hearth-
pan, as though the owner had been touching her tiptoe
against it to keep the chair in gentle motion. One cheek
was on the pillow ; down the other curled a few light
strands of hair that had escaped from her brow.

Thus for an instant. Then a smile began to wreath
about the corner of her lips ; she faintly stirred, opened
her eyes — and lo ! Dr. Sevier, motionless, tranquil, and
grave.

"O Doctor!" The blood surged into her face and down upon her neck. She put her hands over her eyes, and her face into the pillow. "O Doctor!"—rising to a sitting posture,—"I thought, of course, it was my husband."

The Doctor replied while she was speaking:—

"My carriage broke down." He drew a chair toward the fireplace, and asked, with his face toward the dying fire:—

"How are you feeling to-day, madam,—stronger?"

"Yes; I can almost say I'm well." The blush was still on her face as he turned to receive her answer, but she smiled with a bright courageousness that secretly amused and pleased him. "I thank you, Doctor, for my recovery; I certainly should thank you." Her face lighted up with that soft radiance which was its best quality, and her smile became half introspective as her eyes dropped from his, and followed her outstretched hand as it re-arranged the farther edges of the dressing-gown one upon another.

"If you will take better care of yourself hereafter, madam," responded the Doctor, thumping and brushing from his knee some specks of mud that he may have got when his carriage broke down, "I will thank you. But"—brush—brush—"I—doubt it."

"Do you think you should?" she asked, leaning forward from the back of the great chair and letting her wrists drop over the front of its broad arms.

"I do," said the Doctor, kindly. "Why shouldn't I? This present attack was by your own fault." While he spoke he was looking into her eyes, contracted at their corners by her slight smile. The face was one of those that show not merely that the world is all unknown to 'hem, but that it always will be so. It beamed with inquisitive intelligence, and yet had the innocence almost of infancy. The Doctor made a discovery; that it was this that made her beautiful. "She *is* beautiful," he insisted to himself when his critical faculty dissented.

"You needn't doubt me, Doctor. I'll try my best to take care. Why, of course I will, — for John's sake." She looked up into his face from the tassel she was twisting around her finger, touching the floor with her slippers' toe and faintly rocking.

"Yes, there's a chance there," replied the grave man, seemingly not overmuch pleased; "I dare say everything you do or leave undone is for his sake."

The little wife betrayed for a moment a pained perplexity, and then exclaimed: —

"Well, of course!" and waited his answer with bright eyes.

"I have known women to think of their own sakes," was the response.

She laughed, and with unprecedented sparkle replied: —

"Why, whatever's his sake is my sake. I don't see the difference. Yes, I see, of course, how there might be a difference; but I don't see how a woman"— She ceased, still smiling, and, dropping her eyes to her hands, slowly stroked one wrist and palm with the tassel of her husband's robe.

The Doctor rose, turned his back to the mantel-piece, and looked down upon her. He thought of the great, wide world: its thorny ways, its deserts, its bitter waters, its unrighteousness, its self-seeking greeds, its weaknesses, its under and over reaching, its unfaithfulness; and then again of this — child, thrust all at once a thousand miles into it, with never — so far as he could see — an implement, a weapon, a sense of danger, or a refuge;

well pleased with herself, as it seemed, lifted up into the bliss of self-obliterating wifehood, and resting in her husband with such an assurance of safety and happiness as a saint might pray for grace to show to Heaven itself. He stood silent, feeling too grim to speak, and presently Mrs. Richling looked up with a sudden liveliness of eye and a smile that was half apology and half persistence.

"Yes, Doctor, I'm going to take care of myself."

"Mrs. Richling, is your father a man of fortune?"

"My father is not living," said she, gravely. "He died two years ago. He was the pastor of a small church. No, sir; he had nothing but his small salary, except that for some years he taught a few scholars. He taught me." She brightened up again. "I never had any other teacher."

The Doctor folded his hands behind him and gazed abstractedly through the upper sash of the large French windows. The street-door was heard to open.

"There's John," said the convalescent, quickly, and the next moment her husband entered. A tired look vanished from his face as he saw the Doctor. He hurried to grasp his hand, then turned and kissed his wife. The physician took up his hat.

"Doctor," said the wife, holding the hand he gave her, and looking up playfully, with her cheek against the chairback, "you surely didn't suspect me of being a rich girl, did you?"

"Not at all, madam." His emphasis was so pronounced that the husband laughed.

"There's one comfort in the opposite condition, Doctor," said the young man.

"Yes?"

"Why, yes; you see, it requires no explanation."

"Yes, it does," said the physician; "it is just as bind-
ing on people to show good cause why they are poor as it
is to show good cause why they're rich.   Good-day,
madam." The two men went out together. His word
would have been good-by, but for the fear of fresh
acknowledgments.

CHAPTER V.

HARD QUESTIONS.

DR. SEVIER had a simple abhorrence of the expression of personal sentiment in words. Nothing else seemed to him so utterly hollow as the attempt to indicate by speech a regard or affection which was not already demonstrated in behavior. So far did he keep himself aloof from insincerity that he had barely room enough left to be candid.

"I need not see your wife any more," he said, as he went down the stairs with the young husband at his elbow; and the young man had learned him well enough not to oppress him with formal thanks, whatever might have been said or omitted upstairs.

Madame Zénobie contrived to be near enough, as they reached the lower floor, to come in for a share of the meagre adieu. She gave her hand with a dainty grace and a bow that might have been imported from Paris.

Dr. Sevier paused on the front step, half turned toward the open door where the husband still tarried. That was not speech; it was scarcely action; but the young man understood it and was silent. In truth, the Doctor himself felt a pang in this sort of farewell. A physician's way through the world is paved, I have heard one say, with these broken bits of other's lives, of all colors and all degrees of beauty. In his reminiscences, when he can do no better, he gathers them up, and, turning them over and over in the darkened chamber of his retrospection

rees patterns of delight lit up by the softened rays of by-
gone time. But even this renews the pain of separation,
and Dr. Sevier felt, right here at this door-step, that, if
this was to be the last of the Richlings, he would feel the
twinge of parting every time they came up again in his
memory.

He looked at the house opposite, — where there was
really nothing to look at, — and at a woman who happened
to be passing, and who was only like a thousand others
with whom he had nothing to do.

"Richling," he said, "what brings you to New Orleans,
any way?"

Richling leaned his cheek against the door-post.

"Simply seeking my fortune, Doctor."

"Do you think it is here?"

"I'm pretty sure it is; the world owes me a living."

The Doctor looked up.

"When did you get the world in your debt?"

Richling lifted his head pleasantly, and let one foot
down a step.

"It owes me a chance to earn a living, doesn't it?"

"I dare say," replied the other; "that's what it generally owes."

"That's all I ask of it," said Richling; "if it will let
us alone we'll let it alone."

"You've no right to allow either," said the physician.
"No, sir; no," he insisted, as the young man looked incredulous. There was a pause. "Have you any capital?"
asked the Doctor.

"Capital! No," — with a low laugh.

"But surely you have something to" —

"Oh, yes, — a little!"

The Doctor marked the southern "Oh." There is no
"O" in Milwaukee.

"You don't find as many vacancies as you expected to see, I suppose — h-m-m?"

There was an under-glow of feeling in the young man's tone as he replied : —

"I was misinformed."

"Well," said the Doctor, staring down-street, "you'll find something. What can you do?"

"Do? Oh, I'm willing to do anything!"

Dr. Sevier turned his gaze slowly, with a shade of disappointment in it. Richling rallied to his defences.

"I think I could make a good book-keeper, or correspondent, or cashier, or any such"—

The Doctor interrupted, with the back of his head toward his listener, looking this time up the street, riverward : —

"Yes ; — or a shoe, — or a barrel, — h-m-m?"

Richling bent forward with the frown of defective hearing, and the physician raised his voice : —

"Or a cart-wheel — or a coat?"

"I can make a living," rejoined the other, with a needlessly resentful-heroic manner, that was lost, or seemed to ɔe, on the physician.

"Richling," — the Doctor suddenly faced around and fixed a kindly severe glance on him, — "why didn't you bring letters?"

"Why," — the young man stopped, looked at his feet, and distinctly blushed. "I think," he stammered — "it seems to me" — he looked up with a faltering eye — "don't you think — I think a man ought to be able to recommend *himself*."

The Doctor's gaze remained so fixed that the self-recommended man could not endure it silently.

"*I* think so," he said, looking down again and swing-

ing his foot. Suddenly he brightened. "Doctor, isn't
this your carriage coming?"

"Yes; I told the boy to drive by here when it was
mended, and he might find me." The vehicle drew up
and stopped. "Still, Richling," the physician continued,
as he stepped toward it, "you had better get a letter or
two, yet; you might need them."

The door of the carriage clapped to. There seemed a
touch of vexation in the sound. Richling, too, closed
his door, but in the soft way of one in troubled meditation. Was this a proper farewell? The thought came
to both men.

"Stop a minute!" said Dr. Sevier to his driver. He
leaned out a little at the side of the carriage and looked
back. "Never mind; he has gone in."

The young husband went upstairs slowly and heavily,
more slowly and heavily than might be explained by his
all-day unsuccessful tramp after employment. His wife
still rested in the rocking-chair. He stood against it,
and she took his hand and stroked it.

"Tired?" she asked, looking up at him. He gazed
into the languishing fire.

"Yes."

"You're not discouraged, are you?"

"Discouraged? N-no. And yet," he said, slowly
shaking his head, "I can't see why I don't find something to do."

"It's because you don't hunt for it," said the wife.

He turned upon her with flashing countenance only to
meet her laugh, and to have his head pulled down to her
lips. He dropped into the seat left by the physician,
laid his head back in his knit hands, and crossed his feet
under the chair.

"John, I do *like* Dr. Sevier.'

"Why?" The questioner looked at the ceiling.

"Why, don't you like him?" asked the wife, and, as John smiled, she added, "You know you like him."

The husband grasped the poker in both hands, dropped his elbows upon his knees, and began touching the fire, saying slowly: —

"I believe the Doctor thinks I'm a fool."

"That's nothing," said the little wife; "that's only because you married me."

The poker stopped rattling between the grate-bars; the husband looked at the wife. Her eyes, though turned partly away, betrayed their mischief. There was a deadly pause; then a rush to the assault, a shower of Cupid's arrows, a quick surrender.

But we refrain. Since ever the world began it is Love's real, not his sham, battles that are worth the telling.

CHAPTER VI.

NESTING.

A FORTNIGHT passed. What with calls on his private skill, and appeals to his public zeal, Dr. Sevier was always loaded like a dromedary. Just now he was much occupied with the affairs of the great American people. For all he was the furthest remove from a mere party contestant or spoilsman, neither his righteous pugnacity nor his human sympathy would allow him to " let politics alone." Often across this preoccupation there flitted a thought of the Richlings.

At length one day he saw them. He had been called by a patient, lodging near Madame Zénobie's house. The proximity of the young couple occurred to him at once, but he instantly realized the extreme poverty of the chance that he should see them. To increase the improbability, the short afternoon was near its close, — an hour when people generally were sitting at dinner.

But what a coquette is that same chance! As he was driving up at the sidewalk's edge before his patient's door, the Richlings came out of theirs, the husband talking with animation, and the wife, all sunshine, skipping up to his side, and taking his arm with both hands, and attending eagerly to his words.

"Heels!" muttered the Doctor to himself, for the sound of Mrs. Richling's gaiters betrayed that fact. Heels were an innovation still new enough to rouse the resentment of masculine conservatism. But for them she would have pleased his sight entirely. Bonnets, for years microscopic, had again become visible, and her girlish face was prettily set in one whose flowers and ribbon, just joyous and no more, were reflected again in the double-skirted silk *barége;* while the dark mantilla that drooped away from the broad lace collar, shading, without hiding, her "Parodi" waist, seemed made for that very street of heavy-grated archways, iron-railed balconies, and high lattices. The Doctor even accepted patiently the free northern step, which is commonly so repugnant to the southern eye.

A heightened gladness flashed into the faces of the two young people as they descried the physician.

"Good-afternoon," they said, advancing.

"Good-evening," responded the Doctor, and shook hands with each. The meeting was an emphatic pleasure to him. He quite forgot the young man's lack of credentials.

"Out taking the air?" he asked.

"Looking about," said the husband.

"Looking up new quarters," said the wife, knitting her fingers about her husband's elbow and drawing closer to it.

"Were you not comfortable?"

"Yes; but the rooms are larger than we need."

"Ah!" said the Doctor; and there the conversation sank. There was no topic suited to so fleeting a moment, and when they had smiled all round again Dr. Sevier lifted his hat. Ah, yes, there was one thing.

"Have you found work?" asked the Doctor of Richling

The wife glanced up for an instant into her husband's face, and then down again.

"No," said Richling, "not yet. If you should hear

of anything, Doctor"— He remembered the Doctor's
word about letters, stopped suddenly, and seemed as if
he might even withdraw the request; but the Doctor
said : —

" I will; I will let you know." He gave his hand to
Richling. It was on his lips to add : "And should you
need," etc. ; but there was the wife at the husband's side.
So he said no more. The pair bowed their cheerful
thanks ; but beside the cheer, or behind it, in the husband's face, was there not the look of one who feels the
odds against him? And yet, while the two men's hands
still held each other, the look vanished, and the young
man's light grasp had such firmness in it that, for this
cause also, the Doctor withheld his patronizing utterance. He believed he would himself have resented it had
he been in Richling's place.

The young pair passed on, and that night, as Dr.
Sevier sat at his fireside, an uncompanioned widower, he
saw again the young wife look quickly up into her husband's face, and across that face flit and disappear its
look of weary dismay, followed by the air of fresh
courage with which the young couple had said good-by.

" I wish I had spoken," he thought to himself; "I
wish I had made the offer."

And again : —

" I hope he didn't tell her what I said about the letters.
Not but I was right, but it'll only wound her."

But Richling had told her ; he always " told her everything ; " she could not possibly have magnified wifehood
more, in her way, than he did in his. May be both ways
were faulty ; but they were extravagantly, youthfully
confident that they were not.

Unknown to Dr. Sevier, the Richlings had returned

from their search unsuccessful. Finding prices too much alike in Custom-house street they turned into Burgundy. From Burgundy they passed into Du Maine. As they went, notwithstanding disappointments, their mood grew gay and gayer. Everything that met the eye was quaint and droll to them: men, women, things, places,— all were more or less outlandish. The grotesqueness of the African, and especially the French-tongued African, was to Mrs. Richling particularly irresistible. Multiplying upon each and all of these things was the ludicrousness of the pecuniary strait that brought themselves and these things into contact. Everything turned to fun.

Mrs. Richling's mirthful mood prompted her by and by to begin letting into her inquiries and comments covert double meanings, intended for her husband's private understanding. Thus they crossed Bourbon street.

About there their mirth reached a climax; it was in a small house, a sad, single-story thing, cowering between two high buildings, its eaves, four or five feet deep, overshadowing its one street door and window.

"Looks like a shade for weak eyes," said the wife.

They had debated whether they should enter it or not. He thought no, she thought yes; but he would not insist and she would not insist; she wished him to do as he thought best, and he wished her to do as she thought best, and they had made two or three false starts and retreats before they got inside. But they were in there at length, and busily engaged inquiring into the availability of a small, lace-curtained, front room, when Richling took his wife so completely off her guard by addressing her as "Madam," in the tone and manner of Dr. Sevier, that she laughed in the face of the householder, who had been trying to talk English with a French accent and a hare-lip, and they fled with haste to the sidewalk and around the corner, where they could smile and smile without being villains.

"We must stop this," said the wife, blushing. "We *must* stop it. We're attracting attention."

And this was true at least as to one ragamuffin, who stood on a neighboring corner staring at them. Yet there is no telling to what higher pitch their humor might have carried them if Mrs. Richling had not been weighted down by the constant necessity of correcting her husband's statement of their wants. This she could do, because his exactions were all in the direction of her comfort.

"But, John," she would say each time as they returned to the street and resumed their quest, "those things cost; you can't afford them, can you?"

"Why, you can't be comfortable without them," he would answer.

"But that's not the question, John. We *must* take cheaper lodgings, mustn't we?"

Then John would be silent, and by littles their gayety would rise again.

One landlady was so good-looking, so manifestly and entirely Caucasian, so melodious of voice, and so modest in her account of the rooms she showed, that Mrs. Richling was captivated. The back room on the second floor, overlooking the inner court and numerous low roofs beyond, was suitable and cheap.

"Yes," said the sweet proprietress, turning to Richling, who hung in doubt whether it was quite good enough, "yesseh, I think you be pretty well in that room yeh.[1] Yesseh, I'm shoe you be *verrie* well; yesseh."

"Can we get them at once?"

---

[1] "Yeh" — *ye*, as in *yearn*.

" Yes? At once? Yes? Oh, yes?"

No downward inflections from her.

" Well," — the wife looked at the husband; he nodded, — " well, we'll take it."

" Yes?" responded the landlady; " well?" leaning against a bedpost and smiling with infantile diffidence, " you dunt want no ref'ence?"

" No," said John, generously, " oh, no; we can trust each other that far, eh?"

" Oh, yes?" replied the sweet creature; then suddenly changing countenance, as though she remembered something. " But daz de troub' — de room not goin' be vacate for t'ree mont'."

She stretched forth her open palms and smiled, with one arm still around the bedpost.

" Why," exclaimed Mrs. Richling, the very statue of astonishment, " you said just now we could have it at once!"

" Dis room? *Oh,* no; nod *dis* room."

" I don't see how I could have misunderstood you."

The landlady lifted her shoulders, smiled, and clasped her hands across each other under her throat. Then throwing them apart she said brightly : —

" No, I say at Madame La Rose. Me, my room is all fill'. At Madame La Rose, I say, I think you be pritty well. I'm shoe you be verrie well at Madame La Rose. I'm sorry. But you kin paz yondeh — 'tiz juz ad the cawneh? And I am shoe I think you be pritty well at Madame La Rose."

She kept up the repetition, though Mrs. Richling, incensed, had turned her back, and Richling was saying good-day.

" She did say the room was vacant!" exclaimed the little wife, as they reached the sidewalk. But the next moment there came a quick twinkle from her eye, and, waving her husband to go on without her, she said, " You kin paz yondeh ; at Madame La Rose I am shoe you be pritty sick." Thereupon she took his arm, — making everybody stare and smile to see a lady and gentleman arm in arm by daylight, — and they went merrily on their way.

The last place they stopped at was in Royal street. The entrance was bad. It was narrow even for those two. The walls were stained by dampness, and the smell of a totally undrained soil came up through the floor. The stairs ascended a few steps, came too near a low ceiling, and shot forward into cavernous gloom to find a second rising place farther on. But the rooms, when reached, were a tolerably pleasant disappointment, and the proprietress a person of reassuring amiability.

She bestirred herself in an obliging way that was the most charming thing yet encountered. She gratified the young people every moment afresh with her readiness to understand or guess their English queries and remarks, hung her head archly when she had to explain away little objections, delivered her No sirs with gravity and her Yes sirs with bright eagerness, shook her head slowly with each negative announcement, and accompanied her affirmations with a gracious bow and a smile full of rice powder.

She rendered everything so agreeable, indeed, that it almost seemed impolite to inquire narrowly into matters, and when the question of price had to come up it was really difficult to bring it forward, and Richling quite lost sight of the economic rules to which he had silent y acceded in the *Rue Du Maine*.

" And you will carpet the floor?" he asked, hovering off of the main issue.

"Put coppit? Ah! cettainlee!" she replied, with a lovely bow and a wave of the hand toward Mrs. Richling, whom she had already given the same assurance.

"Yes," responded the little wife, with a captivated smile, and nodded to her husband.

"We want to get the decentest thing that is cheap," he said, as the three stood close together in the middle o. the room.

The landlady flushed.

"No, no, John," said the wife, quickly, "don't you know what we said?" Then, turning to the proprietress, she hurried to add, "We want the cheapest thing that is decent."

But the landlady had not waited for the correction.

"*Dissent!* You want somesin *dissent!*" She moved a step backward on the floor, scoured and smeared with brick-dust, her ire rising visibly at every heart-throb, and pointing her outward-turned open hand energetically downward, added:—

"'Tis yeh!" She breathed hard. "*Mais*, no; you don't *want* somesin dissent. No!" She leaned forward interogatively: "You want somesin tchip?" She threw both elbows to the one side, cast her spread hands off in the same direction, drew the cheek on that side down into the collar-bone, raised her eyebrows, and pushed her upper lip with her lower, scornfully.

At that moment her ear caught the words of the wife's apologetic amendment. They gave her fresh wrath and new opportunity. For her new foe was a woman, and a woman trying to speak in defence of the husband against whose arm she clung.

"Ah-h-h!" Her chin went up; her eyes shot lightning; she folded her arms fiercely, and drew herself to her best height; and, as Richling's eyes shot back in rising indignation, cried: —

"Ziss pless? 'Tis not ze pless! Zis pless — is diss'nt pless! I am diss'nt woman, me! Fo' w'at you come in yeh?"

"My dear madam! My husband " —

"Dass you' uzban'?" pointing at him.

"Yes!" cried the two Richlings at once.

The woman folded her arms again, turned half-aside, and, lifting her eyes to the ceiling, simply remarked, with an ecstatic smile: —

"Humph!" and left the pair, red with exasperation, to find the street again through the darkening cave of the stairway.

It was still early the next morning, when Richling entered his wife's apartment with an air of brisk occupation. She was pinning her brooch at the bureau glass.

"Mary," he exclaimed, "put something on and come see what I've found! The queerest, most romantic old thing in the city; the most comfortable — and the cheapest! Here, is this the wardrobe key? To save time I'll get your bonnet."

"No, no, no!" cried the laughing wife, confronting him with sparkling eyes, and throwing herself before the wardrobe; "I can't let you touch my bonnet!"

There is a limit, it seems, even to a wife's subserviency.

However, in a very short time afterward, by the feminine measure, they were out in the street, and people were again smiling at the pretty pair to see her arm in his, and she actually *keeping step*. 'Twas very funny.

As they went John described his discovery: A pair of huge, solid green gates immediately on the sidewalk, in the dull façade of a tall, red brick building with old

carved vinework on its window and door frames. Hinges
a yard long on the gates; over the gates a semicircular
grating of iron bars an inch in diameter; in one of these
gates a wicket, and on the wicket a heavy, battered, highly
burnished brass knocker. A short-legged, big-bodied, and
very black slave to usher one through the wicket into a
large, wide, paved corridor, where from the middle joist
overhead hung a great iron lantern. Big double doors at
the far end, standing open, flanked with diamond-paned
side-lights of colored glass, and with an arch at the same,
fan-shaped, above. Beyond these doors and showing
through them, a flagged court, bordered all around by a
narrow, raised parterre under pomegranate and fruit-laden
orange, and over-towered by vine-covered and latticed
walls, from whose ragged eaves vagabond weeds laughed
down upon the flowers of the parterre below, robbed of late
and early suns. Stairs old fashioned, broad; rooms, their
choice of two; one looking down into the court, the other
into the street; furniture faded, capacious; ceilings high;
windows, each opening upon its own separate small balcony, where, instead of balustrades, was graceful iron
scroll-work, centered by some long-dead owner's monogram
two feet in length; and on the balcony next the division
wall, close to another on the adjoining property, a quarter
circle of iron-work set like a blind-bridle, and armed with
hideous prongs for house-breakers to get impaled on.

"Why, in there," said Richling, softly, as they hurried
in, "we'll be hid from the whole world, and the whole
world from us."

The wife's answer was only the upward glance of her
blue eyes into his, and a faint smile.

The place was all it had been described to be, and
more, — except in one particular.

"And my husband tells me " — The owner of said

husband stood beside him, one foot a little in advance of the other, her folded parasol hanging down the front of her skirt from her gloved hands, her eyes just returning to the landlady's from an excursion around the ceiling, and her whole appearance as fresh as the pink flowers that nestled between her brow and the rim of its precious covering. She smiled as she began her speech, but not enough to spoil what she honestly believed to be a very business-like air and manner. John had quietly dropped out of the negotiations, and she felt herself put upon her mettle as his agent. "And my husband tells me the price of this front room is ten dollars a month."

"Munse?"

The respondent was a very white, corpulent woman, who constantly panted for breath, and was everywhere sinking down into chairs, with her limp, unfortified skirt dropping between her knees, and her hands pressed on them exhaustedly.

"Munse?" She turned from husband to wife, and back again, a glance of alarmed inquiry.

Mary tried her hand at French.

"Yes; *oui, madame*. Ten dollah the month—*le mois*."

Intelligence suddenly returned. Madame made a beautiful, silent O with her mouth and two others with her eyes.

"Ah *non!* By munse? No, madame. Ah-h! impossybl'! By *wick*, yes; ten dollah de wick! Ah!"

She touched her bosom with the wide-spread fingers of one hand and threw them toward her hearers.

The room-hunters got away, yet not so quickly but they heard behind and above them her scornful laugh, addressed to the walls of the empty room.

A day or two later they secured an apartment, cheap, and — morally — decent; but otherwise — ah!

CHAPTER VII.

DISAPPEARANCE.

IT was the year of a presidential campaign. The party that afterward rose to overwhelming power was, for the first time, able to put its candidate fairly abreast of his competitors. The South was all afire. Rising up or sitting down, coming or going, week-day or Sabbath-day, eating or drinking, marrying or burying, the talk was all of slavery, abolition, and a disrupted country.

Dr. Sevier became totally absorbed in the issue. He was too unconventional a thinker ever to find himself in harmony with all the declarations of any party, and yet it was a necessity of his nature to be in the *mêlée*. He had his own array of facts, his own peculiar deductions; his own special charges of iniquity against this party and of criminal forbearance against that; his own startling political economy; his own theory of rights; his own interpretations of the Constitution; his own threats and warnings; his own exhortations, and his own prophecies, of which one cannot say all have come true. But he poured them forth from the mighty heart of one who loved his country, and sat down with a sense of duty fulfilled and wiped his pale forehead while the band played a polka.

It hardly need be added that he proposed to dispense with politicians, or that, when " the boys " presently counted him into their party team for campaign haranguing, he let them clap the harness upon him and splashed along in the mud with an intention as pure as snow.

" Hurrah for " —

Whom it is no matter now. It was not Fremont.
Buchanan won the race. Out went the lights, down came
the platforms, rockets ceased to burst; it was of no use
longer to "Wait for the wagon"; "Old Dan Tucker"
got " out of the way," small boys were no longer fellow-
citizens, dissolution was postponed, and men began to
have an eye single to the getting of money.

A mercantile friend of Dr. Sevier had a vacant clerkship which it was necessary to fill. A bright recollection
flashed across the Doctor's memory.

" Narcisse ! "

" Yesseh ! "

" Go to Number 40 Custom-house street and inquire
for Mr. Fledgeling ⚡ or, if he isn't in, for Mrs. Fledge
— humph ! Richling, I mean ; I" —

Narcisse laughed aloud.

" Ha-ha-ha ! daz de way, sometime' ! My hant she got
a honcl' — he says, once 'pon a time " —

" Never mind ! Go at once ! "

" All a-ight, seh ! "

" Give him this card " —

" Yesseh ! "

"These people" —

" Yesseh ! "

" Well, wait till you get your errand, can't you ?
These " —

" Yesseh ! "

" These people want to see him."

" All a-ight, seh ! "

Narcisse threw open and jerked off a worsted jacket,
took his coat down from a peg, transferred a snowy
handkerchief from the breast-pocket of the jacket to that
of the coat, felt in his pantaloons to be sure that he had

his match-case and cigarettes, changed his shoes, got his hat from a high nail by a little leap, and put it on a head as handsome as Apollo's.

"Doctah Seveeah," he said, "in fact, I fine that a ve'y gen'lemany young man, that Mistoo Itchlin, weely, Doctah."

The Doctor murmured to himself from the letter he was writing.

"Well, *au 'evoi*, Doctah; I'm goin'."

Out in the corridor he turned and jerked his chin up and curled his lip, brought a match and cigarette together in the lee of his hollowed hand, took one first, fond draw, and went down the stairs as if they were on fire.

At Canal street he fell in with two noble fellows of his own circle, and the three went around by way of Exchange alley to get a glass of soda at McCloskey's old down-town stand. His two friends were out of employment at the moment, — making him, consequently, the interesting figure in the trio as he inveighed against his master.

"Ah, phooh!" he said, indicating the end of his speech by dropping the stump of his cigarette into the sand on the floor and softly spitting upon it, — "*le* Shylock *de la rue* Carondelet!" — and then in English, not to lose the admiration of the Irish waiter: —

"He don't want to haugment me! I din hass 'im, because the 'lection. But you juz wait till dat firce of Jannawerry!"

The waiter swathed the zinc counter, and inquired why Narcisse did not make his demands at the present moment.

"W'y I don't hass 'im now? Because w'en I hass 'im he know' he's got to *do* it! You thing I'm goin' to kill myseff workin'?"

Nobody said yes, and by and by he found himself alive

in the house of Madame Zénobie. The furniture was being sold at auction, and the house was crowded with all sorts and colors of men and women. A huge sideboard was up for sale as he entered, and the crier was crying : —

" Faw-ty-fi' dollah ! faw-ty-fi' dollah, ladies an' gentymen ! On'y faw-ty-fi' dollah fo' thad magniffyzan sidebode ! *Quarante-cinque piastres, seulement, messieurs ! Les* knobs *vaut bien cette prix !* Gentymen, de knobs is worse de money ! Ladies, if you don' stop dat talkin', I will not sell one thing mo' ! *Et quarante cinque piastres* — faw-ty-fi' dollah " —

" Fifty ! " cried Narcisse, who had not owned that much at one time since his father was a constable ; realizing which fact, he slipped away upstairs and found Madame Zénobie half crazed at the slaughter of her assets.

She sat in a chair against the wall of the room the Richlings had occupied, a spectacle of agitated dejection. Here and there about the apartment, either motionless in chairs, or moving noiselessly about, and pulling and pushing softly this piece of furniture and that, were numerous vulture-like persons of either sex, waiting the up-coming of the auctioneer. Narcisse approached her briskly.

" Well, Madame Zénobie ! " — he spoke in French — " is it you who lives here ? Don't you remember me ? What ! No ? You don't remember how I used to steal figs from you ? "

The vultures slowly turned their heads. Madame Zénobie looked at him in a dazed way.

No, she did not remember. So many had robbed her — all her life.

" But you don't look at me, Madame Zénobie. Don't you remember, for example, once pulling a little boy — as little as *that* — out of your fig-tree, and taking the half of a shingle, split lengthwise, in your hand, and his head under your arm, — swearing you would do it if you died for it, — and bending him across your knee," — he began a vigorous but graceful movement of the right arm, which few members of our fallen race could fail to recognize, — " and you don't remember me, my old friend?"

She looked up into the handsome face with a faint smile of affirmation. He laughed with delight.

" The shingle was *that* wide. Ah! Madame Zénobie, you did it well!" He softly smote the memorable spot, first with one hand and then with the other, shrinking forward spasmodically with each contact, and throwing utter woe into his countenance. The general company smiled. He suddenly put on great seriousness.

"Madame Zénobie, I hope your furniture is selling well?" He still spoke in French.

She cast her eyes upward pleadingly, caught her breath, threw the back of her hand against her temple, and dashed it again to her lap, shaking her head.

Narcisse was sorry.

" I have been doing what I could for you, downstairs, — running up the prices of things. I wish I could stay to do more, for the sake of old times. I came to see Mr. Richling, Madame Zénobie; is he in? Dr. Sevier wants him."

Richling? Why, the Richlings did not live there! The Doctor must know it. Why should she be made responsible for this mistake? It was his oversight. They had moved long ago. Dr. Sevier had seen them looking for apartments. Where did they live now? Ah, me! *she* could not tell. Did Mr. Richling owe the Doctor something?

"Owe? Certainly not. The Doctor — on the contrary " —

Ah! well, indeed, she didn't know where they lived, it is true; but the fact was, Mr. Richling happened to be there just then! — *à-ç't'eure!* He had come to get a few trifles left by his madame.

Narcisse made instant search. Richling was not on the upper floor. He stepped to the landing and looked down. There he went!

"Mistoo 'Itchlin!"

Richling failed to hear. Sharper ears might have served him better. He passed out by the street door. Narcisse stopped the auction by the noise he made coming downstairs after him. He had some trouble with the front door, — lost time there, but got out.

Richling was turning a corner. Narcisse ran there and looked; looked up — looked down — looked into every store and shop on either side of the way clear back to Canal street; crossed it, went back to the Doctor's office, and reported. If he omitted such details as having seen and then lost sight of the man he sought, it may have been in part from the Doctor's indisposition to give him speaking license. The conclusion was simple: the Richlings could not be found.

The months of winter passed. No sign of them.

"They've gone back home," the Doctor often said to himself. How much better that was than to stay where they had made a mistake in venturing, and become the nurslings of patronizing strangers! He gave his admiration free play, now that they were quite gone. True courage that Richling had — courage to retreat when retreat is best! And his wife — ah! what a reminder of — hush, memory!

"Yes, they must have gone home!" The Doctor spoke

very positively, because, after all, he was haunted by doubt.

One spring morning he uttered a soft exclamation as he glanced at his office-slate. The first notice on it read : —

Please call as soon as you can at number 292 St. Mary street, corner of Prytania. Lower corner — opposite the asylum.

JOHN RICHLING.

The place was far up in the newer part of the American quarter. The signature had the appearance as if the writer had begun to write some other name, and had changed it to Richling.

CHAPTER VIII.

A QUESTION OF BOOK-KEEPING.

A DAY or two after Narcisse had gone looking for
Richling at the house of Madame Zénobie, he might
have found him, had he known where to search, in
Tchoupitoulas street.

Whoever remembers that thoroughfare as it was in
those days, when the commodious " cotton-float " had not
quite yet come into use, and Poydras and other streets
did not so vie with Tchoupitoulas in importance as they
do now, will recall a scene of commercial hurly-burly that
inspired much pardonable vanity in the breast of the
utilitarian citizen. Drays, drays, drays ! Not the light
New York things ; but big, heavy, solid affairs, many of
them drawn by two tall mules harnessed tandem. Drays
by threes and by dozens, drays in opposing phalanxes,
drays in long processions, drays with all imaginable kinds
of burden ; cotton in bales, piled as high as the omnibuses ;
leaf tobacco in huge hogsheads ; cases of linens and silks ;
stacks of rawhides ; crates of cabbages ; bales of prints
and of hay ; interlocked heaps of blue and red ploughs ;
bags of coffee, and spices, and corn ; bales of bagging ;
barrels, casks, and tierces ; whiskey, pork, onions, oats,
bacon, garlic, molasses, and other delicacies ; rice, sugar,
— what was there not ? Wines of France and Spain in
pipes, in baskets, in hampers, in octaves ; queensware
from England ; cheeses, like cart-wheels, from Switzerland ; almonds, lemons, raisins, olives, boxes of citron

casks of chains; specie from Vera Cruz; cries of drivers,
cracking of whips, rumble of wheels, tremble of earth,
frequent gorge and stoppage. It seemed an idle tale to
say that any one could be lacking bread and raiment.
"We are a great city," said the patient foot-passengers,
waiting long on street corners for opportunity to cross the
way.

On one of these corners paused Richling. He had not
found employment, but you could not read that in his
face; as well as he knew himself, he had come forward
into the world prepared amiably and patiently to be, to
do, to suffer anything, provided it was not wrong or
ignominious. He did not see that even this is not enough
in this rough world; nothing had yet taught him that one
must often gently suffer rudeness and wrong. As to
what constitutes ignominy he had a very young man's —
and, shall we add? a very American — idea. He could
not have believed, had he been told, how many establish-
ments he had passed by, omitting to apply in them for
employment. He little dreamed he had been too select.
He had entered not into any house of the Samaritans, to
use a figure; much less, to speak literally, had he gone
to the lost sheep of the house of Israel. Mary, hiding
away in uncomfortable quarters a short stone's throw
from Madame Zénobie's, little imagined that, in her broad
irony about his not hunting for employment, there was
really a tiny seed of truth. She felt sure that two or
three persons who had seemed about to employ him had
failed to do so because they detected the defect in his
hearing, and in one or two cases she was right.

Other persons paused on the same corner where Rich-
ling stood, under the same momentary embarrassment.
One man, especially busy-looking, drew very near him.
And then and there occurred this simple accident, — that

at last he came in contact with the man who had work to
give him. This person good-humoredly offered an
impatient comment on their enforced delay. Richling
answered in sympathetic spirit, and the first speaker re
sponded with a question : —

"Stranger in the city?"

"Yes."

"Buying goods for up-country?"

It was a pleasant feature of New Orleans life that
sociability to strangers on the street was not the exclusive
prerogative of gamblers' decoys.

"No; I'm looking for employment."

"Aha!" said the man, and moved away a little. But
in a moment Richling, becoming aware that his questioner
was glancing all over him with critical scrutiny, turned,
and the man spoke.

"D'you keep books?"

Just then a way opened among the vehicles; and the
man, young and muscular, darted into it, and Richling
followed.

"I *can* keep books," he said, as they reached the
farther curb-stone.

The man seized him by the arm.

"D'you see that pile of codfish and herring where that
tall man is at work yonder with a marking-pot and brush?
Well, just beyond there is a boarding-house, and then a
hardware store; you can hear them throwing down sheets
of iron. Here; you can see the sign. See? Well, the
next is my store. Go in there — upstairs into the office —
and wait till I come."

Richling bowed and went. In the office he sat down
and waited what seemed a very long time. Could he have
misunderstood? For the man did not come. There was
a person sitting at a desk on the farther side of the office.

writing, who had not lifted his head from first to last. Richling said : —

"Can you tell me when the proprietor will be in?"

The writer's eyes rose, and dropped again upon his writing.

"What do you want with him?"

"He asked me to wait here for him."

"Better wait, then."

Just then in came the merchant. Richling rose, and he uttered a rude exclamation : —

"*I* forgot you completely! Where did you say you kept books at, last?"

"I've not kept anybody's books yet, but I can do it."

The merchant's response was cold and prompt. He did not look at Richling, but took a sample vial of molasses from a dirty mantel-piece and lifted it between his eyes and the light, saying : —

"You can't do any such thing. I don't want you."

"Sir," said Richling, so sharply that the merchant looked round, "if you don't want me I don't want you ; but you mustn't attempt to tell me that what I say is not true!" He had stepped forward as he began to speak, but he stopped before half his words were uttered, and saw his folly. Even while his voice still trembled with passion and his head was up, he colored with mortification. That feeling grew no less when his offender simply looked at him, and the man at the desk did not raise his eyes. It rather increased when he noticed that both of them were young — as young as he.

"I don't doubt your truthfulness," said the merchant, marking the effect of his forbearance ; "but you ought to know you can't come in and take charge of a large set of books in the midst of a busy season, when you've never kept books before."

" I don't know it at all."

" Well, I do," said the merchant, still more coldly than before. " There are my books," he added, warming, and pointed to three great canvassed and black-initialled volumes standing in a low iron safe, " left only yesterday in such a snarl, by a fellow who had ' never kept books, but knew how,' that I shall have to open another set ! After this I shall have a book-keeper who has kept books."

He turned away.

Some weeks afterward Richling recalled vividly a thought that had struck him only faintly at this time : that, beneath much superficial severity and energy, there was in this establishment a certain looseness of management. It may have been this half-recognized thought that gave him courage, now, to say, advancing another step : —

" One word, if you please."

" It's no use, my friend."

" It may be."

" How ? "

" Get an experienced book-keeper for your new set of books "—

" You can bet your bottom dollar ! " said the merchant. turning again and running his hands down into his lower pockets. " And even he'll have as much as he can do "—

" That is just what I wanted you to say," interrupted Richling, trying hard to smile ; " then you can let me straighten up the old set."

" Give a new hand the work of an expert ! "

The merchant almost laughed out. He shook his head and was about to say more, when Richling persisted : —

" If I don't do the work to your satisfaction don't pay me a cent."

' I never make that sort of an arrangement ; no, sir !

Unfortunately it had not been Richling's habit to show this pertinacity, else life might have been easier to him as a problem; but these two young men, his equals in age, were casting amused doubts upon his ability to make good his professions. The case was peculiar. He reached a hand out toward the books.

"Let me look over them for one day; if I don't convince you the next morning in five minutes that I can straighten them I'll leave them without a word."

The merchant looked down an instant, and then turned to the man at the desk.

"What do you think of that, Sam?"

Sam set his elbows upon the desk, took the small end of his pen-holder in his hands and teeth, and, looking up, said : —

"I don't know; you might — try him."

"What did you say your name was?" asked the other, again facing Richling. "Ah, yes! Who are your references, Mr. Richmond?"

"Sir?" Richling leaned slightly forward and turned his ear.

"I say, who knows you?"

"Nobody."

"Nobody! Where are you from?"

"Milwaukee."

The merchant tossed out his arm impatiently.

"Oh, I can't do that kind o' business."

He turned abruptly, went to his desk, and, sitting down half-hidden by it, took up an open letter.

"I bought that coffee, Sam," he said, rising again and moving farther away.

"Umhum," said Sam; and all was still.

Richling stood expecting every instant to turn on the next and go. Yet he went not. Under the dusty front windows of the counting-room the street was roaring below. Just beyond a glass partition at his back a great windlass far up under the roof was rumbling with the descent of goods from a hatchway at the end of its tense rope. Salesmen were calling, trucks were trundling, shipping clerks and porters were replying. One brawny fellow he saw, through the glass, take a herring from a broken box, and stop to feed it to a sleek, brindled mouser. Even the cat was valued; but he — he stood there absolutely zero. He saw it. He saw it as he never had seen it before in his life. This truth smote him like a javelin: that all this world wants is a man's permission to do without him. Right then it was that he thought he swallowed all his pride; whereas he only tasted its bitter brine as like a wave it took him up and lifted him forward bodily. He strode up to the desk beyond which stood the merchant, with the letter still in his hand, and said : —

"I've not gone yet! I may have to be turned off by you, but not in this manner ! "

The merchant looked around at him with a smile of surprise, mixed with amusement and commendation, but said nothing. Richling held out his open hand.

" I don't ask you to trust me. Don't trust me. Try me ! "

He looked distressed. He was not begging, but he seemed to feel as though he were.

The merchant dropped his eyes again upon the letter, and in that attitude asked : —

" What do you say, Sam?"

" He can't hurt anything," said Sam.

The merchant looked suddenly at Richling.

" You're not from Milwaukee. You're a Southern man."

Richling changed color.

"I said Milwaukee."

"Well," said the merchant, 'I hardly know. Come and see me further about it to-morrow morning. I haven't time to talk now."

"Take a seat," he said, the next morning, and drew up a chair sociably before the returned applicant. "Now, suppose I was to give you those books, all in confusion as they are, what would you do first of all?"

Mary fortunately had asked the same question the night before, and her husband was entirely ready with an answer which they had studied out in bed.

"I should send your deposit-book to bank to be balanced, and, without waiting for it, I should begin to take a trial-balance off the books. If I didn't get one pretty soon, I'd drop that for the time being, and turn in and render the accounts of everybody on the books, asking them to examine and report."

"All right," said the merchant, carelessly; "we'll try you."

"Sir?" Richling bent his ear.

"*All right; we'll try you!* I don't care much about recommendations. I generally most always make up my opinion about a man from looking at him. I'm that sort of a man."

He smiled with inordinate complacency.

So, week by week, as has been said already, the winter passed,— Richling on one side of the town, hidden away in his work, and Dr. Sevier on the other, very positive that the "young pair" must have returned to Milwaukee.

At length the big books were readjusted in all their hundreds of pages, were balanced, and closed. Much satisfaction was expressed; but another man had meantime taken charge of the new books,—one who influences business, and Richling had nothing to do but put on his hat.

However, the house cheerfully recommended him to a neighboring firm, which also had disordered books to be righted; and so more weeks passed. Happy weeks! Happy days! Ah, the joy of them! John bringing home money, and Mary saving it!

"But, John, it seems such a pity not to have stayed with A, B, & Co.; doesn't it?"

"I don't think so. I don't think they'll last much longer."

And when he brought word that A, B, & Co. had gone into a thousand pieces Mary was convinced that she had a very far-seeing husband.

By and by, at Richling's earnest and restless desire, they moved their lodgings again. And thus we return by a circuit to the morning when Dr. Sevier, taking up his slate, read the summons that bade him call at the corner of St. Mary and Prytania streets.

CHAPTER IX.

WHEN THE WIND BLOWS.

THE house stands there to-day. A small, pinched, frame, ground-floor-and-attic, double tenement, with its roof sloping toward St. Mary street and overhanging its two door-steps that jut out on the sidewalk. There the Doctor's carriage stopped, and in its front room he found Mary in bed again, as ill as ever. A humble German woman, living in the adjoining half of the house, was attending to the invalid's wants, and had kept her daughter from the public school to send her to the apothecary with the Doctor's prescription.

"It is the poor who help the poor," thought the physician.

"Is this your home?" he asked the woman softly, as he sat down by the patient's pillow. He looked about upon the small, cheaply furnished room, full of the neat makeshifts of cramped housewifery.

"It's mine," whispered Mary. Even as she lay there in peril of her life, and flattened out as though Juggernaut had rolled over her, her eyes shone with happiness and scintillated as the Doctor exclaimed in undertone :—

"Yours !" He laid his hand upon her forehead. "Where is Mr. Richling?"

"At the office." Her eyes danced with delight. She would have begun, then and there, to tell him all that had happened, — "had taken care of herself all along," she said, "until they began to move. In moving, had been *obliged* to overwork — hardly *fixed* yet "—

But the Doctor gently checked her and bade her be quiet.

"I will," was the faint reply; "I will; but—just one thing, Doctor, please let me say."

"Well?"

"John"—

"Yes, yes; I know; he'd be here, only you wouldn't let him stay away from his work."

She smiled assent, and he smiled in return.

"'Business is business,'" he said.

She turned a quick, sparkling glance of affirmation, as if she had lately had some trouble to maintain that ancient truism. She was going to speak again, but the Doctor waved his hand downward soothingly toward the restless form and uplifted eyes.

"All right," she whispered, and closed them.

The next day she was worse. The physician found himself, to use his words, "only the tardy attendant of offended nature." When he dropped his finger-ends gently upon her temple she tremblingly grasped his hand.

"You'll save me?" she whispered.

"Yes," he replied; "we'll do that—the Lord helping us."

A glad light shone from her face as he uttered the latter clause. Whereat he made haste to add:—

"I don't pray, but I'm sure you do."

She silently pressed the hand she still held.

On Sunday he found Richling at the bedside. Mary had improved considerably in two or three days. She lay quite still as they talked, only shifting her glance softly from one to the other as one and then the other spoke. The Doctor heard with interest Richling's full account of all that had occurred since he had met them last together. Mary's eyes filled with merriment when

John told the droller part of their experiences in the hard quarters from which they had only lately removed. But the Doctor did not so much as smile. Richling finished, and the physician was silent.

" Oh, we're getting along," said Richling, stroking the small, weak hand that lay near him on the coverlet. But still the Doctor kept silence.

"Of course," said Richling, very quietly, looking at his wife, " we mustn't be surprised at a backset now and then. But we're getting on."

Mary turned her eyes toward the Doctor. Was he not going to assent at all? She seemed about to speak. He bent his ear, and she said, with a quiet smile : —

" ' When the wind blows, the cradle will rock.' "

The physician gave only a heavy-eyed " Humph ! " and a faint look of amusement.

" What did she say? " said Richling ; the words had escaped his ear. The Doctor repeated it, and Richling, too, smiled.

Yet it was a good speech, — why not? But the patient also smiled, and turned her eyes toward the wall with a disconcerted look, as if the smile might end in tears. For herein lay the very difficulty that always brought the Doctor's carriage to the door, — the cradle would not rock.

For a few days more that carriage continued to appear, and then ceased. Richling dropped in one morning at Number 3½ Carondelet, and settled his bill with Narcisse.

The young Creole was much pleased to be at length brought into actual contact with a man of his own years, who, without visible effort, had made an impression on Dr. Sevier.

Until the money had been paid and the bill receipted nothing more than a formal business phrase or two passed between them. But as Narcisse delivered the receipted bill, with an elaborate gesture of courtesy, and Richling began to fold it for his pocket, the Creole remarked : —

"I 'qpe you will excuse the 'an'-a-'iting."

Richling reopened the paper; the penmanship was beautiful.

"Do you ever write better than this?" he asked. "Why, I wish I could write half as well!"

"No; I do not fine that well a-'itten. I cannot see 'ow that is, — I nevva 'ite to the satizfagtion of my abil'ty soon in the mawnin's. I am dest'oying my chi'og'aphy at that desk yeh."

"Indeed?" said Richling; "why, I should think" —

"Yesseh, 'tis the tooth. But consunning the chi'og'aphy, Mistoo Itchlin, I 'ave descovvud one thing to a maul cettainty, and that is, if I 'ave something to 'ite to a young lady, I always dizguise my chi'og'aphy. Ha-ah! I 'ave learn that! You will be aztonish' to see in 'ow many diffe'n' fawm' I can make my 'an'-a-'iting to appeah. That paz thoo my fam'ly, in fact, Mistoo Itchlin. My hant, she's got a honcle w'at use' to be cluck in a bank, w'at could make the si'natu'e of the pwesiden', as well as of the cashieh, with that so absolute puffegtion, that they tu'n 'im out of the bank! Yesseh. In fact, I thing you ought to know 'ow to 'ite a ve'y fine 'an', Mistoo Itchlin."

"N-not very," said Richling; "my hand is large and legible, but not well adapted for — book-keeping; it's too heavy."

"You 'ave the 'ight physio'nomie, I am shu'. You will pe'haps believe me with difficulty, Mistoo Itchlin, but I assu' you I can tell if a man 'as a fine chi'og'aphy aw no, by juz lookin' upon his liniment. Do you know that Benjamin Fwanklin 'ote a v'ey fine chi'og'aphy, in

fact? Also, Voltaire. Yesseh. An' Napoleon Bona-
parte. Lawd By'on muz 'ave 'ad a beaucheouz chi'og'a-
phy. 'Tis impossible not to be, with that face. He is
my favo ite poet, that Lawd By'on. Moze people pwefeh
'im to Shakspere, in fact. Well, you muz go? I am ve'y
'appy to meck yo' acquaintanze, Mistoo Itchlin, seh. I
am so'y Doctah Seveeah is not theh pwesently. The negs
time you call, Mistoo Itchlin, you muz not be too much
aztonizh to fine me gone from yeh. Yesseh. He's got to
haugment me ad the en' of that month, an' we 'ave to-day
the fifteenth Mawch. Do you smoke, Mistoo Itchlin?"
He extended a package of cigarettes. Richling accepted
one. "I smoke lawgely in that weatheh," striking a
match on his thigh. "I feel ve'y sultwy to-day. Well,"
— he seized the visitor's hand, — " au'evoi', Mistoo Itchlin." And Narcisse returned to his desk happy in the
conviction that Richling had gone away dazzled.

CHAPTER X.

GENTLES AND COMMONS.

DR. SEVIER sat in the great easy-chair under the drop-light of his library table trying to read a book. But his thought was not on the page. He expired a long breath of annoyance, and lifted his glance backward from the bottom of the page to its top.

Why must his mind keep going back to that little cottage in St. Mary street? What good reason was there? Would they thank him for his solicitude? Indeed! He almost smiled his contempt of the supposition. Why, when on one or two occasions he had betrayed a least little bit of kindly interest, — what? Up had gone their youthful vivacity like an umbrella. Oh, yes! — like all young folks — *their* affairs were intensely private. Once or twice he had shaken his head at the scantiness of all their provisions for life. Well? They simply and unconsciously stole a hold upon one another's hand or arm, as much as to say, " To love is enough." When, gentlemen of the jury, it isn't enough!

" Pshaw ! " The word escaped him audibly. He drew partly up from his half recline, and turned back a leaf of the book to try once more to make out the sense of it.

But there was Mary, and there was her husband. Especially Mary. Her image came distinctly between his eyes and the page. There she was, just as on his last visit, — a superfluous one — no charge, — sitting and plying her needle, unaware of his approach, gently moving her rocking-chair, and softly singing, "Flow on, thou shining river,"—the song his own wife used to sing. "O child, child! do you think it's always going to be shining'?" They shouldn t be so contented. Was pride under that cloak? Oh, no, no! But even if the content was genuine, it wasn't good. Why, they oughtn't to be *able* to be happy so completely out of their true sphere. It showed insensibility. But, there again,— Richling wasn't insensible, much less Mary.

The Doctor let his book sink, face downward, upon his knee.

"They're too big to be playing in the sand." He took up the book again. "'Tisn't my business to tell them so." But before he got the volume fairly before his eyes his professional bell rang, and he tossed the book upon the table.

"Well, why don't you bring him in?" he asked, in a tone of reproof, of a servant who presented a card; and in a moment the visitor entered.

He was a person of some fifty years of age, with a patrician face, in which it was impossible to tell where benevolence ended and pride began. His dress was of fine cloth, a little antique in cut, and fitting rather loosely on a form something above the medium height, of good width, but bent in the shoulders, and with arms that had been stronger. Years, it might be, or possibly some un- flinching struggle with troublesome facts, had given many lines of his face a downward slant. He apologized for the hour of his call, and accepted with thanks the chair offered him.

"You are not a resident of the city?" asked Dr. Sevier.

"I am from Kentucky." The voice was rich, and the

stranger's general air one of rather conscious social eminence.

"Yes?" said the Doctor, not specially pleased, and looked at him closer. He wore a black satin neck-stock, and dark-blue buttoned gaiters. His hair was dyed brown. A slender frill adorned his shirt-front.

"Mrs." — the visitor began to say, not giving the name, but waving his index-finger toward his card, which Dr. Sevier had laid upon the table, just under the lamp, — "my wife, Doctor, seems to be in a very feeble condition. Her physicians have advised her to try the effects of a change of scene, and I have brought her down to your busy city, sir."

The Doctor assented. The stranger resumed : —

"Its hurry and energy are a great contrast to the plantation life, sir."

"They're very unlike," the physician admitted.

"This chafing of thousands of competitive designs," said the visitor, "this great fretwork of cross purposes, is a decided change from the quiet order of our rural life. Hmm! There everything is under the administration of one undisputed will, and is executed by the unquestioning obedience of our happy and contented slave peasantry. I prefer the country. But I thought this was just the change that would arouse and electrify an invalid who has really no tangible complaint."

"Has the result been unsatisfactory?"

"Entirely so. I am unexpectedly disappointed." The speaker's thought seemed to be that the climate of New Orleans had not responded with that hospitable alacrity which was due so opulent, reasonable, and universally obeyed a guest.

There was a pause here, and Dr. Sevier looked around

at the book which lay at his elbow. But the visitor did
not resume, and the Doctor presently asked : —

" Do you wish me to see your wife ? "

" I called to see you alone first," said the other, " because there might be questions to be asked which were
better answered in her absence."

" Then you think you know the secret of her illness, do
you ? "

" I do. I think, indeed I may say I know, it is — be-
reavement."

The Doctor compressed his lips and bowed.

The stranger drooped his head somewhat, and, resting
his elbows on the arms of his chair, laid the tips of his
thumbs and fingers softly together.

" The truth is, sir, she cannot recover from the loss of
our son."

" An infant ? " asked the Doctor. His bell rang again
as he put the question.

" No, sir ; a young man, — one whom I had thought a
person of great promise ; just about to enter life."

" When did he die ? "

" He has been dead nearly a year. I " — The speaker
ceased as the mulatto waiting-man appeared at the open
door, with a large, simple, German face looking easily
over his head from behind.

" Toctor," said the owner of this face, lifting an immense open hand, " Toctor, uf you bleace, Toctor, you
vill bleace ugscooce me."

The Doctor frowned at the servant for permitting the
interruption. But the gentleman beside him said : —

" Let him come in, sir ; he seems to be in haste, sir,
and I am not, — I am not, at all."

" Come in," said the physician.

The new-comer stepped into the room. He was about six feet three inches in height, three feet six in breadth, and the same in thickness. Two kindly blue eyes shone softly in an expanse of face that had been clean-shaven every Saturday night for many years, and that ended in a retreating chin and a dewlap. The limp, white shirt-collar just below was without a necktie, and the waist of his pantaloons, which seemed intended to supply this deficiency, did not quite, but only almost reached up to the unoccupied blank. He removed from his respectful head a soft gray hat, whitened here and there with flour.

"Yentlemen," he said, slowly, " you vill ugscooce me to interruptet you, — yentlemen."

" Do you wish to see me? " asked Dr. Sevier.

The German made an odd gesture of deferential assent, lifting one open hand a little in front of him to the level of his face, with the wrist bent forward and the fingers pointing down.

" Uf you bleace, Toctor, I toose ; undt tat's te fust time I effer *tit* vanted a toctor. Undt you mus' ugscooce me, Toctor, to callin' on you, ovver I vish you come undt see mine " —

To the surprise of all, tears gushed from his eyes.

" Mine poor vife, Toctor ! " He turned to one side, pointed his broad hand toward the floor, and smote his forehead.

" I yoost come in fun mine paykery undt comin' into mine howse, fen — I see someting " — he waved his hand downward again —" someting — layin' on te — floor — face pleck ans a nigger's ; undt fen I look to see who udt iss, — *udt is Mississ Reisen !* Toctor, I vish you come right off ! I couldn't shtayndt udt you toandt come right avay ! "

" I'll come," said the Doctor, without rising ; " just

write your name and address on that little white slate yonder."

"Toctor," said the German, extending and dipping his hat, "I'm ferra much a-velcome to vou, Toctor; undt tat's yoost fot te pottekerra by mine corner sayt you vould too. He sayss, 'Reisen,' he sayss, 'you yoost co to Toctor Tsewier.'" He bent his great body over the farther end of the table and slowly worked out his name, street, and number. "Dtere udt iss, Toctor; I put udt town on teh schlate; ovver, I hope you ugscooce te hayndtwriding."

"Very well. That's right. That's all."

The German lingered. The Doctor gave a bow of dismission.

"That's all, I say. I'll be there in a moment. That's all. Dan, order my carriage!"

"Yentlemen, you vill ugscooce me?"

The German withdrew, returning each gentleman's bow with a faint wave of the hat.

During this interview the more polished stranger had sat with bowed head, motionless and silent, lifting it only once and for a moment at the German's emotional outburst. Then the upward and backward turned face was marked with a commiseration partly artificial, but also partly natural. He now looked up at the Doctor.

"I shall have to leave you," said the Doctor.

"Certainly, sir," replied the other; "by all means!" The willingness was slightly overdone and the benevolence of tone was mixed with complacency. "By all means," he said again; "this is one of those cases where it is only a proper grace in the higher to yield place to the lower." He waited for a response, but the Doctor merely frowned into space and called for his boots. The visitor resumed: —

" I have a good deal of feeling, sir, for the unlettered and the vulgar. They have their station, but they have also — though doubtless in smaller capacity than we — their pleasures and pains."

Seeing the Doctor ready to go, he began to rise.

" I may not be gone long," said the physician, rather coldly ; " if you choose to wait " —

" I thank you ; n-no-o " — The visitor stopped between a sitting and a rising posture.

" Here are books," said the Doctor, " and the evening papers, — 'Picayune,' ' Delta,' ' True Delta.' " It seemed for a moment as though the gentleman might sink into his seat again. "And there's the ' New York Herald.' "

" No, sir ! " said the visitor quickly, rising and smoothing himself out ; " nothing from that quarter, if you please." Yet he smiled. The Doctor did not notice that, while so smiling, he took his card from the table. There was something familiar in the stranger's face which the Doctor was trying to make out. They left the house together. Outside the street door the physician made apologetic allusion to their interrupted interview.

" Shall I see you at my office to-morrow ? I would be happy " —

The stranger had raised his hat. He smiled again, as pleasantly as he could, which was not delightful, and said, after a moment's hesitation : —

" — Possibly."

CHAPTER XI.

A PANTOMIME.

IT chanced one evening about this time — the vernal equinox had just passed — that from some small cause Richling, who was generally detained at the desk until a late hour, was home early. The air was soft and warm, and he stood out a little beyond his small front door-step, lifting his head to inhale the universal fragrance, and looking in every moment, through the unlighted front room, toward a part of the diminutive house where a mild rattle of domestic movements could be heard, and whence he had, a little before, been adroitly requested to absent himself. He moved restlessly on his feet, blowing a soft tune.

Presently he placed a foot on the step and a hand on the door-post, and gave a low, urgent call.

A distant response indicated that his term of suspense was nearly over. He turned about again once or twice, and a moment later Mary appeared in the door, came down upon the sidewalk, looked up into the moonlit sky and down the empty, silent street, then turned and sat down, throwing her wrists across each other in her lap, and lifting her eyes to her husband's with a smile that confessed her fatigue.

The moon was regal. It cast its deep contrasts of clear-cut light and shadow among the thin, wooden, unarchitectural forms and weed-grown vacancies of the half-settled neighborhood, investing the matter-of-fact with

mystery, and giving an unexpected charm to the unpic-
turesque. It was — as Richling said, taking his place
beside his wife — midspring in March. As he spoke he
noticed she had brought with her the odor of flowers.
They were pinned at her throat.

"Where did you get them?" he asked, touching them
with his fingers.

Her face lighted up.

"Guess."

How could he guess? As far as he knew neither she
nor he had made an acquaintance in the neighborhood.
He shook his head, and she replied : —

"The butcher."

"You're a queer girl," he said, when they had
laughed.

"Why?"

"You let these common people take to you so."

She smiled, with a faint air of concern.

"You don't dislike it, do you?" she asked.

"Oh, no," he said, indifferently, and spoke of other
things.

And thus they sat, like so many thousands and thousands of young pairs in this wide, free America, offering
the least possible interest to the great human army round
about them, but sharing, or believing they shared, in the
fruitful possibilities of this land of limitless bounty,
fondling their hopes and recounting the petty minutiæ of
their daily experiences. Their converse was mainly in
the form of questions from Mary and answers from
John.

"And did he say that he would?" etc. "And didn't
you insist that he should?" etc. "I don't understand
how he could require you to," etc., etc. Looking at everything from John's side, as if there never could be any other,

until at last John himself laughed softly when she asked why he couldn't take part of some outdoor man's work, and give him part of his own desk-work in exchange, and why he couldn't say plainly that his work was too sedentary.

Then she proposed a walk in the moonlight, and insisted she was not tired; she wanted it on her own account. And so, when Richling had gone into the house and returned with some white worsted gauze for her head and neck and locked the door, they were ready to start.

They were tarrying a moment to arrange this wrapping when they found it necessary to move aside from where they stood in order to let two persons pass on the sidewalk.

These were a man and woman, who had at least reached middle age. The woman wore a neatly fitting calico gown; the man, a short pilot-coat. His pantaloons were very tight and pale. A new soft hat was pushed forward from the left rear corner of his closely cropped head, with the front of the brim turned down over his right eye. At each step he settled down with a little jerk alternately on this hip and that, at the same time faintly dropping the corresponding shoulder. They passed. John and Mary looked at each other with a nod of mirthful approval. Why? Because the strangers walked silently hand-in-hand.

It was a magical night. Even the part of town where they were, so devoid of character by day, had become all at once romantic with phantasmal lights and glooms, echoes and silences. Along the edge of a wide chimney-top on one blank, new hulk of a house, that nothing else could have made poetical, a mocking-bird hopped and ran back and forth, singing as if he must sing or die. The mere names of the streets they traversed suddenly became sweet food for the fancy. Down at the first corner below they turned into one that had been an old country road, and was still named Felicity.

Richling called attention to the word painted on a board. He merely pointed to it in playful silence, and then let his hand sink and rest on hers as it lay in his elbow. They were walking under the low boughs of a line of fig-trees that overhung a high garden wall. Then some gay thought took him; but when his downward glance met the eyes uplifted to meet his they were grave, and there came an instantaneous tenderness into the exchange of looks that would have been worse than uninteresting to you or me. But the next moment she brightened up, pressed herself close to him, and caught step. They had not owned each other long enough to have settled into sedate possession, though they sometimes thought they had done so. There was still a tingling ecstasy in one another's touch and glance that prevented them from quite behaving themselves when under the moon.

For instance, now, they began, though in cautious undertone, to sing. Some person approached them, and they hushed. When the stranger had passed, Mary began again another song, alone : —

" Oh, don't you remember sweet Alice, Ben Bolt? "

" Hush!" said John, softly.

She looked up with an air of mirthful inquiry, and he added : —

" That was the name of Dr. Sevier's wife."

" But he doesn't hear me singing."

" No; but it seems as if he did."

And they sang no more.

They entered a broad, open avenue, with a treeless, grassy way in the middle, up which came a very large and lumbering street-car, with smokers' benches on the roof, and drawn by tandem horses.

"Here we turn down," said Richling, "into the way of the Naiads." (That was the street's name.) "They're not trying to get me away."

He looked down playfully. She was clinging to him with more energy than she knew.

"I'd better hold you tight," she answered. Both laughed. The nonsense of those we love is better than the finest wit on earth. They walked on in their bliss. Shall we follow? Fie!

They passed down across three or four of a group of parallel streets named for the nine muses. At Thalia they took the left, went one square, and turned up by another street toward home.

Their conversation had flagged. Silence was enough. The great earth was beneath their feet, firm and solid; the illimitable distances of the heavens stretched above their heads and before their eyes. Here was Mary at John's side, and John at hers; John her property and she his, and time flowing softly, shiningly on. Yea, even more. If one might believe the names of the streets, there were Naiads on the left and Dryads on the right; a little farther on, Hercules; yonder corner the dark trysting-place of Bacchus and Melpomene; and here, just in advance, the corner where Terpsichore crossed the path of Apollo.

They came now along a high, open fence that ran the entire length of a square. Above it a dense rank of bitter orange-trees overhung the sidewalk, their dark mass of foliage glittering in the moonlight. Within lay a deep, old-fashioned garden. Its white shell walks gleamed in

many directions. A sweet breath came from its parterres
of mingled hyacinths and jonquils that hid themselves
every moment in black shadows of ligustrums and laures-
tines.   Here, in severe order, a pair of palms, prim as
mediæval queens, stood over against each other; and in
the midst of the garden, rising high against the sky, appeared the pillared veranda and immense, four-sided roof
of an old French colonial villa, as it stands unchanged
to-day.

The two loiterers slackened their pace to admire the
scene. There was much light shining from the house.
Mary could hear voices, and, in a moment, words. The
host was speeding his parting guests.

" The omnibus will put you out only one block from
the hotel," some one said.

Dr. Sevier, returning home from a visit to a friend in
Polymnia street, had scarcely got well seated in the omnibus before he witnessed from its window a singular
dumb show. He had handed his money up to the driver
as they crossed Euterpe street, had received the change
and deposited his fare as they passed Terpsichore, and
was just siting down when the only other passenger in the
vehicle said, half-rising : —

" Hello ! there's going to be a shooting scrape ! "

A rather elderly man and woman on the sidewalk, both
of them extremely well dressed, and seemingly on the eve
of hailing the omnibus, suddenly transferred their attention to a younger couple a few steps from them, who
appeared to have met them entirely by accident. The
elderly lady threw out her arms toward the younger man
with an expression on her face of intensest mental suffering. She seemed to cry out; but the deafening rattle
of the omnibus, as it approached them, intercepted the

sound. All four of the persons seemed, in various ways, to experience the most violent feelings. The young man more than once moved as if about to start forward, yet did not advance; his companion, a small, very shapely woman, clung to him excitedly and pleadingly. The older man shook a stout cane at the younger, talking furiously as he did so. He held the elderly lady to him with his arm thrown about her, while she now cast her hands upward, now covered her face with them, now wrung them, clasped them, or extended one of them in seeming accusation against the younger person of her own sex. In a moment the omnibus was opposite the group. The Doctor laid his hand on his fellow-passenger's arm.

" Don't get out. There will be no shooting."

The young man on the sidewalk suddenly started forward, with his companion still on his farther arm, and with his eyes steadily fixed on those of the elder and taller man, a clenched fist lifted defensively, and with a tense, defiant air walked hurriedly and silently by within easy sweep of the uplifted staff. At the moment when the slight distance between the two men began to increase, the cane rose higher, but stopped short in its descent and pointed after the receding figure.

" I command you to leave this town, sir ! "

Dr. Sevier looked. He looked with all his might, drawing his knee under him on the cushion and leaning out. The young man had passed. He still moved on, turning back as he went a face full of the fear that men show when they are afraid of their own violence ; and, as the omnibus clattered away, he crossed the street at the upper corner and disappeared in the shadows.

"That's a very strange thing," said the other passenger to Dr. Sevier, as they resumed the corner seats by the door.

" It certainly is ! " replied the Doctor, and averted his
face.   For when the group and he were nearest together
and the moon shone brightly upon the four, he saw, beyond all question, that the older man was his visitor of a
few evenings before and that the younger pair were John
and Mary Richling.

CHAPTER XII.

"SHE'S ALL THE WORLD."

EXCELLENT neighborhood, St. Mary street, and Prytania was even better. Everybody was very retired though, it seemed. Almost every house standing in the midst of its shady garden, — sunny gardens are a newer fashion of the town, — a bell-knob on the gatepost, and the gate locked. But the Richlings cared nothing for this; not even what they should have cared. Nor was there any unpleasantness in another fact.

"Do you let this window stand wide this way when you are at work here, all day?" asked the husband. The opening alluded to was on Prytania street, and looked across the way to where the asylumed widows of "St Anna's" could glance down into it over their poor little window-gardens.

"Why, yes, dear!" Mary looked up from her little cane rocker with that thoughtful contraction at the outer corners of her eyes and that illuminated smile that between them made half her beauty. And then, somewhat more gravely and persuasively: "Don't you suppose they like it? They must like it. I think we can do that much for them. Would you rather I'd shut it?"

For answer John laid his hand on her head and gazed into her eyes.

"Take care," she whispered; "they'll see you."

He let his arm drop in amused despair.

"Why, what's the window open for? And, anyhow, they're all abed and asleep these two hours."

They did like it, those aged widows. It fed their
hearts' hunger to see the pretty unknown passing and re-
passing that open window in the performance of her
morning duties, or sitting down near it with her needle,
still crooning her soft morning song, — poor, almost as
poor as they, in this world's glitter; but rich in hope and
courage, and rich beyond all count in the content of one
who finds herself queen of ever so little a house, where
love is.

"Love is enough!" said the widows.

And certainly she made it seem so. The open window brought, now and then, a moisture to the aged eyes,
yet they liked it open.

But, without warning one day, there was a change. It
was the day after Dr. Sevier had noticed that queer street
quarrel. The window was not closed, but it sent out no
more light. The song was not heard, and many small,
faint signs gave indication that anxiety had come to be a
guest in the little house. At evening the wife was seen in
her front door and about its steps, watching in a new,
restless way for her husband's coming; and when he came
it could be seen, all the way from those upper windows,
where one or two faces appeared now and then, that he
was troubled and careworn. There were two more days
like this one; but at the end of the fourth the wife read
good tidings in her husband's countenance. He handed
her a newspaper, and pointed to a list of departing
passengers.

"They're gone!" she exclaimed.

He nodded, and laid off his hat. She cast her arms
about his neck, and buried her head in his bosom. You
could almost have seen Anxiety flying out at the window
By morning the widows knew of a certainty that the
cloud had melted away.

In the counting-room one evening, as Richling said good-night with noticeable alacrity, one of his employers, sitting with his legs crossed over the top of a desk, said to his partner : —

" Richling works for his wages."

" That's all," replied the other ; " he don't see his interests in ours any more than a tinsmith would, who comes to mend the roof."

The first one took a meditative puff or two from his cigar, tipped off its ashes, and responded : —

" Common fault. He completely overlooks his immense indebtedness to the world at large, and his dependence on it. He's a good fellow, and bright ; but he actually thinks that he and the world are starting even."

" His wife's his world," said the other, and opened the Bills Payable book. Who will say it is not well to sail in an ocean of love? But the Richlings were becalmed in theirs, and, not knowing it, were satisfied.

Day in, day out, the little wife sat at her window, and drove her needle. Omnibuses rumbled by ; an occasional wagon or cart set the dust a-flying ; the street venders passed, crying the praises of their goods and wares ; the blue sky grew more and more intense as weeks piled up upon weeks ; but the empty repetitions, and the isolation and, worst of all, the escape of time, — she smiled at all, and sewed on and crooned on, in the sufficient thought that John would come, each time, when only hours enough had passed away forever.

Once she saw Dr. Sevier's carriage. She bowed brightly, but he — what could it mean? — he lifted his hat with such austere gravity. Dr. Sevier was angry. He had no definite charge to make, but that did not lessen his displeasure. After long, unpleasant wondering, and long trusting to see Richling some day on the street, he had at length driven by this way purposely to see if they had indeed left town, as they had been so imperiously commanded to do.

This incident, trivial as it was, roused Mary to thought; and all the rest of the day the thought worked with energy to dislodge the frame of mind that she had acquired from her husband.

When John came home that night and pressed her to his bosom she was silent. And when he held her off a little and looked into her eyes, and she tried to better her smile, those eyes stood full to the lashes and she looked down.

"What's the matter?" asked he, quickly.

"Nothing!" She looked up again, with a little laugh.

He took a chair and drew her down upon his lap.

"What's the matter with my girl?"

"I don't know."

"How, — you don't know?"

"Why, I simply don't. I can't make out what it is. If I could I'd tell you; but I don't know at all." After they had sat silent a few moments : —

"I wonder" — she began.

"You wonder what?" asked he, in a rallying tone.

"I wonder if there's such a thing as being too contented."

Richling began to hum, with a playful manner : —

"' And she's all the world to me.'

Is that being too" —

"Stop!" said Mary "That's it." She laid her hand upon his shoulder. "You've said it. That's what I ought not to be!"

"Why, Mary, what on earth" — His face flamed up

"John, I'm willing to be *more* than all the rest of the world to you. I always must be that. I'm going to be that forever. And you"—she kissed him passionately—"you're all the world to me! But I've no right to be *all* the world to *you*. And you mustn't allow it. It's making it too small!"

"Mary, what are you saying?"

"Don't, John. Don't speak that way. I'm not saying anything. I'm only trying to say something, I don't know what."

"Neither do I," was the mock-rueful answer.

"I only know," replied Mary, the vision of Dr. Sevier's carriage passing before her abstracted eyes, and of the Doctor's pale face bowing austerely within it, "that if you don't take any part or interest in the outside world it'll take none in you; do you think it will?"

"And who cares if it doesn't?" cried John, clasping her to his bosom.

"I do," she replied. "Yes, I do. I've no right to steal you from the rest of the world, or from the place in it that you ought to fill. John"—

"That's my name."

"Why can't I do something to help you?"

John lifted his head unnecessarily.

"No!"

"Well, then, let's think of something we can do, without just waiting for the wind to blow us along,—I mean," she added appeasingly, "I mean without waiting to be employed by others."

"Oh, yes; but that takes capital!"

"Yes, I know; but why don't you think up something, —some new enterprise or something,—and get somebody with capital to go in with you?"

He shook his head.

" You're out of your depth. And that wouldn't make so much difference, but you're out of mine. It isn't enough to think of something; you must know how to do it. And what do I know how to do? Nothing! Nothing that's worth doing!"

" I know one thing you could do."

" What's that?"

" You could be a professor in a college."

John smiled bitterly.

" Without antecedents?" he asked.

Their eyes met; hers dropped, and both voices were silent. Mary drew a soft sigh. She thought their talk had been unprofitable. But it had not. John laid hold of work from that day on in a better and wiser spirit.

CHAPTER XIII.

THE BOUGH BREAKS.

BY some trivial chance, she hardly knew what, Mary found herself one day conversing at her own door with the woman whom she and her husband had once smiled at for walking the moonlit street with her hand in willing and undisguised captivity. She was a large and strong, but extremely neat, well-spoken, and good-looking Irish woman, who might have seemed at ease but for a faintly betrayed ambition.

She praised with rather ornate English the good appearance and convenient smallness of Mary's house; said her own was the same size. That person with whom she sometimes passed "of a Sundeh" — yes, and moonlight evenings — that was her husband. He was "ferst ingineeur" on a steamboat. There was a little, just discernible waggle in her head as she stated things. It gave her decided character.

"Ah! engineer," said Mary.

"*Ferst* ingineeur," repeated the woman; "you know there bees ferst ingineeurs, an' secon' ingineeurs, an' therd ingineeurs. Yes." She unconsciously fanned herself with a dust-pan that she had just bought from a tin peddler.

She lived only some two or three hundred yards away, around the corner, in a tidy little cottage snuggled in among larger houses in Coliseum street. She had had children, but she had lost them; and Mary's sympathy

when she told her of them — the girl and two boys — won
the woman as much as the little lady's pretty manners had
dazed her. It was not long before she began to drop in
upon Mary in the hour of twilight, and sit through it without speaking often, or making herself especially interesting in any way, but finding it pleasant, notwithstanding.

"John," said Mary, — her husband had come in unexpectedly, — "our neighbor, Mrs. Riley."

John's bow was rather formal, and Mrs. Riley soon rose
and said good-evening.

"John," said the wife again, laying her hands on his
shoulders as she tiptoed to kiss him, "what troubles
you?" Then she attempted a rallying manner : "Don't
my friends suit you?"

He hesitated only an instant, and said : —

"Oh, yes, that's all right!"

"Well, then, I don't see why you look so."

"I've finished the task I was to do."

"What! you haven't" —

"I'm out of employment."

They went and sat down on the little haircloth sofa
that Mrs. Riley had just left.

"I thought they said they would have other work for
you."

"They said they might have; but it seems they
haven't."

"And it's just in the opening of summer, too," said
Mary ; "why, what right" —

"Oh!"—a despairing gesture and averted gaze —
"they've a perfect right if they think best. I asked them
that myself at first — not too politely, either; but I soon
saw I was wrong."

They sat without speaking until it had grown quite
dark. Then John said, with a long breath, as he rose : —

"It passes my comprehension."

"What passes it?" asked Mary, detaining him by one hand.

"The reason why we are so pursued by misfortunes."

"But, John," she said, still holding him, "*is* it misfortune? When I know so well that you deserve to succeed, I think maybe it's good fortune in disguise, after all. Don't you think it's possible? You remember how it was last time, when A., B., & Co. failed. Maybe the best of all is to come now!" She beamed with courage. "Why, John, it seems to me I'd just go in the very best of spirits, the first thing to-morrow, and tell Dr. Sevier you are looking for work. Don't you think 't might" —

"I've been there."

"Have you? What did he say?"

"He wasn't in."

There was another neighbor, with whom John and Mary did not get acquainted. Not that it was more his fault than theirs; it may have been less. Unfortunately for the Richlings there was in their dwelling no toddling, self-appointed child commissioner to find his way in unwatched moments to the play-ground of some other toddler, and so plant the good seed of neighbor acquaintanceship.

This neighbor passed four times a day. A man of fortune, aged a hale sixty or so, who came and stood on the corner, and sometimes even rested a foot on Mary's doorstep, waiting for the Prytania omnibus, and who, on his returns, got down from the omnibus step a little gingerly, went by Mary's house, and presently shut himself inside a very ornamental iron gate, a short way up St. Mary street. A child would have made him acquainted. Even as it was, they did not escape his silent notice. It was pleasant

for him, from whose life the early dew had been dried
away by a well-risen sun, to recall its former freshness
by glimpses of this pair of young beginners. It was like
having a bird's nest under his window.

John, stepping backward from his door one day, saying
a last word to his wife, who stood on the threshold,
pushed against this neighbor as he was moving with somewhat cumbersome haste to catch the stage, turned quickly,
and raised his hat.

" Pardon ! "

The other uncovered his bald head and circlet of white,
silken locks, and hurried on to the conveyance.

" President of one of the banks down-town," whispered
John.

That is the nearest they ever came to being acquainted.
And even this accident might not have occurred had not
the man of snowy locks been glancing at Mary as he
passed instead of at his omnibus.

As he sat at home that evening he remarked : —

"Very pretty little woman that, my dear, that lives
in the little house at the corner ; who is she ? "

The lady responded, without lifting her eyes from the
newspaper in which she was interested ; she did not
know.   The husband mused and twirled his penknife
between a finger and thumb.

" They seem to be starting at the bottom," he observed.

" Yes ? "

" Yes ; much the same as we did."

" I haven't noticed them particularly."

" They're worth noticing," said the banker.

He threw one fat knee over the other, and laid his head
on the back of his easy-chair.

The lady's eyes were still on her paper, but she
asked : —

" Would you like me to go and see them ? "

" No, no — unless you wish."

She dropped the paper into her lap with a smile and a sigh.

" Don't propose it. I have so much going to do "— She paused, removed her glasses, and fell to straightening the fringe of the lamp-mat. " Of course, if you think they're in need of a friend ; but from your description " —

" No," he answered, quickly, "not at all. They've friends, no doubt. Everything about them has a neat, happy look. That's what attracted my notice. They've got friends, you may depend." He ceased, took up a pamphlet, and adjusted his glasses. " I think I saw a sofa going in there to-day as I came to dinner. A little expansion, I suppose."

" It was going out," said the only son, looking up from a story-book.

But the banker was reading. He heard nothing, and the word was not repeated. He did not divine that a little becalmed and befogged bark, with only two lovers in her, too proud to cry " Help ! " had drifted just yonder upon the rocks, and, spar by spar and plank by plank, was dropping into the smooth, unmerciful sea.

Before the sofa went there had gone, little by little, some smaller valuables.

" You see," said Mary to her husband, with the bright hurry of a wife bent upon something high-handed, " we both have to have furniture ; we must have it ; and I don't have to have jewelry. Don't you see?"

" No, I "—

" Now, John ! " There could be but one end to the debate ; she had determined that. The first piece was a bracelet. "No, I wouldn't pawn it," she said. "Better sell it outright at once."

But Richling could not but cling to hope and to the adornments that had so often clasped her wrists and throat or pinned the folds upon her bosom. Piece by piece he pawned them, always looking out ahead with strained vision for the improbable, the incredible, to rise to his relief.

"Is *nothing* going to happen, Mary?"

Yes; nothing happened — except in the pawn-shop.

So, all the sooner, the sofa had to go.

"It's no use talking about borrowing," they both said. Then the bureau went. Then the table. Then, one by one, the chairs. Very slyly it was all done, too. Neighbors mustn't know. "Who lives there?" is a question not asked concerning houses as small as theirs; and a young man, in a well-fitting suit of only too heavy goods, removing his winter hat to wipe the standing drops from his forehead; and a little blush-rose woman at his side, in a mist of cool muslin and the cunningest of millinery, — these, who always paused a moment, with a lost look, in the vestibule of the sepulchral-looking little church on the corner of Prytania and Josephine streets, till the sexton ushered them in, and who as often contrived, with no end of ingenuity, despite the little woman's fresh beauty, to get away after service unaccosted by the elders, — who could imagine that *these* were from so deep a nook in poverty's vale?

There was one person who guessed it: Mrs. Riley, who was not asked to walk in any more when she called at the twilight hour. She partly saw and partly guessed the truth, and offered what each one of the pair had been secretly hoping somebody, anybody, would offer — a loan.

But when it actually confronted them it was sweetly declined.

"Wasn't it kind?" said Mary; and John said emphatically, "Yes." Very soon it was their turn to be kind to Mrs. Riley. They attended her husband's funeral. He had been killed by an explosion. Mrs. Riley beat upon the bier with her fists, and wailed in a far-reaching voice : —

"O Mike, Mike! Me jew'l, me jew'l! Why didn't ye wait to see the babe that's unborn?"

And Mary wept. And when she and John reëntered their denuded house she fell upon his neck with fresh tears, and kissed him again and again, and could utter no word, but knew he understood. Poverty was so much better than sorrow! She held him fast, and he her, while he tenderly hushed her, lest a grief, the very opposite of Mrs. Riley's, should overtake her.

CHAPTER XIV.

HARD SPEECHES AND HIGH TEMPER.

DR. SEVIER found occasion, one morning, to speak at some length, and very harshly, to his book-keeper. He had hardly ceased when John Richling came briskly in.

"Doctor," he said, with great buoyancy, "how do you do?"

The physician slightly frowned.

"Good-morning, Mr. Richling."

Richling was tamed in an instant; but, to avoid too great a contrast of manner, he retained a semblance of sprightliness, as he said : —

"This is the first time I have had this pleasure since you were last at our house, Doctor."

"Did you not see me one evening, some time ago, in the omnibus?" asked Dr. Sevier.

"Why, no," replied the other, with returning pleasure ; "was I in the same omnibus?"

"You were on the sidewalk."

"No-o," said Richling, pondering. "I've seen you in your carriage several times, but you "—

"I didn't see you."

Richling was stung. The conversation failed. He recommenced it in a tone pitched intentionally too low for the alert ear of Narcisse.

"Doctor, I've simply called to say to you that I'm out of work and looking for employment again."

"Um—hum," said the Doctor, with a cold fulness of voice that hurt Richling afresh. "You'll find it hard to get anything this time of year," he continued, with no attempt at undertone; "it's very hard for anybody to get anything these days, even when well recommended."

Richling smiled an instant. The Doctor did not, but turned partly away to his desk, and added, as if the smile had displeased him: —

"Well, maybe you'll not find it so."

Richling turned fiery red.

"Whether I do or not," he said, rising, "my affairs sha'n't trouble anybody. Good-morning!"

He started out.

"How's Mrs. Richling?" asked the Doctor.

"She's well," responded Richling, putting on his hat and disappearing in the corridor. Each footstep could be heard as he went down the stairs

"He's a fool!" muttered the physician.

He looked up angrily, for Narcisse stood before him.

"Well, Doctah," said the Creole, hurriedly arranging his coat-collar, and drawing his handkerchief, "I'm goin' ad the poss-office."

"See here, sir!" exclaimed the Doctor, bringing his fist down upon the arm of his chair, "every time you've gone out of this office for the last six months you've told me you were going to the post-office; now don't you ever tell me that again!"

The young man bowed with injured dignity and responded: —

"All a-ight, seh."

He overtook Richling just outside the street entrance. Richling had halted there, bereft of intention, almost of outward sense, and choking with bitterness. It seemed to him as if in an instant all his misfortunes, disappointments, and humiliations, that never before had seemed so many or so great, had been gathered up into the knowledge of that hard man upstairs, and, with one unmerciful downward wrench, had received his seal of approval. Indignation, wrath, self-hatred, dismay, in undefined confusion, usurped the faculties of sight and hearing and motion.

"Mistoo Itchlin,' said Narcisse, "I 'ope you fine you'seff O.K., seh, if you'll egscuse the slang expwession."

Richling started to move away, but checked himself.

"I'm well, sir, thank you, sir; yes, sir, I'm very well."

"I billieve you, seh. You ah lookin' well."

Narcisse thrust his hands into his pockets, and turned upon the outer sides of his feet, the embodiment of sweet temper. Richling found him a wonderful relief at the moment. He quit gnawing his lip and winking into vacancy, and felt a malicious good-humor run into all his veins.

"I dunno 'ow 'tis, Mistoo Itchlin," said Narcisse, "but I muz tell you the tooth; you always 'ave to me the appe'ance ligue the chile of p'ospe'ity."

"Eh?" said Richling, hollowing his hand at his ear,— "child of "—

' P'ospe'ity?"

"Yes — yes," replied the deaf man vaguely, "I — have a relative of that name."

"Oh!" exclaimed the Creole, "thass good faw luck! Mistoo Itchlin, look' like you a lil mc' hawd to yeh — but egscuse me. I s'pose you muz be advansing in business, Mistoo Itchlin. I say I s'pose you muz be gittin' along!"

"I? Yes; yes, I must."

He started.

" I'm 'appy to yeh it ! " said Narcisse.

His innocent kindness was a rebuke. Richling began to offer a cordial parting salutation, but Narcisse said : —

" You goin' that way? Well, I kin go that way."

They went.

" I was goin' ad the poss-office, but " — he waved his hand and curled his lip. " Mistoo Itchlin, in fact, if you yeh of something suitable to me I would like to yeh it. I am not satisfied with that pless yondeh with Doctah Seveeah. I was compel this mawnin', biffo you came in, to 'epoove 'im faw 'is 'oodness. He called me a jackass, in fact. I woon allow that. I 'ad to 'epoove 'im. ' Doctah Seveeah,' says I, ' don't you call me a jackass ag'in ! ' An' 'e din call it me ag'in. No, seh. But 'e din like to 'ush up. Thass the rizz'n 'e was a lil miscutteous to you. Me, I am always polite. As they say, ' A nod is juz as good as a kick f'om a bline hoss.' You are fon' of maxim, Mistoo Itchlin? Me, I'm ve'y fon' of them. But they's got one maxim what you may 'ave 'eard — I do not fine that maxim always come t'ue. 'Ave you evva yeah that maxim, ' A fool faw luck ' ? That don't always come t'ue. I 'ave discove'd that."

" No," responded Richling, with a parting smile, " that doesn't always come true."

Dr. Sevier denounced the world at large, and the American nation in particular, for two days. Within himself, for twenty-four hours, he grumly blamed Richling for their rupture ; then for twenty-four hours reproached himself, and, on the morning of the third day knocked at the door, corner of St. Mary and Prytania.

No one answered. He knocked again. A woman in bare feet showed herself at the corresponding door-way in the farther half of the house.

" Nobody don't live there no more, sir," she said.

" Where have they gone? "

" Well, reely, I couldn't tell you, sir. Because, reely, I don't know nothing about it. I haint but jest lately moved in here myself, and I don't know nothing about nobody around here scarcely at all."

The Doctor shut himself again in his carriage and let himself be whisked away, in great vacuity of mind.

" They can't blame anybody but themselves," was, by-and-by, his rallying thought. " Still " — he said to himself after another vacant interval, and said no more. The thought that whether *they* could blame others or not did not cover all the ground, rested heavily on him.

CHAPTER XV.

THE CRADLE FALLS.

IN the rear of the great commercial centre of New Orleans, on that part of Common street where it suddenly widens out, broad, unpaved, and dusty, rises the huge dull-brown structure of brick, famed, well-nigh as far as the city is known, as the Charity Hospital.

Twenty-five years ago, when the emigrant ships used to unload their swarms of homeless and friendless strangers into the streets of New Orleans to fall a prey to yellow-fever or cholera, that solemn pile sheltered thousands on thousands of desolate and plague-stricken Irish and Germans, receiving them unquestioned, until at times the very floors were covered with the sick and dying, and the sawing and hammering in the coffin-shop across the inner court ceased not day or night. Sombre monument at once of charity and sin! For, while its comfort and succor cost the houseless wanderer nothing, it lived and grew, and lives and grows still, upon the licensed vices of the people,—drinking, harlotry, and gambling.

The Charity Hospital of St. Charles — such is its true name — is, however, no mere plague-house. Whether it ought to be, let doctors decide. How good or necessary such modern innovations as "ridge ventilation," "movable bases," the "pavilion plan," "trained nurses," etc., may be, let the Auxiliary Sanitary Association say. There it stands as of old, innocent of all sins that may be involved in any of these changes, rising story over

story, up and up : here a ward for poisonous fevers, and
there a ward for acute surgical cases ; here a story full of
simple ailments, and there a ward specially set aside for
women.

In 1857 this last was Dr. Sevier's ward. Here, at his
stated hour one summer morning in that year, he tarried
a moment, yonder by that window, just where you enter
the ward and before you come to the beds. He had fallen
into discourse with some of the more inquiring minds
among the train of students that accompained him, and
waited there to finish and cool down to a physician's
proper temperature. The question was public sanitation.

He was telling a tall Arkansan, with high-combed hair,
self-conscious gloves, and very broad, clean-shaven lower
jaw, how the peculiar formation of delta lands, by which
they drain away from the larger watercourses, instead of
into them, had made the swamp there in the rear of the
town, for more than a century, " the common dumping-
ground and cesspool of the city, sir ! "

Some of the students nodded convincedly to the
speaker ; some looked askance at the Arkansan, who put
one forearm meditatively under his coat-tail ; some
looked through the window over the regions alluded to,
and some only changed their pose and looked around for
a mirror.

The Doctor spoke on. Several of his hearers were
really interested in the then unusual subject, and listened
intelligently as he pointed across the low plain at hundreds
of acres of land that were nothing but a morass, partly
filled in with the foulest refuse of a semi-tropical city, and
beyond it where still lay the swamp, half cleared of its
forest and festering in the sun — " every drop of its
waters, and every inch of its mire," said the Doctor,
" saturated with the poisonous drainage of the town ! "

"I happen," interjected a young city student; but the others bent their ear to the Doctor, who continued: —

"Why, sir, were these regions compactly built on, like similar areas in cities confined to narrow sites, the mortality, with the climate we have, would be frightful."

"I happen to know," essayed the city student; but the Arkansan had made an interrogatory answer to the Doctor, that led him to add: —

"Why, yes; you see the houses here on these lands are little, flimsy, single ground-story affairs, loosely thrown together, and freely exposed to sun and air."

"I hap—," said the city student.

"And yet," exclaimed the Doctor, "Malaria is king!"

He paused an instant for his hearers to take in the figure.

"Doctor, I happen to" —

Some one's fist from behind caused the speaker to turn angrily, and the Doctor resumed: —

"Go into any of those streets off yonder, — Trémé, Prieur, Marais. Why, there are often ponds under the houses! The floors of bedrooms are within a foot or two of these ponds! The bricks of the surrounding pavements are often covered with a fine, dark moss! Water seeps up through the sidewalks! That's his realm, sir! Here and there among the residents — every here and there — you'll see his sallow, quaking subjects dragging about their work or into and out of their beds, until a fear of a fatal ending drives them in here. Congestion? Yes, sometimes congestion pulls them under suddenly, and they're gone before they know it. Sometimes their vitality wanes slowly, until Malaria beckons in Consumption."

"Why, Doctor," said the city student, ruffling with pride of his town, "there are plenty of cities as bad as this. I happen to know, for 'nstance" —

Dr. Sevier turned away in quiet contempt.

"It will not improve our town to dirty others, or to clean them, either."

He moved down the ward, while two or three members among the moving train, who never happened to know anything, nudged each other joyfully.

The group stretched out and came along, the Doctor first and the young men after, some of one sort, some of another, — the dull, the frivolous, the earnest, the kind, the cold, — following slowly, pausing, questioning, discoursing, advancing, moving from each clean, slender bed to the next, on this side and on that, down and up the long sanded aisles, among the poor, sick women.

Among these, too, there was variety. Some were stupid and ungracious, hardened and dulled with long penury as some in this world are hardened and dulled with long riches. Some were as fat as beggars; some were old and shrivelled; some were shrivelled and young; some were bold; some were frightened; and here and there was one almost fair.

Down at the far end of one aisle was a bed whose occupant lay watching the distant, slowly approaching group with eyes of unspeakable dread. There was not a word or motion, only the steadfast gaze. Gradually the throng drew near. The faces of the students could be distinguished. This one was coarse; that one was gentle; another was sleepy; another trivial and silly; another heavy and sour; another tender and gracious. Presently the tones of the Doctor's voice could be heard, soft, clear, and without that trumpet quality that it had beyond the sick-room. How slowly, yet how surely, they came! The patient's eyes turned away toward the ceiling; they could not bear the slowness of the encounter. They closed; the lips moved in prayer. The group came to the bed that was only the fourth away; then to the third; then to the second. There they pause some minutes. Now the Doctor approaches the very next bed. Suddenly he notices this patient. She is a small woman, young, fair to see, and, with closed eyes and motionless form, is suffering an agony of consternation. One startled look, a suppressed exclamation, two steps forward, — the patient's eyes slowly open. Ah, me! It is Mary Richling.

"Good-morning, madam," said the physician, with a cold and distant bow; and to the students, "We'll pass right along to the other side," and they moved into the next aisle.

"I am a little pressed for time this morning," he presently remarked, as the students showed some unwillingness to be hurried. As soon as he could he parted with them and returned to the ward alone.

As he moved again down among the sick, straight along this time, turning neither to right nor left, one of the Sisters of Charity — the hospital and its so-called nurses are under their oversight — touched his arm. He stopped impatiently.

"Well, Sister" — (bowing his ear).

"I — I — the — the" — His frown had scared away her power of speech.

"Well, what is it, Sister?"

"The — the last patient down on this side" —

He was further displeased. "*I'll* attend to the patients, Sister," he said; and then, more kindly, "I'm going there now. No, you stay here, if you please." And he left her behind.

He came and stood by the bed. The patient gazed on him.

"Mrs. Richling," he softly began, and had to cease.

She did not speak or move; she tried to smile, but her eyes filled, her lips quivered.

"My dear madam," exclaimed the physician, in a low voice, "what brought you here?"

The answer was inarticulate, but he saw it on the moving lips.

"Want," said Mary.

"But your husband?" He stooped to catch the husky answer.

"Home."

"Home?" He could not understand. "Not gone to —back —up the river?"

She slowly shook her head: "No, home. In Prieur street."

Still her words were riddles. He could not see how she had come to this. He stood silent, not knowing how to utter his thought. At length he opened his lips to speak, hesitated an instant, and then asked: —

"Mrs. Richling, tell me plainly, has your husband gone wrong?"

Her eyes looked up, a moment, upon him, big and staring, and suddenly she spoke: —

"O Doctor! My husband go wrong? John go wrong?" The eyelids closed down, the head rocked slowly from side to side on the flat hospital pillow, and the first two tears he had ever seen her shed welled from the long lashes and slipped down her cheeks.

"My poor child!" said the Doctor, taking her hand in his. "No, no! God forgive me! He hasn't gone wrong; he's not going wrong. You'll tell me all about it when you're stronger."

The Doctor had her removed to one of the private rooms of the pay-ward, and charged the Sisters to take special care of her. "Above all things," he murmured, with a beetling frown, "tell that thick-headed nurse not to let her know that this is at anybody's expense. Ah, yes; and when her husband comes, tell him to see me at my office as soon as he possibly can."

As he was leaving the hospital gate he had an afterthought : " I might have left a note." He paused, with his foot on the carriage-step. " I suppose they'll tell him," — and so he got in and drove off, looking at his watch.

On his second visit, although he came in with a quietly inspiring manner, he had also, secretly, the feeling of a culprit. But, midway of the room, when the young head on the pillow turned its face toward him, his heart rose. For the patient smiled. As he drew nearer she slid out her feeble hand. " I'm glad I came here," she murmured.

" Yes," he replied ; " this room is much better than the open ward."

" I didn't mean this room," she said. " I meant the whole hospital."

" The whole hospital ! " He raised his eyebrows, as to a child.

" Ah ! Doctor," she responded, her eyes kindling, though moist.

" What, my child ? "

She smiled upward to his bent face.

" The poor — mustn't be ashamed of the poor, must they ? "

The Doctor only stroked her brow, and presently turned and addressed his professional inquiries to the nurse. He went away. Just outside the door he asked the nurse : —

" Hasn't her husband been here ? "

" Yes," was the reply, " but she was asleep, and he only stood there at the door and looked in a bit. He trembled," the unintelligent woman added, for the Doctor seemed waiting to hear more, — " he trembled all over ;

and that's all he did, excepting his saying her name over
to himself like, over and over, and wiping of his eyes."

"And nobody told him anything?"

"Oh, not a word, sir!" came the eager answer.

"You didn't tell him to come and see me?"

The woman gave a start, looked dismayed, and
began: —

"N-no, sir; you didn't tell" —

"Um — hum," growled the Doctor. He took out a
card and wrote on it. "Now see if you can remember to
give him that."

CHAPTER XVI.

MANY WATERS.

AS the day faded away it began to rain. The next morning the water was coming down in torrents. Richling, looking out from a door in Prieur street, found scant room for one foot on the inner edge of the sidewalk; all the rest was under water. By noon the sidewalks were completely covered in miles of streets. By two in the afternoon the flood was coming into many of the houses. By three it was up at the door-sill on which he stood. There it stopped.

He could do nothing but stand and look. Skiffs, canoes, hastily improvised rafts, were moving in every direction, carrying the unsightly chattels of the poor out of their overflowed cottages to higher ground. Barrels, boxes, planks, hen-coops, bridge lumber, piles of straw that waltzed solemnly as they went, cord-wood, old shingles, door-steps, floated here and there in melancholy confusion; and down upon all still drizzled the slackening rain. At length it ceased.

Richling still stood in the door-way, the picture of mute helplessness. Yes, there was one other thing he could do; he could laugh. It would have been hard to avoid it sometimes, there were such ludicrous sights, — such slips and sprawls into the water; so there he stood in that peculiar isolation that deaf people content themselves with, now looking the picture of anxious waiting, now indulging a low, deaf man's chuckle when something made the rowdies and slattens of the street roar.

Presently he noticed, at a distance up the way, a young man in a canoe, passing, much to their good-natured chagrin, a party of three in a skiff, who had engaged him in a trial of speed. From both boats a shower of hilarious French was issuing. At the nearest corner the skiff party turned into another street and disappeared, throwing their lingual fireworks to the last. The canoe came straight on with the speed of a fish. Its dexterous occupant was no other than Narcisse.

There was a grace in his movement that kept Richling's eyes on him, when he would rather have withdrawn into the house. Down went the paddle always on the same side, noiselessly, in front; on darted the canoe; backward stretched the submerged paddle and came out of the water edgewise at full reach behind, with an almost imperceptible swerving motion that kept the slender craft true to its course. No rocking; no rush of water before or behind; only the one constant glassy ripple gliding on either side as silently as a beam of light. Suddenly, without any apparent change of movement in the sinewy wrists, the narrow shell swept around in a quarter circle, and Narcisse sat face to face with Richling.

Each smiled brightly at the other. The handsome Creole's face was aglow with the pure delight of existence.

"Well, Mistoo Itchlin, 'ow you enjoyin' that watah? As fah as myseff am concerned, 'I am afloat, I am afloat on the fee-us 'olling tide.' I don't think you fine that stweet pwetty dusty to-day, Mistoo Itchlin?"

Richling laughed.

"It don't inflame my eyes to-day," he said.

"You muz egscuse my i'ony, Mistoo Itchlin; I can't 'ep that sometime'. It come natu'al to me, in fact. I was on'y speaking i'oniously juz now in calling allusion to that dust; because, of co'se, theh s no dust to-day,

because the g'ound is all covvud with watah, in fact.
Some people don't understand that figgah of i'ony."

" I don't understand as much about it myself as I'd like
to," said Richling.

" Me, I'm ve'y fon' of it," responded the Creole. " I
was making seve'al i'onies ad those fwen' of mine juz now.
We was 'unning a 'ace. An' thass anotheh thing I am
fon' of. I would 'ather 'un a 'ace than to wuck faw a
livin'. Ha! ha! ha! I should thing so! Anybody would,
in fact. But thass the way with me — always making
some i'onies." He stopped with a sudden change of
countenance, and resumed gravely: " Mistoo Itchlin,
looks to me like you' lookin' ve'y salad." He fanned himself with his hat. " I dunno 'ow 'tis with you, Mistoo
Itchlin, but I fine myseff ve'y oppwessive thiz evening."

" I don't find you so," said Richling, smiling broadly.

And he did not. The young Creole's burning face and
resplendent wit were a sunset glow in the darkness of this
day of overpowering adversity. His presence even supplied, for a moment, what seemed a gleam of hope. Why
wasn't there here an opportunity to visit the hospital?
He need not tell Narcisse the object of his visit.

" Do you think," asked Richling, persuasively, crouch
ing down upon one of his heels, " that I could sit in that
thing without turning it over?"

" In that pee-ogue?" Narcisse smiled the smile of
the proficient as he waved his paddle across the canoe.
" Mistoo Itchlin," — the smile passed off, — " I dunno
if you'll billiv me, but at the same time I muz tell you the
tooth?" —

He paused inquiringly.

" Certainly," said Richling, with evident disappoint
ment.

" Well, it's juz a poss'bil'ty that you'll wefwain fum

spillin' out fum yeh till the negs cawneh. Thass the manneh of those who ah not acquainted with the pee-ogue. ' Lost to sight, to memo'y deah ' — if you'll egscuse the maxim. Thass Chawles Dickens mague use of that egs-pwession."

Richling answered with a gay shake of the head. " I'll keep out of it." If Narcisse detected his mortified cha-grin, he did not seem to. It was hard ; the day's last hope was blown out like a candle in the wind. Richling dared not risk the wetting of his suit of clothes ; they were his sole letter of recommendation and capital in trade.

"Well, *au 'evoi*', Mistoo Itchlin." He turned and moved off — dip, glide, and away.

Dr. Sevier stamped his wet feet on the pavement of the hospital porch. It was afternoon of the day following that of the rain. The water still covering the streets about the hospital had not prevented his carriage from splashing through it on his double daily round. A nar-row and unsteady plank spanned the immersed sidewalk. Three times, going and coming, he had crossed it safely, and this fourth time he had made half the distance well enough ; but, hearing distant cheers and laughter, he looked up street ; when — splatter ! — and the cheers were re-doubled.

" Pretty thing to laugh at !" he muttered. Two or three bystanders, leaning on their umbrellas in the lodge at the gate and in the porch, where he stood stamping, turned their backs and smoothed their mouths.

" Hah !" said the tall Doctor, stamping harder Stamp ! — stamp ! He shook his leg. — " Bah !" He stamped the other long, slender, wet foot and looked down at it, turning one side and then the other. — " F-fah !" —

The first one again. — "Psha!" — The other. — Stamp!
— stamp! — "*Right — into* it! — up to my *ankles!*" He
looked around with a slight scowl at one man, who seemed
taken with a sudden softening of the spine and knees,
and who turned his back quickly and fell against another,
who, also with his back turned, was leaning tremulously
against a pillar.

But the object of mirth did not tarry. He went as he
was to Mary's room, and found her much better — as,
indeed, he had done at every visit. He sat by her bed
and listened to her story.

"Why, Doctor, you see, we did nicely for a while.
John went on getting the same kind of work, and pleasing
everybody, of course, and all he lacked was finding something permanent. Still, we passed through one month
after another, and we really began to think the sun was
coming out, so to speak."

"Well, I thought so, too," put in the Doctor. "I
thought if it didn't you'd let me know."

"Why, no, Doctor, we couldn't do that; you couldn't
be taking care of well people."

"Well," said the Doctor, dropping that point, "I
suppose as the busy season began to wane that mode of
livelihood, of course, disappeared."

"Yes," — a little one-sided smile, — "and so did our
money. And then, of course," — she slightly lifted and
waved her hand.

"You had to live," said Dr. Sevier, sincerely.

She smiled again, with abstracted eyes. "We thought
we'd like to," she said. "I didn't mind the loss of the
things so much, — except the little table we ate from.
You remember that little round table, don't you?"

The visitor had not the heart to say no He nodded.

"When that went there was but one thing left that could go."

"Not your bed?"

"The bedstead; yes."

"You didn't sell your bed, Mrs. Richling?"

The tears gushed from her eyes. She made a sign of assent.

"But then," she resumed, "we made an excellent arrangement with a good woman who had just lost her husband, and wanted to live cheaply, too."

"What amuses you, madam?"

"Nothing great. But I wish you knew her. She's funny. Well, so we moved down-town again. Didn't cost much to move."

She would smile a little in spite of him.

"And then?" said he, stirring impatiently and leaning forward. "What then?"

"Why, then I worked a little harder than I thought,— pulling trunks around and so on,— and I had this third attack."

The Doctor straightened himself up, folded his arms, and muttered:—

"Oh!— oh! *Why* wasn't I instantly sent for?"

The tears were in her eyes again, but—

"Doctor," she answered, with her odd little argumentative smile, "how could we? We had nothing to pay with. It wouldn't have been just."

"Just!" exclaimed the physician, angrily.

"Doctor," said the invalid, and looked at him.

"Oh— all right!"

She made no answer but to look at him still more pleadingly.

"Wouldn't it have been just as fair to let me be generous, madam?" His faint smile was bitter. "For once? Simply for once?"

"We couldn't make that proposition, could we, Doctor?"

He was checkmated.

"Mrs. Richling," he said suddenly, clasping the back of his chair as if about to rise, "tell me, — did you or your husband act this way for anything I've ever said or done?"

"No, Doctor! no, no; never! But"—

"But kindness should seek — not be sought," said the physician, starting up.

"No, Doctor, we didn't look on it so. Of course we didn't. If there's any fault it's all mine. For it was my own proposition to John, that as we *had* to seek charity we should just be honest and open about it. I said, 'John, as I need the best attention, and as that can be offered free only in the hospital, why, to the hospital I ought to go.'"

She lay still, and the Doctor pondered. Presently he said : —

"And Mr. Richling — I suppose he looks for work all the time?"

"From daylight to dark!"

"Well, the water is passing off. He'll be along by and by to see you, no doubt. Tell him to call, first thing to-morrow morning, at my office." And with that the Doctor went off in his wet boots, committed a series of indiscretions, reached home, and fell ill.

In the wanderings of fever he talked of the Richlings, and in lucid moments inquired for them.

"Yes, yes," answered the sick Doctor's physician, "they're attended to. Yes, all their wants are supplied. Just dismiss them from your mind." In the eyes of this physician the Doctor's life was invaluable, and these patients, or pensioners, an unknown and, most likely, an inconsiderable quantity; two sparrows, as it were, worth a farthing. But the sick man lay thinking. He frowned.

"I wish they would go home."

"I have sent them."

"You have? Home to Milwaukee?"

"Yes."

"Thank God!"

He soon began to mend. Yet it was weeks before he could leave the house. When one day he reëntered the hospital, still pale and faint, he was prompt to express to the Mother-Superior the comfort he had felt in his sickness to know that his brother physician had sent those Richlings to their kindred.

The Sister shook her head. He saw the deception in an instant. As best his strength would allow, he hurried to the keeper of the rolls. There was the truth. Home? Yes, — to Prieur street, — discharged only one week before. He drove quickly to his office.

"Narcisse, you will find that young Mr. Richling living in Prieur street, somewhere between Conti and St. Louis. I don't know the house; you'll have to find it. Tell him I'm in my office again, and to come and see me."

Narcisse was no such fool as to say he knew the house. He would get the praise of finding it quickly.

"I'll do my mose awduous, seh," he said, took down his coat, hung up his jacket, put on his hat, and went straight to the house and knocked. Got no answer. Knocked again, and a third time; but in vain. Went next door and inquired of a pretty girl, who fell in love with him at a glance.

"Yes, but they had moved. She wasn't *jess ezac'ly*

sure where they *had* moved to, *unless-n* it was in that little house yondeh between St. Louis and Toulouse ; and if they wasn't there she didn't know *where* they was. People ought to leave words where they's movin' at, but they don't. You're very welcome," she added, as he expressed his thanks ; and he would have been welcome had he questioned her for an hour. His parting bow and smile stuck in her heart a six-months.

He went to the spot pointed out. As a Creole he was used to seeing very respectable people living in very small and plain houses This one was not too plain even foi his ideas of Richling, though it was but a little one-street-door-and-window affair, with an alley on the left running back into the small yard behind. He knocked. Again no one answered. He looked down the alley and saw, moving about the yard, a large woman, who, he felt certain, could not be Mrs. Richling.

Two little short-skirted, bare-legged girls were playing near him. He spoke to them in French. Did they know where Monsieu' Itchlin lived? The two children repeated the name, looking inquiringly at each other.

" *Non, miché.*" — " No, sir, they didn't know."

" *Qui reste ici?*" he asked. " Who lives here?"

" *Ici?   Madame qui reste là c'est Mizziz Ri-i-i-ly!*" said one.

" Yass," said the other, breaking into English and rubbing a musquito off of her well-tanned shank with the sole of her foot, " tis Mizziz Ri-i-i-ly what live there. She jess move een. She's got a lill baby. —Oh! you means dat lady what was in de Chatty Hawspill!"

" No, no! A real, nice *lady*. She nevva saw thai Cha'ity Hospi'l."

The little girls shook their heads. They couldn't imagine a person who had never seen the Charity Hospital.

"Was there nobody else who had moved into any of these houses about here lately?" He spoke again in French. They shook their heads. Two boys came forward and verified the testimony. Narcisse went back with his report: "Moved, — not found."

"I fine that ve'y d'oll, Doctah Seveeah," concluded the unaugmented, hanging up his hat; "some peop' always 'ard to fine. I h-even notiz that sem thing w'en I go to colic' some bill. I dunno 'ow 'tis, Doctah, but I assu' you I kin tell that by a man's physio'nomy. Nobody teach me that. 'Tis my own in*geen*u'ty 'as made me to discoveh that, in fact."

The Doctor was silent. Presently he drew a piece of paper toward him and, dipping his pen into the ink, began to write: —

"Information wanted of the whereabouts of John Richling" —

"Narcisse," he called, still writing, "I want you to take an advertisement to the 'Picayune' office."

"With the gweatez of pleazheh, seh." The clerk began his usual shifting of costume. "Yesseh! I assu' you, Doctah, that is a p'oposition moze enti'ly to my satizfagtion; faw I am suffe'ing faw a smoke, and deztitute of a ciga'ette! I am aztonizh' 'ow I did that, to egshauz them unconsciouzly, in fact." He received the advertisement in an envelope, whipped his shoes a little with his handkerchief, and went out. One would think to hear him thundering down the stairs, that it was twenty-five cents' worth of ice.

"Hold o—" The Doctor started from his seat, then turned and paced feebly up and down. Who, besides Richling, might see that notice? What might be its unexpected results? Who was John Richling? A man with a secret at the best; and a secret, in Dr. Sevier's

eyes, was detestable. Might not Richling be a man who
had fled from something? "No! no!" The Doctor
spoke aloud. He had promised to think nothing ill of
him. Let the poor children have their silly secret. He
spoke again: "They'll find out the folly of it by and
by." He let the advertisement go; and it went

CHAPTER XVII

RAPHAEL RISTOFALO.

RICHLING had a dollar in his pocket. A man touched him on the shoulder.

But let us see. On the day that John and Mary had sold their only bedstead, Mrs. Riley, watching them, had proposed the joint home. The offer had been accepted with an eagerness that showed itself in nervous laughter. Mrs. Riley then took quarters in Prieur street, where John and Mary, for a due consideration, were given a single neatly furnished back room. The bedstead had brought seven dollars. Richling, on the day after the removal, was in the commercial quarter, looking, as usual, for employment.

The young man whom Dr. Sevier had first seen, in the previous October, moving with a springing step and alert, inquiring glances from number to number in Carondelet street was slightly changed. His step was firm, but something less elastic, and not quite so hurried. His face was more thoughtful, and his glance wanting in a certain dancing freshness that had been extremely pleasant. He was walking in Poydras street toward the river.

As he came near to a certain man who sat in the entrance of a store with the freshly whittled corner of a chair between his knees, his look and bow were grave, but amiable, quietly hearty, deferential, and also self-respectful — and uncommercial : so palpably uncommercial that the sitter did not rise or even shut his knife.

He slightly stared. Richling, in a low, private tone, was asking him for employment.

"What?" turning his ear up and frowning downward.

The application was repeated, the first words with a slightly resentful ring, but the rest more quietly.

The store-keeper stared again, and shook his head slowly.

"No, sir," he said, in a barely audible tone. Richling moved on, not stopping at the next place, or the next, or the next; for he felt the man's stare all over his back until he turned the corner and found himself in Tchoupitoulas street. Nor did he stop at the first place around the corner. It smelt of deteriorating potatoes and up-river cabbages, and there were open barrels of onions set ornamentally aslant at the entrance. He had a fatal conviction that his services would not be wanted in malodorous places.

"Now, isn't that a shame?" asked the chair-whittler, as Richling passed out of sight. "Such a gentleman as that, to be beggin' for work from door to door!"

"He's not beggin' f'om do' to do'," said a second, with a Creole accent on his tongue, and a match stuck behind his ear like a pen. "Beside, he's too *much* of a gennlemun."

"That's where you and him differs," said the first. He frowned upon the victim of his delicate repartee with make-believe defiance. Number Two drew from an outside coat-pocket a wad of common brown wrapping-paper, tore from it a small, neat parallelogram, dove into an opposite pocket for some loose smoking-tobacco, laid a pinch of it in the paper, and, with a single dexterous turn of the fingers, thumbs above, the rest beneath, — it looks simple, but 'tis an amazing art, — made a cigarette Then he took down his match, struck it under his short coat-skirt, lighted his cigarette, drew an inhalation through it that consumed a third of its length, and sat there, with his eyes half-closed, and all that smoke somewhere inside of him.

"That young man," remarked a third, wiping a tooth-pick on his thigh and putting it in his vest-pocket, as he stepped to the front, "don't know how to *look* fur work. There's one way fur a day-laborer to look fur work, and there's another way fur a gentleman to look fur work, and there's another way fur a — a — a man with money to look fur somethin' to put his money into. *It's just like fishing!*" He threw both hands outward and downward, and made way for a porter's truck with a load of green meat. The smoke began to fall from Number Two's nostrils in two slender blue streams. Number Three continued : —

"You've got to know what kind o' hooks you want, and what kind o' bait you want, and then, after *that*, you've " —

Numbers One and Two did not let him finish.

" — Got to know how to fish," they said; "that's so!" The smoke continued to leak slowly from Number Two's nostrils and teeth, though he had not lifted his cigarette the second time.

"Yes, you've got to know how to fish," reaffirmed the third. "If you don't know how to fish, it's as like as not that nobody can tell you what's the matter; an' yet, all the same, you aint goin' to ketch no fish."

"Well, now," said the first man, with an unconvinced swing of his chin, "*spunk* 'll sometimes pull a man through; and you can't say he aint spunky." Number Three admitted the corollary. Number Two looked up: his chance had come.

"He'd a w'ipped you faw a dime," said he to Number

One, took a comforting draw from his cigarette, and felt a great peace.

"I take notice he's a little deaf," said Number Three, still alluding to Richling.

"That'd spoil him for me," said Number One.

Number Three asked why.

"Oh, I just wouldn't have him about me. Didn't you ever notice that a deaf man always seems like a sort o' stranger? I can't bear 'em."

Richling meanwhile moved on. His critics were right. He was not wanting in courage; but no man from the moon could have been more an alien on those sidewalks. He was naturally diligent, active, quick-witted, and of good, though maybe a little too scholarly address; quick of temper, it is true, and uniting his quickness of temper with a certain bashfulness, — an unlucky combination, since, as a consequence, nobody had to get out of its way; but he was generous in fact and in speech, and never held malice a moment. But, besides the heavy odds which his small secret seemed to be against him, estopping him from accepting such valuable friendships as might otherwise have come to him, and besides his slight deafness, he was by nature a recluse, or, at least, a dreamer. Every day that he set foot on Tchoupitoulas, or Carondelet, or Magazine, or Fulton, or Poydras street he came from a realm of thought, seeking service in an empire of matter.

There is a street in New Orleans called Triton *Walk*. That is what all the ways of commerce and finance and daily bread-getting were to Richling. He was a merman —ashore. It was the feeling rather than the knowledge of this that prompted him to this daily, aimless trudging after mere employment. He had a proper pride; once in a while a little too much; nor did he clearly see his deficiencies; and yet the unrecognized consciousness that he had not the commercial instinct made him willing — as Number Three would have said — to "cut bait" for any fisherman who would let him do it.

He turned without any distinct motive and, retracing his steps to the corner, passed up across Poydras street. A little way above it he paused to look at some machinery in motion. He liked machinery, — for itself rather than for its results. He would have gone in and examined the workings of this apparatus had it not been for the sign above his head, "No Admittance." Those words always seemed painted for him. A slight modification in Richling's character might have made him an inventor. Some other faint difference, and he might have been a writer, a historian, an essayist, or even — there is no telling — a well-fed poet. With the question of food, raiment, and shelter permanently settled, he might have become one of those resplendent flash lights that at intervals dart their beams across the dark waters of the world's ignorance, hardly from new continents, but from the observatory, the study, the laboratory. But he was none of these. There had been a crime committed somewhere in his bringing up, and as a result he stood in the thick of life's battle, weaponless. He gazed upon machinery with childlike wonder; but when he looked around and saw on every hand men, — good fellows who ate in their shirt-sleeves at restaurants, told broad jokes, spread their mouths and smote their sides when they laughed, and whose best wit was to bombard one another with bread-crusts and hide behind the sugar-bowl; men whom he could have taught in every kind of knowledge that they were capable of grasping, except the knowledge of how to get money, — when he saw these men, as it seemed to him, grow rich daily by simply flipping beans into each other's faces, or slapping each other on the back, the wonder of machinery was eclipsed. Do as they did? He? He could no more reach a conviction as to what the price of corn would be to-morrow than he could remember what the price of sugar was yesterday.

He called himself an accountant, gulping down his secret pride with an amiable glow that commanded, instantly, an amused esteem. And, to judge by his evident familiarity with Tonti's beautiful scheme of mercantile records, he certainly—those guessed whose books he had extricated from confusion—had handled money and money values in days before his unexplained coming to New Orleans. Yet a close observer would have noticed that he grasped these tasks only as problems, treated them in their mathematical and enigmatical aspect, and solved them without any appreciation of their concrete values. When they were done he felt less personal interest in them than in the architectural beauty of the store-front, whose window-shutters he had never helped to close without a little heart-leap of pleasure.

But, standing thus, and looking in at the machinery, a man touched him on the shoulder.

"Good-morning," said the man. He wore a pleasant air. It seemed to say, "I'm nothing much, but you'll recognize me in a moment; I'll wait." He was short, square, solid, beardless; in years, twenty-five or six. His skin was dark, his hair almost black, his eyebrows strong. In his mild black eyes you could see the whole Mediterranean. His dress was coarse, but clean; his linen soft and badly laundered. But under all the rough garb and careless, laughing manner was visibly written again and again the name of the race that once held the world under its feet.

" You don't remember me?" he added, after a moment.

" No," said Richling, pleasantly, but with embarrassment. The man waited another moment, and suddenly Richling recalled their earlier meeting. The man, representing a wholesale confectioner in one of the smaller cities up the river, had bought some cordials and syrups of the house whose books Richling had last put in order.

" Why, yes I do, too!" said Richling. "You left your pocket-book in my care for two or three days; your own private money, you said."

" Yes." The man laughed softly. " Lost that money. Sent it to the boss. Boss died — store seized — everything gone." His English was well pronounced, but did not escape a pretty Italian accent, too delicate for the printer's art.

" Oh! that was too bad!" Richling laid his hand upon an awning-post and twined an arm and leg around it as though he were a vine. " I — I forget your name."

" Ristofalo. Raphael Ristofalo. Yours is Richling. Yes, knocked me flat. Not got cent in world." The Italian's low, mellow laugh claimed Richling's admiration.

" Why, when did that happen?" he asked.

" Yes'day," replied the other, still laughing.

" And how are you going to provide for the future?" Richling asked, smiling down into the face of the shorter man. The Italian tossed the future away with the back of his hand.

" I got nothin' do with that." His words were low, but very distinct.

Thereupon Richling laughed, leaning his cheek against the post.

" Must provide for the present," said Raphael Ristofalo. Richling dropped his eyes in thought. The present! He had never been able to see that it was the present which must be provided against, until, while he was training his guns upon the future, the most primitive wants of the present burst upon him right and left like whooping savages.

"Can you lend me dollar?" asked the Italian. "Give you back dollar an' quarter to-morrow."

Richling gave a start and let go the post. "Why, Mr. Risto — falo, I — I —, the fact is, I" — he shook his head — "I haven't much money."

"Dollar will start me," said the Italian, whose feet had not moved an inch since he touched Richling's shoulder. "Be aw righ' to-morrow."

"You can't invest one dollar by itself," said the incredulous Richling.

"Yes. Return her to-morrow."

Richling swung his head from side to side as an expression of disrelish. "I haven't been employed for some time."

"I goin' t'employ myself," said Ristofalo.

Richling laughed again. There was a faint betrayal of distress in his voice as it fell upon the cunning ear of the Italian; but he laughed too, very gently and innocently, and stood in his tracks.

"I wouldn't like to refuse a dollar to a man who needs it," said Richling. He took his hat off and ran his fingers through his hair. "I've seen the time when it was much easier to lend than it is just now." He thrust his hand down into his pocket and stood gazing at the sidewalk.

The Italian glanced at Richling askance, and with one sweep of the eye from the softened crown of his hat to the slender, white bursted slit in the outer side of either well-polished shoe, took in the beauty of his face and a full understanding of his condition. His hair, somewhat dry, had fallen upon his forehead. His fine, smooth

skin was darkened by the exposure of his daily wanderings. His cheek-bones, a trifle high, asserted their place
above the softly concave cheeks. His mouth was closed
and the lips were slightly compressed; the chin small,
gracefully turned, not weak, — not strong. His eyes were
abstracted, deep, pensive. His dress told much. The
fine plaits of his shirt had sprung apart and been neatly
sewed together again. His coat was a little faulty in the
set of the collar, as if the person who had taken the garment apart and turned the goods had not put it together
again with practised skill. It was without spot and the
buttons were new. The edges of his shirt-cuffs had been
trimmed with the scissors. Face and vesture alike revealed to the sharp eye of the Italian the woe underneath.
"He has a wife," thought Ristofalo.

Richling looked up with a smile. "How can you be
so sure you will make, and not lose?"

"I never fail." There was not the least shade of
boasting in the man's manner. Richling handed out his
dollar. It was given without patronage and taken with
simple thanks.

"Where goin' to meet to-morrow morning?" asked
Ristofalo. "Here?"

"Oh! I forgot," said Richling. "Yes, I suppose so;
and then you'll tell me how you invested it, will you?"

"Yes, but you couldn't do it."

"Why not?"

Raphael Ristofalo laughed. "Oh! fifty reason'."

CHAPTER XVIII.

HOW HE DID IT.

RISTOFALO and Richling had hardly separated, when it occurred to the latter that the Italian had first touched him from behind. Had Ristofalo recognized him with his back turned, or had he seen him earlier and followed him? The facts were these: about an hour before the time when Richling omitted to apply for employment in the ill-smelling store in Tchoupitoulas street, Mr. Raphael Ristofalo halted in front of the same place, — which appeared small and slovenly among its more pretentious neighbors, — and stepped just inside the door to where stood a single barrel of apples, — a fruit only the earliest varieties of which were beginning to appear in market. These were very small, round, and smooth, and with a rather wan blush confessed to more than one of the senses that they had seen better days. He began to pick them up and throw them down — one, two, three, four, seven, ten; about half of them were entirely sound

"How many barrel' like this?"

"No got-a no more; dass all," said the dealer. He was a Sicilian. "Lame duck," he added. "Oäl de rest gone."

"How much?" asked Ristofalo, still handling the fruit.

The Sicilian came to the barrel, looked in, and said, w th a gesture of indifference: —

"'M — doll' an' 'alf."

Ristofalo offered to take them at a dollar if he might wash and sort them under the dealer's hydrant, which could be heard running in the back yard. The offer would have been rejected with rude scorn but for one thing: it was spoken in Italian. The man looked at him with pleased surprise, and made the concession. The porter of the store, in a red worsted cap, had drawn near. Ristofalo bade him roll the barrel on its chine to the rear and stand it by the hydrant.

"I will come back pretty soon," he said, in Italian, and went away.

By and by he returned, bringing with him two swarthy, heavy-set, little Sicilian lads, each with his inevitable basket and some clean rags. A smile and gesture to the store-keeper, a word to the boys, and in a moment the barrel was upturned, and the pair were washing, wiping, and sorting the sound and unsound apples at the hydrant.

Ristofalo stood a moment in the entrance of the store. The question now was where to get a dollar. Richling passed, looked in, seemed to hesitate, went on, turned, and passed again, the other way. Ristofalo saw him all the time and recognized him at once, but appeared not to observe him.

"He will do," thought the Italian. "Be back few minute'," he said, glancing behind him.

"Or-r righ'," said the store-keeper, with a hand-wave of good-natured confidence. He recognized Mr. Raphael Ristofalo's species.

The Italian walked up across Poydras street, saw Richling stop and look at the machinery, approached, and touched him on the shoulder.

On parting with him he did not return to the store where he had left the apples. He walked up Tchoupitoulas street about a mile, and where St. Thomas street

branches acutely from it, in a squalid district full of the
poorest Irish, stopped at a dirty fruit-stand and spoke
in Spanish to its Catalan proprietor. Half an hour later
twenty-five cents had changed hands, the Catalan's fruit
shelves were bright with small pyramids — sound side
foremost — of Ristofalo's second grade of apples, the
Sicilian had Richling's dollar, and the Italian was gone
with his boys and his better grade of fruit. Also, a grocer
had sold some sugar, and a druggist a little paper of
some harmless confectioner's dye.

Down behind the French market, in a short, obscure
street that runs from Ursulines to Barracks street, and is
named in honor of Albert Gallatin, are some old buildings of three or four stories' height, rented, in John
Richling's day, to a class of persons who got their
livelihood by sub-letting the rooms, and parts of rooms,
to the wretchedest poor of New Orleans, — organ-grind-
ers, chimney-sweeps, professional beggars, street musi-
cians, lemon-peddlers, rag-pickers, with all the yet dirtier
herd that live by hook and crook in the streets or under
the wharves; a room with a bed and stove, a room
without, a half-room with or without ditto, a quarter-
room with or without a blanket or quilt, and with only a
chalk-mark on the floor instead of a partition. Into one
of these went Mr. Raphael Ristofalo, the two boys, and
the apples. Whose assistance or indulgence, if any, he
secured in there is not recorded; but when, late in
the afternoon, the Italian issued thence — the boys,
meanwhile, had been coming and going — an unusual
luxury had been offered the roustabouts and idlers of the
steamboat landings, and many had bought and eaten
freely of the very small, round, shiny, sugary, and artificially crimson roasted apples, with neatly whittled white-
pine stems to poise them on as they were lifted to the

consumer's watering teeth. When, the next morning,
Richling laughed at the story, the Italian drew out two
dollars and a half, and began to take from it a dollar.

"But you have last night's lodging and so forth yet to
pay for."

"No. Made friends with Sicilian luggerman. Slept
in his lugger." He showed his brow and cheeks speckled
with mosquito-bites. "Ate little hard-tack and coffee
with him this morning. Don't want much." He offered
the dollar with a quarter added. Richling declined the
bonus.

"But why not?"

"Oh, I just couldn't do it," laughed Richling; "that's
all."

"Well," said the Italian, "lend me that dollar one day
more, I return you dollar and half in its place to-
morrow."

The lender had to laugh again. "You can't find an
odd barrel of damaged apples every day."

"No. No apples to-day. But there's regiment soldiers
at lower landing; whole steamboat load; going to sail
this evenin' to Florida. They'll eat whole barrel hard-
boil' eggs."—And they did. When they sailed, the
Italian's pocket was stuffed with small silver.

Richling received his dollar and fifty cents. As he
did so, "I would give, if I had it, a hundred dollars for
half your art," he said, laughing unevenly. He was
beaten, surpassed, humbled. Still he said, "Come, don't
you want this again? You needn't pay me for the use
of it."

But the Italian refused. He had outgrown his patron.
A week afterward Richling saw him at the Picayune Tier,
superintending the unloading of a small schooner-load of

bananas. He had bought the cargo, and was reselling to small fruiterers.

"Make fifty dolla' to-day," said the Italian, marking his tally-board with a piece of chalk.

Richling clapped him joyfully on the shoulder, but turned around with inward distress and hurried away. He had not found work.

Events followed of which we have already taken knowledge. Mary, we have seen, fell sick and was taken to the hospital.

"I shall go mad!" Richling would moan, with his dishevelled brows between his hands, and then start to his feet, exclaiming, "I must not! I must not! I must keep my senses!" And so to the commercial regions or to the hospital.

Dr. Sevier, as we know, left word that Richling should call and see him; but when he called, a servant — very curtly, it seemed to him — said the Doctor was not well and didn't want to see anybody. This was enough for a young man who *hadn't* his senses. The more he needed a helping hand the more unreasonably shy he became of those who might help him.

"Will nobody come and find us?" Yet he would not cry "Whoop!" and how, then, was anybody to come?

Mary returned to the house again (ah! what joys there are in the vale of tribulation!), and grew strong, — stronger, she averred, than ever she had been.

"And now you'll *not* be cast down, *will* you?" she said, sliding into her husband's lap. She was in an uncommonly playful mood.

"Not a bit of it," said John. "Every dog has his day. I'll come to the top. You'll see."

"Don't I know that?" she responded, "Look here, now," she exclaimed, starting to her feet and facing him.

"*I'll* recommend you to anybody. *I've* got confidence in you!" Richling thought she had never looked quite so pretty as at that moment. He leaped from his chair with a laughing ejaculation, caught and swung her an instant from her feet, and landed her again before she could cry out. If, in retort, she smote him so sturdily that she had to retreat backward to rearrange her shaken coil of hair, it need not go down on the record; such things will happen. The scuffle and suppressed laughter were detected even in Mrs. Riley's room.

"Ah!" sighed the widow to herself, "wasn't it Kate Riley that used to get the sweet, haird knocks!" Her grief was mellowing.

Richling went out on the old search, which the advancing summer made more nearly futile each day than the day before.

Stop. What sound was that?

"Richling! Richling!"

Richling, walking in a commercial street, turned. A member of the firm that had last employed him beckoned him to halt.

"What are you doing now, Richling? Still acting deputy assistant city surveyor *pro tem.?*"

"Yes."

"Well, see here! Why haven't you been in the store to see us lately? Did I seem a little preoccupied the last time you called?"

"I" — Richling dropped his eyes with an embarrassed smile — "*I was* afraid I was in the way — or should be."

"Well and suppose you were? A man that's looking for work must put himself in the way. But come with me. I think I may be able to give you a lift."

"How's that?" asked Richling, as they started off abreast.

"There's a house around the corner here that will give you some work, — temporary anyhow, and may be permanent."

So Richling was at work again, hidden away from Dr. Sevier between journal and ledger. His employers asked for references. Richling looked dismayed for a moment, then said, "I'll bring somebody to recommend me," went away, and came back with Mary.

"All the recommendation I've got," said he, with timid elation. There was a laugh all round.

"Well, madam, if you say he's all right, we don't doubt he is!"

CHAPTER XIX.

ANOTHER PATIENT.

" DOCTAH SEVEEAH," said Narcisse, suddenly, as
he finished sticking with great fervor the postage-
stamps on some letters the Doctor had written, and
having studied with much care the phraseology of what
he had to say, and screwed up his courage to the pitch of
utterance, " I saw yo' notiz on the noozpapeh this
mornin'."

The unresponding Doctor closed his eyes in unutterable
weariness of the innocent young gentleman's prepared
speeches.

" Yesseh. 'Tis a beaucheouz notiz. I fine that w'itten
with the gweatez accu'acy of diction, in fact. I made a
twanslation of that faw my hant. Thaz a thing I am
fon' of, twanslation. I dunno 'ow 'tis, Doctah," he continued, preparing to go out, — "I dunno 'ow 'tis, but I
thing, you goin' to fine that Mistoo Itchlin ad the en'.
I dunno 'ow 'tis. Well, I'm goin' ad the " —

The Doctor looked up fiercely.

"Bank," said Narcisse, getting near the door.

" All right!" grumbled the Doctor, more politely.

" Yesseh — befo' I go ad the poss-office."

A great many other persons had seen the advertisement.
There were many among them who wondered if Mr. John
Richling could be sucn a fool as to fall into that trap.
There were others — some of them women, alas! — who
wondered how it was that nobody advertised for informa-

tion concerning them, and who wished, yes, "wished to God," that such a one, or such a one, who had had his money-bags locked up long enough, would die, and then you'd see who'd be advertised for. Some idlers looked in vain into the city directory to see if Mr. John Richling were mentioned there. But Richling himself did not see the paper. His employers, or some fellow-clerk, might have pointed it out to him, but — we shall see in a moment.

Time passed. It always does. At length, one morning, as Dr. Sevier lay on his office lounge, fatigued after his attentions to callers, and much enervated by the prolonged summer heat, there entered a small female form, closely veiled. He rose to a sitting posture.

"Good-morning, Doctor," said a voice, hurriedly, behind the veil. "Doctor," it continued, choking, — "Doctor" —

"Why, Mrs. Richling!"

He sprang and gave her a chair. She sank into it.

"Doctor, — O Doctor! John is in the Charity Hospital!"

She buried her face in her handkerchief and sobbed aloud. The Doctor was silent a moment, and then asked: —

"What's the matter with him?"

"Chills."

It seemed as though she must break down again, but the Doctor stopped her savagely.

"Well, my dear madam, don't cry! Come, now, you're making too much of a small matter. Why, what are chills? We'll break them in forty-eight hours. He'll have the best of care. You needn't cry! Certainly this isn't as bad as when you were there."

She was still, but shook her head. She couldn't agree to that.

" Doctor, will you attend him? "

" Mine is a female ward. "

" I know ; but " —

" Oh — if you wish it — certainly ; of course I will.
But now, where have you moved, Mrs. Richling? I sent "
— He looked up over his desk toward that of Narcisse.

The Creole had been neither deaf nor idle. Hospital?
Then those children in Prieur street had told him right.
He softly changed his coat and shoes. As the physician
looked over the top of the desk Narcisse's silent form,
just here at the left, but out of the range of vision,
passed through the door and went downstairs with the
noiselessness of a moonbeam.

Mary explained the location and arrangement of her
residence.

" Yes, " she said, " that's the way your clerk must
have overlooked us. We live behind — down the alley-
way. "

" Well, at any rate, madam, " said the Doctor, " you
are here now, and before you go I want to " — He drew
out his pocket-book.

There was a quick gesture of remonstrance and a look
of pleading.

" No, no, Doctor, please don't ! please don't ! Give
my poor husband one more chance ; don't make me take
that. I don't refuse it for pride's sake ! "

" I don't know about that, " he replied ; " why do you
do it ? "

" For his sake, Doctor. I know just as well what he'd
say — we've no right to take it anyhow. We don't know
when we could pay it back. " Her head sank. She wiped
a tear from her hand.

" Why, I don't care if you never pay it back ! " The
Doctor reddened angrily.

Mary raised her veil.

"Doctor," — a smile played on her lips, —- "I want to say one thing." She was a little care-worn and grief-worn; and yet, Narcisse, you should have seen her; you would not have slipped out.

"Say on, madam," responded the Doctor.

"If we have to ask anybody, Doctor, it will be you. John had another situation, but lost it by his chills. He'll get another. I'm sure he will." A long, broken sigh caught her unawares. Dr. Sevier thrust his pocket-book back into its place, compressing his lips and giving his head an unpersuaded jerk. And yet, was she not right, according to all his preaching? He asked himself that. "Why didn't your husband come to see me, as I requested him to do, Mrs. Richling?"

She explained John's being turned away from the door during the Doctor's illness. "But anyhow, Doctor, John has always been a little afraid of you."

The Doctor's face did not respond to her smile.

"Why, you are not," he said.

"No." Her eyes sparkled, but their softer light quickly returned. She smiled and said: —

"I will ask a favor of you now, Doctor."

They had risen, and she stood leaning sidewise against his low desk and looking up into his face.

"Can you get me some sewing? John says I may take some."

The Doctor was about to order two dozen shirts instan-ter, but common sense checked him, and he only said: —

"I will. I will find you some. And I shall see your husband within an hour. Good-by." She reached the door. "God bless you!" he added.

"What, sir?" she asked, looking back.

But the Doctor was reading.

CHAPTER XX.

ALICE.

A LITTLE medicine skilfully prescribed, the proper nourishment, two or three days' confinement in bed, and the Doctor said, as he sat on the edge of Richling's couch : —

"No, you'd better stay where you are to-day; but to-morrow, if the weather is good, you may sit up."

Then Richling, with the unreasonableness of a convalescent, wanted to know why he couldn't just as well go home. But the Doctor said again, no.

"Don't be impatient; you'll have to go anyhow before I would prefer to send you. It would be invaluable to you to pass your entire convalescence here, and go home only when you are completely recovered. But I can't arrange it very well. The Charity Hospital is for sick people."

"And where is the place for convalescents?"

"There is none," replied the physician.

"I shouldn't want to go to it, myself," said Richling, lolling pleasantly on his pillow; "all I should ask is strength to get home, and I'd be off."

The Doctor looked another way.

"The sick are not the wise," he said, abstractedly. "However, in your case, I should let you go to your wife as soon as you safely could." At that he fell into so long a reverie that Richling studied every line of his face again and again.

A very pleasant thought was in the convalescent's mind the while. The last three days had made it plain to him that the Doctor was not only his friend, but was willing that Richling should be his.

At length the physician spoke : —

"Mary is wonderfully like Alice, Richling."

"Yes?" responded Richling, rather timidly. And the Doctor continued : —

"The same age, the same stature, the same features. Alice was a shade paler in her style of beauty, just a shade. Her hair was darker; but otherwise her whole effect was a trifle quieter, even, than Mary's. She was beautiful,— outside and in. Like Mary, she had a certain richness of character—but of a different sort. I suppose I would not notice the difference if they were not so much alike. She didn't stay with me long."

"Did you lose her — here?" asked Richling, hardly knowing how to break the silence that fell, and yet lead the speaker on.

"No. In Virginia." The Doctor was quiet a moment, and then resumed : —

"I looked at your wife when she was last in my office, Richling; she had a little timid, beseeching light in her eyes that is not usual with her — and a moisture, too; and — it seemed to me as though Alice had come back. For my wife lived by my moods. Her spirits rose or fell just as my whim, conscious or unconscious, gave out light or took on shadow." The Doctor was still again, and Richling only indicated his wish to hear more by shifting himself on his elbow.

"Do you remember, Richling, when the girl you had been bowing down to and worshipping, all at once, in a single wedding day, was transformed into your adorer?"

"Yes, indeed," responded the convalescent, with

beaming face. "Wasn't it wonderful? I couldn't credit my senses. But how did you — was it the same"—

"It's the same, Richling, with every man who has really secured a woman's heart with her hand. It was very strange and sweet to me Alice would have been a spoiled child if her parents could have spoiled her; and when I was courting her she was the veriest little empress that ever walked over a man."

"I can hardly imagine," said Richling, with subdued amusement, looking at the long, slender form before him. The Doctor smiled very sweetly.

"Yes." Then, after another meditative pause: "But from the moment I became her husband she lived in continual trepidation. She so magnified me in her timid fancy that she was always looking tremulously to me to see what should be her feeling. She even couldn't help being afraid of me. I hate for any one to be afraid of me."

"Do you, Doctor?" said Richling, with surprise and evident introspection.

"Yes."

Richling felt his own fear changing to love.

"When I married," continued Dr. Sevier, "I had thought Alice was one that would go with me hand in hand through life, dividing its cares and doubling its joys, as they say; I guiding her and she guiding me. But if I had let her, she would have fallen into me as a planet might fall into the sun. I didn't want to be the sun to her. I didn't want her to shine only when I shone on her, and be dark when I was dark. No man ought to want such a thing. Yet she made life a delight to me; only she wanted that development which a better training, or even a harder training, might have given her; that subserving of the emotionst to the" — he waved his hand — " l

can't philosophize about her.   We loved one another with
our might, and she's in heaven."

Richling felt an inward start.   The Doctor interrupted
his intended speech.

" Our short experience together, Richling, is the one
great light place in my life ; and to me, to-day, sere as I
am, the sweet — the sweetest sound — on God's green
earth" — the corners of his mouth quivered — " is the name
of Alice.   Take care of Mary, Richling ; she's a priceless
treasure.   Don't leave the making and sustaining of the
home sunshine all to her, any more than you'd like her to
leave it all to you."

" I'll not, Doctor ; I'll not."   Richling pressed the
Doctor's hand fervently ; but the Doctor drew it away
with a certain energy, and rose, saying : —

" Yes, you can sit up to-morrow."

The day that Richling went back to his malarious home
in Prieur street Dr. Sevier happened to meet him just
beyond the hospital gate.   Richling waved his hand.   He
looked weak and tremulous.   " Homeward bound," he
said, gayly.

The physician reached forward in his carriage and bade
his driver stop.   " Well, be careful of yourself ; I'm
coming to see you in a day or two."

CHAPTER XXI.

THE SUN AT MIDNIGHT.

D R. SEVIER was daily overtasked. His campaigns against the evils of our disordered flesh had even kept him from what his fellow-citizens thought was only his share of attention to public affairs.

"Why," he cried to a committee that came soliciting his coöperation, "here's one little unprofessional call that I've been trying every day for two weeks to make — and ought to have made — and must make ; and I haven't got a step toward it yet. Oh, no, gentlemen !" He waved their request away.

He was very tired. The afternoon was growing late. He dismissed his jaded horse toward home, walked down to Canal street, and took that yellow Bayou-Road omnibus whose big blue star painted on its corpulent side showed that quadroons, etc., were allowed a share of its accommodation, and went rumbling and tumbling over the cobble-stones of the French quarter.

By and by he got out, walked a little way southward in the hot, luminous shade of low-roofed tenement cottages that closed their window-shutters noiselessly, in sensitive-plant fashion, at his slow, meditative approach, and slightly and as noiselessly reopened them behind him, showing a pair of wary eyes within. Presently he recognized just ahead of him, standing out on the sidewalk, the little house that had been described to him by Mary.

In a door-way that opened upon two low wooden

sidewalk steps stood Mrs. Riley, clad in a crisp black and white calico, a heavy, fat babe poised easily in one arm. The Doctor turned directly toward the narrow alley, merely touching his hat to her as he pushed its small green door inward, and disappeared, while she lifted her chin at the silent liberty and dropped her eyelids.

Dr. Sevier went down the cramped, ill-paved passage very slowly and softly. Regarding himself objectively, he would have said the deep shade of his thoughts was due partly, at least, to his fatigue. But that would hardly have accounted for a certain faint glow of indignation that came into them. In truth, he began distinctly to resent this state of affairs in the life of John and Mary Richling. An ill-defined anger beat about in his brain in search of some tangible shortcoming of theirs upon which to thrust the blame of their helplessness. "Criminal helplessness," he called it, mutteringly. He tried to define the idea — or the idea tried to define itself — that they had somehow been recreant to their social caste, by getting down into the condition and estate of what one may call the alien poor. Carondelet street had in some way specially vexed him to-day, and now here was this. It was bad enough, he thought, for men to slip into riches through dark back windows; but here was a brace of youngsters who had glided into poverty, and taken a place to which they had no right to stoop. Treachery, — that was the name for it. And now he must be expected, — the Doctor quite forgot that nobody had asked him to do it, — he must be expected to come fishing them out of their hole, like a rag-picker at a trash barrel.

— "Bringing me into this wretched alley!" he silently thought. His foot slipped on a mossy brick. Oh, no doubt they thought they were punishing some negligent friend or friends by letting themselves down into this sort of thing. Never mind! He recalled the tender, confiding, friendly way in which he had talked to John, sitting on the edge of his hospital bed. He wished, now, he had every word back he had uttered. They might hide away to the full content of their poverty-pride. Poverty-pride: he had invented the term; it was the opposite pole to purse-pride — and just as mean, — no, meaner. There! Must he yet slip down? He muttered an angry word. Well, well, this was making himself a little the cheapest he had ever let himself be made. And probably this was what they wanted! Misery's revenge. Umhum! They sit down in sour darkness, eh! and make relief seek them. It wouldn't be the first time he had caught the poor taking savage comfort in the blush which their poverty was supposed to bring to the cheek of better-kept kinsfolk. True, he didn't know this was the case with the Richlings. But wasn't it? Wasn't it? And have they a dog, that will presently hurl himself down this alley at one's legs? He hopes so. He would so like to kick him clean over the twelve-foot close plank fence that crowded his right shoulder. Never mind! His anger became solemn.

The alley opened into a small, narrow yard, paved with ashes from the gas-works. At the bottom of the yard a rough shed spanned its breadth, and a woman was there, busily bending over a row of wash-tubs.

The Doctor knocked on a door near at hand, then waited a moment, and, getting no response, turned away toward the shed and the deep, wet, burring sound of a wash-board. The woman bending over it did not hear his footfall. Presently he stopped. She had just straightened up, lifting a piece of the washing to the height of her head, and letting it down with a swash and slap upon the board. It was a woman's garment, but certainly not hers. For she was small and slight. Her hair was hidden under a towel. Her skirts were shortened to a pair of dainty ankles by an extra under-fold at the neat, round waist. Her feet were thrust into a pair of sabots. She paused a moment in her work, and, lifting with both smoothly rounded arms, bared nearly to the shoulder, a large apron from her waist, wiped the perspiration from her forehead. It was Mary.

The red blood came up into the Doctor's pale, thin face. This was too outrageous. This was insult! He stirred as if to move forward. He would confront her. Yes, just as she was. He would speak. He would speak bluntly. He would chide sternly. He had the right. The only friend in the world from whom she had not escaped beyond reach, — he would speak the friendly, angry word that would stop this shocking —

But, truly, deeply incensed as he was, and felt it his right to be, hurt, wrung, exasperated, he did not advance. She had reached down and taken from the wash-bench the lump of yellow soap that lay there, and was soaping the garment on the board before her, turning it this way and that. As she did this she began, all to herself and for her own ear, softly, with unconscious richness and tenderness of voice, to sing. And what was her song?

"Oh, don't you remember sweet Alice, Ben Bolt?"

Down drooped the listener's head. Remember? Ah, memory! — The old, heart-rending memory! Sweet Alice!

"Sweet Alice, whose hair was so brown?"

Yes, yes; so brown! — so brown!

"She wept with delight when you gave her a smile, And trembled with fear at your frown."

Ah! but the frown is gone! There is a look of suppli-
cation now. Sing no more! Oh, sing no more! Yes,
surely, she will stop there!

No. The voice rises gently — just a little — into the
higher key, soft and clear as the note of a distant bird,
and all unaware of a listener. Oh! in mercy's name —

> "In the old church-yard in the valley, Ben Bolt,
>   In a corner obscure and alone,
>   They have fitted a slab of granite so gray,
>   And sweet Alice lies under the stone."

The little toiling figure bent once more across the wash-
board and began to rub. He turned, the first dew of
many a long year welling from each eye, and stole away,
out of the little yard and down the dark, slippery alley,
to the street.

Mrs. Riley still stood on the door-sill, holding the
child.

"Good-evening, madam!"

"Sur, to you." She bowed with dignity.

"Is Mrs. Richling in?"

There was a shadow of triumph in her faint smile.

"She is."

"I should like to see her."

Mrs. Riley hoisted her chin. "I dunno if she's a-seein
comp'ny to-day." The voice was amiably important.
"Wont ye walk in? Take a seat and sit down, sur, and
I'll go and infarm the laydie."

"Thank you," said the Doctor, but continued to stand
Mrs. Riley started and stopped again.

"Ye forgot to give me yer kyaird, sur." She drew
her chin in again austerely.

"Just say Dr. Sevier."

"Certainly, sur; yes, that'll be sufficiend. And dis
pinse with the kyaird." She went majestically.

The Doctor, left alone, cast his uninterested glance around the smart little bare-floored parlor, upon its new, jig-sawed, gray hair-cloth furniture, and up upon a picture of the Pope. When Mrs. Riley, in a moment, returned he stood looking out the door.

"Mrs. Richling consints to see ye, sur. She'll be in turreckly. Take a seat and sit down." She readjusted the infant on her arm and lifted and swung a hair-cloth arm-chair toward him without visible exertion. "There's no use o' having chayers if ye don't sit on um," she added affably.

The Doctor sat down, and Mrs. Riley occupied the exact centre of the small, wide-eared, brittle-looking sofa, where she filled in the silent moments that followed by pulling down the skirts of the infant's apparel, oppressed with the necessity of keeping up a conversation and with the want of subject-matter. The child stared at the Doctor, and suddenly plunged toward him with a loud and very watery coo.

"Ah-h!" said Mrs. Riley, in ostentatious rebuke. "Mike!" she cried, laughingly, as the action was repeated. "Ye rowdy, air ye go-un to fight the gintleman?"

She laughed sincerely, and the Doctor could but notice how neat and good-looking she was. He condescended to crook his finger at the babe. This seemed to exasperate the so-called rowdy. He planted his pink feet on his mother's thigh and gave a mighty lunge and whoop.

"He's go-un to be a wicked bruiser," said proud Mrs. Riley. "He"—the pronoun stood, this time, for her husband—"he never sah the child. He was kilt with an explosion before the child was barn."

She held the infant on her strong arm as he struggled to throw himself, with wide-stretched jaws, upon her bosom; and mignt have been devoured by the wicked

bruise had not his attention been diverted by the entrance
of Mary, who came in at last, all in fragrant white, with
apologies for keeping the Doctor waiting.

He looked down into her uplifted eyes. What a riddle
is woman! Had he not just seen this one in sabots? Did
she not certainly know, through Mrs. Riley, that he must
have seen her so? Were not her skirts but just now
hitched up with an under-tuck, and fastened with a string?
Had she not just laid off, in hot haste, a suds-bespattered
apron and the garments of toil beneath it? Had not a
towel been but now unbound from the hair shining here
under his glance in luxuriant brown coils? This bright-
ness of eye, that seemed all exhilaration, was it not trepidation instead? And this rosiness, so like redundant
vigor, was it not the flush of her hot task? He fancied he
saw — in truth he may have seen — a defiance in the eyes
as he glanced upon, and tardily dropped, the little water-
soaked hand with a bow.

Mary turned to present Mrs. Riley, who bowed and
said, trying to hold herself with majesty while Mike drew
her head into his mouth: "Sur," then turned with great
ceremony to Mary, and adding, "I'll withdrah," withdrew
with the head and step of a duchess.

"How is your husband, madam?"

"John? — is not well at all, Doctor; though he would
say he was if he were here. He doesn't shake off his
chills. He is out, though, looking for work. He'd go as
long as he could stand."

She smiled; she almost laughed; but half an eye could
see it was only to avoid the other thing.

"Where does he go?"

"Everywhere!" She laughed this time audibly.

"If he went everywhere I should see him," said Dr.
Sevier.

"Ah! naturally," responded Mary, playfully. "But he does go wherever he thinks there's work to be found. He doesn't wander clear out among the plantations, of course, where everybody has slaves, and there's no work but slaves' work. And he says it's useless to think of a clerkship this time of year. It must be, isn't it?"

The Doctor made no answer.

There was a footstep in the alley.

"He's coming now," said Mary, — "that's he. He must have got work to-day. He has an acquaintance, an Italian, who promised to have something for him to do very soon. Doctor," — she began to put together the split fractions of a palm-leaf fan, smiling diffidently at it the while, — "I can't see how it is any discredit to a man not to have a *knack* for making money?"

She lifted her peculiar look of radiant inquiry.

"It is not, madam."

Mary laughed for joy. The light of her face seemed to spread clear into her locks.

"Well, I knew you'd say so! John blames himself; he can make money, you know, Doctor, but he blames himself because he hasn't that natural gift for it that Mr. Ristofalo has. Why, Mr. Ristofalo is simply wonderful!" She smiled upon her fan in amused reminiscence. "John is always wishing he had his gift."

"My dear madam, don't covet it! At least don't exchange it for anything else."

The Doctor was still in this mood of disapprobation when John entered. The radiancy of the young husband's greeting hid for a moment, but only so long, the marks of illness and adversity. Mary followed him with her smiling eyes as the two men shook hands, and John drew a chair near to her and sat down with a sigh of mingled pleasure and fatigue.

She told him of whom she and their vis.tor had just been speaking.

"Raphael Ristofalo!" said John, kindling afresh. "Yes; I've been with him all day. It humiliates me to think of him."

Dr. Sevier responded quietly : —

"You've no right to let it humiliate you, sir."

Mary turned to John with dancing eyes, but he passed the utterance as a mere compliment, and said, through his smiles : —

"Just see how it is to-day. I have been overseeing the unloading of a little schooner from Ruatan island loaded with bananas, cocoanuts, and pine-apples. I've made two dollars ; he has made a hundred."

Richling went on eagerly to tell about the plain, lustre-less man whose one homely gift had fascinated him. The Doctor was entertained. The narrator sparkled and glowed as he told of Ristofalo's appearance, and repro-duced his speeches and manner.

"Tell about the apples and eggs," said the delighted Mary.

He did so, sitting on the front edge of his chair-seat, and sprawling his legs now in front and now behind him as he swung now around to his wife and now to the Doctor. Mary laughed softly at every period, and watched the Doctor, to see his slight smile at each detail of the story. Richling enjoyed telling it ; he had worked ; his earnings were in his pocket ; gladness was easy.

"Why, I'm learning more from Raphael Ristofalo than I ever learned from my school-masters : I'm learning the art of livelihood."

He ran on from Ristofalo to the men among whom he had been mingling all day. He mimicked the strange. long swing of their Sicilian speecn ; told of their swarthy faces and black beards, their rich instinct for color in costume; their fierce conversation and violent gestures; the energy of their movements when they worked, and the profoundness of their repose when they rested; the picturesqueness and grotesqueness of the negroes, too; the huge, flat, round baskets of fruit which the black men carried on their heads, and which the Sicilians bore on their shoulders or the nape of the neck. The "captain" of the schooner was a central figure.

"Doctor," asked Richling, suddenly, "do you know anything about the island of Cozumel?"

"Aha!" thought Mary. So there was something besides the day's earning that elated him.

She had suspected it. She looked at her husband with an expression of the most alert pleasure. The Doctor noticed it.

"No," he said, in reply to Richling's question.

"It stands out in the Gulf of Mexico, off the coast of Yucatan," began Richling.

"Yes, I know that."

"Well, Mary, I've almost promised the schooner captain that we'll go there. He wants to get up a colony."

Mary started.

"Why, John!" She betrayed a look of dismay, glanced at their visitor, tried to say " Have you?" approvingly, and blushed.

The Doctor made no kind of response.

"Now, don't conclude," said John to Mary, coloring too, but smiling. He turned to the physician. "It's a wonderful spot, Doctor."

But the Doctor was still silent, and Richling turned.

"Just to think, Mary, of a place where you can raise all the products of two zones; where health is almost perfect; where the yellow fever has never been; and where there is such beauty as can be only in the tropics and a tropical sea. Why, Doctor, I can't understand why Europeans or Americans haven't settled it long ago."

"I suppose we can find out before we go, can't we?" said Mary, looking timorously back and forth between John and the Doctor.

"The reason is," replied John, "it's so little known. Just one island away out by itself. Three crops of fruit a year. One acre planted in bananas feeds fifty men. All the capital a man need have is an axe to cut down the finest cabinet and dye-woods in the world. The thermometer never goes above ninety nor below forty. You can hire all the labor you want at a few cents a day."

Mary's diligent eye detected a cloud on the Doctor's face. But John, though nettled, pushed on the more rapidly.

"A man can make — easily ! — a thousand dollars the first year, and live on two hundred and fifty. It's the place for a poor man."

He looked a little defiant.

"Of course," said Mary, "I know you wouldn't come to an opinion" — she smiled with the same restless glance — "until you had made all the inquiries necessary. It mu— must — be a delightful place, Doctor?"

Her eyes shone blue as the sky.

"I wouldn't send a convict to such a place," said Dr. Sevier.

Richling flamed up.

"Don't you think," he began to say with visible restraint and a faint, ugly twist of the head, — "don't you think it's a better place for a poor man than a great, heartless town?"

"This isn't a heartless town,' said the Doctor.

"He doesn't mean it as you do, Doctor," interposed Mary, with alarm. "John, you ought to explain."

"Than a great town," said Richling, "where a man of honest intentions and real desire to live and be useful and independent; who wants to earn his daily bread at any honorable cost, and who can't do it because the town doesn't want his services, and will not have them — can go" — He ceased, with his sentence all tangled.

"No!" the Doctor was saying meanwhile. "No! No! No!"

"Here I go, day after day," persisted Richling, extending his arm and pointing indefinitely through the window.

"No, no, you don't, John," cried Mary, with an effort at gayety; "you don't go by the window, John; you go by the door." She pulled his arm down tenderly.

"I go by the alley," said John. Silence followed. The young pair contrived to force a little laugh, and John made an apologetic move.

"Doctor," he exclaimed, with an air of pleasantry, "the whole town's asleep! — sound asleep, like a negro in the sunshine! There isn't work for one man in fifty!" He ended tremulously. Mary looked at him with dropped face but lifted eyes, handling the fan, whose rent she had made worse.

"Richling, my friend," — the Doctor had never used that term before, — "what does your Italian money-maker say to the idea?"

Richling gave an Italian shrug and his own pained laugh.

"Exactly! Why, Mr. Richling, you're on an island now, — an island in mid-ocean. Both of you!" He waved his hands toward the two without lifting his head from the back of the easy-chair, where he had dropped it.

"What do you mean, Doctor?"

"Mean? Isn't my meaning plain enough? I mean you're too independent. You know very well, Richling, that you've started out in life with some fanciful feud against the 'world.' What it is I don't know, but I'm sure it's not the sort that religion requires. You've told this world — you remember you said it to me once — that if it will go one road you'll go another. You've forgotten that, mean and stupid and bad as your fellow-creatures are, they're your brothers and sisters, and that they have claims on you as such, and that you have claims on them as such. — Cozumel! You're there now! Has a friend no rights? I don't know your immediate relatives, and I say nothing about them"—

John gave a slight start, and Mary looked at him suddenly.

"But here am I," continued the speaker. "Is it just to me for you to hide away here in want that forces you and your wife — I beg your pardon, madam — into mortifying occupations, when one word to me — a trivial obligation, not worthy to be called an obligation, contracted with me — would remove that necessity, and tide you over the emergency of the hour?"

Richling was already answering, not by words only, but by his confident smile : —

"Yes, sir ; yes, it is just : ask Mary."

"Yes, Doctor," interposed the wife. "We went over" —

"We went over it together," said John. "We weighed it well. It *is* just, — not to ask aid as long as there's hope without it."

The Doctor responded with the quiet air of one who is sure of his position : —

"Yes, I see. But, of course — I know without asking — you left the question of health out of your reckoning.

Now, Richling, put the whole world, if you choose, in a selfish attitude " —

" No, no," said Richling and his wife. " Ah, no ! " But the Doctor persisted.

" — a purely selfish attitude. Wouldn't it, nevertheless, rather help a well man or woman than a sick one? Wouldn't it pay better?"

" Yes, but " —

" Yes," said the Doctor. " But you're taking the most desperate risks against health and life." He leaned forward in his chair, jerked in his legs, and threw out his long white hands. " You're committing slow suicide."

" Doctor," began Mary ; but her husband had the floor.

" Doctor," he said, " can you put yourself in our place? Wouldn't you rather die than beg? *Wouldn't* you?"

The Doctor rose to his feet as straight as a lance.

" It isn't what you'd rather, sir ! You haven't your choice ! You haven't your choice at all, sir ! When God gets ready for you to die he'll let you know, sir ! And you've no right to trifle with his mercy in the meanwhile. I'm not a man to teach men to whine after each other for aid ; but every principle has its limitations, Mr. Richling. You say you went over the whole subject. Yes ; well, didn't you strike the fact that suicide is an affront to civilization and humanity?"

" Why, Doctor ! " cried the other two, rising also " We're not going to commit suicide."

" No," retorted he, " you're not. That's what I came here to tell you. I'm here to prevent it."

" Doctor," exclaimed Mary, the big tears standing in her eyes, and the Doctor melting before them like wax, " it's not so bad as it looks. I wash — some — because it pays so much better than sewing. I find I'm stronger than any one would believe. I'm stronger than I ever was before in my life. I am, indeed. I *don't* wash *much*. And it's only for the present. We'll all be laughing at this, some time, together." She began a small part of the laugh then and there.

" You'll do it no more," the Doctor replied. He drew out his pocket-book. " Mr. Richling, will you please send me through the mail, or bring me, your note for fifty dollars, — at your leisure, you know, — payable on demand?" He rummaged an instant in the pocket-book, and extended his hand with a folded bank-note between his thumb and finger. But Richling compressed his lips and shook his head, and the two men stood silently confronting each other. Mary laid her hand upon her husband's shoulder and leaned against him, with her eyes on the Doctor's face.

" Come, Richling," — the Doctor smiled, — " your friend Ristofalo did not treat you in this way."

" I never treated Ristofalo so," replied Richling, with a smile tinged with bitterness. It was against himself that he felt bitter; but the Doctor took it differently, and Richling, seeing this, hurried to correct the impression.

" I mean I lent him no such amount as that."

" It was just one-fiftieth of that," said Mary.

" But you gave liberally, without upbraiding," said the Doctor.

" Oh, no, Doctor! no!" exclaimed she, lifting the hand that lay on her husband's near shoulder and reaching it over to the farther one. " Oh! a thousand times no! John never meant that. Did you, John?"

" How could I?" said John. " No!" Yet there was confession in his look. He had not meant it, but he had felt it.

Dr. Sevier sat down, motioned them into their seats, drew the arm-chair close to theirs. Then he spoke. He spoke long, and as he had not spoken anywhere but at the bedside scarce ever in his life before. The young husband and wife forgot that he had ever said a grating word. A soft love-warmth began to fill them through and through. They seemed to listen to the gentle voice of an older and wiser brother. A hand of Mary sank unconsciously upon a hand of John. They smiled and assented, and smiled, and assented, and Mary's eyes brimmed up with tears, and John could hardly keep his down. The Doctor made the whole case so plain and his propositions so irresistibly logical that the pair looked from his eyes to each other's and laughed. " Cozumel ! " They did not utter the name ; they only thought of it both at one moment. It never passed their lips again. Their visitor brought them to an arrangement. The fifty dollars were to be placed to John's credit on the books kept by Narcisse, as a deposit from Richling, and to be drawn against by him in such littles as necessity might demand. It was to be " secured " — they all three smiled at that word — by Richling's note payable on demand. The Doctor left a prescription for the refractory chills.

As he crossed Canal street, walking in slow meditation homeward at the hour of dusk, a tall man standing against a wall, tin cup in hand, — a full-fledged mendicant of the steam-boiler explosion, tin-proclamation type, — asked his alms. He passed by, but faltered, stopped, let his hand down into his pocket, and looked around to see if his pernicious example was observed. None saw him. He felt — he saw himself — a drivelling sentimentalist. But weak, and dazed, sore wounded of the archers, he turned and dropped a dime into the beggar's cup.

Richling was too restless with the joy of relief to sit or stand. He trumped up an errand around the corner, and hardly got back before he contrived another. He went out to the bakery for some crackers — fresh baked — for Mary; listened to a long story across the baker's counter, and when he got back to his door found he had left the crackers at the bakery. He went back for them and returned, the blood about his heart still running and leaping and praising God.

"The sun at midnight!" he exclaimed, knitting Mary's hands in his. "You're very tired. Go to bed. Me? I can't yet. I'm too restless."

He spent more than an hour chatting with Mrs. Riley, and had never found her so "nice" a person before; so easy comes human fellowship when we have had a stroke of fortune. When he went again to his room there was Mary kneeling by the bedside, with her head slipped under the snowy mosquito net, all in fine linen, white as the moonlight, frilled and broidered, a remnant of her wedding glory gleaming through the long, heavy wefts of her unbound hair.

"Why, Mary"—

There was no answer.

"Mary?" he said again, laying his hand upon her head.

The head was slowly lifted. She smiled an infant's smile, and dropped her cheek again upon the bedside. She had fallen asleep at the foot of the Throne.

At that same hour, in an upper chamber of a large, distant house, there knelt another form, with bared, bowed head, but in the garb in which it had come in from the street. Praying? This white thing overtaken by sleep here was not more silent. Yet — yes, praying. But, all the while, the prayer kept running to a little tune, and the words repeating themselves again and again: "Oh, don't you remember sweet Alice — with hair so brown — so brown — so brown? Sweet Alice, with hair so brown?" And God bent his ear and listened.

CHAPTER XXII.

BORROWER TURNED LENDER.

IT was only a day or two later that the Richlings, one afternoon, having been out for a sunset walk, were just reaching Mrs. Riley's door-step again, when they were aware of a young man approaching from the opposite direction with the intention of accosting them. They brought their conversation to a murmurous close.

For it was not what a mere acquaintance could have joined them in, albeit its subject was the old one of meat and raiment. Their talk had been light enough on their starting out, notwithstanding John had earned nothing that day. But it had toned down, or, we might say up, to a sober, though not a sombre, quality. John had in some way evolved the assertion that even the life of the body alone is much more than food and clothing and shelter; so much more, that only a divine provision can sustain it; so much more, that the fact is, when it fails, it generally fails with meat and raiment within easy reach.

Mary devoured his words. His spiritual vision had been a little clouded of late, and now, to see it clear — She closed her eyes for bliss.

"Why, John," she said, "you make it plainer than any preacher I ever heard."

This, very naturally, silenced John. And Mary, hoping to start him again, said: —

"Heaven provides. And yet I'm sure you're right in

seeking our food and raiment?" She looked up inquiringly.

"Yes; like the fowls, the provision is made *for* us through us. The mistake is in making those things the *end* of our search."

"Why, certainly!" exclaimed Mary, softly. She took fresh hold in her husband's arm; the young man was drawing near.

"It's Narcisse!" murmured John. The Creole pressed suddenly forward with a joyous smile, seized Richling's hand, and, lifting his hat to Mary as John presented him, brought his heels together and bowed from the hips.

"I wuz juz coming at yo' 'ouse, Mistoo Itchlin. Yesseh. I wuz juz sitting in my 'oom afteh dinneh, envelop' in my *'obe de chambre*, when all at once I says to myseff, 'Faw distwaction I will go and see Mistoo Itchlin!'"

"Will you walk in?" said the pair.

Mrs. Riley, standing in the door of her parlor, made way by descending to the sidewalk. Her calico was white, with a small purple figure, and was highly starched and beautifully ironed. Purple ribbons were at her waist and throat. As she reached the ground Mary introduced Narcisse. She smiled winningly, and when she said, with a courtesy: "Proud to know ye, sur," Narcisse was struck with the sweetness of her tone. But she swept away with a dramatic tread.

"Will you walk in?" Mary repeated; and Narcisse responded: —

"If you will pummit me yo' attention a few moment'." He bowed again and made way for Mary to precede him.

"Mistoo Itchlin," he continued, going in, "in fact you don't give Misses Witchlin my last name with absolute co'ectness "

"Di l I not?   Why, I hope you'll pardon "—

"Oh, I'm glad of it.   I don' feel lak a pusson is my fwen' whilst they don't call me Nahcisse."   He directed his remark particularly to Mary.

"Indeed?" responded she.   "But, at the same time, Mr. Richling would have"— She had turned to John, who sat waiting to catch her eye with such intense amusement betrayed in his own that she saved herself from laughter and disgrace only by instant silence.

"Yesseh," said Narcisse to Richling, "'tis the tooth."

He cast his eye around upon the prevailing hair-cloth and varnish.

"Misses Witchlin, I muz tell you I like yo' tas'e in that pawlah."

"It's Mrs. Riley's taste," said Mary.

"'Tis a beaucheouz tas'e," insisted the Creole, contemplatively, gazing at the Pope's vestments tricked out with blue, scarlet, and gilt spangles.   "Well, Mistoo Itchlin, since some time I've been stipulating me to do myseff that honoh, seh, to come at yo' 'ouse ; well, ad the end I am yeh.   I think you fine yoseff not ve'y well those days.   Is that nod the case, Mistoo Itchlin?"

"Oh, I'm well enough!"   Richling ended with a laugh, somewhat explosively.   Mary looked at him with forced gravity as he suppressed it.   He had to draw his nose slowly through his thumb and two fingers bef re he could quite command himself.   Mary relieved him by responding : —

"No, Mr. Richling hasn't been well for some time."

Narcisse responded triumphantly : —

"It stwuck me — so soon I pe'ceive you — that you 'ave the ai' of a valedictudina'y.   Thass a ve'y fawtunate that you ah 'esiding in a 'ealthsome pawt of the city, in fact."

Both John and Mary laughed and demurred.

"You don't think?" asked the smiling visitor. "Me, I dunno, — I fine one thing. If a man don't die fum one thing, yet, still, he'll die fum something. I 'ave study that out, Mistoo Itchlin. ' To be, aw to not be, thaz the queztion,' in fact. I don't ca'e if you live one place aw if you live anotheh place, 'tis all the same, — you've got to pay to live!"

The Richlings laughed again, and would have been glad to laugh more ; but each, without knowing it of the other, was reflecting with some mortification upon the fact that, had they been talking French, Narcisse would have bitten his tongue off before any of his laughter should have been at their expense.

"Indeed you have got to pay to live," said John, stepping to the window and drawing up its painted paper shade. "Yes, and " —

"Ah!" exclaimed Mary, with gentle disapprobation. She met her husband's eye with a smile of protest. "John," she said, "Mr. —— " she couldn't think of the name.

"Nahcisse," said the Creole.

"Will think," she continued, her amusement climbing into her eyes in spite of her, "you're in earnest."

"Well, I am, partly. Narcisse knows, as well as we do, that there are two sides to the question." He resumed his seat. "I reckon" —

"Yes," said Narcisse, "and what you muz look out faw, 'tis to git on the soff side."

They all laughed.

"I was going to say," said Richling, "the world takes us as we come, 'sight-unseen.' Some of us pay expenses, some don't."

"Ah! ' rejoined Narcisse, looking up at the white-

washed ceiling, "those egspenze'!" He raised his hand
and dropped it. "I *fine* it so *diffycul'* to defeat those
egspenze'! In fact, Mistoo Itchlin, such ah the state
of my financial emba'assment that I do not go out at all.
I stay in, in fact. I stay at my 'ouse — to light' those
egspenze'!"

They were all agreed that expenses could be lightened
thus.

"And by making believe you don't want things," said
Mary.

"Ah!" exclaimed Narcisse, "I nevvah kin do that!"
and Richling gave a laugh that was not without sympathy.
"But I muz tell you, Mistoo Itchlin, I am aztonizh at
you."

An instant apprehension seized John and Mary. They
knew their ill-concealed amusement would betray them,
and now they were to be called to account. But
no.

"Yesseh," continued Narcisse, "you 'ave the gweatez
o'casion to be the subjec' of congwatulation, Mistoo
Itchlin, to 'ave the poweh to *accum'*late money in those
hawd time' like the pwesen'!"

The Richlings cried out with relief and amused surprise.

"Why, you couldn't make a greater mistake!"

"Mistaken! Hah! W'en I ged that memo'andum
f'om Dr. Seveeah to paz that fifty dollah at yo' cwedit, it
burz f'om me, that egs*clam*ation! 'Acchilly! 'ow that
Mistoo Itchlin deserve the 'espect to save a lill quantity
of money like that!'"

The laughter of John and Mary did not impede his
rhapsody, nor their protestations shake his convictions.

"Why," said Richling, lolling back, "the Doctor has
simply omitted to have you make the entry of" —

But he had no right to interfere with the Doctor's accounts. However, Narcisse was not listening.

"You' compel' to be witch some day, Mistoo Itchlin, ad that wate of p'ogwess; I am convince of that. I can deteg that indis*put*ably in yo' physio'nomie. Me — I *can't* save a cent! Mistoo Itchlin, you would be azton izh to know 'ow bad I want some money, in fact; exceb that I am *too* pwoud to dizclose you that state of my condition!"

He paused and looked from John to Mary, and from Mary to John again.

"Why, I'll declare," said Richling, sincerely, dropping forward with his chin on his hand, "I'm sorry to hear" —

But Narcisse interrupted.

"Diffyculty with me — I am not willing to baw'."

Mary drew a long breath and glanced at her husband. He changed his attitude and, looking upon the floor, said, "Yes, yes." He slowly marked the bare floor with the edge of his shoe-sole. "And yet there are times when duty actually" —

"I believe you, Mistoo Itchlin," said Narcisse, quickly forestalling Mary's attempt to speak. "Ah, Mistoo Itchlin! *if* I had baw'd money ligue the huncle of my hant!" He waved his hand to the ceiling and looked up through that obstruction, as it were, to the witnessing sky. "But I *hade* that — to baw'! I tell you 'ow 'tis with me, Mistoo Itchlin; I nevvah would consen' to baw' money on'y if I pay a big inte'es' on it. An' I'm compel' to tell you one thing, Mistoo Itchlin, in fact: I nevvah would leave money with Doctah Seveeah to invez faw me — no!"

Richling gave a little start, and cast his eyes an instant toward his wife. She spoke.

"We'd rather you wouldn't say that to us, Mister

——" There was a commanding smile at one corner of her lips. " You don't know what a friend " —

Narcisse had already apologized by two or three gestures to each of his hearers.

" Misses Itchlin — Mistoo Itchlin," — he shook his head and smiled skeptically, — " you think you kin admiah Doctah Seveeah mo' than me? 'Tis uzeless to attempt. ' With all 'is fault I love 'im still.' "

Richling and his wife both spoke at once.

" But John and I," exclaimed Mary, electrically, " love him, faults and all ! "

She looked from husband to visitor, and from visitor to husband, and laughed and laughed, pushing her small feet back and forth alternately and softly clapping her hands. Narcisse felt her in the centre of his heart. He laughed. John laughed.

" What I mean, Mistoo Itchlin," resumed Narcisse, preferring to avoid Mary's aroused eye, — " what I mean — Doctah Seveeah don't un'stan' that kine of business co'ectly. Still, ad the same time, if I was you I know I would 'ate faw my money not to be makin' me some inte'es'. I tell you what I would do with you, Mistoo Itchlin, in fact : I kin baw' that fifty dollah f'om you myseff."

Richling repressed a smile. " Thank you ! But I don't care to invest it."

" Pay you ten pe' cent. a month."

" But we can't spare it," said Richling, smiling toward Mary. " We may need part of it ourselves."

" I tell you, 'eally, Mistoo Itchlin, I nevveh baw' money ; but it juz 'appen I kin use that juz at the pwesent."

" Why, John," said Mary, " I think you might as well say plainly that the money is borrowed money."

"That's what it is," responded Richling, and rose to spread the street-door wider open, for the daylight was fading.

"Well, I 'ope you'll egscuse that libbetty," said Narcisse, rising a little more tardily, and slower. "I muz baw' fawty dollah— some place. Give you good secu'ty — give you my note, Mistoo Itchlin, in fact; muz baw fawty — aw thutty-five."

"Why, I'm very sorry," responded Richling, really ashamed that he could not hold his face straight. "I hope you understand " —

"Mistoo Itchlin, 'tis baw'd money. If you had a necessity faw it you would use it. If a fwend 'ave a necessity — 'tis anotheh thing — you don't feel that libbetty — you ah 'ight — I honoh you " —

"I *don't* feel the same liberty."

"Mistoo Itchlin," said Narcisse, with noble generosity, throwing himself a half step forward, "if it was yoze you'd baw' it to me in a minnit! " He smiled with benign delight. "Well, madame, — I bid you good evening, Misses Itchlin. The bes' of fwen's muz pawt, you know." He turned again to Richling with a face all beauty and a form all grace. "I was juz sitting — mistfully — all at once I says to myseff, 'Faw distwaction I'll go an' see Mistoo Itchlin.' I don't *know* 'ow I juz 'appen'! — Well, *au 'evoi*', Mistoo Itchlin."

Richling followed him out upon the door-step. There Narcisse intimated that even twenty dollars for a few days would supply a stern want. And when Richling was compelled again to refuse, Narcisse solicited his company as far as the next corner. There the Creole covered him with shame by forcing him to refuse the loan of ten dollars, and then of five.

It was a full hour before Richling rejoined his wife.

Mrs. Riley had stepped off to some neighbor's door with Mike on her arm. Mary was on the sidewalk.

"John," she said, in a low voice, and with a long anxious look.

"What?"

"He *didn't* take the only dollar of your own in the world?"

"Mary, what could I do? It seemed a crime to give, and a crime not to give. He cried like a child; said it was all a sham about his dinner and his *robe de chambre.*" An aunt, two little cousins, an aged uncle at home — and not a cent in the house! What could I do? He says he'll return it in three days."

"And" — Mary laughed distressfully — "you believed him?" She looked at him with an air of tender, painful admiration, half way between a laugh and a cry.

"Come, sit down," he said, sinking upon the little woooden buttress at one side of the door-step.

Tears sprang into her eyes. She shook her head.

"Let's go inside." And in there she told him sincerely, "No, no, no; she didn't think he had done wrong" — when he knew he had.

CHAPTER XXIII.

WEAR AND TEAR.

THE arrangement for Dr. Sevier to place the loan of fifty dollars on his own books at Richling's credit naturally brought Narcisse into relation with it.

It was a case of love at first sight. From the moment the record of Richling's " little quantity " slid from the pen to the page, Narcisse had felt himself betrothed to it by destiny, and hourly supplicated the awful fates to frown not upon the amorous hopes of him unaugmented. Richling descended upon him once or twice and tore away from his embrace small fractions of the coveted treasure, choosing, through a diffidence which he mistook for a sort of virtue, the time of day when he would not see Dr. Sevier ; and at the third visitation took the entire golden fleece away with him rather than encounter again the always more or less successful courtship of the scorner of loans.

A faithful suitor, however, was not thus easily shaken off. Narcisse became a frequent visitor at the Richlings', where he never mentioned money ; that part was left to moments of accidental meeting with Richling in the street, which suddenly began to occur at singularly short intervals.

Mary labored honestly and arduously to dislike him — to hold a repellent attitude toward him. But he was too much for her. It was easy enough when he was absent ; but one look at his handsome face, so rife with animal innocence, and despite herself she was ready to reward his displays of sentiment and erudition with laughter that, mean what it might, always pleased and flattered him.

"Can you help liking him?" she would ask John. "I can't, to save my life!"

Had the treasure been earnings, Richling said — and believed — he could firmly have repelled Narcisse's importunities. But coldly to withhold an occasional modest heave-offering of that which was the free bounty of another to him was more than he could do.

"But," said Mary, straightening his cravat, "you intend to pay up, and he — you don't think I'm uncharitable, do you?"

"I'd rather give my last cent than think you so," replied John. "Still," — laying the matter before her with both open hands, — "if you say plainly not to give him another cent I'll do as you say. The money's no more mine than yours."

"Well, you can have all my share," said Mary, pleasantly.

So the weeks passed and the hoard dwindled.

"What has it got down to, now?" asked John, frowningly, on more than one morning as he was preparing to go out. And Mary, who had been made treasurer, could count it at a glance without taking it out of her purse.

One evening, when Narcisse called, he found no one at home but Mrs. Riley. The infant Mike had been stuffed with rice and milk and laid away to slumber. The Richlings would hardly be back in less than an hour.

"I'm so'y," said Narcisse, with a baffled frown, as he sat down and Mrs. Riley took her seat opposite. "I came to 'epay 'em some moneys which he made me the loan — juz in a fwenly way. And I came to 'epay 'im

The sum-total, in fact — I suppose he nevva mentioned you about that, eh?"

"No, sir; but, still, if " —

"No, and so I can't pay it to you. I'm so'y. Because I know he woon like it, I know, if he fine that you know he's been bawing money to me. Well, Misses Wiley, in fact, thass a *ve'y* fine gen'leman and lady — that Mistoo and Misses Itchlin, in fact?"

"Well, now, Mr. Narcisse, ye'r about right? She's just too good to live — and he's not much better — ha! ha!" She checked her jesting mood. "Yes, sur, they're very peaceable, quiet people. They're just simply ferst tlass."

"'Tis t'ue," rejoined the Creole, fanning himself with his straw hat and looking at the Pope. "And they handsome and genial, as the lite'ati say on the noozpapeh. Seem like they almoze wedded to each otheh."

"Well, now, sir, that's the ttrooth!" She threw her open hand down with emphasis.

"And isn't that as man and wife should be?"

"Yo' mighty co'ect, Misses Wiley!" Narcisse gave his pretty head a little shake from side to side as he spoke.

"Ah! Mr. Narcisse," — she pointed at herself,— "haven't I been a wife? The husband and wife — they'd aht to jist be each other's guairdjian angels! Hairt to hairt sur; sperit to sperit. All the rist is nawthing, Mister Narcisse." She waved her hands. "Min is different from women, sur." She looked about on the ceiling. Her foot noiselessly patted the floor.

"Yes," said Narcisse, "and thass the cause that they dwess them dif'ent. To show the dif'ence, you know."

"Ah! no. It's not the mortial frame, sur; it's the sperit. The sperit of man is not the sperit of woman. The sperit of woman is not the sperit of man. Each one needs the other, sur. They needs each other, sur, to purify and strinthen and enlairge each other's speritu'l life. Ah, sur! Doo not I feel those things, sur?" She touched her heart with one backward-pointed finger. "*I* doo. It isn't good for min to be alone — much liss for women. Do not misunderstand me, sur; I speak as a widder, sur — and who always will be — ah! yes, I will — ha! ha! ha!" She hushed her laugh as if this were going too far, tossed her head, and continued smiling.

So they talked on. Narcisse did not stay an hour, but there was little of the hour left when he rose to go. They had passed a pleasant time. The Creole, it is true, tried and failed to take the helm of conversation. Mrs. Riley held it. But she steered well. She was still expatiating on the "strinthenin'" spiritual value of the marriage relation when she, too, stood up.

"And that's what Mr. and Madam Richlin's a-doin' all the time. And they do ut to perfiction, sur — jist to perfiction!"

"I doubt it not, Misses Wiley. Well, Misses Wiley, I bid you *au 'evoi'*. I dunno if you'll pummit me, but I am compel to tell you, Misses Wiley, I nevva yeh anybody in my life with such a educated and talented conve'sation like yo'seff. Misses Wiley, at what univussity did you gwaduate?"

"Well, reely, Mister — eh" — she fanned herself with broad sweeps of her purple bordered palm-leaf — "reely, sur, if I don't furgit the name I — I — I'll be switched! Ha! ha! ha!"

Narcisse joined in the laugh.

"Thaz the way, sometime," he said, and then with sudden gravity: "And, by-the-by, Misses Wiley, speakin' of Mistoo Itchlin,— if you could baw' me two dollahs an' a 'alf juz till tomaw mawnin — till I kin sen' it you

fum the office — Because that money I've got faw Mistoo Itchlin is in the shape of a check, and anyhow I'm
c'owding me a little to pay that whole sum-total to Mistoo
Itchlin. I kin sen' it you firs' thing my bank open
tomaw mawnin.''

Do you think he didn't get it?

"What has it got down to now?" John asked again,
a few mornings after Narcisse's last visit. Mary told him.
He stepped a little way aside, averting his face, dropped
his forehead into his hand, and returned.

"I don't see — I don't see, Mary—I"—

"Darling," she replied, reaching and capturing both
his hands, "who does see? The rich *think* they see; but
do they, John? Now, *do* they?"

The frown did not go quite off his face, but he took her
head between his hands and kissed her temple.

"You're always trying to lift me," he said.

"Don't you lift me?" she replied, looking up between
his hands and smiling.

"Do I?"

"You know you do. Don't you remember the day we
took that walk, and you said that after all it never is we
who provide?" She looked at the button of his coat,
which she twirled in her fingers. "That word lifted me."

"But suppose I can't practice the trust I preach?" he
said.

"You do trust, though. You have trusted."

"Past tense," said John. He lifted her hands slowly
away from him, and moved toward the door of their
chamber. He could not help looking back at the eyes
that followed him, and then he could not bear their look.
"I — I suppose a man mustn't trust too much," he sa'd.

"Can he?" asked Mary, leaning against a table.

"Oh, yes, he can," replied John; but his tone lacked conviction.

"If it's the right kind?"

Her eyes were full of tears.

"I'm afraid mine's not the right kind, then," said John, and passed out into and down the street.

But what a mind he took with him — what torture of questions! Was he being lifted or pulled down? His tastes, — were they rising or sinking? Were little negligences of dress and bearing and in-door attitude creeping into his habits? Was he losing his discriminative sense of quantity, time, distance? Did he talk of small achievements, small gains, and small truths, as though they were great? Had he learned to carp at the rich, and to make honesty the excuse for all penury? Had he these various poverty-marks? He looked at himself outside and inside, and feared to answer. One thing he knew, — that he was having great wrestlings.

He turned his thoughts to Ristofalo. This was a common habit with him. Not only in thought, but in person, he hovered with a positive infatuation about this man of perpetual success.

Lately the Italian had gone out of town, into the country of La Fourche, to buy standing crops of oranges. Richling fed his hope on the possibilities that might follow Ristofalo's return. His friend would want him to superintend the gathering and shipment of those crops — when they should be ripe — away yonder in November. Frantic thought! A man and his wife could starve to death twenty times before then.

Mrs. Riley's high esteem for John and Mary had risen from the date of the Doctor's visit, and the good woman thought it but right somewhat to increase the figures of their room-rent to others more in keeping with such high gentility. How fast the little hoard melted away!

And the summer continued on, — the long, beautiful, glaring, implacable summer; its heat quaking on the low roofs; its fig-trees dropping their shrivelled and blackened leaves and writhing their weird, bare branches under the scorching sun; the long-drawn, frying note of its cicada throbbing through the mid-day heat from the depths of the becalmed oak; its universal pall of dust on the myriad red, sleep-heavy blossoms of the oleander and the white tulips of the lofty magnolia; its twinkling pomegranates hanging their apples of scarlet and gold over the garden wall; its little chameleons darting along the hot fence-tops; its far-stretching, empty streets; its wide hush of idleness; its solitary vultures sailing in the upper blue; its grateful clouds; its hot north winds, its cool south winds; its gasping twilight calms; its gorgeous nights, — the long, long summer lingered on into September.

One evening, as the sun was sinking below the broad, flat land, its burning disk reddened by a low golden haze of suspended dust, Richling passed slowly toward his home, coming from a lower part of the town by way of the quadroon quarter. He was paying little notice, or none, to his whereabouts, wending his way mechanically, in the dejected reverie of weary disappointment, and with voiceless inward screamings and groanings under the weight of those thoughts which had lately taken up their stay in his dismayed mind. But all at once his attention was challenged by a strange, offensive odor. He looked up and around, saw nothing, turned a corner, and found himself at the intersection of Trémé and St. Anne streets, just behind the great central prison of New Orleans.

The "Parish Prison" was then only about twenty-five years old; but it had made haste to become offensive to every sense and sentiment of reasonable man. It had been built in the Spanish style, — a massive, dark, grim, huge, four-sided block, the fissure-like windows of its cells looking down into the four public streets which ran immediately under its walls. Dilapidation had followed hard behind ill-building contractors. Down its frowning masonry ran grimy streaks of leakage over peeling stucco and mould-covered brick. Weeds bloomed high aloft in the broken gutters under the scant and ragged eaves Here and there the pale, debauched face of a prisoner peered shamelessly down through shattered glass or rusted grating; and everywhere in the still atmosphere floated the stifling smell of the unseen loathsomeness within.

Richling paused. As he looked up he noticed a bat dart out from a long crevice under the eaves. Two others followed. Then three — a dozen — a hundred — a thousand — millions. All along the two sides of the prison in view they poured forth in a horrid black torrent, — myriads upon myriads. They filled the air. They came and came. Richling stood and gazed; and still they streamed out in gibbering waves, until the wonder was that anything but a witch's dream could contain them.

The approach of another passer roused him, and he started on. The step gained upon him — closed up with him; and at the moment when he expected to see the person go by, a hand was laid gently on his shoulder.

"Mistoo Itchl n, I 'ope you well, seh!"

CHAPTER XXIV.

BROUGHT TO BAY.

ONE may take his choice between the two, but there is no escaping both in this life : the creditor — the borrower. Either, but never neither. Narcisse caught step with Richling, and they walked side by side.

"How I learned to mawch, I billong with a fiah comp'ny," said the Creole. "We mawch eve'y yeah on the fou'th of Mawch." He laughed heartily. "Thass a 'ime ! — Mawch on the fou'th of Mawch ! Thass poetwy, in fact, as you may *say* in a jesting *way* — ha ! ha ! ha ! "

"Yes, and it's truth, besides," responded the drearier man.

"Yes ! " exclaimed Narcisse, delighted at the unusual coincidence, " at the same time 'tis the tooth ! In fact, why should I tell a lie about such a thing like *that?* 'Twould be useless. Pe'haps you may 'ave notiz, Mistoo Itchlin, thad the noozpapehs opine us fiahmen to be the gau'dians of the city."

"Yes," responded Richling. "I think Dr. Sevier calls you the Mamelukes, doesn't he? But that's much the same, I suppose."

"Same thing," replied the Creole. "We combad the fiah fiend. You fine that building ve'y pitto'esque, Mistoo Itchlin?" He jerked his thumb toward the prison, that was still pouring forth its clouds of impish wings. "Yes? 'Tis the same with me. But I tell you one thing, Mistoo Itchlin, I assu' you, and you will believe me, I would 'atheh be lock' *out*side of that building than to be lock' *in*side of the same. 'Cause — you know why? 'Tis ve'y 'umid in that building. An thass a thing w'at I believe, Mistoo Itchlin; I believe w'en a building is v'ey 'umid it is not ve'y 'ealthsome. What is yo' opinion consunning that, Mistoo Itchlin?"

"My opinion?" said Richling, with a smile. "My opinion is that the Parish Prison would not be a good place to raise a family."

Narcisse laughed.

"I thing yo' opinion is co'ect," he said, flatteringly; then growing instantly serious, he added, "Yesseh, I think you' about a-'ight, Mistoo Itchlin; faw even if 'twas not too 'umid, 'twould be too confining, in fact, — speshly faw child'en. I dunno; but thass my opinion. If you ah p'oceeding at yo' residence, Mistoo Itchlin, I'll juz continue my p'omenade in yo' society — if not intooding "—

Richling smiled candidly. "Your company's worth all it costs, Narcisse. Excuse me; I always forget your last name — and your first is so appropriate." It *was* worth all it cost, though Richling could ill afford the purchase. The young Latin's sweet, abysmal ignorance, his infantile amiability, his artless ambition, and heathenish innocence started the natural gladness of Richling's blood to effervescing anew every time they met, and, through the sheer impossibility of confiding any of his troubles to the Creole, made him think them smaller and lighter than they had just before appeared. The very light of Narcisse's countenance and beauty of his form — his smooth, low forehead, his thick, abundant locks, his faintly up-tipped nose and expanded nostrils, his sweet, weak mouth with its impending smile, his beautiful chin and bird's throat, his almond eyes, his full, round arm, and strong thigh — had their emphatic value.

So now, Richling, a moment earlier borne down by the dreadful shadow of the Parish Prison, left it behind him as he walked and laughed and chatted with his borrower. He felt very free with Narcisse, for the reason that would have made a wiser person constrained, — lack of respect for him.

"Mistoo Itchlin, you know," said the Creole, "I like you to call me Nahcisse. But at the same time my las' name is Savillot." He pronounced it Sav-*veel*-yo. "Thass a somewot Spanish name. That double l got a twist in it."

"Oh, call it Papilio!" laughed Richling.

"Papillon!" exclaimed Narcisse, with delight. "The buttehfly! All a-'ight; you kin juz style me that! 'Cause thass my natu'e, Mistoo Itchlin; I gatheh honey eve'y day fum eve'y opening floweh, as the bahd of A-von wemawk."

So they went on.

Ad infinitum? Ah, no! The end was just as plainly in view to both from the beginning as it was when, at length, the two stepping across the street gutter at the last corner between Richling and home, Narcisse laid his open hand in his companion's elbow, and stopped, saying, as Richling turned and halted with a sudden frown of unwillingness: —

"I tell you 'ow 'tis with me, Mistoo Itchlin, I've p'oject that manneh myseff; in weading a book — w'en I see a beaucheouz idee, I juz take a pencil" — he drew one from his pocket — "check! I check it. So w'en I wead the same book again, then I take notiz I've check that idee and I look to see what I check it faw 'Ow you like that invention, eh?"

"Very simple," said Richling, with an unpleasant look of expectancy.

"Mistoo Itchlin," resumed the other, "do you not fine me impooving in my p'onouncement of yo' lang-widge? I fine I don't use such bad land-widge like biffo. I am shue you muz' 'ave notiz since some time I always soun' that awer in yo' name. Mistoo Itchlin, will you 'ave that kin'ness to baw me two-an-a-'alf till the lass of that month?"

Richling looked at him a moment in silence, and then broke into a short, grim laugh.

"It's all gone. There's no more honey in this flower." He set his jaw as he ceased speaking. There was a warm red place on either cheek.

"Mistoo Itchlin," said Narcisse, with sudden, quavering fervor, "you kin len' me two dollahs! I gi'e you my honah the moze sacwed of a gen'leman, Mistoo Itchlin, I nevvah hass you ag'in so long I live!" He extended a pacifying hand. "One moment, Mistoo Itchlin,—one moment,—I implo' you, seh! I assu' you, Mistoo Itchlin, I pay you eve'y cent in the worl' on the laz of that month? Mistoo Itchlin, I am in indignan' circumstan's. Mistoo Itchlin, if you know the distwess—Mistoo Itchlin, if you know—'ow bad I 'ate to baw!" The tears stood in his eyes. "It nea'ly *kill* me to b—" Utterance failed him.

"My friend," began Richling.

"Mistoo Itchlin," exclaimed Narcisse, dashing away the tears and striking his hand on his heart, "I *am* yo' fwend, seh!"

Richling smiled scornfully. "Well, my good friend, if you had ever kept a single promise made to me I need not have gone since yesterday without a morsel of food."

Narcisse tried to respond.

"Hush!" said Richling, and Narcisse bowed while Richling spoke on. "I haven't a cent to buy bread with to carry home. And whose fault is it? Is it my fault — or is it yours?"

"Mistoo Itchlin, seh" —

"Hush!" cried Richling, again; "if you try to speak before I finish I'll thrash you right here in the street!"

Narcisse folded his arms. Richling flushed and flashed with the mortifying knowledge that his companion's behavior was better than his own.

"If you want to borrow more money of me find me a chance to earn it!" He glanced so suddenly at two or three street lads, who were the only on-lookers, that they shrank back a step.

"Mistoo Itchlin," began Narcisse, once more, in a tone of polite dismay, "you aztonizh me. I assu' you, Mistoo Itchlin" —

Richling lifted his finger and shook it. "Don't you tell me that, sir! I will not be an object of astonishment to you! Not to you, sir! Not to you!" He paused, trembling, his anger and his shame rising together.

Narcisse stood for a moment, silent, undaunted, the picture of amazed friendship and injured dignity, then raised his hat with the solemnity of affronted patience and said : —

"Mistoo Itchlin, seein' as 'tis you, a puffic gen'leman, 'oo is not goin' to 'efuse that satisfagtion w'at a gen'leman, always a-'eady to give a gen'leman, — I bid you --faw the pwesen' — good-evenin', seh!" He walked away.

Richling stood in his tracks dumfounded, crushed. His eyes followed the receding form of the borrower until it disappeared around a distant corner, while the eye of his mind looked in upon himself and beheld, with a shame that overwhelmed anger, the folly and the puerility of his outburst. The nervous strain of twenty-four hours' fast, without which he might not have slipped at all, only sharpened his self-condemnation. He turned and walked to his house, and all the misery that had oppressed him before he had seen the prison, and all that had come with that sight, and all this new shame, sank down upon his heart at once. "I am not a man! I am not a whole man!" he suddenly moaned to himself. "Something is wanting — oh! what is it?" — he lifted his eyes to the sky, — "what is it?" — when in truth, there was little wanting just then besides food.

He passed in at the narrow gate and up the slippery alley. Nearly at its end was the one window of the room he called home. Just under it — it was somewhat above his head — he stopped and listened. A step within was moving busily here and there, now fainter and now plainer; and a voice, the sweetest on earth to him, was singing to itself in its soft, habitual way.

He started round to the door with a firmer tread. It stood open. He halted on the threshold. There was a small table in the middle of the room, and there was food on it. A petty reward of his wife's labor had brought it there.

"Mary," he said, holding her off a little, "don't kiss me yet."

She looked at him with consternation. He sat down, drew her upon his lap, and told her, in plain, quiet voice, the whole matter.

"Don't look so, Mary."

"How?" she asked, in a husky voice and with flashing eye.

"Don't breathe so short and set your lips. I never saw you look so, Mary, darling!"

She tried to smile, but her eyes filled.

"If you had been with me," said John, musingly, "it wouldn't have happened."

"If — if "— Mary sat up as straight as a dart, the corners of her mouth twitching so that she could scarcely shape a word, — "if — if I'd been there, I'd have made you *whip* him!" She flouted her handkerchief out of her pocket, buried her face in his neck, and sobbed like a child.

"Oh!" exclaimed the tearful John, holding her away by both shoulders, tossing back his hair and laughing as she laughed, — "Oh! you women! You're all of a sort! You want us men to carry your hymn-books and your iniquities, too!"

She laughed again.

"Well, of course!"

And they rose and drew up to the board.

CHAPTER XXV.

THE DOCTOR DINES OUT.

ON the third day after these incidents, again at the sunset hour, but in a very different part of the town, Dr. Sevier sat down, a guest, at dinner. There were flowers; there was painted and monogrammed china; there was Bohemian glass; there was silver of cunning work with linings of gold, and damasked linen, and oak of fantastic carving. There were ladies in summer silks and elaborate coiffures; the hostess, small, slender, gentle, alert; another, dark, flashing, Roman, tall; another, ripe but not drooping, who had been beautiful, now, for thirty years; and one or two others. There were jewels; there were sweet odors. And there were, also, some good masculine heads: Dr. Sevier's, for instance; and the chief guest's, — an iron-gray, with hard lines in the face, and a scar on the near cheek, — a colonel of the regular army passing through from Florida; and one crown, bald, pink, and shining, encircled by a silken fringe of very white hair: it was the banker who lived in St. Mary street. His wife was opposite. And there was much high-bred grace. There were tall windows thrown wide to make the blaze of gas bearable, and two tall mulattoes in the middle distance bringing in and bearing out viands too sumptuous for any but a French nomenclature.

It was what you would call a quiet affair; quite out of season, and difficult to furnish with even this little handful of guests; but it was a proper and necessary attention to the colonel; conversation not too dull, nor yet too bright for ease, but passing gracefully from one agreeable topic to another without earnestness, a restless virtue, or frivolity, which also goes against serenity. Now it touched upon the prospects of young A. B. in the demise of his uncle; now upon the probable seriousness of C. D. in his attentions to E. F.; now upon G.'s amusing mishaps during a late tour in Switzerland, which had — "how unfortunately!" — got into the papers. Now it was concerning the admirable pulpit manners and easily pardoned vocal defects of a certain new rector. Now it turned upon Stephen A. Douglas's last speech; passed to the questionable merits of a new-fangled punch; and now, assuming a slightly explanatory form from the gentlemen to the ladies, showed why there was no need whatever to fear a financial crisis — which came soon afterward.

The colonel inquired after an old gentleman whom he had known in earlier days in Kentucky.

"It's many a year since I met him," he said. "The proudest man I ever saw. I understand he was down here last season."

" He was," replied the host, in a voice of native kindness, and with a smile on his high-fed face. " He was; but only for a short time. He went back to his estate. That is his world. He's there now."

"It used to be considered one of the finest places in the State." said the colonel.

" It is still," rejoined the host. " Doctor, you know him?"

"I think not," said Dr. Sevier; but somehow he recalled the old gentleman in button gaiters, who had called on him one evening to consult him about his sick wife.

"A good man," said the colonel, looking amused;

" and a superb gentleman. Is he as great a partisan of the church as he used to be?"

" Greater!   Favors an established church of America."

The ladies were much amused. The host's son, a young fellow with sprouting side-whiskers, said he thought he could be quite happy with one of the finest plantations in Kentucky, and let the church go its own gait.

"Humph!" said the father; "I doubt if there's ever a happy breath drawn on the place."

" Why, how is that?" asked the colonel, in a cautious tone.

"Hadn't he heard?" The host was surprised, but spoke low.   "Hadn't he heard about the trouble with their only son? Why, he went abroad and never came back!"

Every one listened.

" It's a terrible thing," said the hostess to the ladies nearest her; "no one ever dares ask the family what the trouble is, — they have such odd, exclusive ideas about their matters being nobody's business. All that can be known is that they look upon him as worse than dead and gone forever."

" And who will get the estate?" asked the banker.

" The two girls.   They're both married."

" They're very much like their father," said the hostess, smiling with gentle significance.

" Very much," echoed the host, with less delicacy. " Their mother is one of those women who stand in terror of their husband's will. Now, if he were to die and leave her with a will of her own she would hardly know what to do with it — I mean with her will — or the property either."

The hostess protested softly against so harsh a speech, and the son, after one or two failures, got in his remark: —

"Maybe the prodigal would come back and be taken in."

But nobody gave this conjecture much attention. The host was still talking of the lady without a will.

"Isn't she an invalid?" Dr. Sevier had asked.

"Yes; the trip down here last season was on her account, — for change of scene. Her health is wretched."

"I'm distressed that I didn't call on her," said the hostess; "but they went away suddenly. My dear, I wonder if they really did encounter the young man here?"

"Pshaw!" said the husband, softly, smiling and shaking his head, and turned the conversation.

In time it settled down with something like earnestness for a few minutes upon a subject which the rich find it easy to discuss without the least risk of undue warmth. It was about the time when one of the graciously murmuring mulattoes was replenishing the glasses, that remark in some way found utterance to this effect, — that the company present could congratulate themselves on living in a community where there was no poor class.

"Poverty, of course, we see; but there is no misery, or nearly none," said the ambitious son of the host.

Dr. Sevier differed with him. That was one of the Doctor's blemishes as a table guest: he would differ with people.

"There is misery," he said; "maybe not the gaunt squalor and starvation of London or Paris or New York; the climate does not tolerate that, — stamps it out before it can assume dimensions; but there is at least misery of that sort that needs recognition and aid from the well-fed."

The lady who had been beautiful so many years had somewhat to say; the physician gave attention, and she spoke: —

" If sister Jane were here, she would be perfectly tri
umphant to hear you speak so, Doctor." She turned to
the hostess, and continued : " Jane is quite an enthusiast,
you know ; a sort of Dorcas, as husband says, modified
and readapted. Yes, she is for helping everybody."

" Whether help is good for them or not," said the lady's
husband, a very straight and wiry man with a garrote
collar.

" It's all one," laughed the lady. " Our new rector told
her plainly, the other day, that she was making a great
mistake ; that she ought to consider whether assistance
assists. It was really amusing. Out of the pulpit and
off his guard, you know, he lisps a little ; and he said she
ought to consider whether ' aththithtanth aththithtth.' "

There was a gay laugh at this, and the lady was called
a perfect and cruel mimic.

" ' Aththithtanth aththithtth ! ' " said two or three to
their neighbors, and laughed again.

" What did your sister say to that ? " asked the banker,
bending forward his white, tonsured head, and smiling
down the board.

" She said she didn't care ; that it kept her own heart
tender, anyhow. ' My dear madam,' said he, ' your heart
wants strengthening more than softening.' He told her
a pound of inner resource was more true help to any poor
person than a ton of assistance."

The banker commended the rector. The hostess, very
sweetly, offered her guarantee that Jane took the rebuke
in good part.

" She did," replied the time-honored beauty ; " she
tried to profit by it. But husband, here, has offered her
a wager of a bonnet against a hat that the rector will
upset her new schemes. Her idea now is to make work
for those whom nobody will employ."

"Jane," said the kind-faced host, "really wants to do good for its own sake."

"I think she's even a little Romish in her notions," said Jane's wiry brother-in-law. "I talked to her as plainly as the rector. I told her, 'Jane, my dear, all this making of work for the helpless poor is not worth one-fiftieth part of the same amount of effort spent in teaching and training those same poor to make their labor intrinsically marketable.'"

"Yes," said the hostess; "but while we are philosophizing and offering advice so wisely, Jane is at work — doing the best she knows how. We can't claim the honor even of making her mistakes."

"'Tisn't a question of honors to us, madam," said Dr. Sevier; "it's a question of results to the poor."

The brother-in-law had not finished. He turned to the Doctor.

"Poverty, Doctor, is an inner condition"—

"Sometimes," interposed the Doctor.

"Yes, generally," continued the brother-in-law, with some emphasis. "And to give help you must, first of all, 'inquire within'— within your beneficiary."

"Not always, sir," replied the Doctor; "not if they're sick, for instance." The ladies bowed briskly and applauded with their eyes. "And not always if they're well," he added. His last words softened off almost into soliloquy.

The banker spoke forcibly:—

"Yes, there are two quite distinct kinds of poverty. One is an accident of the moment; the other is an inner condition of the individual"—

"Of course it is," said sister Jane's brother-in-law, who felt it a little to have been contradicted on the side of kindness by the hard-spoken Doctor. "Certainly! it's a deficiency of inner resources or character, and what to do with it is no simple question."

"That's what I was about to say," resumed the banker; "at least, when the poverty is of that sort. And what discourages kind people is that that's the sort we commonly see. It's a relief to meet the other, Doctor, just as it's a relief to a physician to encounter a case of simple surgery."

"And — and," said the brother-in-law, "what is your rule about plain almsgiving to the difficult sort?"

"My rule," replied the banker, "is, don't do it. Debt is slavery, and there is an ugly kink in human nature that disposes it to be content with slavery. No, sir; gift-making and gift-taking are twins of a bad blood." The speaker turned to Dr. Sevier for approval; but, though the Doctor could not gainsay the fraction of a point, he was silent. A lady near the hostess stirred softly both under and above the board. In her private chamber she would have yawned. Yet the banker spoke again : —

"Help the old, I say. You are pretty safe there. Help the sick. But as for the young and strong, — now, no man could be any poorer than I was at twenty-one, — I say be cautious how you smooth that hard road which is the finest discipline the young can possibly get."

"If it isn't *too* hard," chirped the son of the host.

"Too hard? Well, yes, if it isn't too hard. Still I say, hands off; you needn't turn your back, however." Here the speaker again singled out Dr. Sevier. "Watch the young man out of one corner of your eye; but make him swim!"

"Ah-h!" said the ladies.

"No, no," continued the banker; "I don't say let him drown; but I take it, Doctor, that your alms, for instance, are no alms if they put the poor fellow into your debt and at your back."

"To whom do you refer?" asked Dr. Sevier. Whereat there was a burst of laughter, which was renewed when the banker charged the physician with helping so many persons, "on the sly," that he couldn't tell which one was alluded to unless the name were given.

"Doctor," said the hostess, seeing it was high time the conversation should take a new direction, "they tell me you have closed your house and taken rooms at the St. Charles."

"For the summer," said the physician.

As, later, he walked toward that hotel, he went resolving to look up the Richlings again without delay. The banker's words rang in his ears like an overdose of quinine: "Watch the young man out of one corner of your eye. Make him swim. I don't say let him drown."

"Well, I do watch him," thought the Doctor. "I've only lost sight of him once in a while." But the thought seemed to find an echo against his conscience, and when it floated back it was: "I've only *caught* sight of him once in a while." The banker's words came up again: "Don't put the poor fellow into your debt and at your back." "Just what you've done," said conscience. "How do you know he isn't drowned?" He would see to it.

While he was still on his way to the hotel he fell in with an acquaintance, a Judge Somebody or other, lately from Washington City. He, also, lodged at the St. Charles. They went together. As they approached the majestic porch of the edifice they noticed some confusion at the bottom of the stairs that led up to the rotunda; cabmen and boys were running to a common point, where, in the midst of a small, compact crowd, two or three pairs of arms were being alternately thrown aloft and brought down. Presently the mass took a rapid movement up St. Charles street.

The judge gave his conjecture: "Some poor devil resisting arrest."

Before he and the Doctor parted for the night they went to the clerk's counter.

"No letters for you, Judge; mail failed. Here is a card for you, Doctor."

The Doctor received it. It had been furnished, blank, by the clerk to its writer.

JOHN RICHLING.

At the door of his own room, with one hand on the unturned knob and one holding the card, the Doctor stopped and reflected. The card gave no indication of urgency. Did it? It was hard to tell. He didn't want to look foolish; morning would be time enough; he would go early next morning.

But at daybreak he was summoned post-haste to the bedside of a lady who had stayed all summer in New Orleans so as not to be out of this good doctor's reach at this juncture. She counted him a dear friend, and in similar trials had always required close and continual attention. It was the same now.

Dr. Sevier scrawled and sent to the Richlings a line, saying that, if either of them was sick, he would come at their call. When the messenger returned with word from Mrs. Riley that both of them were out, the Doctor's mind was much relieved. So a day and a night passed, in which he did not close his eyes.

The next morning, as he stood in his office, hat in hand, and a finger pointing to a prescription on his desk, which he was directing Narcisse to give to some one who would call for it, there came a sudden hurried pounding of feminine feet on the stairs, a whiff of robes in the corridor, and Mary Richling rushed into his presence all tears and cries.

"O Doctor! — O Doctor! O God, my husband! my husband! O Doctor, my husband is in the Parish Prison!" She sank to the floor.

The Doctor raised her up. Narcisse hurried forward with his hands full of restoratives.

"Take away those things," said the Doctor, resentfully. "Here! — Mrs. Richling, take Narcisse's arm and go down and get into my carriage. I must write a short note, excusing myself from an appointment, and then I will join you."

Mary stood alone, turned, and passed out of the office beside the young Creole, but without taking his proffered arm. Did she suspect him of having something to do with this dreadful affair?

"Missez Wichlin," said he, as soon as they were out in the corridor, "I dunno if you goin' to billiv me, but I boun' to tell you that nodwithstanning that yo' 'uzban' is displease' with me, an' nodwithstanning 'e's in that calaboose, I h'always fine 'im a puffic gen'leman — that Mistoo Itchlin, — an' I'll sweah 'e *is* a gen'leman!"

She lifted her anguished eyes and looked into his beautiful face. Could she trust him? His little forehead was as hard as a goat's, but his eyes were brimming with tears, and his chin quivered. As they reached the head of the stairs he again offered his arm, and she took it, moaning softly, as they descended: —

"O John! O John! O my husband, my husband!"

CHAPTER XXVI.

THE TROUGH OF THE SEA.

NARCISSE, on receiving his scolding from Richling, had gone to his home in Casa Calvo street, a much greater sufferer than he had appeared to be. While he was confronting his abaser there had been a momentary comfort in the contrast between Richling's ill-behavior and his own self-control. It had stayed his spirit and turned the edge of Richling's sharp denunciations. But, as he moved off the field, he found himself, at every step, more deeply wounded than even he had supposed. He began to suffocate with chagrin, and hurried his steps in sheer distress. He did not experience that dull, vacant acceptance of universal scorn which an unresentful coward feels. His pangs were all the more poignant because he knew his own courage.

In his home he went so straight up to the withered little old lady, in the dingiest of flimsy black, who was his aunt, and kissed her so passionately, that she asked at once what was the matter. He recounted the facts, shedding tears of mortification. Her feeling, by the time he had finished the account, was a more unmixed wrath than his, and, harmless as she was, and wrapped up in her dear, pretty nephew as she was, she yet demanded to know why such a man shouldn't be called out upon the field of honor.

"Ah!" cried Narcisse, shrinkingly. She had touched the core of the tumor. One gets a public tongue-lashing from a man concerning money borrowed; well, how is one going to challenge him without first handing back the borrowed money? It was a scalding thought! The rotten joists beneath the bare scrubbed-to-death floor quaked under Narcisse's to-and-fro stride.

"— And then, anyhow!" — he stopped and extended both hands, speaking, of course, in French, — "anyhow, he is the favored friend of Dr. Sevier. If I hurt him — I lose my situation! If he hurts me — I lose my situation!"

He dried his eyes. His aunt saw the insurmountability of the difficulty, and they drowned feeling in an affectionate glass of green-orangeade.

"But never mind!" Narcisse set his glass down and drew out his tobacco. He laughed spasmodically as he rolled his cigarette. "You shall see. The game is not finished yet."

Yet Richling passed the next day and night without assassination, and on the second morning afterward, as on the first, went out in quest of employment. He and Mary had eaten bread, and it had gone into their life without a remainder either in larder or purse. Richling was all aimless.

"I do wish I had the *art* of finding work," said he. He smiled. "I'll get it," he added, breaking their last crust in two. "I have the science already. Why, look you, Mary, the quiet, amiable, imperturbable, dignified, diurnal, inexorable haunting of men of influence will get you whatever you want."

"Well, why don't you do it, dear? Is there any harm in it? I don't see any harm in it. Why don't you do that very thing?"

"I'm telling you the truth," answered he, ignoring her question. "Nothing else short of overtowering merit will get you what you want half so surely."

"Well, why not do it? Why not?" A fresh, glad courage sparkled in the wife's eyes.

"Why, Mary," said John, "I never in my life tried so hard to do anything else as I've tried to do that! It sounds easy; but try it! You can't conceive how hard it is till you try it. I can't *do* it! I *can't* do it!"

"*I'd* do it!" cried Mary. Her face shone. "*I'd* do it! You'd see if I didn't! Why, John"—

"All right!" exclaimed he; "you sha'n't talk that way to me for nothing. I'll try it again! I'll begin to-day!"

"Good-by," he said. He reached an arm over one of her shoulders and around under the other and drew her up on tiptoe. She threw both hers about his neck. A long kiss—then a short one.

"John, something tells me we're near the end of our troubles."

John laughed grimly. "Ristofalo was to get back to the city to-day: maybe he's going to put us out of our misery. There are two ways for troubles to end." He walked away as he spoke. As he passed under the window in the alley, its sash was thrown up and Mary leaned out on her elbows.

"John!"

"Well?"

They looked into each other's eyes with the quiet pleasure of tried lovers, and were silent a moment. She leaned a little farther down, and said, softly:—

"You mustn't mind what I said just now."

"Why, what did you say?"

"That if it were I, I'd do it. I know you can do anything I can do, and a hundred better things besides."

He lifted his hand to her cheek. "We'll see," he whispered. She drew in, and he moved on.

Morning passed. Noon came. From horizon to horizon the sky was one unbroken blue. The sun spread its bright, hot rays down upon the town and far beyond, ripening the distant, countless fields of the great delta, which by and by were to empty their abundance into the city's lap for the employment, the nourishing, the clothing of thousands. But in the dusty streets, along the ill-kept fences and shadowless walls of the quiet districts, and on the glaring façades and heated pavements of the commercial quarters, it seemed only as though the slowly retreating summer struck with the fury of a wounded Amazon. Richling was soon dust-covered and weary. He had gone his round. There were not many men whom he could even propose to haunt. He had been to all of them. Dr. Sevier was not one. "Not to-day," said Richling.

"It all depends on the way it's done," he said to himself; "it needn't degrade a man if it's done the right way." It was only by such philosophy he had done it at all. Ristofalo he could have haunted without effort; but Ristofalo was not to be found. Richling tramped in vain. It may be that all plans were of equal merit just then. The summers of New Orleans in those times were, as to commerce, an utter torpor, and the autumn reawakening was very tardy. It was still too early for the stirrings of general mercantile life. The movement of the cotton crop was just beginning to be perceptible; but otherwise almost the only sounds were from the hammers of craftsmen making the town larger and preparing it for the activities of days to come.

The afternoon wore along. Not a cent yet to carry home! Men began to shut their idle shops and go to meet their wives and children about their comfortable dinner-tables. The sun dipped low. Hammers and saws

were dropped into tool-boxes, and painters pulled themselves out of their overalls. The mechanic's rank, hot
supper began to smoke on its bare board; but there was
one board that was still altogether bare and to which no
one hastened. Another day and another chance of life
were gone.

Some men at a warehouse door, the only opening in the
building left unclosed, were hurrying in a few bags of
shelled corn. Night was falling. At an earlier hour
Richling had offered the labor of his hands at this very
door and had been rejected. Now, as they rolled in the
last truck-load, they began to ask for rest with all the
gladness he would have felt to be offered toil, singing, —

" To blow, to blow, some time for to blow."

They swung the great leaves of the door together as they
finished their chorus, stood grouped outside a moment
while the warehouseman turned the resounding lock, and
then went away. Richling, who had moved on, watched
them over his shoulder, and as they left turned back. He
was about to do what he had never done before. He went
back to the door where the bags of grain had stood. A
drunken sailor came swinging along. He stood still and
let him pass; there must be no witnesses. The sailor
turned the next corner. Neither up nor down nor across
the street, nor at dust-begrimed, cobwebbed window, was
there any sound or motion. Richling dropped quickly on
one knee and gathered hastily into his pocket a little pile
of shelled corn that had leaked from one of the bags.

That was all. No harm to a living soul; no theft; no
wrong; but ah! as he rose he felt a sudden inward lesion.
Something broke. It was like a ship, in a dream, noiselessly striking a rock where no rock is. It seemed as

though the very next thing was to begin going to pieces. He walked off in the dark shadow of the warehouse, half lifted from his feet by a vague, wide dismay. And yet he felt no greatness of emotion, but rather a painful want of it, as if he were here and emotion were yonder, down-street, or up-street, or around the corner. The ground seemed slipping from under him. He appeared to have all at once melted away to nothing. He stopped. He even turned to go back. He felt that if he should go and put that corn down where he had found it he should feel himself once more a living thing of substance and emotions. Then it occurred to him — no, he would keep it; he would take it to Mary; but himself — he would not touch it; and so he went home.

Mary parched the corn, ground it fine in the coffee-mill and salted and served it close beside the candle. "It's good white corn," she said, laughing. "Many a time when I was a child I used to eat this in my playhouse and thought it delicious. Didn't you? What! not going to eat?"

Richling had told her how he got the corn. Now he told his sensations. "You eat it, Mary," he said at the end; "you needn't feel so about it; but if I should eat it I should feel myself a vagabond. It may be foolish, but I wouldn't touch it for a hundred dollars." A hundred dollars had come to be his synonyme for infinity.

Mary gazed at him a moment tearfully, and rose, with the dish in her hand, saying, with a smile, "I'd look pretty, wouldn't I!"

She set it aside, and came and kissed his forehead. By and by she asked: —

"And so you saw no work, anywhere?"

"Oh, yes!" he replied, in a tone almost free from dejec-on. "I saw any amount of work — preparations for a

big season. I think I certainly shall pick up something
to-morrow — enough, anyhow, to buy something to eat
with. If we can only hold out a little longer — just a
little — I am sure there'll be plenty to do— for everybody."
Then he began to show distress again. "I could have
got work to-day if I had been a carpenter, or if I'd
been a joiner, or a slater, or a bricklayer, or a plasterer, or
a painter, or a hod-carrier. Didn't I try that, and was
refused?"

" I'm glad of it," said Mary.

" 'Show me your hands,' said the man to me. I
showed them. " 'You won't do,' said he."

" I'm glad of it !" said Mary, again.

" No," continued Richling; " or if I'd been a glazier,
or a whitewasher, or a wood-sawyer, or" — he began to
smile in a hard, unpleasant way, — " or if I'd been anything but an American gentleman. But I wasn't, and I
didn't get the work ! "

Mary sank into his lap, with her very best smile.

" John, if you hadn't been an American gentleman "—

" We should never have met," said John. " That's
true ; that's true." They looked at each other, rejoicing
in mutual ownership.

" But," said John, " I needn't have been the typical
American gentleman, — completely unfitted for prosperity
and totally unequipped for adversity."

" That's not your fault," said Mary.

" No, not entirely ; but it's your calamity, Mary. C
Mary ! I little thought "—

She put her hand quickly upon his mouth. His eye
flashed and he frowned.

" Don't do so !" he exclaimed, putting the hand away ;
then blushed for shame, and kissed her.

They went to bed. Bread would have put them to sleep. But after a long time —

"John," said one voice in the darkness, "do you remember what Dr. Sevier told us?"

"Yes, he said we had no right to commit suicide by starvation."

"If you don't get work to-morrow, are you going to see him?"

"I am."

In the morning they rose early.

During these hard days Mary was now and then conscious of one feeling which she never expressed, and was always a little more ashamed of than probably she need have been, but which, stifle it as she would, kept recurring in moments of stress. Mrs. Riley — such was the thought — need not be quite so blind. It came to her as John once more took his good-by, the long kiss and the short one, and went breakfastless away. But was Mrs. Riley as blind as she seemed? She had vision enough to observe that the Richlings had bought no bread the day before, though she did overlook the fact that emptiness would set them astir before their usual hour of rising. She knocked at Mary's inner door. As it opened a quick glance showed the little table that occupied -the centre of the room standing clean and idle.

"Why, Mrs. Riley!" cried Mary; for on one of Mis. Riley's large hands there rested a blue-edged soup-plate, heaping full of the food that goes nearest to the Creole heart — *jambolaya*. There it was, steaming and smelling, — a delicious confusion of rice and red pepper, chicken legs, ham, and tomatoes. Mike, on her opposite arm, was struggling to lave his socks in it.

"Ah!" said Mrs. Riley, with a disappointed lift of the

head, "ye're after eating breakfast already! And the plates all tleared off. Well, ye air smairt! I knowed Mr. Richlin's taste for jumbalie"—

Mary smote her hands together. "And he's just this instant gone! John! John! Why, he's hardly"— She vanished through the door, glided down the alley, leaned out the gate, looking this way and that, tripped down to this corner and looked —"Oh! oh!"— no John there — back and up to the other corner —"Oh! which way did John go?" There was none to answer.

Hours passed; the shadows shortened and shrunk under their objects, crawled around stealthily behind them as the sun swung through the south, and presently began to steal away eastward, long and slender. This was the day that Dr. Sevier dined out, as hereinbefore set forth.

The sun set. Carondelet street was deserted. You could hear your own footstep on its flags. In St. Charles street the drinking-saloons and gamblers' drawing-rooms, and the barber-shops, and the show-cases full of shirt-bosoms and walking-canes, were lighted up. The smell of lemons and mint grew finer than ever. Wide Canal street, out under the darkling crimson sky, was resplendent with countless many-colored lamps. From the river the air came softly, cool and sweet. The telescope man set up his skyward-pointing cylinder hard by the dark statue of Henry Clay; the confectioneries were ablaze and full of beautiful life, and every little while a great, empty cotton-dray or two went thundering homeward over the stony pavements until the earth shook, and speech for the moment was drowned. The St. Charles, such a glittering mass in winter nights, stood out high and dark under the summer stars, with no glow except just in its midst, in the rotunda; and even the rotunda was well-nigh deserted.

The clerk at his counter saw a young man enter the great door opposite, and quietly marked him as he drew near.

Let us not draw the stranger's portrait. If that were a pleasant task the clerk would not have watched him. What caught and kept that functionary's eye was that, whatever else might be revealed by the stranger's aspect, — weariness, sickness, hardship, pain,— the confession was written all over him, on his face, on his garb, from his hat's crown to his shoe's sole, Penniless! Penniless! Only when he had come quite up to the counter the clerk did not see him at all.

" Is Dr. Sevier in?"

" Gone out to dine," said the clerk, looking over the inquirer's head as if occupied with all the world's affairs except the subject in hand.

" Do you know when he will be back?"

" Ten o'clock."

The visitor repeated the hour murmurously and looked something dismayed. He tarried.

"Hem! — I will leave my card, if you please."

The clerk shoved a little box of cards toward him, from which a pencil dangled by a string. The penniless wrote his name and handed it in. Then he moved away, went down the tortuous granite stair, and waited in the obscurity of the dimly lighted porch below. The card was to meet the contingency of the Doctor's coming in by some other entrance. He would watch for him here.

By and by — he was very weary — he sat down on the stairs. But a porter, with a huge trunk on his back, told him very distinctly that he was in the way there, and he rose and stood aside. Soon he looked for another resting-place. He must get off of his feet somewhere, if only for

a few moments. He moved back into the deep gloom
of the stair-way shadow, and sank down upon the pavement. In a moment he was fast asleep.

He dreamed that he, too, was dining out. Laughter
and merry-making were on every side. The dishes of
steaming viands were grotesque in bulk. There were
mountains of fruit and torrents of wine. Strange peop.e
of no identity spoke in senseless vaporings that passed
for side-splitting wit, and friends whom he had not seen
since childhood appeared in ludicrously altered forms and
announced impossible events. Every one ate like a Cos-
sack. One of the party, champing like a boar, pushed
him angrily, and when he, eating like the rest, would
have turned fiercely on the aggressor, he awoke.

A man standing over him struck him smartly with his
foot.

" Get up out o' this !   Get up ! get up ! "

The sleeper bounded to his feet. The man who had
waked him grasped him by the lapel of his coat.

" What do you mean ? " exclaimed the awakened man,
throwing the other off violently.

" I'll show you ! " replied the other, returning with a
rush ; but he was thrown off again, this time with a blow
of the fist.

" You scoundrel ! " cried the penniless man, in a rage ;
" if you touch me again I'll kill you ! "

They leaped together. The one who had proposed to
show what he meant was knocked flat upon the stones.
The crowd that had run into the porch made room for him
to fall. A leather helmet rolled from his head, and the
silver crescent of the police flashed on his breast. The
police were not uniformed in those days.

But he is up in an instant and his adversary is down —
backward, on his elbows. Then the penniless man is up

again; they close and struggle, the night-watchman's club falls across his enemy's head blow upon blow, while the sufferer grasps him desperately, with both hands, by the throat. They tug, they snuffle, they reel to and fro in the yielding crowd; the blows grow fainter, fainter; the grip is terrible; when suddenly there is a violent rupture of the crowd, it closes again, and then there are two against one, and up sparkling St. Charles street, the street of all streets for flagrant, unmolested, well-dressed crime, moves a sight so exhilarating that a score of street lads follow behind and a dozen trip along in front with frequent backward glances: two officers of justice walking in grim silence abreast, and between them a limp, torn, hatless, bloody figure, partly walking, partly lifted, partly dragged, past the theatres, past the lawyers' rookeries of Commercial place, the tenpin alleys, the chop-houses, the bunko shows, and shooting-galleries, on, across Poydras street into the dim openness beyond, where glimmer the lamps of Lafayette square and the white marble of the municipal hall, and just on the farther side of this, with a sudden wheel to the right into Hevia street, a few strides there, a turn to the left, stumbling across a stone step and wooden sill into a narrow, lighted hall, and turning and entering an apartment here again at the right. The door is shut; the name is written down; the charge is made: Vagrancy, assaulting an officer, resisting arrest. An inner door is opened.

"What have you got in number nine?" asks the captain in charge.

"Chuck-full," replies the turnkey.

"Well, number seven?" These were the numbers of cells.

"The rats 'll eat him up in number seven."

"How about number ten?"

"Two drunk-and-disorderlies, one petty larceny, and one embezzlement and breach of trust."

"Put him in there."

.   .   .   .

And this explains what the watchman in Marais street could not understand, — why Mary Richling's window shone all night long.

CHAPTER XXVII.

OUT OF THE FRYING—PAN.

ROUND goes the wheel forever. Another sun rose up, not a moment hurried or belated by the myriads of life-and-death issues that cover the earth and wait in ecstasies of hope or dread the passage of time. Punctually at ten Justice-in-the-rough takes its seat in the Recorder's Court, and a moment of silent preparation at the desks follows the loud announcement that its session has begun. The perky clerks and smirking pettifoggers move apart on tiptoe, those to their respective stations, these to their privileged seats facing the high dais. The lounging police slip down from their reclining attitudes on the heel-scraped and whittled window-sills. The hum of voices among the forlorn humanity that half fills the gradually rising, greasy benches behind, allotted to witnesses and prisoners' friends, is hushed. In a little square, railed space, here at the left, the reporters tip their chairs against the hair-greased wall, and sharpen their pencils. A few tardy visitors, familiar with the place, tiptoe in through the grimy doors, ducking and winking, and softly lifting and placing their chairs, with a mock-timorous upward glance toward the long, ungainly personage who, under a faded and tattered crimson canopy, fills the august bench of magistracy with its high oaken back. On the right, behind a rude wooden paling that rises from the floor to the smoke-stained ceiling, are the peering, bloated faces of the night's prisoners.

The recorder utters a name. The clerk down in front of him cals it aloud. A door in the palings opens, and one of the captives comes forth and stands before the rail. The arresting officer mounts to the witness-stand and confronts him. The oath is rattled and turned out like dice from a box, and the accusing testimony is heard. It may be that counsel rises and cross-examines, if there are witnesses for the defence. Strange and far-fetched questions, from beginners at the law or from old blunderers, provoke now laughter, and now the peremptory protestations of the court against the waste of time. Yet, in general, a few minutes suffices for the whole trial of a case.

" You are sure she picked the handsaw up by the handle, are you?" says the questioner, frowning with the importance of the point.

" Yes."

" And that she coughed as she did so?"

" Well, you see, she kind o' " —

" Yes, or no!"

" No."

" That's all." He waves the prisoner down with an air of mighty triumph, turns to the recorder, " trusts it is not necessary to," etc., and the accused passes this way or that, according to the fate decreed, — discharged, sentenced to fine and imprisonment, or committed for trial before the courts of the State.

" Order in court!" There is too mnch talking. Another comes and stands before the rail, and goes his way. Another, and another; now a ragged boy, now a half-sobered crone, now a battered ruffian, and now a painted girl of the street, and at length one who starts when his name is called, as though something had exploded.

" John Richling!"

He came.

" Stand there ! "

Some one is in the witness-stand, speaking. The prisoner partly hears, but does not see. He stands and holds the rail, with his eyes fixed vacantly on the clerk, who bends over his desk under the seat of justice, writing. The lawyers notice him. His dress has been laboriously genteel, but is torn and soiled. A detective, with small eyes set close together, and a nose like a yacht's rudder, whisperingly calls the notice of one of these spectators who can see the prisoner's face to the fact that, for all its thinness and bruises, it is not a bad one. All can see that the man's hair is fine and waving where it is not matted with blood.

The testifying officer had moved as if to leave the witness-stand, when the recorder restrained him by a gesture, and, leaning forward and looking down upon the prisoner, asked : —

" Have you anything to say to this ? "

The prisoner lifted his eyes, bowed affirmatively, and spoke in a low, timid tone. " May I say a few words to you privately ? "

" No."

He dropped his eyes, fumbled with the rail, and, looking up suddenly, said in a stronger voice, " I want somebody to go to my wife — in Prieur street. She is starving. This is the third day " —

" We're not talking about that," said the recorder. " Have you anything to say against this witness's statement ? "

The prisoner looked upon the floor and slowly shook his head. " I never meant to break the law. I never expected to stand here. It's like an awful dream. Yesterday, at this time, I had no more idea of this — I didn't think I was so near it. It's like getting caught in machinery." He looked up at the recorder again. "I m so confused " — he frowned and drew his hand slowly across his brow — "I can hardly — put my words to gether. I was hunting for work. There is no man in this city who wants to earn an honest living more than I do."

"What's your trade?"

"I have none."

"I supposed not. But you profess to have some occu pation, I dare say. What's your occupation?"

"Accountant."

"Hum! you're all accountants. How long have you been out of employment?"

"Six months."

"Why did you go to sleep under those steps?"

"I didn't intend to go to sleep. I was waiting for a friend to come in who boards at the St. Charles."

A sudden laugh ran through the room. "Silence in court!" cried a deputy.

"Who is your friend?" asked the recorder.

The prisoner was silent.

"What is your friend's name?"

Still the prisoner did not reply. One of the group of pettifoggers sitting behind him leaned forward, touched him on the shoulder, and murmured: "You'd better tell his name. It won't hurt him, and it may help you." The prisoner looked back at the man and shook his head.

"Did you strike this officer?" asked the recorder, touching the witness, who was resting on both elbows in the light arm-chair on the right.

The prisoner made a low response.

"I don't hear you," said the recorder.

"I struck him," replied the prisoner; "I knocked him

down." The court officers below the dais smiled. " I woke and found him spurning me with his foot, and I resented it. I never expected to be a law-breaker. I "— He pressed his temples between his hands and was silent. The men of the law at his back exchanged glances of approval. The case was, to some extent, interesting.

"May it please the court," said the man who had before addressed the prisoner over his shoulder, stepping out on the right and speaking very softly and graciously, " I ask that this man be discharged. His fault seems so much more to be accident than intention, and his suffering so much more than his fault "—

The recorder interrupted by a wave of the hand and a preconceived smile : " Why, according to the evidence, the prisoner was noisy and troublesome in his cell all night."

"O sir," exclaimed the prisoner, " I was thrown in with thieves and drunkards ! It was unbearable in that hole. We were right on the damp and slimy bricks. The smell was dreadful. A woman in the cell opposite screamed the whole night. One of the men in the cell tried to take my coat from me, and I beat him ! "

" It seems to me, your honor," said the volunteer advocate, " the prisoner is still more sinned against than sinning. This is evidently his first offence, and " —

" Do you know even that ? " asked the recorder.

" I do not believe his name can be found on any criminal record. I " —

The recorder interrupted once more. He leaned toward the prisoner.

" Did you ever go by any other name ? "

The prisoner was dumb.

" Isn't John Richling the only name you have ever gone by ? " said his new friend ; but the prisoner silently blushed to the roots of his hair and remained motion-less.

"I think I shall have to send you to prison," said the recorder, preparing to write. A low groan was the prisoner's only response.

"May it please your honor," began the lawyer, taking a step forward; but the recorder waved his pen impatiently.

"Why, the more is said the worse his case gets; he's guilty of the offence charged, by his own confession."

"I am guilty and not guilty," said the prisoner slowly. "I never intended to be a criminal. I intended to be a good and useful member of society; but I've somehow got under its wheels. I've missed the whole secret of living." He dropped his face into his hands. "O Mary, Mary! why are you my wife?" He beckoned to his counsel. "Come here; come here." His manner was wild and nervous. "I want you — I want you to go to Prieur street, to my wife. You know — you know the place, don't you? Prieur street. Ask for Mrs. Riley"—

"Richling," said the lawyer.

"No, no! you ask for Mrs. Riley? Ask her — ask her — oh! where are my senses gone? Ask"—

"May it please the court," said the lawyer, turning once more to the magistrate and drawing a limp handkerchief from the skirt of his dingy alpaca, with a reviving confidence, "I ask that the accused be discharged; he is evidently insane."

The prisoner looked rapidly from counsel to magistrate, and back again, saying, in a low voice, "Oh, no! not that! Oh, no! not that! not that!"

The recorder dropped his eyes upon a paper on the desk before him, and, beginning to write, said. without looking up :—

"Parish Prison — to be examined for insanity."

A cry of remonstrance broke so sharply from the prisoner that even the reporters in their corner checked their energetic streams of lead-pencil rhetoric and looked up.

"You cannot do that!" he exclaimed. "I am not insane! I'm not even confused now! It was only for a minute! I'm not even confused!"

An officer of the court laid his hand quickly and sternly upon his arm; but the recorder leaned forward and motioned him off. The prisoner darted a single flash of anger at the officer, and then met the eye of the justice.

"If I am a vagrant commit me for vagrancy! I expect no mercy here! I expect no justice! You punish me first, and try me afterward, and now you can punish me again; but you can't do that!"

"Order in court! Sit down in those benches!" cried the deputies. The lawyers nodded darkly or blandly, each to each. The one who had volunteered his counsel wiped his bald Gothic brow. On the recorder's lips an austere satire played as he said to the panting prisoner : —

"You are showing not only your sanity, but your contempt of court also."

The prisoner's eyes shot back a fierce light as he retorted : —

"I have no object in concealing either."

The recorder answered with a quick, angry look; but, instantly restraining himself, dropped his glance upon his desk as before, began again to write, and said, with his eyes following his pen : —

"Parish Prison, for thirty days."

The officer grasped the prisoner again and pointed him to the door in the palings whence he had come, and whither he now returned, without a word or note of distress.

Half an hour later the dark omnibus without windows, that went by the facetious name of the "Black Maria" received the convicted ones from the same street door by which they had been brought in out of the world the night before. The waifs and vagabonds of the town gleefully formed a line across the sidewalk from the station-house to the van, and counted with zest the abundant number of passengers that were ushered into it one by one. Heigh ho! In they went: all ages and sorts; both sexes; tried and untried, drunk and sober, new faces and old acquaintances; a man who had been counterfeiting, his wife who had been helping him, and their little girl of twelve, who had done nothing. Ho, ho! Bridget Fury! Ha, ha! Howling Lou! In they go: the passive, the violent, all kinds; filling the two benches against the sides, and then the standing room; crowding and packing, until the officer can shut the door only by throwing his weight against it.

"Officer," said one, whose volunteer counsel had persuaded the reporters not to mention him by name in their thrilling account, — officer," said this one, trying to pause an instant before the door of the vehicle, "is there no other possible way to " —

"Get in! get in!"

Two hands spread against his back did the rest; the door clapped to like the lid of a bursting trunk, the padlock rattled: away they went!

CHAPTER XXVIII.

"OH, WHERE IS MY LOVE?"

AT the prison the scene is repeated in reverse, and the Black Maria presently rumbles away empty. In that building, whose exterior Narcisse found so pictu-resque, the vagrant at length finds food. In that question of food, by the way, another question arose, not as to any degree of criminality past or present, nor as to age, or sex, or race, or station; but as to the having or lacking fifty cents. "Four bits" a day was the open sesame to a department where one could have bedstead and ragged bedding and dirty mosquito-bar, a cell whose window looked down into the front street, food in variety, and a seat at table with the officers of the prison. But those who could not pay were conducted past all these delights, along one of several dark galleries, the turnkeys of which were themselves convicts, who, by a process of reason-ing best understood among the harvesters of perquisites, were assumed to be undergoing sentence.

The vagrant stood at length before a grated iron gate while its bolts were thrown back and it growled on its hinges. What he saw within needs no minute description; it may be seen there still, any day: a large, flagged court, surrounded on three sides by two stories of cells with heavy, black, square doors all a-row and mostly open; about a hundred men sitting, lying, or lounging about in scanty rags, — some gaunt and feeble, some burly and alert, some scarred and maimed, some sallow, some red, some grizzled, some mere lads, some old and bowed, — the sentenced, the untried, men there for the first time, men who were oftener in than out, — burglars, smugglers, house-burners, highwaymen, wife-beaters, wharf-rats, common " drunks," pickpockets, shop-lifters, stealers of bread, garroters, murderers, — in common equality and fraternity. In this resting and refreshing place for vice, this caucus for the projection of future crime, this ghastly burlesque of justice and the protection of society, there was a man who had been convicted of a dreadful murder a year or two before, and sentenced to twenty-one years' labor in the State penitentiary. He had got his sentence commuted to confinement in this prison for twenty-one years of idleness. The captain of the prison had made him " captain of the yard." Strength, ferocity, and a terrific record were the qualifications for this honorary office.

The gate opened. A howl of welcome came from those within, and the new batch, the vagrant among them, entered the yard. He passed, in his turn, to a tank of muddy water in this yard, washed away the soil and blood of the night, and so to the cell assigned him. He was lying face downward on its pavement, when a man with a cudgel ordered him to rise. The vagrant sprang to his feet and confronted the captain of the yard, a giant in breadth and stature, with no clothing but a ragged undershirt and pantaloons.

" Get a bucket and rag and scrub out this cell ! "

He flourished his cudgel. The vagrant cast a quick glance at him, and answered quietly, but with burning face : —

"I 'll die first."

A blow with the cudgel, a cry of rage, a clash together, a push, a sledge-hammer fist in the side, another on the head, a fall out into the yard, and the vagrant lay senseless on the flags.

When he opened his eyes again, and struggled to his feet, a gentle grasp was on his arm. Somebody was steadying him. He turned his eyes. Ah! who is this? A short, heavy, close-shaven man, with a woollen jacket thrown over one shoulder and its sleeves tied together in a knot under the other. He speaks in a low, kind tone :—

" Steady, Mr. Richling ! "

Richling supported himself by a hand on the man's arm, gazed in bewilderment at the gentle eyes that met his, and with a slow gesture of astonishment murmured, " Ristofalo ! " and dropped his head.

The Italian had just entered the prison from another station-house. With his hand still on Richling's shoulder, and Richling's on his, he caught the eye of the captain of the yard, who was striding quietly up and down near by, and gave him a nod to indicate that he would soon adjust everything to that autocrat's satisfaction. Richling, dazed and trembling, kept his eyes still on the ground, while Ristofalo moved with him slowly away from the squalid group that gazed after them. They went toward the Italian's cell.

" Why are you in prison? " asked the vagrant, feebly.

" Oh, nothin' much — witness in shootin' scrape — talk 'bout aft' while."

" O Ristofalo," groaned Richling, as they entered, " my wife ! my wife ! Send some bread to my wife ! "

" Lie down," said the Italian, pressing softly on his shoulders ; but Richling as quietly resisted.

" She is near here, Ristofalo. You can send with the greatest ease ! You can do anything, Ristofalo, — if you only choose ! "

" Lay down," said the Italian again, and pressed more

heavily. The vagrant sank limply to the pavement, his companion quickly untying the jacket sleeves from under his own arms and wadding the garment under Richling's head.

"Do you know what I'm in here for, Ristofalo?" moaned Richling.

"Don't know, don't care. Yo' wife know you here?" Richling shook his head on the jacket. The Italian asked her address, and Richling gave it.

"Goin' tell her come and see you," said the Italian. "Now, you lay still little while; I be back t'rectly." He went out into the yard again, pushing the heavy door after him till it stood only slightly ajar, sauntered easily around till he caught sight of the captain of the yard, and was presently standing before him in the same immovable way in which he had stood before Richling in Tchoupitoulas street, on the day he had borrowed the dollar. Those who idly drew around could not hear his words, but the "captain's" answers were intentionally audible. He shook his head in rejection of a proposal. "No, nobody out the prisoner himself should scrub out the cell. No, the Italian should not do it for him. The prisoner's refusal and resistance had settled that question. No, the knocking down had not balanced accounts at all. There was more scrubbing to be done. It was scrubbing day. Others might scrub the yard and the galleries, but he should scrub out the tank. And there were other things, and worse,— menial services of the lowest kind. He should do them when the time came, and the Italian would have to help him too. Never mind about the law or the terms of his sentence. Those counted for nothing there." Such was the sense of the decrees; the words were such as may be guessed or left unguessed. The scrubbing of the cell must commence at once. The vagrant must make up his mind to suffer. "He had served on jury!" said the man in the undershirt, with a final flourish of his stick. "He's got to pay dear for it."

When Ristofalo returned to his cell, its inmate, after many upstartings from terrible dreams, that seemed to guard the threshold of slumber, had fallen asleep. The Italian touched him gently, but he roused with a wild start and stare.

"Ristofalo," he said, and fell a-staring again.

"You had some sleep," said the Italian.

"It's worse than being awake," said Richling. He passed his hands across his face. "Has my wife been here?"

"No. Haven't sent yet. Must watch good chance. Git captain yard in good-humor first, or else do on sly." The cunning Italian saw that anything looking like early extrication would bring new fury upon Richling. He knew *all* the values of time. "Come," he added, "must scrub out cell now." He ignored the heat that kindled in Richling's eyes, and added, smiling, "You don't do it, I got to do it."

With a little more of the like kindly guile, and some wise and simple reasoning, the Italian prevailed. Together, without objection from the captain of the yard, with many unavailing protests from Richling, who would now do it alone, and with Ristofalo smiling like a Chinaman at the obscene ribaldry of the spectators in the yard, they scrubbed the cell. Then came the tank. They had to stand in it with the water up to their knees, and rub its sides with brickbats. Richling fell down twice in the water, to the uproarious delight of the yard; but his companion helped him up, and they both agreed it was the sliminess of the tank's bottom that was to blame.

·" Soon we get through we goin' to b y drink ɔ' whisky
from jailer," said Ristofalo ; " he keep it for sale. Then,
after that, kin hire somebody to go to your house;
captain yard think we gittin' mo' whisky."

" Hire?" said Richling. " I haven't a cent in the
world."

" I got a little — few dimes," rejoined the other.

" Then why are you here? Why are you in this part
of the prison?"

" Oh, 'fraid to spend it. On'y got few dimes. Broke
ag'in."

Richling stopped still with astonishment, brickbat in
hand. The Italian met his gaze with an illuminated smile.
" Yes," he said, " took all I had with me to bayou La
Fourche. Coming back, slept with some men in boat.
One git up in night-time and steal everything. Then was
a big fight. Think that what fight was about— about
dividing the money. Don't know sure. One man git
killed. Rest run into the swamp and prairie. Officer arrest me for witness. Couldn't trust me to stay in the
city."

" Do you think the one who was killed was the thief ?"

" Don't know sure," said the Italian, with the same
sweet face, and falling to again with his brickbat,—
" hope so ! "

" Strange place to confine a witness ! " said Richling,
holding his hand to his bruised side and slowly straightening his back.

" Oh, yes, good place," replied the other, scrubbing
away ; " git him, in short time, so he swear to anything."

It was far on in the afternoon before the wary Ristofalo ventured to offer all he had in his pocket to a
hanger-on of the prison office, to go first to Richling's
house, and then to an acquaintance of his own, with

messages looking to the procuring of their release. The messenger chose to go first to Ristofalo's friend, and afterward to Mrs. Riley's. It was growing dark when he reached the latter place. Mary was out in the city somewhere, wandering about, aimless and distracted, in search of Richling. The messenger left word with Mrs. Riley. Richling had all along hoped that that good friend, doubtless acquainted with the most approved methods of finding a missing man, would direct Mary to the police station at the earliest practicable hour. But time had shown that she had not done so. No, indeed! Mrs. Riley counted herself too benevolently shrewd for that. While she had made Mary's suspense of the night less frightful than it might have been, by surmises that Mr. Richling had found some form of night-work, — watching some pile of freight or some unfinished building, — she had come, secretly, to a different conviction, predicated on her own married experiences; and if Mr. Richling had, in a moment of gloom, tipped the bowl a little too high, as her dear lost husband, the best man that ever walked, had often done, and had been locked up at night to be let out in the morning, why, give him a chance! Let him invent his own little fault-hiding romance and come home with it. Mary was frantic. She could not be kept in; but Mrs. Riley, by prolonged effort, convinced her it was best not to call upon Dr. Sevier until she could be sure some disaster had actually occurred, and sent her among the fruiterers and oystermen in vain search for Raphael Ristofalo. Thus it was that the Doctor's morning messenger to the Richlings, bearing word that if any one were sick he would call without delay, was met by Mrs. Riley only, and by the reassuring statement that both of them were out. The later messenger, from the two men in prison, brought back word of Mary's absence from the

house, of her physical welfare, and Mrs. Riley's promise
that Mary should visit the prison at the earliest hour
possible. This would not be till the next morning.

While Mrs. Riley was sending this message, Mary, a
great distance away, was emerging from the darkening
and silent streets of the river front and moving with timid
haste across the broad levee toward the edge of the water
at the steamboat landing. In this season of depleted
streams and idle waiting, only an occasional boat lifted
its lofty, black, double funnels against the sky here and
there, leaving wide stretches of unoccupied wharf-front
between. Mary hurried on, clear out to the great wharf's
edge, and looked forth upon the broad, softly moving harbor. The low waters spread out and away, to and around
the opposite point, in wide surfaces of glassy purples and
wrinkled bronze. Beauty, that joy forever, is sometimes
a terror. Was the end of her search somewhere underneath that fearful glory? She clasped her hands, bent
down with dry, staring eyes, then turned again and fled
homeward. She swerved once toward Dr. Sevier's quarters, but soon decided to see first if there were any tidings
with Mrs. Riley, and so resumed her course. Night
overtook her in streets where every footstep before or
behind her made her tremble; but at length she crossed
the threshold of Mrs. Riley's little parlor. Mrs. Riley
was standing in the door, and retreated a step or two
backward as Mary entered with a look of wild inquiry.

" Not come? " cried the wife.

" Mrs. Richlin'," said the widow, hurriedly, " yer husband's alive and found."

Mary seized her frantically by the shoulders, crying
with high-pitched voice : —

" Where is he? — where is he? "

" Ye can't see um till marning, Mrs. Richlin'."

" Where is he?" cried Mary, louder than before.

" Me dear," said Mrs. Riley, " ye kin easy git him out in the marning."

" Mrs. Riley," said Mary, holding her with her eye, " is my husband in prison? — O Lord God!   O God! my God!"

Mrs. Riley wept.   She clasped the moaning, sobbing wife to her bosom, and with streaming eyes said: —

" Mrs. Richlin', me dear, Mrs. Richlin', me dear, what wad I give to have my husband this night where your husband is!"

CHAPTER XXIX.

RELEASE. — NARCISSE.

AS some children were playing in the street before the Parish Prison next morning, they suddenly started and scampered toward the prison's black entrance. A physician's carriage had driven briskly up to it, ground its wheels against the curb-stone, and halted. If any fresh crumbs of horror were about to be dropped, the children must be there to feast on them. Dr. Sevier stepped out, gave Mary his hand and then his arm, and went in with her. A question or two in the prison office, a reference to the rolls, and a turnkey led the way through a dark gallery lighted with dimly burning gas. The stench was suffocating. They stopped at the inner gate.

" Why didn't you bring him to us? " asked the Doctor, scowling resentfully at the facetious drawings and legends on the walls, where the dampness glistened in the sickly light.

The keeper made a low reply as he shot the bolts.

" What ? " quickly asked Mary.

" He's not well," said Dr. Sevier.

The gate swung open. They stepped into the yard and across it. The prisoners paused in a game of ball. Others, who were playing cards, merely glanced up and went on. The jailer pointed with his bunch of keys to a cell before him. Mary glided away from the Doctor and darted in. There was a cry and a wail.

The Doctor followed quickly. Ristofalo passed out as

he entered. Richling lay on a rough gray blanket spread on the pavement with the Italian's jacket under his head. Mary had thrown herself down beside him upon her knees, and their arms were around each other's neck.

"Let me see, Mrs. Richling," said the physician, touching her on the shoulder. She drew back. Richling lifted a hand in welcome. The Doctor pressed it.

"Mrs. Richling," he said, as they faced each other, he on one knee, she on both. He gave her a few laconic directions for the sick man's better comfort. "You must stay here, madam," he said at length; "this man Ristofalo will be ample protection for you; and I will go at once and get your husband's discharge." He went out.

In the office he asked for a seat at a desk. As he finished using it he turned to the keeper and asked, with severe face: —

"What do you do with sick prisoners here, anyway?"

The keeper smiled.

"Why, if they gits right sick, the hospital wagon comes and takes 'em to the Charity Hospital."

"Umhum!" replied the Doctor, unpleasantly, — "in the same wagon they use for a case of scarlet fever or small-pox, eh?"

The keeper, with a little resentment in his laugh, stated that he would be eternally lost if he knew.

"*I* know," remarked the Doctor. "But when a man is only a little sick, — according to your judgment, — like that one in there now, he is treated here, eh?"

The keeper swelled with a little official pride. His tone was boastful.

"We has a complete dispenisary in the prison," he said.

"Yes? Who's your druggist?" Dr. Sevier was in his worst inquisitorial mood.

" One of the prisoners," said the keeper.

The Doctor looked at him steadily. The man, in the blackness of his ignorance, was visibly proud of this bit of economy and convenience.

" How long has he held this position?" asked the physician.

"Oh, a right smart while. He was sentenced for murder, but he's waiting for a new trial."

" And he has full charge of all the drugs?" asked the Doctor, with a cheerful smile.

" Yes, sir." The keeper was flattered.

" Poisons and all, I suppose, eh?" pursued the Doctor.

" Everything."

The Doctor looked steadily and silently upon the officer, and tore and folded and tore again into small bits the prescription he had written. A moment later the door of his carriage shut with a smart clap and its wheels rattled away. There was a general laugh in the office, heavily spiced with maledictions.

" I say, Cap', what d'you reckon he'd 'a' said if he'd 'a' seen the women's department?"

In those days recorders had the power to release prisoners sentenced by them when in their judgment new information justified such action. Yet Dr. Sevier had a hard day's work to procure Richling's liberty. The sun was declining once more when a hack drove up to Mrs. Riley's door with John and Mary in it, and Mrs. Riley was restrained from laughing and crying only by the presence of the great Dr. Sevier and a romantic Italian stranger by the captivating name of Ristofalo. Richling, with repeated avowals of his ability to walk alone, was helped into the house between these two illustrious visitors, Mary hurrying in ahead, and Mrs. Riley shutting

the street door with some resentment of manner toward
the staring children who gathered without. Was there
anything surprising in the fact that eminent persons should
call at her house?"

When there was time for greetings she gave her hand
to Dr. Sevier and asked him how he found himself. To
Ristofalo she bowed majestically. She noticed that he
was handsome and muscular.

At different hours the next day the same two visitors
called. Also the second day after. And the third. And
frequently afterward.

Ristofalo regained his financial feet almost, as one
might say, at a single hand-spring. He amused Mary
and John and Mrs. Riley almost beyond limit with his
simple story of how he did it.

"Ye'd better hurry and be getting up out o' that sick
bed, Mr. Ritchlin'," said the widow, in Ristofalo's absence,
"or that I-talian rascal 'll be making himself entirely too
agree'ble to yer lady here. Ha! ha! It's *she* that he's
a-comin' here to see."

Mrs. Riley laughed again, and pointed at Mary and
tossed her head, not knowing that Mary went through it
all over again as soon as Mrs. Riley was out of the room,
to the immense delight of John.

"And now, madam," said Dr Sevier to Mary, by and
by, "let it be understood once more that even indepen-
dence may be carried to a vicious extreme, and that " —
he turned to Richling, by whose bed he stood — "you and
your wife will not do it again. You've had a narrow
escape. Is it understood?"

"We'll try to be moderate," replied the invalid, play
fully.

"I don't believe you," said the Doctor.

And his scepticism was wise. He continued to watch them, and at length enjoyed the sight of John up and out again with color in his cheeks and the old courage — nay, a new and a better courage — in his eyes.

Said the Doctor on his last visit, "Take good care of your husband, my child." He held the little wife's hand a moment, and gazed out of Mrs. Riley's front door upon the western sky. Then he transferred his gaze to John, who stood, with his knee in a chair, just behind her. He looked at the convalescent with solemn steadfastness. The husband smiled broadly.

"I know what you mean. I'll try to deserve her."

The Doctor looked again into the west.

"Good-by."

Mary tried playfully to retort, but John restrained her, and when she contrived to utter something absurdly complimentary of her husband he was her only hearer.

They went back into the house, talking of other matters. Something turned the conversation upon Mrs. Riley, and from that subject it seemed to pass naturally to Ristofalo. Mary, laughing and talking softly as they entered their room, called to John's recollection the Italian's account of how he had once bought a tarpaulin hat and a cottonade shirt of the pattern called a "jumper," and had worked as a deck-hand in loading and unloading steamboats. It was so amusingly sensible to put on the proper badge for the kind of work sought. Richling mused. Many a dollar he might have earned the past summer, had he been as ingeniously wise, he thought.

"Ristofalo is coming here this evening," said he, taking a seat in the alley window.

Mary looked at him with sidelong merriment. The Italian was coming to see Mrs. Riley.

heavy, rushing blast of the cotton compress, telling that the flood tide of commerce was setting in.

Narcisse surprised the Richlings one evening with a call. They tried very hard to be reserved, but they were too young for that task to be easy. The Creole had evidently come with his mind made up to take unresentfully and override all the unfriendliness they might choose to show. His conversation never ceased, but flitted from subject to subject with the swift waywardness of a humming-bird. It was remarked by Mary, leaning back in one end of Mrs. Riley's little sofa, that " summer dresses were disappearing, but that the girls looked just as sweet in their darker colors as they had appeared in midsummer white. Had Narcisse noticed? Probably he didn't care for " —

" Ho! I notiz them an' they notiz me! An' thass one thing I 'ave notiz about young ladies : they ah juz like those bird' ; in summeh lookin' cool, in winteh waul l. I 'ave notiz that. An' I've notiz anotheh thing which make them juz like those bird'. They halways know if a man is lookin', an' they halways make like they don't see 'im ! I would like to 'ite an i'ony about that — a lill i'ony — in the he'oic measuh. You like that he'oic measuh, Mizzez Witchlin' ? "

As he rose to go he rolled a cigarette, and folded the end in with the long nail of his little finger.

" Mizzez Witchlin', if you will allow me to light my ciga'ette fum yo' lamp — I can't use my sun-glass at night, because the sun is nod theh. But, the sun shining, I use it. I 'ave adop' that method since lately."

" You borrow the sun's rays," said Mary, with wicked sweetness.

" Yes ; 'tis cheapeh than matches in the longue 'un "

"You have discovered that, I suppose," remarked John.

"Me? The sun-glass? No. I believe Ahchimides invend that, in fact. An' yet, out of ten thousan' who use the sun-glass only a few can account 'ow tis done. 'Ow did you think that that's my invention, Mistoo Itchlin? Did you know that I am something of a chimist? I can tu'n litmus papeh 'ed by juz dipping it in SO_3HO. Yesseh."

"Yes," said Richling, "that's one thing that I have noticed, that you're very fertile in devices."

"Yes," echoed Mary, "I noticed that, the first time you ever came to see us. I only wish Mr. Richling was half as much so."

She beamed upon her husband. Narcisse laughed with pure pleasure.

"Well, I am compel' to say you ah co'ect. I am continually makin' some discove'ies. 'Necessity's the motheh of inventions.' Now thass anotheh thing I 'ave notiz — about that month of Octobeh: it always come befo' you think it's comin'. I 'ave notiz that about eve'y month. Now, to-day we ah the twennieth Octobeh! Is it not so?" He lighted his cigarette. "You ah compel' to co'obo'ate me."

CHAPTER XXX.

LIGHTING SHIP.

YES, the tide was coming in. The Richlings' bark was still on the sands, but every now and then a wave of promise glided under her. She might float, now, any day. Meantime, as has no doubt been guessed, she was held on an even keel by loans from the Doctor.

" Why you don't advertise in papers?" asked Ristofalo.

" Advertise? Oh, I didn't think it would be of any use. I advertised a whole week, last summer."

" You put advertisement in wrong time and keep it out wrong time," said the Italian.

" I have a place in prospect, now, without advertising," said Richling, with an elated look.

It was just here that a new mistake of Richling's emerged. He had come into contact with two or three men of that wretched sort that indulge the strange vanity of keeping others waiting upon them by promises of employment. He believed them, liked them heartily because they said nothing about references, and gratefully distended himself with their husks, until Ristofalo opened his eyes by saying, when one of these men had disappointed Richling the third time : —

" Business man don't promise but once."

" You lookin' for book-keeper's place?" asked the Italian at another time. " Why don't dress like a book-keeper?"

"On borrowed money?" asked Richling, evidently look‑ing upon that question as a poser.

"Yes."

"Oh, no," said Richling, with a smile of superiority; but the other one smiled too, and shook his head.

"Borrow mo', if you don't."

Richling's heart flinched at the word. He had thought he was giving his true reason; but he was not. A foolish notion had floated, like a grain of dust, into the over‑delicate wheels of his thought,— that men would employ him the more readily if he looked needy. His hat was unbrushed, his shoes unpolished; he had let his beard come out, thin and untrimmed; his necktie was faded. He looked battered. When the Italian's gentle warning showed him this additional mistake on top of all his others he was dismayed at himself; and when he sat down in his room and counted the cost of an accountant's uniform, so to speak, the remains of Dr. Sevier's last loan to him was too small for it. Thereupon he committed one error more,— but it was the last. He sunk his standard, and began again to look for service among industries that could offer employment only to manual labor. He crossed the river and stirred about among the dry-docks and ship-carpenters' yards of the suburb Algiers. But he could neither hew spars, nor paint, nor splice ropes. He watched a man half a day calking a boat; then he offered himself for the same work, did it fairly, and earned half a day's wages. But then the boat was done, and there was no other calking at the moment along the whole harbor front, except some that was being done on a ship by her own sailors.

"John," said Mary, dropping into her lap the sewing that hardly paid for her candle, "isn't it hard to realize that it isn't twelve months since your hardships commenced? They *can't* last much longer, darling."

"I know that," said John. "And I know I'll find a place presently, and then we'll wake up to the fact that this was actually less than a year of trouble in a lifetime of love."

"Yes," rejoined Mary, "I know your patience will be rewarded."

"But what I want is work now, Mary. The bread of idleness is getting *too* bitter. But never mind; I'm going to work to-morrow; — never mind where. It's all right. You'll see."

She smiled, and looked into his eyes again with a confession of unreserved trust. The next day he reached the — what shall we say? — big end of his last mistake. What it was came out a few mornings after, when he called at Number 5 Carondelet street.

"The Doctah is not in pwesently,' said Narcisse. "He ve'y hawdly comes in so soon as that. He's living home again, once mo', now. He's ve'y un'estless. I tole 'im yestiddy, 'Doctah, I know juz 'ow you feel, seh; 'tis the same way with myseff. You ought to git ma'ied!'"

"Did he say he would?" asked Richling.

"Well, you know, Mistoo Itchlin, so the povvub says, 'Silent give consense.' He juz look at me — nevvah said a word — ha! he couldn'! You not lookin' ve'y well, Mistoo Itchlin. I suppose 'tis that waum weatheh."

"I suppose it is; at least, partly," said Richling, and added nothing more, but looked along and across the ceiling, and down at a skeleton in a corner, that was offering to shake hands with him. He was at a loss how to talk to Narcisse. Both Mary and he had grown a little ashamed of their covert sarcasms, and yet to leave them out was bread without yeast, meat without salt, as far as their own powers of speech were concerned.

"I thought, the other day," he began again, with an effort, "when it blew up cool, that the warm weather was over."

"It seem to be finishin' ad the end, I think," responded the Creole. "I think, like you, that we 'ave 'ad too waum weatheh. Me, I like that weatheh to be cole, me. I halways weigh the mose in cole weatheh. I gain flesh, in fact. But so soon 'tis summeh somethin' become of it. I dunno if 'tis the fault of my close, but I reduct in summeh. Speakin' of close, Mistoo Itchlin, — egscuse me if 'tis a fair question, — w'at was yo' objec' in buyin' that tawpaulin hat an' jacket lass week ad that sto' on the levee? You din know I saw you, but I juz 'appen to see you, in fact." (The color rose in Richling's face, and Narcisse pressed on without allowing an answer.) "Well, thass none o' my biziness, of co'se, but I think you lookin' ve'y bad, Mistoo Itchlin" — He stopped very short and stepped with dignified alacrity to his desk, for Dr. Sevier's step was on the stair.

The Doctor shook hands with Richling and sank into the chair at his desk. "Anything turned up yet, Richling?"

"Doctor," began Richling, drawing his chair near and speaking low.

"Good-mawnin', Doctah," said Narcisse, showing himself with a graceful flourish.

The Doctor nodded, then turned again to Richling. "You were saying" —

"I 'ope you well, seh," insisted the Creole, and as the Doctor glanced toward him impatiently, repeated the sentiment, "'Ope you well, seh."

The Doctor said he was, and turned once more to

Richling. Narcisse bowed away backward and went to his desk, filled to the eyes with fierce satisfaction. He had made himself felt. Richling drew his chair nearer and spoke low : —

"If I don't get work within a day or two I shall have to come to you for money."

"That's all right, Richling." The Doctor spoke aloud ; Richling answered low.

"Oh, no, Doctor, it's all wrong ! Indeed, I can't do it any more unless you will let me earn the money."

"My dear sir, I would most gladly do it ; but I have nothing that you can do."

"Yes, you have, Doctor."

"What is it ?"

"Why, it's this : you have a slave boy driving your carriage."

"Well ?"

"Give him some other work, and let me do that."

Dr. Sevier started in his seat. "Richling, I can't do that. I should ruin you. If you drive my carriage" —

"Just for a time, Doctor, till I find something else."

"No ! no ! If you drive my carriage in New Orleans you'll never do anything else."

"Why, Doctor, there are men standing in the front ranks to-day, who" —

"Yes, yes," replied the Doctor, impatiently, "I know, — who began with menial labor ; but — I can't explain it to you, Richling, but you're not of the same sort ; that's all. I say it without praise or blame ; you must have work adapted to your abilities."

"My abilities !" softly echoed Richling. Tears sprang to his eyes. He held out his open palms, — "Doctor, look there." They were lacerated. He started to rise, but the Doctor prevented him.

"Let me go," said Richling, pleadingly, and with averted face. "Let me go. I'm sorry I showed them. It was mean and foolish and weak. Let me go."

Bu: Dr. Sevier kept a hand on him, and he did not resist. The Doctor took one of the hands and examined it. "Why, Richling, you've been handling freight!"

"There was nothing else."

"Oh, bah!"

"Let me go," whispered Richling. But the Doctor held him.

"You didn't do this on the steam-boat landing, did you, Richling?"

The young man nodded. The Doctor dropped the hand and looked upon its owner with set lips and steady severity. When he spoke he said:—

"Among the negro and green Irish deck-hands, and under the oaths and blows of steam-boat mates! Why, Richling!" He turned half away in his rotary chair with an air of patience worn out.

"You thought I had more sense," said Richling.

The Doctor put his elbows upon his desk and slowly drew his face upward through his hands. "Mr. Richling, what is the matter with you?" They gazed at each other a long moment, and then Dr. Sevier continued: "Your trouble isn't want of sense. I know that very well, Richling." His voice was low and became kind. "But you don't get the use of the sense you have. It isn't available." He bent forward: "Some men, Richling, carry their folly on the surface and their good sense at the bottom," — he jerked his thumb backward toward the distant Narcisse, and added, with a stealthy frown,— "like that little fool in yonder. He's got plenty of sense, but he doesn't load any of it on deck. Some men carry their sense on top and their folly down below" —

Richling smiled broadly through his dejection, and touched his own chest. "Like this big fool here," he said.

"Exactly," said Dr. Sevier. "Now you've developed a defect of the memory. Your few merchantable qualities have been so long out of the market, and you've suffered such humiliation under the pressure of adversity, that you've — you've done a very bad thing."

"Say a dozen," responded Richling, with bitter humor. But the Doctor swung his head in resentment of the levity.

"One's enough. You've allowed yourself to forget your true value."

"I'm worth whatever I'll bring."

The Doctor tossed his head in impatient disdain.

'Pshaw! You'll never bring what you're worth any more than some men are worth what they bring. You don't know how. You never will know."

"Well, Doctor, I do know that I'm worth more than I ever was before. I've learned a thousand things in the last twelvemonth. If I can only get a chance to prove it!" Richling turned red and struck his knee with his fist.

"Oh, yes," said Dr. Sevier; "that's your sense, on top. And then you go — in a fit of the merest impatience, as I do suspect — and offer yourself as a deck-hand and as a carriage-driver. That's your folly, at the bottom. What ought to be done to such a man?" He gave a low, harsh laugh. Richling dropped his eyes. A silence followed.

"You say all you want is a chance," resumed the Doctor.

"Yes," quickly answered Richling, looking up.

"I'm going to give it to you." They looked into each

other's eyes. The Doctor nodded. "Yes, sir." He nodded again.

"Where did you come from, Richling, — when you came to New Orleans, — you and your wife? Milwaukee?"

"Yes."

"Do your relatives know of your present condition?"

"No."

"Is your wife's mother comfortably situated?"

"Yes."

"Then I'll tell you what you must do."

"The only thing I can't do," said Richling.

"Yes, you can. You must. You must send Mrs. Richling back to her mother."

Richling shook his head.

"Well," said the Doctor, warmly, "I say you must. I will lend you the passage-money."

Richling's eye kindled an instant at the Doctor's compulsory tone, but he said, gently: —

"Why, Doctor, Mary will never consent to leave me."

"Of course she will not. But you must make her do it! That's what you must do. And when that's done then you must start out and go systematically from door to door, — of business houses, I mean, — offering yourself for work befitting your station — ahem! —station, I say — and qualifications. I will lend you money to live on until you find permanent employment. Now, now, don't get alarmed! I'm not going to help you any more than I absolutely must!"

"But, Doctor, how can you expect" — But the Doctor interrupted.

"Come, now, none of that! You and your wife are brave; I must say that for you. She has the courage of a gladiator. You can do this if you will."

"Doctor," said Richling, "you are the best of friends; but, you know, the fact is, Mary and I — well, we're still lovers."

"Oh!" The Doctor turned away his head with fresh impatience. Richling bit his lip, but went on: —

"We can bear anything on earth together; but we have sworn to stay together through better and worse" —

"Oh, pf-f-f-f!" said the doctor, closing his eyes and swinging his head away again.

" — And we're going to do it," concluded Richling.

"But you can't do it!" cried the Doctor, so loudly that Narcisse stood up on the rungs of his stool and peered.

"We can't separate."

Dr. Sevier smote the desk and sprang to his feet: —

"Sir, you've got to do it! If you continue in this way, you'll die. You'll die, Mr. Richling — both of you! You'll die! Are you going to let Mary die just because she's brave enough to do it?" He sat down again and busied himself, nervously placing pens on the pen-rack, the stopper in the inkstand, and the like.

Many thoughts ran through Richling's mind in the ensuing silence. His eyes were on the floor. Visions o. parting; of the great emptiness that would be left behind; the pangs and yearnings that must follow, — crowded one upon another. One torturing realization kept ever in the front, — that the Doctor had a well-earned right to advise, and that, if his advice was to be rejected, one must show good and sufficient cause for rejecting it, both in present resources and in expectations. The truth leaped upon him and bore him down as it never had done before, — the truth which he had heard this very Dr. Sevier proclaim, — that debt is bondage. For a moment he rebelled against it; but shame soon displaced mutiny, and he accepted this part, also, of his lot.   At length he rose.

"Well?" said Dr. Sevier.

"May I ask Mary?"

"You will do what you please, Mr. Richling." And then, in a kinder voice, the Doctor added, "Yes; ask her."

They moved together to the office door. The Doctor opened it, and they said good-by, Richling trying to drop a word of gratitude, and the Doctor hurriedly ignoring it.

The next half hour or more was spent by the physician in receiving, hearing, and dismissing patients and their messengers.   By and by no others came. The only audible sound was that of the Doctor's paper-knife as it parted the leaves of a pamphlet.   He was thinking over the late interview with Richling, and knew that, if this silence were not soon interrupted from without, he would have to encounter his book-keeper, who had not spoken since Richling had left.   Presently the issue came.

"Dr. Seveeah," — Narcisse came forward, hat in hand, — "I dunno 'ow 'tis, but Mistoo Itchlin always wemine me of that povvub, 'Ully to bed, ully to 'ise, make a pusson to be 'ealthy an' wealthy an' wise.'"

"I don't know how it is, either," grumbled the Doctor.

"I believe thass not the povvub I was thinking.   I am acquainting myseff with those povvubs; but I'm somewhat gween in that light, in fact.   Well, Doctah, I'm goin' ad the — shoemakeh.   I burs' my shoe vistiddy.   I was juz" —

"Very well, go."

"Yesseh; and from the shoemakeh I'll go" —

The Doctor glanced darkly over the top of the pamphlet.

" — Ad the bank; yesseh," said Narcisse, and went.

CHAPTER XXXI.

AT LAST.

MARY, cooking supper, uttered a soft exclamation of pleasure and relief as she heard John's step under the alley window and then at the door. She turned, with an iron spoon in one hand and a candlestick in the other, from the little old stove with two pot-holes, where she had been stirring some mess in a tin pan.

" Why, you're "— she reached for a kiss —" real late ! "

" I could not come any sooner." He dropped into a chair at the table.

" Busy ? "

" No ; no work to-day."

Mary lifted the pan from the stove, whisked it to the table, and blew her fingers.

" Same subject continued," she said laughingly, pointing with her spoon to the warmed-over food.

Richling smiled and nodded, and then flattened his elbows out on the table and hid his face in them.

This was the first time he had ever lingered away from his wife when he need not have done so. It was the Doctor's proposition that had kept him back. All day long it had filled his thoughts. He felt its wisdom. Its sheer practical value had pierced remorselessly into the deepest convictions of his mind. But his heart could not receive it.

' Well," said Mary, brightly, as she sat down at the

table, " maybe you'll have better luck to-morrow. Don't you think you may?"

' I don't know," said John, straightening up and tossing back his hair. He pushed a plate up to the pan, supplied and passed it. Then he helped himself and fell to eating

"Have you seen Dr. Sevier to-day?" asked Mary, cautiously, seeing her husband pause and fall into distraction.

He pushed his plate away and rose. She met him in the middle of the room. He extended both hands, took hers, and gazed upon her. How could he tell? Would she cry and lament, and spurn the proposition, and fall upon him with a hundred kisses? Ah, if she would! But he saw that Doctor Sevier, at least, was confident she would not; that she would have, instead, what the wife so often has in such cases, the strongest love, it may be, but also the strongest wisdom for that particular sort of issue. Which would she do? Would she go, or would she not?

He tried to withdraw his hands, but she looked beseechingly into his eyes and knit her fingers into his. The question stuck upon his lips and would not be uttered. And why should it be? Was it not cowardice to leave the decision to her? Should not he decide? Oh! if she would only rebel! But would she? Would not her utmost be to give good reasons in her gentle, inquiring way why he should not require her to leave him? And were there any such? No! no! He had racked his brain to find so much as one, all day long.

"John," said Mary, "Dr. Sevier's been talking to you."

"Yes."

"And he wants you to send me back home for a while?"

"How do you know?" asked John, with a start.

"I can read it in your face." She loosed one hand and laid it upon his brow.

"What — what do you think about it, Mary?"

Mary, looking into his eyes with the face of one who pleads for mercy, whispered, "He's right," then buried her face in his bosom and wept like a babe.

"I felt it six months ago," she said later, sitting on her husband's knee and holding his folded hands tightly in hers.

"Why didn't you say so?" asked John.

"I was too selfish," was her reply.

When, on the second day afterward, they entered the Doctor's office Richling was bright with that new hope which always rises up beside a new experiment, and Mary looked well and happy. The Doctor wrote them a letter of introduction to the steam-boat agent.

"You're taking a very sensible course," he said, smoothing the blotting-paper heavily over the letter. "Of course, you think it's hard. It is hard. But distance needn't separate you."

"It can't," said Richling.

"Time," continued the Doctor,— "maybe a few months, — will bring you together again, prepared for a long life of secure union; and then, when you look back upon this, you'll be proud of your courage and good sense. And you'll be " — He enclosed the note, directed the envelope, and, pausing with it still in his hand, turned toward the pair. They rose up. His rare, sick-room smile hovered about his mouth, and he said : —

"You'll be all the happier — all three of you."

The husband smiled. Mary colored down to the throat and looked up on the wall, where Harvey was explaining to his king the circulation of the blood. There was quite a pause, neither side caring to utter the first adieu.

"If a physician could call any hour his own," presently said the Doctor, "I should say I would come down to the boat and see you off. But I might fail in that. Good-by!"

"Good-by, Doctor!" — a little tremor in the voice, — "take care of John."

The tall man looked down into the upturned blue eyes.

"Good-by!" He stooped toward her forehead, but she lifted her lips and he kissed them. So they parted.

The farewell with Mrs. Riley was mainly characterized by a generous and sincere exchange of compliments and promises of remembrance. Some tears rose up; a few ran over.

At the steam-boat wharf there were only the pair themselves to cling one moment to each other and then wave that mute farewell that looks through watery eyes and sticks in the choking throat. Who ever knows what good-by means?

"Doctor," said Richling, when he came to accept those terms in the Doctor's proposition which applied more exclusively to himself, — "no, Doctor, not that way, please." He put aside the money proffered him. "This is what I want to do: I will come to your house every morning and get enough to eat to sustain me through the day, and will continue to do so till I find work."

"Very well," said the Doctor.

The arrangement went into effect. They never met at dinner; but almost every morning the Doctor, going into the breakfast-room, met Richling just risen from his earlier and hastier meal.

"Well? Anything yet?"

"Nothing yet."

And, unless there was some word from Ma y, nothing more would be said. So went the month of November.

But at length, one day toward the close of the Doctor's office hours, he noticed the sound of an agile foot springing up his stairs three steps at a stride, and Richling entered, panting and radiant.

"Doctor, at last! At last!"

"At last, what?"

"I've found employment! I have, indeed! One line from you, and the place is mine! A good place, Doctor, and one that I can fill. The very thing for me! Adapted to my abilities!" He laughed so that he coughed, was still, and laughed again. "Just a line, if you please, Doctor."

CHAPTER XXXII.

A RISING STAR.

IT had been many a day since Dr. Sevier had felt such pleasure as thrilled him when Richling, half beside himself with delight, ran in upon him with the news that he had found employment. Narcisse, too, was glad. He slipped down from his stool and came near enough to contribute his congratulatory smiles, though he did not venture to speak. Richling nodded him a happy howd'ye-do, and the Creole replied by a wave of the hand.

In the Doctor's manner, on the other hand, there was a decided lack of response that made Richling check his spirits and resume more slowly, —

"Do you know a man named Reisen?"

"No," said the Doctor.

"Why, he says he knows you."

"That may be."

"He says you treated his wife one night when she was very ill" —

"What name?"

"Reisen."

The Doctor reflected a moment.

"I believe I recollect him. Is he away up on Benjamin street, close to the river, among the cotton-presses?"

"Yes. Thalia street they call it now. He says" —

"Does he keep a large bakery?" interrupted the Doctor.

"The 'Star Bakery,'" said Richling, brightening

again. "He says he knows you, and tha., if you will give me just one line of recommendation, he will put me in charge of his accounts and give me a trial. And a trial's all I want, Doctor. I'm not the least fearful of the result."

"Richling," said Dr. Sevier, slowly picking up his paper-folder and shaking it argumentatively, "where are the letters I advised you to send for?"

Richling sat perfectly still, taking a long, slow breath through his nostrils, his eyes fixed emptily on his questioner. He was thinking, away down at the bottom of his heart, — and the Doctor knew it, — that this was the unkindest question, and the most cold-blooded, that he had ever heard. The Doctor shook his paper-folder again.

"You see, now, as to the bare fact, I don't know you."

Richling's jaw dropped with astonishment. His eye lighted up resentfully. But the speaker went on: —

"I esteem you highly. I believe in you. I would trust you, Richling," — his listener remembered how the speaker *had* trusted him, and was melted, — "but as to recommending you, why, that is like going upon the witness-stand, as it were, and I cannot say that I know anything."

Richling's face suddenly flashed full of light. He touched the Doctor's hand.

"That's it! That's the very thing, sir! Write that!"

The Doctor hesitated. Richling sat gazing at him, afraid to move an eye lest he should lose an advantage. The Doctor turned to his desk and wrote.

On the next morning Richling did not come for his

breakfast; and, not many days after, Dr. Sevier received through the mail the following letter: —

NEW ORLEANS, December 2, 1857.

DEAR DOCTOR, — I've got the place. I'm Reisen's book-keeper. I'm earning my living. And I like the work. Bread, the word bread, that has so long been terrible to me, is now the sweetest word in the language. For eighteen months it was a prayer; now it's a proclamation.

I've not only got the place, but I'm going to keep it. I find I have new powers; and the first and best of them is the power to throw myself into my work and make it *me*. It's not a task; it's a mission. Its being bread, I suppose, makes it easier to seem so; but it should be so if it was pork and garlic, or rags and raw-hides.

My maxim a year ago, though I didn't know it then, was to do what I liked. Now it's to like what I do. I understand it now. And I understand now, too, that a man who expects to retain employment must yield a profit. He must be worth more than he costs. I thank God for the discipline of the last year and a half. I thank him that I did not fall where, in my cowardice, I so often prayed to fall, into the hands of foolish benefactors. You wouldn't believe this of me, I know; but it's true. I have been taught what life is; I never would have learned it any other way.

And still another thing: I have been taught to know what the poor suffer. I know their feelings, their temptations, their hardships, their sad mistakes, and the frightful mistakes and oversights the rich make concerning them, and the ways to give them true and helpful help. And now, if God ever gives me competency, whether he gives me abundance or not, I know what he intends me to do. I was once, in fact and in sentiment, a brother to the rich; but I know that now he has trained me to be a brother to the poor. Don't think I am going to be foolish. I remember that I'm brother to the rich too; but I'll be the other as well. How wisely has God — what am I saying? Poor fools that we humans are! We can hardly venture to praise God's wisdom to-day when we think we see it, lest it turn out to be only our own folly to-morrow.

But I find I'm only writing to myself, Doctor, not to you; so I stop. Mary is well, and sends you much love.

Yours faithfully,

JOHN RICHLING

"Very little about Mary," murmured Dr. Sevier. Yet he was rather pleased than otherwise with the letter. He thrust it into his breast-pocket. In the evening, at his fireside, he drew it out again and re-read it.

"Talks as if he had got into an impregnable castle," thought the Doctor, as he gazed into the fire. "Book-keeper to a baker," he muttered, slowly folding the sheet again. It somehow vexed him to see Richling so happy in so low a station. But — "It's the joy of what he has escaped *from*, not *to*," he presently remembered.

A fortnight or more elapsed. A distant relative of Dr. Sevier, a man of his own years and profession, was his guest for two nights and a day as he passed through the city, eastward, from an all-summer's study of fevers in Mexico. They were sitting at evening on opposite sides of the library fire, conversing in the leisurely ease of those to whom life is not a novelty.

"And so you think of having Laura and Bess come out from Charleston, and keep house for you this winter? Their mother wrote me to that effect."

"Yes," said Dr. Sevier. "Society here will be a great delight to them. They will shine. And time will be less monotonous for me. It may suit me, or it may not."

"I dare say it may," responded the kinsman, whereas in truth he was very doubtful about it.

He added something, a moment later, about retiring for the night, and his host had just said, "Eh?" when a slave, in a five-year-old dress-coat, brought in the card of a person whose name was as well known in New Orleans in those days as St. Patrick's steeple or the statue of Jackson in the old Place d'Armes. Dr. Sevier turned it over and looked for a moment ponderingly upon the domestic.

The relative rose.

" You needn't go," said Dr. Sevier; but he said " he had intended," etc., and went to his chamber.

The visitor entered. He was a dark, slender, iron gray man, of finely cut, regular features, and seeming to be much more deeply wrinkled than on scrutiny he proved to be. One quickly saw that he was full of reposing energy. He gave the feeling of your being very near some weapon, of dreadful efficiency, ready for instant use whenever needed. His clothing fitted him neatly; his long, gray mustache was the only thing that hung loosely about him; his boots were fine. If he had told a child that all his muscles and sinews were wrapped with fine steel wire the child would have believed him, and continued to sit on his knee all the same. It is said, by those who still survive him, that in dreadful places and moments the flash of his fist was as quick, as irresistible, and as all-sufficient, as lightning, yet that years would sometimes pass without its ever being lifted.

Dr. Sevier lifted his slender length out of his easy-chair, and bowed with severe gravity.

" Good-evening, sir," he said, and silently thought, " Now, what can Smith Izard possibly want with me?"

It may have been perfectly natural that this man's presence shed off all idea of medical consultation; but why should it instantly bring to the Doctor's mind, as an answer to his question, another man as different from this one as water from fire?

The detective returned the Doctor's salutation, and they became seated. Then the visitor craved permission to ask a confidential question or two for information which he was seeking in his official capacity. His manners were a little old-fashioned, but perfect of their kind. The Doctor consented. The man put his hand into his breast-pocket, and drew out a daguerreotype case, touched its spring, and as it opened in his palm extended it to the Doctor. The Doctor took it with evident reluctance. It contained the picture of a youth who was just reaching manhood. The detective spoke : —

" They say he ought to look older than that now."

" He does," said Dr. Sevier.

" Do you know his name?" inquired the detective.

" No."

" What name do you know him by?"

" John Richling."

" Wasn't he sent down by Recorder Munroe, last summer, for assault, etc.?"

" Yes. I got him out the next day. He never should have been put in."

To the Doctor's surprise the detective rose to go.

" I'm much obliged to you, Doctor."

" Is that all you wanted to ask me?"

" Yes, sir."

" Mr. Izard, who is this young man? What has he done?"

" I don't know, sir. I have a letter from a lawyer in Kentucky who says he represents this young man's two sisters living there, — half-sisters, rather, — stating that his father and mother are both dead, — died within three days of each other."

" What name?"

" He didn't give the name. He sent this daguerreotype, with instructions to trace up the young man, if possible. He said there was reason to believe he was in New Orleans. He said, if I found him, just to see him privately, tell him the news, and invite him to come back home. But he said if the young fellow had got into any kind of trouble that might somehow reflect on the family, you know. like getting arrested for something or other, you know, or some such thing, then I was just to drop the thing quietly, and say nothing about it to him or anybody else."

"And doesn't that seem a strange way to manage a matter like that, — to put it into the hands of a detective?"

"Well, I don't know," said Mr. Izard. "We're used to strange things, and this isn't so very strange. No, it's very common. I suppose he knew that if he gave it to me it would be attended to in a quiet and innocent sort o' way. Some people hate mighty bad to get talked about. Nobody's seen that picture but you and one 'aid,' and just as soon as he saw it he said, 'Why, that's the chap that Dr. Sevier took out of the Parish Prison last September.' And there won't anybody else see it."

"Don't you intend to see Richling?" asked the Doctor, following the detective toward the door.

"I don't see as it would be any use," said the detective, "seeing he's been sent down, and so on. I'll write to the lawyer and state the facts, and wait for orders."

"But do you know how slight the blame was that got him into trouble here?"

"Yes. The 'aid' who saw the picture told me all about that. It was a shame. I'll say so. I'll give all the particulars. But I tell you, I just guess — they'll drop him."

"I dare say," said Dr. Sevier.

"Well, Doctor," said Mr. Izard, "hope I haven't annoyed you."

"No," replied the Doctor.

But he had; and the annoyance had not ceased to be felt when, a few mornings afterward, Narcisse suddenly doubled — trebled it by saying : —

"Doctah Seveeah," — it was a cold day and the young

Creole stood a moment with his back to the office fire, to which he had just given an energetic and prolonged poking, — "a man was yeh, to see you, name' Bison. 'F want' to see you about Mistoo Itchlin."

The Doctor looked up with a start, and Narcisse continued : —

"Mistoo Itchlin is wuckin' in 'is employment. I think 'e's please' with 'im."

"Then why does he come to see me about him?" asked the Doctor, so sharply that Narcisse shrugged as he replied : —

"Reely, I cann' tell you; but thass one thing, Doctah, I dunno if you 'ave notiz : the worl' halways take a gweat deal of welfa'e in a man w'en 'e's 'ising. I do that myseff. Some'ow I cann' 'e'p it." This bold speech was too much for him. He looked down at his symmetrical legs and went back to his desk.

The Doctor was far from reassured. After a silence he called out : —

"Did he say he would come back?" A knock at the door arrested the answer, and a huge, wide, broad-faced German entered diffidently. The Doctor recognized Reisen. The visitor took off his flour-dusted hat and bowed with great deference.

"Toc-tor," he softly drawled, "I yoost taught 1 trop in on you to say a verte to you apowt teh chung yentleman vot you hef rickomendet to me."

"I didn't recommend him to you, sir. I wrote you distinctly that I did not feel at liberty to recommend him."

"Tat iss teh troot, Toctor Tseweer; tat iss teh ectsectly troot. Shtill I taught I'll yoost trop in on you to say a verte to you, — Toctor, — apowt Mister " — He hung his large head at one side to remember.

"Richling," said the Doctor, impatiently.

"Yes, sir. Apowt Mister Richlun. I heff a tifficuldy to rigolict naymps. I yoost taught I voot trop in und trop a verte to you apowt Mr. Richlun, vot maypy you titn't herr udt before, yet."

"Yes," said the Doctor, with ill-concealed contempt. "Well, speak it out, Mr. Reisen; time is precious."

The German smiled and made a silly gesture of assent.

"Yes, udt is brecious. Shtill I taught I voot take enough time to yoost trop in undt say to you tat I heffent het Mr. Richlun in my etsteplitchmendt a veek undtil I finte owdt someting apowt him, tot, uf you het a-knowdt ud, voot hef mate your letter maypy a little tifferendt written, yet."

Now, at length, Dr. Sevier's annoyance was turned to dismay. He waited in silence for Reisen to unfold his enigma, but already his resentment against Richling was gathering itself for a spring. To the baker, however, he betrayed only a cold hostility.

"I kept a copy of my letter to you, Mr. Reisen, and there isn't a word in it which need have misled you, sir."

The baker waved his hand amicably.

"Sure, Tocter Tseweer, I toandt hef nutting to gomblain akinst teh vertes of tat letter. You voss mighty puttickly. Ovver, shtill, I hef sumpting to tell you vot ef you het a-knowdt udt pefore you writed tose vertes, alreatty, t'ey voot a little tifferendt pin."

"Well, sir, why don't you tell it?"

Reisen smiled. "Tat iss teh ectsectly vot I am coing to too. I yoost taught I'll trop in undt tell you, Toctor, tat I heffent het Mr. Richlun in my etsteplitchmendt a veek undtil I findte owdt tat he's a — berfect — tressure."

Doctor Sevier started half up from his chair, dropped

into it again, wheeled half away, and back again with the blood surging into his face and exclaimed : —

"Why, what do you mean by such drivelling nonsense, sir? You've given me a positive fright!" He frowned the blacker as the baker smiled from ear to ear.

"Vy, Toctor, I hope you ugscooce me! I yoost taught you voot like to herr udt. Undt Missis Reisen sayce, 'Reisen, you yoost co undt tell um. I taught udt voot pe blessant to you to know tatt you hett sendt me teh fynust pisness mayn I effer het apowdt me. Undt uff he iss onnust he iss a berfect tressure, undt uff he aint a berfect tressure,'"—he smiled anew and tendered his capacious hat to his listener, —"you yoost kin take tiss, Toctor, undt kip udt undt vare udt! Toctor, I vish you a merrah Chris'mus!"

CHAPTER XXXIII.

BEES, WASPS, AND BUTTERFLIES.

THE merry day went by. The new year, 1858, set in.
Everything gathered momentum. There was a
panic and a crash. The brother-in-law of sister Jane —
he whom Dr. Sevier met at that quiet dinner-party —
struck an impediment, stumbled, staggered, fell under
the feet of the racers, and crawled away minus not money
and credit only, but all his philosophy about helping the
poor, maimed in spirit, his pride swollen with bruises, his
heart and his speech soured beyond all sweetening.

Many were the wrecks. But over their débris, Mercury
and Venus — the busy season and the gay season — ran
lightly, hand in hand. Men getting money and women
squandering it. Whole nights in the ball-room. Gold
pouring in at the hopper and out at the spout, — Carondelet street emptying like a yellow river into Canal street.
Thousands for vanity ; thousands for pride ; thousands for
influence and for station ; thousands for hidden sins ; a
slender fraction for the wants of the body ; a slenderer
for the cravings of the soul. Lazarus paid to stay away
from the gate. John the Baptist, in raiment of broad-
cloth, a circlet of white linen about his neck, and his
meat strawberries and ice-cream. The lower classes
mentioned mincingly ; awkward silences or visible winc-
ings at allusions to death, and converse on eternal things
banished as if it were the smell of cabbage. So looked
the gay world, at least, to Dr. Sevier.

He saw more of it than had been his wont for many seasons. The two young-lady cousins whom he had brought and installed in his home thirsted for that gorgeous, nocturnal moth life in which no thirst is truly slaked, and dragged him with them into the iridescent, gas-lighted spider-web of society.

"Now, you know you like it!" they said.

"A little of it, yes. But I don't see how you can like it, who virtually live in it and upon it. Why, I would as soon try to live upon cake and candy!"

"Well, we can live very nicely upon cake and candy," retorted they.

"Why, girls, it's no more life than spice is food. What lofty motive — what earnest, worthy object " —

But they drowned his homily in a carol, and ran away arm in arm to dress for another ball. One of them stopped in the door with an air of mock bravado: —

"What do we care for lofty motives or worthy objects?"

A smile escaped from him as she vanished. His condemnation was flavored with charity. "It's their mating season," he silently thought, and, not knowing he did it, sighed.

"There come Dr. Sevier and his two pretty cousins," was the ball-room whisper. "Beautiful girls — rich widower without children — great catch! *Passé*, how? Well, maybe so; not as much as he makes himself out, though." "*Passé*, yes," said a merciless belle to a blade of her own years; "a man of strong sense is *passé* at any age." Sister Jane's name was mentioned in the same connection, but that illusion quickly passed. The cousins denied indignantly that he had any matrimonial intention. Somebody dissipated the rumor by a syllogism: A man hunting a second wife always looks like a fool ; the Doctor doesn't look a bit like a fool, ergo " —

He grew very weary of the giddy rout, standing in it like a rock in a whirlpool. He did rejoice in the Carnival, but only because it was the end.

"Pretty? yes, as pretty as a bonfire," he said. "I can't enjoy much fiddling while Rome is burning."

"But Rome isn't always burning," said the cousins.

" Yes, it is ! Yes, it is ! "

The wickeder of the two cousins breathed a penitential sigh, dropped her bare, jewelled arms out of her cloak, and said : —

"Now tell us *once* more about Mary Richling." He had bored them to death with Mary.

Lent was a relief to all three. One day, as the Doctor was walking along the street, a large hand grasped his elbow and gently arrested his steps. He turned.

"Well, Reisen, is that you?"

The baker answered with his wide smile. "Yes, Toctor, tat iss me, sure. You titn't tink udt iss Mr. Richlun, tit you?"

"No. How is Richling?"

"Vell, Mr. Richlun kitten along so-o-o-so-o-o. He iss not ferra shtrong ; ovver he vurks like a shteam-inchyine."

"I haven't seen him for many a day," said Dr. Sevier.

The baker distended his eyes, bent his enormous digestive apparatus forward, raised his eyebrows, and hung his arms free from his sides. "He toandt kit a minudt to shpare in teh tswendy-four hourss. Sumptimes he sayss, ' Mr. Reisen, I can't shtop to talk mit you.' Sindts Mr. Richlun pin py my etsteplitchmendt, I tell you teh troot, Toctor Tseweer, I am yoost meckin' monneh haynd ofer fist ! " He swung his chest forward again, drew in his lower regions, revolved his fists around each other for a moment, and then let them fall open at his sides, with the added assurance, "Now you kott teh ectsectly troot."

The Doctor started away, but the baker detained him by a touch: —

"You toandt kott enna verte to sendt to Mr. Richlun, Toctor!"

"Yes. Tell him to come and pass an hour with me some evening in my library."

The German lifted his hand in delight.

"Vy, tot's yoost teh dting! Mr. Richlun alvayss pin 'sayin', 'I vish he aysk me come undt see um;' undt I sayss, 'You holdt shtill, yet, Mr. Richlun; teh next time I see um I make um aysk you.' Vell, now, titn't I tunned udt?" He was happy.

"Well, ask him," said the Doctor, and got away.

"No fool is an utter fool," pondered the Doctor, as he went. Two friends had been kept long apart by the fear of each, lest he should seem to be setting up claims based on the past. It required a simpleton to bring them together.

CHAPTER XXXIV.

TOWARD THE ZENITH

" RICHLING, I am glad to see you!"

Dr. Sevier had risen from his luxurious chair beside a table, the soft downward beams of whose lamp partly showed, and partly hid, the rich appointments of his library. He grasped Richling's hand, and with an extensive stride drew forward another chair on its smooth-running castors.

Then inquiries were exchanged as to the health of one and the other. The Doctor, with his professional eye, noticed, as the light fell full upon his visitor's buoyant face, how thin and pale he had grown. He rose again, and stepping beyond Richling with a remark, in part complimentary and in part critical, upon the balmy April evening, let down the sash of a window where the smell of honeysuckles was floating in.

"Have you heard from your wife lately?" he asked, as he resumed his seat.

"Yesterday," said Richling. "Yes, she's very well; been well ever since she left us. She always sends love to you."

"Hum," responded the physician. He fixed his eyes on the mantel and asked abstractedly, "How do you bear the separation?"

"Oh!" Richling laughed, "not very heroically. It's a great strain on a man's philosophy."

TOWARD THE ZENITH. 263

"Work is the only antidote," said the Doctor, not moving his eyes.

"Yes, so I find it," answered the other. "It's bearable enough while one is working like mad; but sooner or later one must sit down to meals, or lie down to rest, you know"—

"Then it hurts," said the Doctor.

"It's a lively discipline," mused Richling.

"Do you think you learn anything by it?" asked the other, turning his eyes slowly upon him. "That's what it means, you notice."

"Yes, I do," replied Richling, smiling; "I learn the very thing I suppose you're thinking of,—that separation isn't disruption, and that no pair of true lovers are quite fitted out for marriage until they can bear separation if they must."

"Yes," responded the physician; "if they can muster the good sense to see that they'll not be so apt to marry prematurely. I needn't tell you I believe in marrying for love; but these needs-must marriages are so ineffably silly. You 'must' and you 'will' marry, and 'nobody shall hinder you!' And you do it! And in three or four or six months"—he drew in his long legs energetically from the hearth-pan—"*death* separates you!—death, sometimes, resulting directly from the turn your haste has given to events! Now, where is your 'must' and 'will'?" He stretched his legs out again, and laid his head on his cushioned chair-back.

"I have made a narrow escape," said Richling.

"I wasn't so fortunate," responded the Doctor, turning solemnly toward his young friend. "Richling, just seven months after I married Alice I buried her. I'm not going into particulars—of course; but the sickness that carried her off was distinctly connected with the haste of our marriage. Your Bible, Richling, that you lay such store by, is right; we should want things as if we didn't want them. That isn't the quotation, exactly, but it's the idea. I swore I couldn't and wouldn't live without her; but, you see, this is the fifteenth year that I have had to do it."

" I should think it would have unmanned you for life," said Richling.

" It made a man of me! I've never felt young a day since, and yet I've never seemed to grow a day older. It brought me all at once to my full manhood. I have never consciously disputed God's arrangements since. The man who does is only a wayward child."

" It's true," said Richling, with an air of confession, " it's true; " and they fell into silence.

Presently Richling looked around the room. His eyes brightened rapidly as he beheld the ranks and tiers of good books. He breathed an audible delight. The multitude of volumes rose in the old-fashioned way, in ornate cases of dark wood from floor to ceiling, on this hand, on that, before him, behind; some in gay covers,— green, blue, crimson,— with gilding and embossing; some in the sumptuous leathers of France, Russia, Morocco, Turkey; others in worn attire, battered and venerable, dingy but precious,— the gray heads of the council.

The two men rose and moved about among those silent wits and philosophers, and, from the very embarrassment of the inner riches, fell to talking of letter-press and bindings, with maybe some effort on the part of each to seem the better acquainted with Caxton, the Elzevirs, and other like immortals. They easily passed to a competitive enumeration of the rare books they had seen or not seen here and there in other towns and countries. Richling admitted he had travelled, and the conversation turned

upon noted buildings and famous old nooks in distant
cities where both had been. So they moved slowly back
to their chairs, and stood by them, still contemplating the
books. But as they sank again into their seats the one
thought which had fastened itself in the minds of both
found fresh expression.

Richling began, smilingly, as if the subject had not
been dropped at all,—" I oughtn't to speak as if I didn't
realize my good fortune, for I do."

"I believe you do," said the Doctor, reaching toward
the fire-irons.

"Yes. Still, I lose patience with myself to find myself
taking Mary's absence so hard."

"All hardships are comparative," said the Doctor.

"Certainly they are," replied Richling. "I lie sometimes and think of men who have been political prisoners,
shut away from wife and children, with war raging outside and no news coming in."

"Think of the common poor," exclaimed Dr. Sevier,—
"the thousands of sailors' wives and soldiers' wives.
Where does that thought carry you?"

"It carries me," responded the other, with a low laugh,
"to where I'm always a little ashamed of myself."

"I didn't mean it to do that," said the Doctor; "I
can imagine how you miss your wife. I miss her myself."

"Oh! but she's here on this earth. She's alive and
well. Any burden is light when I think of that — pardon
me, Doctor!"

"Go on, go on. Anything you please about her, Richling." The Doctor half sat, half lay in his chair, his
eyes partly closed. "Go on," he repeated.

"I was only going to say that long before Mary went
away, many a time when she and I were fighting starva-

tion at close quarters, I have looked at her and said to myself, 'What if I were in Dr. Sevier's place?' and it gave me strength to rise up and go on."

"You were right."

"I know I was. I often wake now at night and turn and find the place by my side empty, and I can hardly keep from calling her aloud. It wrenches me, but before long I think she's no such great distance away, since we're both on the same earth together, and by and by she'll be here at my side; and so it becomes easy to me once more." Richling, in the self-occupation of a lover, forgot what pains he might be inflicting. But the Doctor did not wince.

"Yes," said the physician, "of course you wouldn't want the separation to be painless; and it promises a reward, you know."

"Ah!" exclaimed Richling, with an exultant smile and motion of the head, and then dropped his eyes in meditation. The Doctor looked at him steadily.

"Richling, you've gathered some terribly hard experiences. But hard experiences are often the foundation-stones of a successful life. You can make them all profitable. You can make them draw you along, so to speak. But you must hold them well in hand, as you would a dangerous team, you know,— coolly and alertly, firmly and patiently,—and never let the reins slack till you've driven through the last gate."

Richling replied, with a pleasant nod, "I believe I shall do it. Did you notice what I wrote you in my letter? I have got the notion strongly that the troubles we have gone through — Mary and I — were only our necessary preparation — not so necessary for her as for me "—

"No," said Dr. Sevier, and Richling continued, with a smile : —

"To fit us for a long and useful life, and especially a life that will be full of kind and valuable services to the poor. If that isn't what they were sent for "— he dropped into a tone of reflection — "then I don't understand them."

"And suppose you don't understand," said the Doctor, with his cold, grim look.

"Oh!" rejoined Richling, in amiable protest; "but a man would like to understand."

"Like to — yes," replied the Doctor; "but be careful. The spirit that *must* understand is the spirit that can't trust." He paused. Presently he said, "Richling!"

Richling answered by an inquiring glance.

"Take better care of your health," said the physician.

Richling smiled — a young man's answer — and rose to say good-night.

/

CHAPTER XXXV.

TO SIGH, YET FEEL NO PAIN.

MRS. RILEY missed the Richlings, she said, more than tongue could tell. She had easily rented the rooms they left vacant; that was not the trouble. The new tenant was a sallow, gaunt, wind-dried seamstress of sixty, who paid her rent punctually, but who was —

" Mighty poor comp'ny to thim as 's been used to the upper tin, Mr. Ristofalo."

Still she was a protection. Mrs. Riley had not regarded this as a necessity in former days, but now, somehow, matters seemed different. This seamstress had, moreover, a son of eighteen years, principally skin and bone, who was hoping to be appointed assistant hostler at the fire-engine house of " Volunteer One," and who meantime hung about Mrs. Riley's dwelling and loved to relieve her of the care of little Mike. This also was something to be appreciated. Still there was a void.

" Well, Mr. Richlin' ! " cried Mrs. Riley, as she opened her parlor door in response to a knock. " Well, I'll be switched ! ha ! ha ! I didn't think it was you at all. Take a seat and sit down ! "

It was good to see how she enjoyed the visit. Whenever she listened to Richling's words she rocked in her rocking-chair vigorously, and when she spoke stopped its motion and rested her elbows on its arms.

" And how *is* Mrs. Richlin' ? And so she sent her love to me, did she, now ? The blessed angel ! Now, ye're not just a-makin' that up? No, I know ye wouldn't do sich a thing as that, Mr. Richlin'. Well, you must give her mine back again. I've nobody else on e'rth to give ud to, and never will have." She lifted her nose with amiable stateliness, as if to imply that Richling might not believe this, but that it was true, nevertheless.

"You may change your mind, Mrs. Riley, some day," returned Richling, a little archly.

"Ha! ha!" She tossed her head and laughed with good-natured scorn. "Nivver a fear o' that, Mr. Richlin'!" Her brogue was apt to broaden when pleasure pulled down her dignity. "And, if I did, it wuddent be for the likes of no I-talian Dago, if id's him ye're a-dthrivin' at,— not intinding anny disrespect to your friend, Mr. Richlin', and indeed I don't deny he's a perfect gintleman, — but, indeed, Mr. Richlin', I'm just after thinkin' that you and yer lady wouldn't have no self-respect for Kate Riley if she should be changing her name."

"Still you were thinking about it," said Richling, with a twinkle.

"Ah! ha! ha! Indeed I wasn', an' ye needn' be t'rowin' anny o' yer slyness on me. Ye know ye'd have no self-respect fur me. No; now ye know ye wuddent, — wud ye?"

"Why, Mrs. Riley, of course we would. Why — why not?" He stood in the door-way, about to take his leave. "You may be sure we'll always be glad of anything that will make you the happier." Mrs. Riley looked so grave that he checked his humor.

"But in the nixt life, Mr. Richlin', how about that?"

"There? I suppose we shall simply each love all in absolute perfection. We'll " —

"We'll never know the differ," interposed Mrs. Riley

"That's it," said Richling, smiling again. "And so I say,— and I've always said,— if a person *feels* like marrying again, let him do it."

"Have ye, now? Well, ye're just that good, Mr Richlin'."

"Yes," he responded, trying to be grave, "that's about my measure."

"Would *you* do ut?"

"No, I wouldn't. I couldn't. But I should like — in good earnest, Mrs. Riley, I should like, now, the comfort of knowing that you were not to pass all the rest of your days in widowhood."

"Ah! ged out, Mr. Richlin'!" She failed in her effort to laugh. "Ah! ye're sly!" She changed her attitude and drew a breath.

"No," said Richling, "no, honestly. I should feel that you deserved better at this world's hands than that, and that the world deserved better of you. I find two people don't make a world, Mrs. Riley, though often they think they do. They certainly don't when one is gone."

"Mr. Richlin'," exclaimed Mrs. Riley, drawing back and waving her hand sweetly, "stop yer flattery! Stop ud! Ah! ye're a-feeling yer oats, Mr. Richlin'. An' ye're a-showin' em too, ye air. Why, I hered ye was lookin' terrible, and here ye're lookin' just splendud!"

"Who told you that?" asked Richling.

"Never mind! Never mind who he was — ha, ha, ha!" She checked herself suddenly. "Ah, me! It's a shame for the likes o' me to be behavin' that foolish!" She put on additional dignity. "I will always be the Widow Riley." Then relaxing again into sweetness: "Marridge is a lottery, Mr. Richlin'; indeed an' it is; and ye know mighty well that he ye're after 'oking me about is no more nor a fri'nd." She looked sweet enough for somebody to kiss.

"I don't know so certainly about that," said her visitor, stepping down upon the sidewalk and putting on his hat. " If I may judge by " — He paused and glanced at the window.

"Ah, now, Mr. Richlin', na-na-now, Mr. Richlin', ye daurn't say ud! Ye daurn't!" She smiled and blushed and arched her neck and rose and sank upon herself with sweet delight.

"I say if I may judge by what he has said to me," insisted Richling.

Mrs. Riley glided down across the door-step, and, with all the insinuation of her sex and nation, demanded: —

"What'd he tell ye? Ah! he didn't tell ye nawthing! Ha, ha! there wasn' nawthing to tell!" But Richling slipped away.

Mrs. Riley shook her finger: " Ah, ye're a wicket joker, Mr. Richlin'. I didn't think that o' the likes of a gintleman like you, anyhow!" She shook her finger again as she withdrew into the house, smiling broadly all the way in to the cradle, where she kissed and kissed again her ruddy, chubby, sleeping boy.

Ristofalo came often. He was a man of simple words, and of few thoughts of the kind that were available in conversation; but his personal adventures had begun almost with infancy, and followed one another in close and strange succession over lands and seas ever since. He could therefore talk best about himself, though he talked modestly. "These things to hear would Desdemona seriously incline," and there came times when even a tear was not wanting to gem the poetry of the situation.

"And ye might have saved yerself from all that," was

sometimes her note of sympathy. But when he asked
how she silently dried her eyes.

Sometimes his experiences had been intensely ludicrous,
and Mrs. Riley would laugh until in pure self-oblivion she
smote her thigh with her palm, or laid her hand so smartly
against his shoulder as to tip him half off his seat.

"Ye didn't!"

"Yes."

"Ah! Get out wid ye, Raphael Ristofalo, — to be
telling me that for the trooth!"

At one such time she was about to give him a second
push, but he took the hand in his, and quietly kept it to
the end of his story.

He lingered late that evening, but at length took his hat
from under his chair, rose, and extended his hand.

"Man alive!" she cried, "that's my *hand*, sur, I'd
have ye to know. Begahn wid ye! Lookut heere!
What's the reason ye make it so long atween yer visits,
eh? Tell me that. Ah — ah — ye've no need fur to tell
me, Mr. Ristofalo! Ah — now don't tell a lie!"

"Too busy. Come all time — wasn't too busy."

"Ha, ha! Yes, yes; ye're too busy. Of coorse ye're
too busy. Oh, yes! ye *air* too busy — a-courtin' thim
I-talian froot gerls around the Frinch Mairket. Ah! I'll
bet two bits ye're a bouncer! Ah, don't tell me. I know
ye, ye villain! Some o' thim's a-waitin' fur ye now, ha,
ha! Go! And don't ye nivver come back heere anny
more. D'ye mind?"

"Aw righ'." The Italian took her hand for the third
time and held it, standing in his simple square way before
her and wearing his gentle smile as he looked her in the
eye. "Good-by, Kate."

Her eye quailed. Her hand pulled a little helplessly
and in a meek voice she said : —

" That's not right for you to do me that a·way, Mr. Ristofalo. I've got a handle to my name, sur."

She threw some gentle rebuke into her glance, and turned it upon him. He met it with that same amiable absence of emotion that was always in his look.

" Kate too short by itself?" he asked. " Aw righ'; make it Kate Ristofalo. "

" No," said Mrs. Riley, averting and drooping her face.

" Take good care of you," said the Italian : " you and Mike. Always be kind. Good care."

Mrs. Riley turned with sudden fervor.

" Good cayre! — Mr. Ristofalo," she exclaimed, lifting her free hand and touching her bosom with the points of her fingers, " ye don't know the hairt of a woman, surr! No-o-o, surr! It's *love* we wants! 'The hairt as has trooly loved nivver furgits, but as trooly loves ahn to the tlose!'"

" Yes," said the Italian; " yes," nodding and ever smiling, " dass aw righ'."

But she : —

" Ah! it's no use fur you to be a-talkin' an' a-palla-verin' to Kate Riley when ye don't be lovin' her, Mr. Ristofalo, an' ye know ye don't."

A tear glistened in her eye.

" Yes, love you," said the Italian; "course, love you."

He did not move a foot or change the expression of a feature.

" H-yes! " said the widow. H-yes!" she panted. H-yes, a little! A little, Mr. Ristofalo! But I want " — she pressed her hand hard upon her bosom, and raised her eyes aloft — " I want to be — h — h — h-adaured above all the e'rth!"

" Aw righ'," said Ristofalo; " das aw righ'; yes — door above all you worth."

" Raphael Ristofalo," she said, " ye're a-deceivin' me !
Ye came heere whin nobody axed ye, — an' that ye know
is a fact, surr, — an' made yerself agree'ble to a poor,
unsuspectin' widdah, an' [*tears*] rabbed me o' mie hairt,
ye did ; whin I nivver intinded to git married ag'in."

" Don't cry, Kate — Kate Ristofalo," quietly observed
the Italian, getting an arm around her waist, and laying
a hand on the farther cheek. " Kate Ristofalo."

" Shut ! " she exclaimed, turning with playful fierce-
ness, and proudly drawing back her head ; " shut !   Hah !
It's Kate Ristofalo, is it?   Ah, ye think so?   Hah-h !
It'll be ad least two weeks yet before the priest will be
after giving you the right to call me that ! "

And, in fact, an entire fortnight did pass before they
were married.

CHAPTER XXXVI.

WHAT NAME?

RICHLING in Dr. Sevier's library, one evening in early May, gave him great amusement by an account of the Ristofalo-Riley wedding. He had attended it only the night before. The Doctor had received an invitation, but had pleaded previous engagements.

"But I am glad you went," he said to Richling; "however, go on with your account."

"Oh! I was glad to go. And I'm certainly glad I went."

Richling proceeded with the recital. The Doctor smiled. It was very droll, — the description of persons and costumes. Richling was quite another than his usual restrained self this evening. Oddly enough, too, for this was but his second visit; the confinement of his work was almost like an imprisonment, it was so constant. The Doctor had never seen him in just such a glow. He even mimicked the brogue of two or three Irish gentlemen, and the soft, outlandish swing in the English of one or two Sicilians. He did it all so well that, when he gave an instance of some of the broad Hibernian repartee he had heard, the Doctor actually laughed audibly. One of his young-lady cousins on some pretext opened a door, and stole a glance within to see what could have produced a thing so extraordinary.

"Come in, Laura; come in! Tell Bess to come in."

The Doctor introduced Richling with due ceremony

Richling could not, of course, after this accession of numbers, go on being funny. The mistake was trivial, but all saw it. Still the meeting was pleasant. The girls were very intelligent and vivacious. Richling found a certain refreshment in their graceful manners, like what we sometimes feel in catching the scent of some long-forgotten perfume. They had not been told all his history, but had heard enough to make them curious to see and speak to him. They were evidently pleased with him, and Dr. Sevier, observing this, betrayed an air that was much like triumph. But after a while they went as they had come.

" Doctor," said Richling, smiling until Dr. Sevier wondered silently what possessed the fellow, " excuse me for bringing this here. But I find it so impossible to get to your office " — He moved nearer the Doctor's table and put his hand into his bosom.

" What's that? " asked the Doctor, frowning heavily. Richling smiled still broader than before.

" This is a statement," he said.

" Of what? "

" Of the various loans you have made me, with interest to date."

" Yes? " said the Doctor, frigidly.

" And here," persisted the happy man, straightening out a leg as he had done the first time they ever met, and drawing a roll of notes from his pocket, is the total amount."

" Yes? " The Doctor regarded them with cold contempt. " That's all very pleasant for you, I suppose, Richling, — shows you're the right kind of man, I suppose, and so on. I know that already, however. Now just put all that back into your pocket ; the sight of it isn't pleasant. You certainly don't imagine I'm going to take it, do you?"

"You promised to take it when you lent it."

"Humph! Well, I didn't say when."

"As soon as I could pay it," said Richling.

"I don't remember," replied the Doctor, picking up a newspaper. "I release myself from that promise."

"I don't release you," persisted Richling; "neither does Mary."

The Doctor was quiet awhile before he answered. He crossed his knees, a moment after folded his arms, and presently said:—

"Foolish pride, Richling."

"We know that," replied Richling; "we don't deny that that feeling creeps in. But we'd never do anything that's right if we waited for an unmixed motive, would we?"

"Then you think my motive—in refusing it—is mixed, probably."

"Ho-o-oh!" laughed Richling. The gladness within him would break through. "Why, Doctor, nothing could be more different. It doesn't seem to me as though you ever had a mixed motive."

The Doctor did not answer. He seemed to think the same thing.

"We know very well, Doctor, that if we should accept this kindness we might do it in a spirit of proper and commendable—a—humble-mindedness. But it isn't mere pride that makes us insist."

"No?" asked the Doctor, cruelly. "What is it else?"

"Why, I hardly know what to call it, except that it's a conviction that—well, that to pay is best; that it's the nearest to justice we can get, and that"—he spoke faster—"that it's simply duty to choose justice when we can and mercy when we must. There, I've hit it out!" He laughed again. "Don't you see, Doctor? Justice when we may — mercy when we must! It's your own principles!"

The Doctor looked straight at the mantel-piece as he asked: —

"Where did you get that idea?"

"I don't know; partly from nowhere, and" —

"Partly from Mary," interrupted the Doctor. He put out his long white palm. "It's all right. Give me the money." Richling counted it into his hand. He rolled it up and stuffed it into his portemonnaie.

"You like to part with your hard earnings, do you, Richling?"

"Earnings can't be hard," was the reply; "it's borrowings that are hard."

The Doctor assented.

"And, of course," said Richling, "I enjoy paying old debts." He stood and leaned his head in his hand with his elbow on the mantel. "But, even aside from that, I'm happy."

"I see you are!" remarked the physician, emphatically, catching the arms of his chair and drawing his feet closer in. "You've been smiling worse than a boy with a love-letter."

"I've been hoping you'd ask me what's the matter."

"Well, then, Richling, what is the matter?"

"Mary has a daughter."

"What!" cried the Doctor, springing up with a radiant face. and grasping Richling's hand in both his own.

Richling laughed aloud, nodded, laughed again, and gave either eye a quick, energetic wipe with all his fingers.

"Doctor," he said, as the physician sank back into his chair, "we want to name" — he hesitated, stood on one foot and leaned again against the shelf — " we want to call her by the name of — if we may " —

The Doctor looked up as if with alarm, and John said, timidly, — " Alice ! "

Dr. Sevier's eyes — what was the matter? His mouth quivered. He nodded and whispered huskily : —

" All right."

After a long pause Richling expressed the opinion that he had better be going, and the Doctor did not indicate any difference of conviction. At the door the Doctor asked : —

" If the fever should break out this summer, Richling, will you go away?"

" No."

CHAPTER XXXVII.

PESTILENCE.

ON the twentieth of June, 1858, an incident occurred in New Orleans which challenged special attention from the medical profession. Before the month closed there was a second, similar to the first. The press did not give such matters to the public in those days; it would only make the public — the advertising public — angry. Times have changed since — faced clear about; but at that period Dr. Sevier, who hated a secret only less than a falsehood, was right in speaking as he did.

"Now you'll see," he said, pointing downward aslant, "the whole community stick its head in the sand!" He sent for Richling.

"I give you fair warning," he said. "It's coming."

"Don't cases occur sometimes in an isolated way without — anything further?" asked Richling, with a promptness which showed he had already been considering the matter.

"Yes."

"And might not this " —

"Richling, I give you fair warning."

"Have you sent your cousins away, Doctor?"

"They go to-morrow." After a silence the Doctor added: "I tell you now, because this is the time to decide what you will do. If you are not prepared to take all the risks and stay them through, you had better go at once."

"What proportion of those who are taken sick of it die?" asked Richling.

"The proportion varies in different seasons; say about one in seven or eight. But your chances would be hardly so good, for you're not strong, Richling, nor well either."

Richling stood and swung his hat against his knee.

"I really don't see, Doctor, that I have any choice at all. I couldn't go to Mary — when she has but just come through a mother's pains and dangers — and say, ' I've thrown away seven good chances of life to run away from one bad one.' Why, to say nothing else, Reisen can't spare me." He smiled with boyish vanity.

"O Richling, that's silly !"

"I — I know it," exclaimed the other, quickly; "I see it is. If he could spare me, of course he wouldn't be paying me a salary." But the Doctor silenced him by a gesture.

"The question is not whether he can spare you, at all. It's simply, can you spare him?"

"Without violating any pledge, you mean," added Richling.

"Of course," assented the physician.

"Well, I can't spare him, Doctor. He has given me a hold on life, and no one chance in seven, or six, or five is going to shake me loose. Why, I tell you I couldn't look Mary in the face !"

"Have your own way," responded the Doctor. "There are some things in your favor. You frail fellows often pull through easier than the big, full-blooded ones."

"Oh, it's Mary's way too, I feel certain !" retorted Richling, gayly, "and I venture to say " — he coughed and smiled again — "it's yours."

"I didn't say it wasn't," replied the unsmiling Doctor,

reaching for a pen and writing a prescription. "Here; get that and take it according to direction. It's for that cold."

"If I should take the fever," said Richling, coming out of a revery, "Mary will want to come to me."

"Well, she mustn't come a step!" exclaimed the Doctor.

"You'll forbid it, will you not, Doctor? Pledge me!"

"I do better, sir; I pledge myself."

So the July suns rose up and moved across the beautiful blue sky; the moon went through all her majestic changes; on thirty-one successive midnights the Star Bakery sent abroad its grateful odors of bread, and as the last night passed into the first twinkling hour of morning the month chronicled one hundred and thirty-one deaths from yellow fever. The city shuddered because it knew, and because it did not know, what was in store. People began to fly by hundreds, and then by thousands. Many were overtaken and stricken down as they fled. Still men plied their vocations, children played in the streets, and the days came and went, fair, blue tremulous with sunshine, or cool and gray and sweet with summer rain. How strange it was for nature to be so beautiful and so unmoved! By and by one could not look down a street, on this hand or on that, but he saw a funeral. Doctors' gigs began to be hailed on the streets and to refuse to stop, and houses were pointed out that had just become the scenes of strange and harrowing episodes.

"Do you see that bakery, — the 'Star Bakery'? Five funerals from that place — and another goes this afternoon."

Before this was said August had completed its record of eleven hundred deaths, and September had begun the long list that was to add twenty-two hundred more. Reisen had been the first one ill in the establishment. He had been losing friends, — one every few days ; and he thought it only plain duty, let fear or prudence say what they might, to visit them at their bedsides and follow them to their tombs. It was not only the outer man of Reisen, but the heart as well, that was elephantine. He had at length come home from one of these funerals with pains in his back and limbs, and the various familiar accompaniments.

"I feel right clumsy," he said, as he lifted his great feet and lowered them into the mustard foot-bath.

"Doctor Sevier," said Richling, as he and the physician paused half way between the sick-chambers of Reisen and his wife, "I hope you'll not think it foolhardy for me to expose myself by nursing these people" —

"No," replied the veteran, in a tone of indifference, and passed on ; the tincture of self-approval that had "mixed" with Richling's motives went away to nothing.

Both Reisen and his wife recovered. But an apple-cheeked brother of the baker, still in a green cap and coat that he had come in from Germany, was struck from the first with that mortal terror which is so often an evil symptom of the disease, and died, on the fifth day after his attack, in raging delirium. Ten of the workmen, bakers and others, followed him. Richling alone, of all in the establishment, while the sick lay scattered through the town on uncounted thousands of beds, and the month of October passed by, bringing death to eleven hundred more, escaped untouched of the scourge.

"I can't understand it," he said.

"Demand an immediate explanation," said Dr. Sevier, with sombre irony.

How did others fare? Ristofalo had, time and again, sailed with the fever, nursed it, slept with it. It passed him by again. Little Mike took it, lay two or three days very still in his mother's strong arms, and recovered Madame Ristofalo had had it in "fifty-three." She became a heroic nurse to many, and saved life after life among the poor.

The trials of those days enriched John Richling in the acquaintanceship and esteem of Sister Jane's little lisping rector. And, by the way, none of those with whom Dr. Sevier dined on that darkest night of Richling's life became victims. The rector had never encountered the disease before, but when Sister Jane and the banker, and the banker's family and friends, and thousands of others, fled, he ran toward it, David-like, swordless and armorless. He and Richling were nearly of equal age. Three times, four times, and again, they met at dying-beds. They became fond of each other.

Another brave nurse was Narcisse. Dr. Sevier, it is true, could not get rid of the conviction for years afterward that one victim would have lived had not Narcisse talked him to death. But in general, where there was some one near to prevent his telling all his discoveries and inventions, he did good service, and accompanied it with very chivalric emotions.

"Yesseh," he said, with a strutting attitude that somehow retained a sort of modesty, "I 'ad the gweatess success. Hah! a nuss is a nuss those time'. Only some time' 'e's not. 'Tis accawding to the povvub, — what is that povvub, now, ag'in?" The proverb did not answer his call, and he waved it away. "Yesseh, eve'ybody wanting me at once — couldn' supply the deman'."

Richling listened to him with new pleasure and rising esteem.

"You make me envy you," he exclaimed, honestly.

"Well, I s'pose you may say so, Mistoo Itchlin, faw I nevva nuss a sing-le one w'at din paid me ten dollahs a night. Of co'se! 'Consistency, thou awt a jew'l.' It's juz as the povvub says, 'All work an' no pay keep Jack a small boy.' An' yet," he hurriedly added, remembering his indebtedness to his auditor, " 'tis aztonizhin' 'ow 'tis expensive to live. I haven' got a picayune of that money pwesently! I'm aztonizh myse'f!"

CHAPTER XXXVIII.

"I MUST BE CRUEL ONLY TO BE KIND."

THE plague grew sated and feeble. One morning frost sent a flight of icy arrows into the town, and it vanished. The swarthy girls and lads that sauntered homeward behind their mothers' cows across the wide suburban stretches of marshy commons heard again the deep, unbroken, cataract roar of the reawakened city.

We call the sea cruel, seeing its waters dimple and smile where yesterday they dashed in pieces the ship that was black with men, women, and children. But what shall we say of those billows of human life, of which we are ourselves a part, that surge over the graves of its own dead with dances and laughter and many a coquetry, with panting chase for gain and preference, and pious regrets and tender condolences for the thousands that died yesterday — and need not have died?

Such were the questions Dr. Sevier asked himself as he laid down the newspaper full of congratulations upon the return of trade's and fashion's boisterous flow, and praises of the deeds of benevolence and mercy that had abounded throughout the days of anguish.

Certain currents in these human rapids had driven Richling and the Doctor wide apart. But at last, one day, Richling entered the office with a cheerfulness of countenance something overdone, and indicative to the Doctor's eye of inward trepidation.

"Doctor," he said hurriedly, "preparing to leave the office? It was the only moment I could command" —

"Good-morning, Richling."

"I've been trying every day for a week to get down here," said Richling, drawing out a paper. "Doctor" — with his eyes on the paper, which he had begun to unfold.

"Richling" — It was the Doctor's hardest voice. Richling looked up at him as a child looks at a thunder-cloud. The Doctor pointed to the document: —

"Is that a subscription paper?"

"Yes."

"You needn't unfold it, Richling." The Doctor made a little pushing motion at it with his open hand. "From whom does it come?"

Richling gave a name. He had not changed color when the Doctor looked black, but now he did; for Dr. Sevier smiled. It was terrible.

"Not the little preacher that lisps?" asked the physician.

"He lisps sometimes," said Richling, with resentful subsidence of tone and with dropped eyes, preparing to return the paper to his pocket.

"Wait," said the Doctor, more gravely, arresting the movement with his index finger. "What is it for?"

"It's for the aid of an asylum overcrowded with orphans in consequence of the late epidemic." There was still a tightness in Richling's throat, a faint bitterness in his tone, a spark of indignation in his eye. But these the Doctor ignored. He reached out his hand, took the folded paper gently from Richling, crossed his knees, and, resting his elbows on them and shaking the paper in a prefatory way, spoke: —

"Richling, in old times we used to go into monasteries; now we subscribe to orphan asylums. Nine months ago

I warned this community that if it didn't take the necessary precautions against the foul contagion that has since swept over us it would pay for its wicked folly in the lives of thousands and the increase of fatherless and helpless children. I didn't know it would come this year, but I knew it might come any year. Richling, we deserved it!"

Richling had never seen his friend in so forbidding an aspect. He had come to him boyishly elated with the fancied excellence and goodness and beauty of the task he had assumed, and a perfect confidence that his noble benefactor would look upon him with pride and upon the scheme with generous favor. When he had offered to present the paper to Dr. Sevier he had not understood the little rector's marked alacrity in accepting his service. Now it was plain enough. He was well-nigh dumfounded. The responses that came from him came mechanically, and in the manner of one who wards off unmerited buffetings from one whose unkindness may not be resented.

"You can't think that only those died who were to blame?" he asked, helplessly; and the Doctor's answer came back instantly:—

"Ho, no! look at the hundreds of little graves! No, sir. If only those who were to blame had been stricken, I should think the Judgment wasn't far off. Talk of God's mercy in times of health! There's no greater evidence of it than to see him, in these awful visitations, refusing still to discriminate between the innocent and the guilty! Richling, only Infinite Mercy joined to Infinite Power, with infinite command of the future, could so forbear!"

Richling could not answer. The Doctor unfolded the paper and began to read: "'God, in his mysterious providence'—O sir!"

" What!" demanded Richling.

"O sir, what a foul, false charge! There's nothing mysterious about it.   We've trampled the book of Nature's laws in the mire of our streets, and dragged her penalties down upon our heads!   Why, Richling," — he shifted his attitude, and laid the edge of one hand upon the paper that lay in the other, with the air of commencing a demonstration, — "you're a Bible man, eh?   Well, yes, I think you are ; but I want you never to forget that the book of Nature has its commandments, too ; and the man who sins against *them* is a sinner.   There's no dispensation of mercy in that Scripture to Jew or Gentile, though the God of Mercy wrote it with his own finger.   A community has got to know those laws and keep them, or take the consequences — and take them here and now — on this globe — *presently!*"

" You mean, then," said Richling, extending his hand for the return of the paper, " that those whose negligence filled the asylums should be the ones to subscribe."

" Yes," replied the Doctor, " yes!" drew back his hand with the paper still in it, turned to his desk, opened the list, and wrote.   Richling's eyes followed the pen ; his heart came slowly up into his throat.

" Why, Doc — Doctor, that's more than any one else has " —

" They have probably made some mistake," said Dr. Sevier, rubbing the blotting-paper with his finger. " Richling, do you think it's your mission to be a philanthropist?"

" Isn't it everybody's mission?" replied Richling.

" That's not what I asked you."

" But you ask a question," said Richling, smiling down upon the subscription-paper as he folded it, " that nobody would like to answer."

"Very well, then, you needn't answer. But, Richling,"
— he pointed his long finger to the pocket of Richling's
coat, where the subscription-list had disappeared, — "this
sort of work — whether you distinctly propose to be a
philanthropist or not — is right, of course. It's good.
But it's the mere alphabet of beneficence. Richling,
whenever philanthropy takes the *guise* of philanthropy,
look out. Confine your philanthropy — you can't do it
entirely, but as much as you can — confine your philanthropy to the *motive*. It's the temptation of philanthro-
pists to set aside the natural constitution of society
wherever it seems out of order, and substitute some
philanthropic machinery in its place. It's all wrong,
Richling. Do as a good doctor would. Help nature."

Richling looked down askance, pushed his fingers
through his hair perplexedly, drew a deep breath, lifted
his eyes to the Doctor's again, smiled incredulously, and
rubbed his brow.

"You don't see it?" asked the physician, in a tone of
surprise.

"O Doctor," — throwing up a despairing hand, —
"we're miles apart. I don't see how any work could be
nobler. It looks to me" — But Dr. Sevier interrupted.

"— From an emotional stand-point, Richling. Richling," — he changed his attitude again, — "if you *want*
to be a philanthropist, be cold-blooded."

Richling laughed outright, but not heartily.

"Well!" said his friend, with a shrug, as if he dismissed the whole matter. But when Richling moved, as
if to rise, he restrained him. "Stop! I know you're in
a hurry, but you may tell Reisen to blame me."

"It's not Reisen so much as it's the work," replied
Richling, but settled down again in his seat.

"Richling, human benevolence — public benevolence —

in its beginning was a mere nun on the battle-field, bind
ing up wounds and wiping the damp from dying brows
But since then it has had time and opportunity to become
strong, bold, masculine, potential.   Once it had only the
knowledge and power to alleviate evil consequences; now
it has both the knowledge and the power to deal with evil
causes.   Now, I say to you, leave this emotional A B C
of human charity to nuns and mite societies.   It's a good
work; let them do it.   Give them money, if you can."

"I see what you mean — I think," said Richling,
slowly, and with a pondering eye.

"I'm glad if you do," rejoined the Doctor, visibly
relieved.

"But that only throws a heavier responsibility upon
strong men, if I understand it," said Richling, half inter-
rogatively.

"Certainly!   Upon strong spirits, male or female.
Upon spirits that can drive the axe low down into the
causes of things, again and again and again, steadily, patiently, until at last some great evil towering above them
totters and falls crashing to the earth, to be cut to pieces
and burned in the fire.   Richling, gather fagots for pastime
if you like, though it's poor fun; but don't think that's
your mission!   *Don't* be a fagot-gatherer!   What are you
smiling at?"

"Your good opinion of me," answered Richling.
"Doctor, I don't believe I'm fit for anything but a fagot-
gatherer.   But I'm willing to try."

"Oh, bah!"   The Doctor admired such humility as
little as it deserved.   "Richling, reduce the number of
helpless orphans!   Dig out the old roots of calamity!   A
spoon is not what you want; you want a *mattock*.   Reduce
crime and vice!   Reduce squalor!   Reduce the poor man's
death-rate!   Improve his tenements!   improve his hos-

pitals! carry sanitation into his workshops! Teach the
trades! Prepare the poor for possible riches, and the
rich for possible poverty! Ah — ah — Richling, I preach
well enough, I think, but in practice I have missed it
myself! Don't repeat my error!"

"Oh, but you haven't missed it!" cried Richling.

"Yes, but I have," said the Doctor. "Here I am,
telling you to let your philanthropy be cold-blooded;
why, I've always been hot-blooded."

"I like the hot best," said Richling, quickly.

"You ought to hate it," replied his friend. "It's
been the root of all your troubles. Richling, God Almighty is unimpassioned. If he wasn't he'd be weak.
You remember Young's line: 'A God all mercy is a God
unjust.' The time has come when beneficence, to be real,
must operate scientifically, not emotionally. Emotion is
good; but it must follow, not guide. Here! I'll give
you a single instance. Emotion never sells where it can
give: that is an old-fashioned, effete benevolence. The
new, the cold-blooded, is incomparably better: it never —
to individual or to community — gives where it can sell.
Your instincts have applied the rule to yourself; apply it
to your fellow-man."

"Ah!" said Richling, promptly, "that's another thing.
It's not my business to apply it to them."

"It *is* your business to apply it to them. You have
no right to do less."

"And what will men say of me? At least — not that,
but"—

The Doctor pointed upward. ' They will say, 'I
know thee, that thou art an hard man.'" His voice
trembled "But, Richling," he resumed with fresh firmness, "if you want to lead a long and useful life, — you
say you do, — you must take my advice; you must deny

yourself for a while; you must shelve these fine notions
for a time. I tell you once more, you must endeavor to
reëstablish your health as it was before — before they
locked you up, you know. When that is done you can
commence right there if you choose; I wish you would
Give the public — sell would be better, but it will hardly
buy — a prison system less atrocious, less destructive of
justice, and less promotive of crime and vice, than the
one it has. By-the-by, I suppose you know that Raphael
Ristofalo went to prison last night again?"

Richling sprang to his feet. "For what? He hasn't" —

"Yes, sir; he has discovered the man who robbed him,
and has killed him."

Richling started away, but halted as the Doctor spoke
again, rising from his seat and shaking out his legs.

"He's not suffering any hardship. He's shrewd, you
know, — has made arrangements with the keeper by
which he secures very comfortable quarters. The star-
chamber, I think they call the room he is in. He'll suffer
very little restraint. Good-day!"

He turned, as Richling left, to get his own hat and
gloves. "Yes," he thought, as he passed slowly downstairs to his carriage, "I have erred." He was not only
teaching, he was learning. To fight evil was not enough.
People who wanted help for orphans did not come to him
— they sent. They drew back from him as a child
shrinks from a soldier. Even Alice, his buried Alice,
had wept with delight when he gave her a smile, and
trembled with fear at his frown. To fight evil is not
enough. Everybody seemed to feel as though that were
a war against himself. Oh for some one always to understand — never to fear — the frowning good intention of
the lonely man!

CHAPTER XXXIX.

"PETTENT PRATE."

IT was about the time, in January, when clerks and correspondents were beginning to write '59 without first getting it '58, that Dr. Sevier, as one morning he approached his office, noticed with some grim amusement, standing among the brokers and speculators of Carondelet street, the baker, Reisen. He was earnestly conversing with and bending over a small, alert fellow, in a rakish beaver and very smart coat, with the blue flowers of modesty bunched saucily in one button-hole.

Almost at the same moment Reisen saw the Doctor. He called his name aloud, and for all his ungainly bulk would have run directly to the carriage in the middle of the street, only that the Doctor made believe not to see, and in a moment was out of reach. But when, two or three hours later, the same vehicle came, tipping somewhat sidewise against the sidewalk at the Charity Hospital gate, and the Doctor stepped from it, there stood Reisen in waiting.

"Toctor," he said, approaching and touching his hat, "I like to see you a minudt, uff you bleace, shtrict prifut."

They moved slowly down the unfrequented sidewalk, along the garden wall.

"Before you begin, Reisen, I want to ask you a question. I've noticed for a month past that Mr. Richling rides in your bread-carts alongside the drivers on their rounds. Don't you know you ought not to require such a thing as that from a person like Mr. Richling? Mr. Richling's a gentleman, Reisen, and you make him mount up in those bread-carts, and jump out every few minutes to deliver bread!"

The Doctor's blood was not cold.

"Vell, now!" drawled the baker, as the corners of his mouth retreated toward the back of his neck, "end't tat teh funn'est ting, ennahow! Vhy, tat iss yoost teh ferra ting fot I comin' to shpeak mit you apowdt udt!" He halted and looked at the Doctor to see how this coincidence struck him; but the Doctor merely moved on. "*I* toant make him too udt," he continued, starting again; "he cumps to me sindts apowdt two-o-o mundts aco — ven I shtill feelin' a liddle veak, yet, fun teh yalla-feewa — undt yoost paygs me to let um too udt. 'Mr. Richlun,' sayss I to him, 'I toandt kin untershtayndt for vot you vawnts to too sich a ritickliss, Mr. Richlun!' Ovver he sayss, 'Mr. Reisen,' — he alvays callss me 'Mister,' undt tat iss one dting in puttickly vot I alvays tit li-i-iked apowdt Mr. Richlun, — 'Mr. Reisen,' he sayss, 'toandt you aysk me te reason, ovver yoost let me co ahate undt too udt!' Undt I voss a coin' to kiff udt up, alretty; ovver ten cumps in *Missess* Reisen, — who iss a heap shmarter mayn as fot Reisen iss, I yoost tell you te ectsectly troot, — and she sayss, 'Reisen, you yoost tell Mr. Richlun, Mr. Richlun, you toadnt coin' to too sich a ritickliss!'"

The speaker paused for effect.

"Undt ten Mr. Richlun, he talks! — Schweedt? — Oh yendlemuns, toandt say nutting!" The baker lifted up his palm and swung it down against his thigh with a blow that sent the flour out in a little cloud. "I tell you, Toctor Tseweer, ven tat mayn vawndts to too udt, he kin

yoost talk te mo-ust like a Christun fun enna mayn I
neffa he-ut in mine li-i-fe! 'Missess Reisen,' he sayss,
'I vawndts to too udt pecauce I vawndts to too udt.'
Vell, how you coin' to arg-y ennating eagval mit Mr.
Richlun? So teh upshodt iss he coes owdt in teh prate-
cawts tistripputin' te prate!" Reisen threw his arms far
behind him, and bowed low to his listener.

Dr. Sevier had learned him well enough to beware of
interrupting him, lest when he resumed it would be at the
beginning again. He made no answer, and Reisen went
on: —

"Bressently"— He stopped his slow walk, brought
forward both palms, shrugged, dropped them, bowed,
clasped them behind him, brought the left one forward,
dropped it, then the right one, dropped it also, frowned,
smiled, and said: —

"Bressently"— then a long silence — "effrapotty in
my etsteplitchmendt" — another long pause— "hef
yoost teh same ettechmendt to Mr. Richlun," — another
interval, — "tey hef yoost tso much effection fur *him* "—
another silence — "ass tey hef" — another, with a smile
this time — "fur — te teffle himpselluf!" An oven
opened in the baker's face, and emitted a softly rattling
expiration like that of a bursted bellows. The Doctor
neither smiled nor spoke. Reisen resumed: —

"I seen udt. I seen udt. Ovver I toandt coult untershtayndt udt. Ovver one tay cumps in mine little poy in
to me fen te pakers voss all ashleep, 'Pap-a, Mr.
Richlun sayss you shouldt come into teh offuss.' I
kumpt in. Mr. Richlun voss tare, shtayndting yoost so
—yoost so — py teh shtofe; undt, Toctor Tseweer, 1
yoost tell you te ectsectly troot, he toaldt in fife minudts —
six minudts — seven minudts, udt may pe — undt shoadt
me how effrapotty, high undt low, little undt pick, Tom,

Tick, undt Harra, pin ropping me sindts more ass fife years ! "

The longest pause of all followed this disclosure. The baker had gradually backed the Doctor up against the wall, spreading out the whole matter with his great palms turned now upward and now downward, the bulky contents of his high-waisted, barn-door trowsers now bulged out and now withdrawn, to be protruded yet more a moment later. He recommenced by holding out his down-turned hand some distance above the ground.

" I yoompt tot hoigh ! " He blew his cheeks out, and rose a half-inch off his heels in recollection of the mighty leap. "Ovver Mr. Richlun sayss, — he sayss, ' Kip shtill, Mr. Reisen ; ' undt I kibt shtill."

The baker's auditor was gradually drawing him back toward the hospital gate ; but he continued speaking : —

" Py undt py, vun tay, I kot someting to say to Mr. *Richlun*, yet. Undt I sendts vert to Mr. *Richlun* tat *he* shouldt come into teh offuss. He cumps in. ' Mr. Richlun,' I sayss, sayss I to him, ' Mr. Richlun, I kot udt ! ' " The baker shook his finger in Dr. Sevier's face. " ' I kot udt, udt layst, Mr. Richlun ! I yoost het a *suspish'n* sindts teh first tay fot I employedt you, ovver now I *know* I kot udt ! ' Vell, sir, he yoost turnun so rate ass a flennen shirt ! — ' Mr. Reisen,' sayss he to me, ' fot iss udt fot you kot ? ' Undt sayss I to him, ' Mr. Richlun, udt iss you ! Udt is *you* fot I kot ! ' "

Dr. Sevier stood sphinx-like, and once more Reisen went on.

" ' Yes, Mr. Richlun,' " still addressing the Doctor as though he were his book-keeper, " ' I yoost layin, on my pett effra nighdt — effra nighdt, vi-i-ite ava-a-ake ! undt in apowdt a veek I make udt owdt ut layst tot you, Mr.

Richlun,'— I lookt um shtraight in te eye, undt he lookt me shtraight te same,—'tot, Mr. Richlun, *you*,' sayss I, ' not dtose fellehs fot pin py me sindts more ass fife yearss, put *you*, Mr. Richlun, iss teh mayn! —teh mayn fot I — kin *trust!*'" The baker's middle parts bent out and his arms were drawn akimbo. Thus for ten seconds.

"'Undt now, Mr. Richlun, do you kot teh shtrengdt for to shtart a noo pissness?' — Pecause, Toctor, udt pin seem to me Mr. Richlun kitten more undt more shecklun, undt toandt take tot meticine fot you kif um (ovver he sayss he toos). So ten he sayss to me, ' Mister Reisen, I am yoost so sollut undt shtrong like a pilly-coat! Fot is teh noo pissness?' —' Mr. Richlun,' sayss I,'ve goin' to make pettent prate!'"

"What?" asked the Doctor, frowning with impatience and venturing to interrupt at last.

" *Pet-tent prate!* "

The listener frowned heavier and shook his head.

" *Pettent prate!* "

"Oh! patent bread; yes. Well?"

"Yes," said Reisen, " prate mate mit a mutcheen; mit copponic-essut kass into udt ploat pefore udt is paked. I pought teh pettent tiss mawning fun a yendleman in Garontelet shtreedt, alretty, naympt Kknox."

" And what have I to do with all this?" asked the Doctor, consulting his watch, as he had already done twice before.

"Vell," said Reisen, spreading his arms abroad, " I yoost taught you like to herr udt."

"But what do you want to see me for? What have you kept me all this time to tell me — or ask me?"

"Toctor,— you ugscooce me — ovver "— the baker held the Doctor by the elbow as he began to turn away

— " Toctor Tseweer,"— the great face lighted up with a smile, the large body doubled partly together, and the broad left hand was held ready to smite the thigh,— " you shouldt see Mr. Richlun ven he fowndt owdt udt is goin' to lower teh price of prate! I taught he iss goin' to kiss Mississ Reisen!"

CHAPTER XL.

SWEET BELLS JANGLED.

THOSE who knew New Orleans just before the civil war, even though they saw it only along its river-front from the deck of some steam-boat, may easily recall a large sign painted high up on the side of the old "Tri-angle Building," which came to view through the dark web of masts and cordage as one drew near St. Mary's Market. "Steam Bakery" it read. And such as were New Orleans householders, or by any other chance en-joyed the experience of making their way in the early morning among the hundreds of baskets that on hundreds of elbows moved up and down along and across the quaint gas-lit arcades of any of the market-houses, must re-member how, about this time or a little earlier, there began to appear on one of the tidiest of bread-stalls in each of these market-houses a new kind of bread. It was a small, densely compacted loaf of the size and shape of a badly distorted brick. When broken, it divided into layers, each of which showed — "teh bprindt of teh kkneading-mutcheen," said Reisen to Narcisse; "yoost like a tsoda crecker!"

These two persons had met by chance at a coffee-stand one beautiful summer dawn in one of the markets, — the Tréiné, most likely, — where, perched on high stools at a zinc-covered counter, with the smell of fresh blood on the right and of stale fish on the left, they had finished half their cup of *cafè au lait* before they awoke to the exhilarating knowledge of each other's presence.

" Yesseh," said Narcisse, " now since you 'ave we-mawk the mention of it, I think I have saw that va'iety of bwead."

" Oh, surely you poundt to a-seedt udt. A uckly little prown dting " —

" But cook well," said Narcisse.

" Yayss," drawled the baker. It was a fact that he had to admit.

" An' good flou'," persisted the Creole.

" Yayss," said the smiling manufacturer. He could not deny that either.

" An' honness weight! " said Narcisse, planting his empty cup in his saucer, with the energy of his asservation ; " an', Mr. Bison, thass a ve'y seldom thing."

" Yayss," assented Reisen, " ovver tat prate is mighdy dtry, undt shtickin' in teh dtroat."

" No, seh! " said the flatterer, with a generous smile. " Egscuse me — I diffeh fum you. 'Tis a beaucheouz bwead. Yesseh. And eve'y loaf got the name beaucheouzly pwint on the top, with ' Patent ' — sich an' sich a time. 'Tis the tooth, Mr. Bison, I'm boun' to congwatu-*late* you on that bwead."

" O-o-oh! tat iss not *mine* prate," exclaimed the baker. " Tat iss not fun mine etsteplitchmendt. Oh, no! Tatt iss te prate — I'm yoost dtellin' you — tat iss te prate fun tat fellah py teh Sunk-Mary's Morrikit-house! Tat's teh shteam prate.' I to-undt know for vot effrapotty puys tat prate ennahow! Ovver you yoost vait dtill you see *mine* prate! "

" Mr. Bison," said Narcisse, " Mr. Bison," — he had been trying to stop him and get in a word of his own, but could not, — " I don't know if you — Mr. — Mr.

Bison, in fact, you din unde'stood me. Can that be poss'ble that you din notiz that I was speaking in my i'ony about that bwead? Why, of co'se! Thass juz my i'onious cuztom, Mr. Bison. Thass one thing I dunno if you 'ave notiz about that 'steam bwead,' Mr. Bison, but with me that bwead always stick in my th'oat; an' yet I kin swallow mose anything, in fact. No, Mr. Bison, yo' bwead is deztyned to be the bwead; and I tell you how 'tis with me, I juz gladly eat yo' bwead eve'y time I kin git it! Mr. Bison, in fact you don't know me ve'y in- *timi*tly, but you will oblige me ve'y much indeed to baw me five dollahs till tomaw — save me fum d'awing a check!"

The German thrust his hand slowly and deeply into his pocket. "I alvayss like to oplyche a yendleman," — he smiled benignly, drew out a toothpick, and added, — "ovver I nivveh bporrah or lend to ennabodda."

"An' then," said Narcisse, promptly, "'tis imposs'ble faw anybody to be offended. Thass the bess way, Mr. Bison."

"Yayss," said the baker, "I tink udt iss." As they were parting, he added: "Ovver you vait dtill you see *mine* prate!"

"I'll do it, seh! — And, Mr. Bison, you muzn't think anything about that, my not bawing that five dollars fum you, Mr. Bison, because that don't make a bit o' dif'ence; an' thass one thing I like about you, Mr. Bison, you don't baw yo' money to eve'y Dick, Tom, an' Hawwy, do you?"

"No, I dtoandt. Ovver, you yoost vait" —

And certainly, after many vexations, difficulties, and delays, that took many a pound of flesh from Reisen's form, the pretty, pale-brown, fragrant white loaves of "aërated bread" that issued from the Star Bakery in

Benjamin street were something pleasant to see, though they did not lower the price.

Richling's old liking for mechanical apparatus came into play. He only, in the establishment, thoroughly understood the new process, and could be certain of daily, or rather nightly, uniform results. He even made one or two slight improvements in it, which he contemplated with ecstatic pride, and long accounts of which he wrote to Mary.

In a generous and innocent way Reisen grew a little jealous of his accountant, and threw himself into his business as he had not done before since he was young, and in the ardor of his emulation ignored utterly a state of health that was no better because of his great length and breadth.

"Toctor Tseweer!" he said, as the physician appeared one day in his office. "Vell, now, I yoost pet finfty tawllars tat iss Mississ Reisen sendts for you tat I'm sick! Ven udt iss not such a dting!" He laughed immoderately. "Ovver I'm gladt you come, Toctor, ennahow, for you pin yoost in time to see ever'ting runnin'. I vish you yoost come undt see udt!" He grinned in his old, broad way; but his face was anxious, and his bared arms were lean. He laid his hand on the Doctor's arm, and then jerked it away, and tried to blow off the floury print of his fingers. "Come!" He beckoned. "Come; I show you somedting putiful. Toctor, I *vizh* you come!"

The Doctor yielded. Richling had to be called upon at last to explain the hidden parts and processes.

"It's yoost like putt'n' te shpirudt into teh potty," said the laughing German. "Now, tat prate kot life in udt yoost teh same like your own selluf, Toctor. Tot prate kot yoost so much sense ass Reisen kot. Ovver,

Toctor — Toctor " — the Doctor was giving his attention
to Richling, who was explaining something — " Toctor,
toandt you come here uxpectin' to see nopoty sick, less-n
udt iss Mr. Richlun." He caught Richling's face roughly
between his hands, and then gave his back a caressing
thwack. " Toctor, vot you dtink? Ve goin' teh run prate-
cawts mit copponic-essut kass. Tispense mit hawses ! "
He laughed long but softly, and.smote Richling again as
the three walked across the bakery yard abreast.

" Well? " said Dr. Sevier to Richling, in a low tone,
" always working toward the one happy end."

Richling had only time to answer with his eyes, when
the baker, always clinging close to them, said, " Yes ; if
I toandt look oudt yet, he pe rich pefore Reisen."

The Doctor looked steadily at Richling, stood still, and
said, " Don't hurry."

But Richling swung playfully half around on his heel,
dropped his glance, and jerked his head sidewise, as one
who neither resented the advice nor took it. A minute
later he drew from his breast-pocket a small, thick letter
stripped of its envelope, and handed it to the Doctor,
who put it into his pocket, neither of them speaking. The
action showed practice. Reisen winked one eye laboriously at the Doctor and chuckled.

" See here, Reisen," said the Doctor, " I want you to
pack your trunk, take the late boat, and go to Biloxi or
Pascagoula, and spend a month fishing and sailing."

The baker pushed his fingers up under his hat, scratched
his head, smiled widely, and pointed at Richling.

" Sendt him."

The Doctor went and sat down with Reisen, and used
every form of inducement that could be brought to bear ;
but the German had but one answer : Richling, Richling,
not he. The Doctor left a prescription, which the baker

took until he found it was making him sleep while Richling was at work, whereupon he amiably threw it out of his window.

It was no surprise to Dr. Sevier that Richling came to him a few days later with a face all trouble.

How are you, Richling? How's Reisen?"

Doctor," said Richling, "I'm afraid Mr. Reisen is"— Their eyes met.

"Insane," said the Doctor.

"Yes."

"Does his wife know whether he has ever had such symptoms before — in his life?"

"She says he hasn't."

"I suppose you know his pecuniary condition perfectly; has he money?"

"Plenty."

"He'll not consent to go away anywhere, I suppose, will he?"

"Not an inch."

"There's but one sensible and proper course, Richling; he must be taken at once, by force if necessary, to a first-class insane hospital."

"Why, Doctor, why? Can't we treat him better at home?"

The Doctor gave his head its well-known swing of impatience. "If you want to be *criminally* in error try that!"

"I don't want to be in error at all," retorted Richling.

"Then don't lose twelve hours that you can save, but send him off as soon as process of court will let you."

"Will you come at once and see him?" asked Richling, rising up.

"Yes, I'll be there nearly as soon as you will. Stop; you had better ride with me; I have something special to say." As the carriage started off, the Doctor leaned back in its cushions, folded his arms, and took a long, meditative breath. Richling glanced at him and said : —

"We're both thinking of the same person."

"Yes," replied the Doctor; "and the same day, too, I suppose : the first day I ever saw her; the only other time that we ever got into this carriage together. Hmm! hmm! With what a fearful speed time flies!"

"Sometimes," said the yearning husband, and apologized by a laugh. The Doctor grunted, looked out of the carriage window, and, suddenly turning, asked : —

"Do you know that Reisen instructed his wife about six months ago, in the event of his death or disability, to place all her interests in your hands, and to be guided by your advice in everything?"

"Oh!" exclaimed Richling, "he can't do that! He should have asked my consent."

"I suppose he knew he wouldn't get it. He's a cunning simpleton."

"But, Doctor, if you knew this" — Richling ceased

"Six months ago. Why didn't I tell you?" said the physician. "I thought I would, Richling, though Reisen bade me not, when he told me; I made no promise. But time, that you think goes slow, was too fast for me."

"I shall refuse to serve," said Richling, soliloquizing aloud. "Don't you see, Doctor, the delicacy of the position?"

"Yes, I do; but you don't. Don't you see it would be just as delicate a matter for you to refuse?"

Richling pondered, and presently said, quite slowly : —

"It will look like coming down out of the tree to catch the apples as they fall," he said. "Why," he added with impatience, "it lays me wide open to suspicion and slander."

"Does it?" asked the Doctor, heartlessly. "There's nothing remarkable in that. Did any one ever occupy a responsible position without those conditions?"

"But, you know, I have made some unscrupulous enemies by defending Reisen's interests."

"Um-hmm; what did you defend them for?"

Richling was about to make a reply; but the Doctor wanted none. "Richling," he said, "the most of men have burrows. They never let anything decoy them so far from those burrows but they can pop into them at a moment's notice. Do you take my meaning?"

"Oh, yes!" said Richling, pleasantly; "no trouble to understand you this time. I'll not run into any burrow just now. I'll face my duty and think of Mary."

He laughed.

"Excellent pastime," responded Dr. Sevier.

They rode on in silence.

"As to"—began Richling again,—"as to such matters as these, once a man confronts the question candidly, there is really no room, that I can see, for a man to choose: a man, at least, who is always guided by conscience."

"If there were such a man," responded the Doctor.

"True," said John.

"But for common stuff, such as you and I are made of, it must sometimes be terrible."

"I dare say," said Richling. "It sometimes requires cold blood to choose aright."

"As cold as granite," replied the other.

They arrived at the bakery.

"O Doctor," said Mrs. Reisen, proffering her hand as he entered the house, "my poor hussband iss crazy!" She dropped into a chair and burst into tears. She was a large woman, with a round, red face and triple chin, but with a more intelligent look and a better command of English than Reisen. "Doctor, I want you to cure him ass quick ass possible."

"Well, madam, of course; but will you do what I say?"

"I will, certain shure. I do it yust like you tellin' me."

The Doctor gave her such good advice as became a courageous physician.

A look of dismay came upon her. Her mouth dropped open. "Oh, no, Doctor!" She began to shake her head. "I'll never do tha-at; oh, no; I'll never send my poor hussband to the crazy-house! Oh, no, sir; I'll do not such a thing!" There was some resentment in her emotion. Her nether lip went up like a crying babe's, and she breathed through her nostrils audibly.

"Oh, yes, I know!" said the poor creature, turning her face away from the Doctor's kind attempts to explain, and lifting it incredulously as she talked to the wall, — "I know all about it. I'm not a-goin' to put no sich a disgrace on my poor hussband; no, indeed!" She faced around suddenly and threw out her hand to Richling, who leaned against a door twisting a bit of string between his thumbs. "Why, he wouldn't go, nohow, even if I gave my consents. You caynt coax him out of his room yet. Oh, no, Doctor! It's my duty to keep him wid me an' try to cure him first a little while here at home. That aint no trouble to me; I don't never mind no trouble if I can be any help to my hussband." She addressed the wall again.

"Well, madam," replied the physician, with unusual tenderness of tone, and looking at Richling while he spoke, "of course you'll do as you think best."

"Oh! my poor Reisen!" exclaimed the wife, wringing her hands.

" Yes," said the physician, rising and looking out of the window, " I am afraid it will be ruin to Reisen."

" No, it won't be such a thing," said Mrs. Reisen, turning this way and that in her chair as the physician moved from place to place. " Mr. Richlin'," — turning to him, — " Mr. Richlin' and me kin run the business yust so good as Reisen." She shifted her distressed gaze back and forth from Richling to the Doctor. The latter turned to Richling : —

" I'll have to leave this matter to you."

Richling nodded.

" Where is Reisen?" asked the Doctor. " In his own room, upstairs?" The three passed through an inner door.

CHAPTER XLI.

MIRAGE.

"THIS spoils some of your arrangements, doesn't it?" asked Dr. Sevier of Richling, stepping again into his carriage. He had already said the kind things, concerning Reisen, that physicians commonly say when they have little hope. "Were you not counting on an early visit to Milwaukee?"

Richling laughed.

"That illusion has been just a little beyond reach for months." He helped the Doctor shut his carriage-door.

"But now, of course —" said the physician.

"Of course it's out of the question," replied Richling; and the Doctor drove away, with the young man's face in his mind bearing an expression of simple emphasis that pleased him much.

Late at night Richling, in his dingy little office, unlocked a drawer, drew out a plump package of letters, and began to read their pages, — transcripts of his wife's heart, pages upon pages, hundreds of precious lines, dates crowding closely one upon another. Often he smiled as his eyes ran to and fro, or drew a soft sigh as he turned the page, and looked behind to see if any one had stolen in and was reading over his shoulder. Sometimes his smile broadened; he lifted his glance from the sheet and fixed it in pleasant revery on the blank wall before him. Often the lines were entirely taken up with mere utterances of affection. Now and then they were all about little Alice, who had

fretted all the night before, her gums being swollen and
tender on the upper left side near the front; or who had
fallen violently in love with the house-dog, by whom, in
turn, the sentiment was reciprocated; or whose eyes were
really getting bluer and bluer, and her cheeks fatter and
fatter, and who seemed to fear nothing that had existence.
And the reader of the lines would rest one elbow on the
desk, shut his eyes in one hand, and see the fair young head
of the mother drooping tenderly over that smaller head in
her bosom. Sometimes the tone of the lines was hopefully
grave, discussing in the old tentative, interrogative key
the future and its possibilities. Some pages were given
to reminiscences, — recollections of all the droll things and
all the good and glad things of the rugged past. Every
here and there, but especially where the lines drew toward
the signature, the words of longing multiplied, but always
full of sunshine; and just at the end of each letter love
spurned its restraints, and rose and overflowed with sweet
confessions.

Sometimes these re-read letters did Richling good;
not always. Maybe he read them too often. It was
only the very next time that the Doctor's carriage stood
before the bakery that the departing physician turned
before he reëntered the vehicle, and — whatever Richling
had been saying to him — said abruptly: —

"Richling, are you falling out of love with your work?"

"Why do you ask me that?" asked the young man,
coloring.

"Because I no longer see that joy of deliverance with
which you entered upon this humble calling. It seems to
have passed like a lost perfume, Richling. Have you let
your toil become a task once more?"

Richling dropped his eyes and pushed the ground with
the toe of his boot.

"I didn't want you to find that out, Doctor."

"I was afraid, from the first, it would be so," said the physician.

"I don't see why you were."

"Well, I saw that the zeal with which you first laid hold of your work was not entirely natural. It was good, but it was partly artificial, — the more credit to you on that account. But I saw that by and by you would have to keep it up mainly by your sense of necessity and duty. 'That'll be the pinch,' I said; and now I see it's come. For a long time you idealized the work; but at last its real dulness has begun to overcome you, and you're discontented — and with a discontentment that you can't justify, can you?"

"But I feel myself growing smaller again."

"No wonder. Why, Richling, it's the discontent makes that."

"Oh, no! The discontent makes me long to expand. I never had so much ambition before. But what can I do here? Why, Doctor, I ought to be — I might be"—

The physician laid a hand on the young man's shoulder.

"Stop, Richling. Drop those phrases and give us a healthy 'I am,' and 'I must,' and 'I will.' Don't — *don't* be like so many! You're not of the many. Richling, in the first illness in which I ever attended your wife, she watched her chance and asked me privately — implored me — not to let her die, for your sake. I don't suppose that tortures could have wrung from her, even if she realized it, — which I doubt, — the true reason. But don't you feel it? It was because your moral nature needs her so badly. Stop — let me finish. You need Mary back here now to hold you square to your course by the tremendous power of her timid little 'Don't you think?' and 'Doesn't it seem?'"

"Doctor," replied Richling, with a smile of expostulation, "you touch one's pride."

"Certainly I do. You're willing enough to say that you love her and long for her, but not that your moral manhood needs her. And yet isn't it true?"

"It sha'n't be true," said Richling, swinging a playful fist. "'Forewarned is forearmed;' I'll not allow it. I'm man enough for that." He laughed, with a touch of pique.

"Richling," — the Doctor laid a finger against his companion's shoulder, preparing at the same time to leave him, — "don't be misled. A man who doesn't need a wife isn't fit to have one."

"Why, Doctor," replied Richling, with sincere amiability, "you're the man of all men I should have picked out to prove the contrary."

"No, Richling, no. I wasn't fit, and God took her."

In accordance with Dr. Sevier's request Richling essayed to lift the mind of the baker's wife, in the matter of her husband's affliction, to that plane of conviction where facts, and not feelings, should become her motive; and when he had talked until his head reeled, as though he had been blowing a fire, and she would not blaze for all his blowing — would be governed only by a stupid sentimentality; and when at length she suddenly flashed up in silly anger and accused him of interested motives; and when he had demanded instant retraction or release from her employment; and when she humbly and affectionately apologized, and was still as deep as ever in hopeless, clinging sentimentalisms, repeating the dictums of her simple and ignorant German neighbors and intimates, and calling them in to argue with him, the feeling that the Doctor's exhortation had for the moment driven away came back with more force than ever, and he could only turn again to his ovens and account-books with a feeling of annihilation.

"Where am I? What am I?" Silence was the only answer. The separation that had once been so sharp a pain had ceased to cut, and was bearing down upon him now with that dull, grinding weight that does the damage in us.

Presently came another development: the lack of money, that did no harm while it was merely kept in the mind, settled down upon the heart.

"It may be a bad thing to love, but it's a good thing to have," he said, one day, to the little rector, as this friend stood by him at a corner of the high desk where Richling was posting his ledger.

"But not to seek," said the rector.

Richling posted an item and shook his head doubtingly.

"That depends, I should say, on how much one seeks it, and how much of it he seeks."

"No," insisted the clergyman. Richling bent a look of inquiry upon him, and he added:—

"The principle is bad, and you know it, Richling. 'Seek ye first'—you know the text, and the assurance that follows with it—'all these things shall be added'"—

"Oh, yes; but still"—

"'But still!'" exclaimed the little preacher; "why must everybody say 'but still'? Don't you see that that 'but still' is the refusal of Christians to practise Christianity?"

Richling looked, but said nothing; and his friend hoped the word had taken effect. But Richling was too deeply bitten to be cured by one or two good sayings. After a moment he said:—

"I used to wonder to see nearly everybody struggling

to be rich, but I don't now. I don't justify it, but I understand it. It's flight from oblivion. It's the natural longing to be seen and felt."

"Why isn't it enough to be felt?" asked the other. "Here, you make bread and sell it. A thousand people eat it from your hand every day. Isn't that something?"

"Yes; but it's all the bread. The bread's everything; I'm nothing. I'm not asked to do or to be. I may exist or not; there will be bread all the same. I see my remark pains you, but I can't help it. You've never tried the thing. You've never encountered the mild contempt that people in ease pay to those who pursue the 'industries.' You've never suffered the condescension of rank to the ranks. You don't know the smart of being only an arithmetical quantity in a world of achievements and possessions."

"No," said the preacher, "maybe I haven't. But I should say you are just the sort of man that ought to come through all that unsoured and unhurt. Richling," — he put on a lighter mood, — "you've got a moral indigestion. You've accustomed yourself to the highest motives, and now these new notions are not the highest, and you know and feel it. They don't nourish you. They don't make you happy. Where are your old sentiments? What's become of them?"

"Ah!" said Richling, "I got them from my wife. And the supply's nearly run out."

"Get it renewed!" said the little man, quickly, putting on his hat and extending a farewell hand. "Excuse me for saying so. I didn't intend it; I dropped in to ask you again the name of that Italian whom you visit at the prison, — the man I promised you I'd go and talk to Yes — Ristofalo; that's it. Good-by."

That night Richling wrote to his wife. What he wrote goes not down here; but he felt as he wrote that his mood was not the right one, and when Mary got the letter she answered by first mail: —

Will you not let me come to you? Is it not surely best? Say but the word, and I'll come. It will be the steamer to Chicago, railroad to Cairo, and a St. Louis boat to New Orleans. Alice will be both company and protection, and no burden at all. O my beloved husband! I am just ungracious enough to think, some days, that these times of separation are the hardest of all. When we were suffering sickness and hunger together — well, we were *together*. Darling, if you'll just say come, I'll come in an *instant*. Oh, how gladly! Surely, with what you tell me you've saved, and with your place so secure to you, can't we venture to begin again? Alice and I can live with you in the bakery. O my husband! if you but say the word, a little time — a few days will bring us into your arms. And yet, do not yield to my impatience; I trust your wisdom, and know that what you decide will be best. Mother has been very feeble lately, as I have told you; but she seems to be improving, and now I see what I've half suspected for a long time, and ought to have seen sooner, that my husband — my dear, dear husband — needs me most; and I'm coming — I'm *coming*, John, if you'll only say come.

> Your loving
>   MARY."

CHAPTER XLII.

RISTOFALO AND THE RECTOR.

BE Richling's feelings what they might, the Star Bakery shone in the retail firmament of the commercial heavens with new and growing brilliancy. There was scarcely time to talk even with the tough little rector who hovers on the borders of this history, and he might have become quite an alien had not Richling's earnest request made him one day a visitor, as we have seen him express his intention of being, in the foul corridors of the parish prison, and presently the occupant of a broken chair in the apartment apportioned to Raphael Ristofalo and two other prisoners. "Easy little tasks you cut out for your friends," said the rector to Richling when next they met. "I got preached *to* — not to say edified. I'll share my edification with you!" He told his experience.

It was a sinister place, the prison apartment. The hand of Kate Ristofalo had removed some of its unsightly conditions and disguised others; but the bounds of the room, walls, ceiling, windows, floor, still displayed, with official unconcern, the grime and decay that is commonly thought good enough for men charged, rightly or wrongly, with crime.

The clergyman's chair was in the centre of the floor. Ristofalo sat facing him a little way off on the right. A youth of nineteen sat tipped against the wall on the left, and a long-limbed, big-boned, red-shirted young Irishman occupied a poplar table, hanging one of his legs across a

corner of it and letting the other down to the floor. Ris
tofalo remarked, in the form of polite acknowledgment
that the rector had preached to the assembled inmates of
the prison on the Sunday previous.

"Did I say anything that you thought was true?"
asked the minister.

The Italian smiled in the gentle manner that never
failed him.

"Didn't listen much," he said. He drew from a
pocket of his black velveteen pantaloons a small crumpled
tract. It may have been a favorite one with the clergyman, for the youth against the wall produced its counter-
part, and the man on the edge of the table lay back on
his elbow, and, with an indolent stretch of the opposite
arm and both legs, drew a third one from a tin cup that
rested on a greasy shelf behind him. The Irishman held
his between his fingers and smirked a little toward the
floor. Ristofalo extended his toward the visitor, and
touched the caption with one finger: "Mercy offered."

"Well," asked the rector, pleasantly, "what's the
matter with that?"

"Is no use yeh. Wrong place — this prison."

"Um-hm," said the tract-distributor, glancing down
at the leaf and smoothing it on his knee while he took
time to think. "Well, why shouldn't mercy be offered
here?"

"No," replied Ristofalo, still smiling; "ought offer
justice first."

"Mr. Preacher," asked the young Irishman, bringing
both legs to the front, and swinging them under the table,
"d'ye vote?"

"Yes; I vote."

"D'ye call yerself a cidizen — with a cidizen's rights
an' djuties?"

"I do."

"That's right." There was a deep sea of insolence in the smooth-faced, red-eyed smile that accompanied the commendation. "And how manny times have ye bean in this prison?"

"I don't know; eight or ten times. That rather beats you, doesn't it?"

Ristofalo smiled, the youth uttered a high rasping cackle, and the Irishman laughed the heartiest of all.

"A little," he said; "a little. But nivver mind. Ye say ye've bin here eight or tin times; yes. Well, now, will I tell ye what I'd do afore and iver I'd kim back here ag'in, — if I was you now? Will I tell ye?"

"Well, yes," replied the visitor, amiably; "I'd like to know."

"Well, surr, I'd go to the mair of this city and to the judge of the criminal coort, and to the gov'ner of the Sta-ate, and to the ligislatur, if needs be, and I'd say, 'Gintlemin, I can't go back to that prison! There is more crimes a-being committed by the people outside ag'in the fellies in theyre than — than — than the — the fellies in theyre has committed ag'in the people! I'm ashamed to preach theyre! I'm afeered to do ud!'" The speaker slipped off the table, upon his feet. "'There's murrder a-goun' on in theyre! There's more murrder a-bein' done in theyre nor there is outside! Justice is a-bein' murdered theyre ivery hour of day and night!'"

He brandished his fist with the last words, but dropped it at a glance from Ristofalo, and began to pace the floor along his side of the room, looking with a heavy-browed smile back and forth from one fellow-captive to the other. He waited till the visitor was about to speak, and then interrupted, pointing at him suddenly: —

" Ye're a Prodez'n preacher ! I'll bet ye fifty dollars ye have a rich cherch ! Full of leadin' cidizens ! "

" You're correct."

" Well, I'd go an' — an' — an' I'd say, ' Dawn't ye nivver ax me to go into that place ag'in a-pallaverin' about mercy, until ye gid ud chaynged from the hell on earth it is to a house of justice, wheyre min gits the sintences that the coorts decrees ! ' *I* don't complain in here. *He* don't complain," pointing to Ristofalo ; "ye'll nivver hear a complaint from him. But go look in that yaird ! " He threw up both hands with a grimace of disgust — " Aw ! " — and ceased again, but continued his walk, looked at his fellows, and resumed : —

" *I* listened to yer sermon. I heerd ye talkin' about the souls of uz. Do ye think ye kin make anny of thim min believe ye cayre for the souls of us whin ye do nahthing for the *bodies* that's before yer eyes tlothed in rrags and stairved, and made to sleep on beds of brick and stone, and to receive a hundred abuses a day that was nivver intended to be a pairt of *anny*body's sintince — and manny of'm not tried yit, an' nivver a-goun' to have annythin' proved ag'in 'm ? How *can* ye come offerin' uz merrcy ? For ye don't come out o' the tloister, like a poor Cat'lic priest or Sister. Ye come rright out o' the hairt o' the community that's a-committin' more crimes ag'in uz in here than all of us together has iver committed outside. Aw ! — Bring us a better airticle of yer own justice ferst — I doan't cayre how *crool* it is, so ut's *justice* — an' *thin* preach about God's mercy. I'll listen to ye."

Ristofalo had kept his eyes for the most of the time on the floor, smiling sometimes more and sometimes less. Now, however, he raised them and nodded to the clergyman. He approved all that had been said. The Irishman went and sat again on the table and swung his legs. The visitor was not allowed to answer before, and must answer now. He would have been more comfortable at the rectory.

"My friend," he began, "suppose, now, I should say that you are pretty nearly correct in everything you'v said?"

The prisoner, who, with hands grasping the table's edge on either side of him, was looking down at his swinging brogans, simply lifted his lurid eyes without raising his head, and nodded. "It would be right," he seemed to intimate, "but nothing great."

"And suppose I should say that I'm glad I've heard it, and that I even intend to make good use of it?"

His hearer lifted his head, better pleased, but not without some betrayal of the distrust which a lower nature feels toward the condescensions of a higher. The preacher went on : —

"Would you try to believe what I have to add to that?"

"Yes, I'd try," replied the Irishman, looking facetiously from the youth to Ristofalo. But this time the Italian was grave, and turned his glance expectantly upon the minister, who presently replied : —

"Well, neither my church nor the community has sent me here at all."

The Irishman broke into a laugh.

"Did God send ye?" He looked again to his comrades, with an expanded grin. The youth giggled. The clergyman met the attack with serenity, waited a moment and then responded : —

"Well, in one sense, I don't mind saying — yes."

"Well," said the Irishman, still full of mirth, and

swinging his legs with fresh vigor, "he'd aht to 'a' sint ye to the ligislatur."

"I'm in hopes he will," said the little rector; "but" — checking the Irishman's renewed laughter — "tell me why should other men's injustice in here stop me from preaching God's mercy?"

"Because it's pairt *your* injustice! Ye *do* come from yer cherch, an' ye *do* come from the community, an' ye can't deny ud, an' ye'd ahtn't to be comin' in here with yer sweet tahk and yer eyes tight shut to the crimes that's bein' committed ag'in uz for want of an outcry against 'em by you preachers an' prayers an' thract-disthributors." The speaker ceased and nodded fiercely. Then a new thought occurred to him, and he began again abruptly: —

"Look ut here! Ye said in yer serrmon that as to Him" — he pointed through the broken ceiling — "we're all criminals alike, didn't ye?"

"I did," responded the preacher, in a low tone.

"Yes," said Ristofalo; and the boy echoed the same word.

"Well, thin, what rights has some to be out an' some to be in?"

"Only one right that I know of," responded the little man; "still that is a good one."

"And that is — ?" prompted the Irishman.

"Society's right to protect itself."

"Yes," said the prisoner, "to protect itself. Thin what right has it to keep a prison like this, where every man an' woman as goes out of ud goes out a blacker devil, and cunninger devil, and a more dangerous devil, nor when he came in? Is that anny protection? Why shouldn't such a prison tumble down upon the heads of thim as built it? Say."

"I expect you'll have to ask somebody else," said the rector. He rose.

"Ye're not a-goun'!" exclaimed the Irishman, in broad affectation of surprise.

"Yes."

"Ah! come, now! Ye're not goun' to be beat that a-way by a wild Mick o' the woods?" He held himself ready for a laugh.

"No, I'm coming back," said the smiling clergyman, and the laugh came.

"That's right! But"—as if the thought was a sudden one—"I'll be dead by thin, willn't I? Of coorse I will."

"Yes?" rejoined the clergyman. "How's that?"

The Irishman turned to the Italian.

"Mr. Ristofalo, we're a-goin to the pinitintiary, aint we?"

Ristofalo nodded.

"Of coorse we air! Ah! Mr. Preechur, that's the place!"

"Worse than this?"

"Worse? Oh, no! It's better. This is slow death, but that's quick and short—and sure. If it don't git ye in five year', ye're ar allygatur. This place? It's heaven to ud!"

CHAPTER XLIII.

SHALL SHE COME OR STAY?

RICHLING read Mary's letter through three times without a smile. The feeling that he had prompted the missive — that it was partly his — stood between him and a tumult of gladness. And yet when he closed his eyes he could see Mary, all buoyancy and laughter, spurning his claim to each and every stroke of the pen. It was all hers, all!

As he was slowly folding the sheet Mrs. Reisen came in upon him. It was one of those excessively warm spring evenings that sometimes make New Orleans fear it will have no May. The baker's wife stood with her immense red hands thrust into the pockets of an expansive pinafore, and her three double chins glistening with perspiration. She bade her manager a pleasant good-evening.

Richling inquired how she had left her husband.

"Kviet, Mr. Richlin', kviet. Mr. Richlin', I pelief Reisen kittin petter. If he don't gittin' better, how come he'ss every day a little more kvieter, and sit' still and don't say nutting to nobody?"

"Mrs. Reisen, my wife is asking me to send for her" — Richling gave the folded letter a little shake as he held it by one corner — "to come down here and live again."

"Now, Mr. Richlin'?"

"Yes."

"Well, I will shwear!" She dropped into a seat.

"Right in de bekinning o' summer time! Vell, vell, vell! And you told me Mrs. Richling is a sentsible voman! Vell, I don't belief dat I efer see a young voman w'at aint de pickest kind o' fool apowt her huss-bandt! Vell, vell!—And she comin' down heah 'n' choost kittin' all your money shpent, 'n' den her mudter kittin' vorse 'n' she got 'o go pack akin!"

"Why, Mrs. Reisen," exclaimed Richling, warmly, "you speak as if you didn't want her to come." He contrived to smile as he finished.

"Vell,—of—course! *You* don't vant her to come, do you?"

Richling forced a laugh.

"Seems to me 'twould be natural if I did, Mrs. Reisen. Didn't the preacher say, when we were married, 'Let no man put asunder'?"

"Oh, now, Mr. Richlin', dere aindt nopotty a-koin' to put you under!—'less'n it's your vife. Vot she want to come down for? Don't I takin' koot care you?" There was a tear in her eye as she went out.

An hour or so later the little rector dropped in.

"Richling, I came to see if I did any damage the last time I was here. My own words worried me."

"You were afraid," responded Richling, "that I would understand you to recommend me to send for my wife."

"Yes."

"I didn't understand you so."

"Well, my mind's relieved."

"Mine isn't," said Richling. He laid down his pen and gathered his fingers around one knee. "Why shouldn't I send for her?"

"You will, some day."

"But I mean now."

The clergyman shook his head pleasantly.

"I don't think that's what you mean."

"Well, let that pass. I know what I do mean. I mean to get out of this business. I've lived long enough with these savages." A wave of his hand indicated the whole *personnel* of the bread business.

"I would try not to mind their savageness, Richling," said the little preacher, slowly. "The best of us are only savages hid under a harness. If we're not, we've somehow made a loss. Richling looked at him with amused astonishment, but he persisted. "I'm in earnest! We've had something refined out of us that we shouldn't have parted with. Now, there's Mrs. Reisen. I like her. She's a good woman. If the savage can stand you, why can't you stand the savage?"

"Yes, true enough. Yet — well, I must get out of this, anyway."

The little man clapped him on the shoulder.

"*Climb* out. See here, you Milwaukee man," — he pushed Richling playfully, — "what are *you* doing with these Southern notions of ours about the ' yoke of menial service,' anyhow?"

"I was not born in Milwaukee," said Richling.

"And you'll not die with these notions, either," retorted the other. "Look here, I am going. Good-by. You've got to get rid of them, you know, before your wife comes. I'm glad you are not going to send for her now."

"I didn't say I wasn't."

"I wouldn't."

"Oh, you don't know what you'd do," said Richling.

The little preacher eyed him steadily for a moment, and then slowly returned to where he still sat holding his knee.

They had a long talk in very quiet tones. At the end the rector asked : —

" Didn't you once meet Dr. Sevier's two nieces — at his house?"

" Yes," said Richling.

" Do you remember the one named Laura? — the dark, flashing one?"

" Yes."

" Well, — oh, pshaw! I could tell you something funny, but I don't care to do it."

What he did not care to tell was, that she had promised him five years before to be his wife any day when he should say the word. In all that time, and this very night, one letter, one line almost, and he could have ended his waiting; but he was not seeking his own happiness.

They smiled together. " Well, good-by again. Don't think I'm always going to persecute you with my solicitude."

" I'm not worth it," said Richling, slipping slowly down from his high stool and letting the little man out into the street.

A little way down the street some one coming out of a dark alley just in time to confront the clergyman extended a hand in salutation.

" Good-evenin', Mr. Blank."

He took the hand. It belonged to a girl of eighteen, bareheaded and barefooted, holding in the other hand a small oil-can. Her eyes looked steadily into his.

" You don't know me," she said, pleasantly.

" Why, yes, now I remember you. You're Maggie."

" Yes," replied the girl. " Don't you recollect — in the mission-school? Don't you recollect you married me and Larry? That's two years ago." She almost laughed out with pleasure.

" And where's Larry?"

" Why, don't you recollect? He's on the sloop-o'-war

Preble." Then she added more gravely: "I aint seen him in twenty months. But I know he's all right. I aint a-scared about *that* — only if he's alive and well; yes, sir. Well, good-evenin', sir. Yes, sir; I think I'll come to the mission nex' Sunday — and I'll bring the baby, will I? All right, sir. Well, so long, sir. Take care of yourself, sir."

What a word that was! It echoed in his ear all the way home: "Take care of *yourself*." What boast is there for the civilization that refines away the unconscious heroism of the unfriended poor?

He was glad he had not told Richling all his little secret. But Richling found it out later from Dr. Sevier.

CHAPTER XLIV.

WHAT WOULD YOU DO?

THREE days Mary's letter lay unanswered. About
dusk of the third, as Richling was hurrying across
the yard of the bakery on some errand connected with the
establishment, a light touch was laid upon his shoulder;
a peculiar touch, which he recognized in an instant. He
turned in the gloom and exclaimed, in a whisper:—

"Why, Ristofalo!"

"Howdy?" said Raphael, in his usual voice.

"Why, how did you get out?" asked Richling. "Have
you escaped?"

"No. Just come out for little air. Captain of the
prison and me. Not captain, exactly; one of the keepers.
Goin' back some time to-night." He stood there in his
old-fashioned way, gently smiling, and looking as immovable as a piece of granite. "Have you heard from
wife lately?"

"Yes," said Richling. "But — why — I don't understand. You and the jailer out together?"

"Yes, takin' a little stroll 'round. He's out there in
the street. You can see him on door-step 'cross yonder.
Pretty drunk, eh?" The Italian's smile broadened for a
moment, then came back to its usual self again. "I jus'
lef' Kate at home. Thought I'd come see you a little
while."

"Return calls?" suggested Richling.

"Yes, return call. Your wife well?"

" Yes. But — why, this is the drollest " — He stopped short, for the Italian's gravity indicated his opinion that there had been enough amusement shown. " Yes, she's well, thank you. By-the-by, what do you think of my letting her come out here now and begin life over again? Doesn't it seem to you it's high time, if we're ever going to do it at all?"

" What you think?" asked Ristofalo.

" Well, now, you answer my question first."

" No, you answer me first."

" I can't. I haven't decided. I've been three days thinking about it. It may seem like a small matter to hesitate so long over " — Richling paused for his hearer to dissent.

" Yes," said Ristofalo, " pretty small." His smile remained the same. " She ask you? Reckon you put her up to it, eh?"

" I don't see why you should reckon that," said Richling, with resentful coldness.

" I dunno," said the Italian; " thought so — that's the way fellows do sometimes." There was a pause. Then he resumed: " I wouldn't let her come yet. Wait."

" For what?"

" See which way the cat goin' to jump."

Richling laughed unpleasantly.

" What do you mean by that?" he inquired.

" We goin' to have war," said Raphael Ristofalo.

" Ho! ho! ho! Why, Ristofalo, you were never more mistaken in your life!"

" I dunno," replied the Italian, sticking in his tracks; " think it pretty certain. I read all the papers every day; nothin' else to do in parish prison. Think we see war nex' winter."

" Ristofalo, a man of your sort can hardly conceive

the amount of bluster this country can stand without coming to blows. We Americans are not like you Italians."

"No," responded Ristofalo, 'not much like." His smile changed peculiarly "Wasn't for Kate, I go to Italia now."

"Kate and the parish prison," said Richling.

"Oh!"—the old smile returned,—"I get out that place any time I want."

"And you'd join Garibaldi, I suppose?" The news had just come of Garibaldi in Sicily.

"Yes," responded the Italian. There was a twinkle deep in his eyes as he added: "I know Garibaldi."

"Indeed!"

"Yes. Sailed under him when he was ship-cap'n. He knows me."

"And I dare say he'd remember you," said Richling, with enthusiasm.

"He remember me," said the quieter man. "Well,—must go. Good-e'nin'. Better tell yo' wife wait a while."

"I—don't know. I'll see. Ristofalo"—

"What?"

"I want to quit this business."

"Better not quit. Stick to one thing."

"But you never did that. You never did one thing twice in succession."

"There's heap o' diff'ence."

"I don't see it. What is it?"

But the Italian only smiled and shrugged, and began to move away. In a moment he said:—

"You see, Mr. Richlin', you sen' for yo' wife, you can't risk change o' business. You change business, you can't risk sen' for yo' wife. Well, good-night."

Richling was left to his thoughts. Naturally they were

of the man whom he still saw, in his imagination, picking his jailer up off the door-step and going back to prison. Who could say that this man might not any day make just such a lion's leap into the world's arena as Garibaldi had made, and startle the nations as Garibaldi had done? What was that red-shirted scourge of tyrants that this man might not be? Sailor, soldier, hero, patriot, prisoner! See Garibaldi: despising the restraints of law; careless of the simplest conventionalities that go to make up an honest gentleman; doing both right and wrong — like a lion; everything in him leonine. All this was in Ristofalo's reach. It was all beyond Richling's. Which was best, the capability or the incapability? It was a question he would have liked to ask Mary.

Well, at any rate, he had strength now for one thing — "one pretty small thing." He would answer her letter. He answered it, and wrote: "Don't come; wait a little while." He put aside all those sweet lovers' pictures that had been floating before his eyes by night and day, and bade her stay until the summer, with its risks to health, should have passed, and she could leave her mother well and strong.

It was only a day or two afterward that he fell sick. It was provoking to have such a cold and not know how he caught it, and to have it in such fine weather. He was in bed some days, and was robbed of much sleep by a cough. Mrs. Reisen found occasion to tell Dr. Sevier of Mary's desire, as communicated to her by "Mr. Richlin'," and of the advice she had given him.

"And he didn't send for her, I suppose."

"No, sir."

"Well, Mrs. Reisen, I wish you had kept your advice to yourself." The Doctor went to Richling's bedside.

"Richling, why don t you send for your wife?"

The patient floundered in the bed and drew himself up on his pillow.

"O Doctor, just listen!" He smiled incredulously. "Bring that little woman and her baby down here just as the hot season is beginning?" He thought a moment, and then continued : "I'm afraid, Doctor, you're prescribing for homesickness. Pray don't tell me that's my ailment."

"No, it's not. You have a bad cough, that you must take care of ; but still, the other is one of the counts in your case, and you know how quickly Mary and — the little girl would cure it."

Richling smiled again.

"I can't do that, Doctor ; when I go to Mary, or send for her, on account of homesickness, it must be hers, not mine."

"Well, Mrs. Reisen," said the Doctor, outside the street door, "I hope you'll remember my request."

"I'll tdo udt, Dtoctor," was the reply, so humbly spoken that he repented half his harshness.

"I suppose you've often heard that 'you can't make a silk purse of a sow's ear,' haven't you?" he asked.

"Yes ; I pin right often heeard udt." She spoke as though she was not wedded to any inflexible opinion concerning the proposition.

"Well, Mrs. Reisen, as a man once said to me, 'neither can you make a sow's ear out of a silk purse.'"

"Vell, to be cettaintly!" said the poor woman, drawing not the shadow of an inference ; "how kin you?"

"Mr. Richling tells me he will write to Mrs. Richling to prepare to come down in the fall."

"Vell," exclaimed the delighted Mrs. Reisen, in her husband's best manner, "t'at's te etsectly I atwised him!" And, as the Doctor drove away, she rubbed her mighty hands around each other in restored complacency Two or three days later she had the additional pleasure of seeing Richling up and about his work again. It was upon her motherly urging that he indulged himself, one calm, warm afternoon, in a walk in the upper part of the city.

CHAPTER XLV.

NARCISSE WITH NEWS.

IT was very beautiful to see the summer set in. Trees everywhere. You looked down a street, and, unless it were one of the two broad avenues where the only street-cars ran, it was pretty sure to be so overarched with boughs that, down in the distance, there was left but a narrow streak of vivid blue sky in the middle. Well-nigh every house had its garden, as every garden its countless flowers. The dark orange began to show its growing weight of fruitfulness, and was hiding in its thorny interior the nestlings of yonder mocking-bird, silently foraging down in the sunny grass. The yielding branches of the privet were bowed down with their plumy panicles, and swayed heavily from side to side, drunk with gladness and plenty. Here the peach was beginning to droop over a wall. There, and yonder again, beyond, ranks of fig-trees, that had so muffled themselves in their foliage that not the nakedness of a twig showed through, had yet more figs than leaves. The crisp, cool masses of the pomegranate were dotted with scarlet flowers. The cape jasmine wore hundreds of her own white favors, whose fragrance forerun the sight. Every breath of air was a new perfume. Roses, an innumerable host, ran a fairy riot about all grounds, and clambered from the lowest door-step to the highest roof. The oleander, wrapped in one great garment of red blossoms, nodded in the sun, and stirred and winked in the faint stirrings of the air

The pale banana slowly fanned herself with her own broad leaf. High up against the intense sky, its hard, burnished foliage glittering in the sunlight, the magnolia spread its dark boughs, adorned with their queenly white flowers. Not a bird nor an insect seemed unmated. The little wren stood and sung to his sitting wife his loud, ecstatic song, made all of her own name, — Matilda, Urilda, Lucinda, Belinda, Adaline, Madaline, Caroline, or Melinda, as the case might be, — singing as though every bone of his tiny body were a golden flute. The humming-birds hung on invisible wings, and twittered with delight as they feasted on woodbine and honeysuckle. The pigeon on the roof-tree cooed and wheeled about his mate, and swelled his throat, and tremulously bowed and walked with a smiting step, and arched his purpling neck, and wheeled and bowed and wheeled again. Pairs of butter-flies rose in straight upward flight, fluttered about each other in amorous strife, and drifted away in the upper air. And out of every garden came the voices of little children at play, — the blessedest sound on earth.

" O Mary, Mary ! why should two lovers live apart on this beautiful earth? Autumn is no time for mating. Who can tell what autumn will bring?"

The revery was interrupted.

" M'stoo Itchlin, 'ow you enjoyin' yo' 'ealth in that beaucheous weatheh juz at the pwesent? Me, I'm well. Yes, I'm always well, in fact. At the same time nevva-theless, I fine myseff slightly sad. I s'pose 'tis natu'al — a man what love the 'itings of Lawd By'on as much as me. You know, of co'se, the melancholic intelligens?"

" No," said Richling ; " has any one " —

" Lady By'on, seh. Yesseh. ' In the mids' of life' — you know where we ah, Mistoo Itchlin, I su-pose?"

" Is Lady Byron dead?"

" Yesseh." Narcisse bowed solemnly. "Gone, Mistoo Itchlin. Since the seventeenth of last; yesseh. ' Kig the bucket,' as the povvub say." He showed an extra band of black drawn neatly around his new straw hat. "I thought it but p'opeh to put some moaning — as a species of twibute." He restored the hat to his head. "You like the tas'e of that, Mistoo Itchlin?"

Richling could but confess the whole thing was delicious.

"Yo humble servan', seh," responded the smiling Creole, with a flattered bow. Then, assuming a gravity becoming the historian, he said: —

"In fact, 'tis a gweat mistake, that statement that Lawd By'on evva qua'led with his lady, Mistoo Itchlin. But I s'pose you know 'tis but a slandeh of the pwess. Yesseh. As, faw instance, thass anotheh slandeh of the pwess that the delegates qua'led ad the Chawleston convention. They only pwetend to qua'l; so, by that way, to mizguide those Abolish-nists. Mistoo Itchlin, I am p'ojecting to 'ite some obitua' 'emawks about that Lady By'on, but I scass know w'etheh to 'ite them in the poetic style aw in the p'osaic. Which would you conclude, Mistoo Itchlin?"

Richling reflected with downcast eyes.

"It seems to me," he said, when he had passed his hand across his mouth in apparent meditation and looked up, — "seems to me I'd conclude both, without delay."

"Yes? But accawding to what fawmule, Mistoo Itchlin? ' Ay, 'tis theh is the 'ub,' in fact, as Lawd By'on say. Is it to migs the two style' that you advise?"

"That's the favorite method," replied Richling.

"Well, I dunno 'ow 'tis, Mistoo Itchlin, but I fine the moze facil'ty in the poetic. 'Tis t'ue, in the poetic you

got to look out concehning the *'ime*. You got to keep
the eye skin' faw it, in fact. But in the p'osaic, on the
cont'a-ay, 'tis juz the opposite; you got to keep the eye
skin' faw the *sense*. Yesseh. Now, if you migs the two
style' — well — 'ow's that, Mistoo Itchlin, if you migs
them? Seem' to me I dunno."

"Why, don't you see?" asked Richling. "If you
mix them, you avoid both necessities. You sail trium
phantly between Scylla and Charybdis without so much
as skinning your eye."

Narcisse looked at him a moment with a slightly searching glance, dropped his eyes upon his own beautiful feet,
and said, in a meditative tone : —

"I believe you co'ect." But his smile was gone, and
Richling saw he had ventured too far.

"I wish my wife were here," said Richling; "she
might give you better advice than I."

"Yes," replied Narcisse, "I believe you co'ect ag'in,
Mistoo Itchlin. 'Tis but since yeste'd'y that I jus appen
to hea' Dr. Seveah d'op a saying 'esembling to that.
Yesseh, she's a v'ey 'emawkable, Mistoo Itchlin."

"Is that what Dr. Sevier said?" Richling began to
fear an ambush.

"No, seh. What the Doctah say — 'twas me'ly to
'emawk in his jocose way — you know the Doctah's lill
callous, jocose way, Mistoo Itchlin."

He waved either hand outward gladsomely.

"Yes," said Richling, "I've seen specimens of it."

"Yesseh. He was ve'y complimenta'y, in fact, the
Doctah. 'Tis the trooth. He says, 'She'll make a man
of Witchlin if anythin' can.' Juz in his jocose way, you
know."

The Creole's smile had returned in concentrated sweetness   He stood silent, his face beaming with what

seemed his confidence that Richling would be delighted. Richling recalled the physician's saying concerning this very same little tale-bearer, — that he carried his nonsense on top and his good sense underneath.

"Dr. Sevier said that, did he?" asked Richling, after a time.

"'Tis the vehbatim, seh. Convussing to yo' 'eve'end fwend. You can ask him; he will co'obo'ate me in fact. Well, Mistoo Itchlin, it supp'ise me you not tickle at that. Me, I may say, I wish·I had a wife to make a man out of me."

"I wish you had," said Richling. But Narcisse smiled on.

"Well, *au 'evoi'*." He paused an instant with an earnest face. "Pehchance I'll meet you this evening, Mistoo Itchlin? Faw doubtless, like myseff, you will assist at the gweat a-ally faw the Union, the Const'ution, and the enfo'cemen' of the law. Dr. Seveah will ad-dwess."

"I don't know that I care to hear him," replied Richling.

"Goin' to be a gwan' out-po'-ing, Mistoo Itchlin. Citizens of Noo 'Leans without the leas' 'espec' faw fawmeh polly-tickle diff'ence. Also fiah-works. 'Come one, come all,' as says the gweat Scott — includin' yo'seff, Mistoo Itchlin. No? Well, *au 'evoi'*, Mistoo Itchlin."

CHAPTER XLVI.

A PRISON MEMENTO.

THE political pot began to seethe. Many yet wil. remember how its smoke went up. The summer — summer of 1860 — grew fervent. Its breath became hot and dry. All observation — all thought — turned upon the fierce campaign. Discussion dropped as to whether Heenan would ever get that champion's belt, which even the little rector believed he had fairly won in the international prize-ring. The news brought by each succeeding European steamer of Garibaldi's splendid triumphs in the cause of a new Italy, the fierce rattle of partisan warfare in Mexico, that seemed almost within hearing, so nearly was New Orleans concerned in some of its movements, — all things became secondary and trivial beside the developments of a political canvass in which the long-foreseen, long-dreaded issues between two parts of the nation were at length to be made final. The conventions had met, the nominations were complete, and the clans of four parties and fractions of parties were "meeting," and "rallying," and "uprising," and "outpouring."

All life was strung to one high pitch. This contest was everything, — nay, everybody, — men, women, and children. They were all for the Constitution; they were all for the Union; and each, even Richling, for the enforcement of — his own ideas. On every bosom, "no matteh the sex," and no matter the age, hung one of those little round, ribbanded medals, with a presidential candidate on one side and his vice-presidential man Friday on the other. Needless to say that Ristofalo's Kate, instructed by her husband, imported the earliest and many a later invoice of them, and distributing her peddlers at choice thronging-places, "everlastin'ly," as she laughingly and confidentially informed Dr. Sevier, "raked in the sponjewlicks." They were exposed for sale on little stalls on populous sidewalks and places of much entry and exit.

The post-office in those days was still on Royal street, in the old Merchants' Exchange. The small hand-holes of the box-delivery were in the wide tessellated passage that still runs through the building from Royal street to Exchange alley. A keeper of one of these little stalls established himself against a pillar just where men turned into and out of Royal street, out of or into this passage. One day, in this place, just as Richling turned from a delivery window to tear the envelope of a letter bearing the Milwaukee stamp, his attention was arrested by a man running by him toward Exchange alley, pale as death, and followed by a crowd that suddenly broke into a cry, a howl, a roar: "Hang him! Hang him!"

"Come!" said a small, strong man, seizing Richling's arm and turning him in the common direction. If the word was lost on Richling's defective hearing, not so the touch; for the speaker was Ristofalo. The two friends ran with all their speed through the passage and out into the alley. A few rods away the chased wretch had been overtaken, and was made to face his pursuers. When Richling and Ristofalo reached him there was already a rope about his neck.

The Italian's leap, as he closed in upon the group around the victim, was like a tiger's. The men ha

touched did not fall; they were rather hurled, driving
backward those whom they were hurled against. A man
levelled a revolver at him; Richling struck it a blow that
sent it over twenty men's heads. A long knife flashed in
Ristofalo's right hand. He stood holding the rope in his
left, stooping slightly forward, and darting his eyes about
as if selecting a victim for his weapon. A stranger
touched Richling from behind, spoke a hurried word in
Italian, and handed him a huge dirk. But in that same
moment the affair was over. There stood Ristofalo,
gentle. self-contained, with just a perceptible smile turned
upon the crowd, no knife in his hand, and beside him the
slender, sinewy, form, and keen gray eye of Smith Izard.

The detective was addressing the crowd. While he was
speaking, half a score of police came from as many directions. When he had finished, he waved his slender hand
at the mass of heads.

"Stand back. Go about your business." And they
began to go. He laid a hand upon the rescued stranger
and addressed the police.

"Take this rope off. Take th:s man to the station and
keep him until it's safe to let him go."

The explanation by which he had so quickly pacified
the mob was a simple one. The rescued man was a seller
of campaign medals. That morning, in opening a fresh
supply of his little stock, he had failed to perceive that,
among a lot of "Breckenridge and Lane" medals, there
had crept in one of Lincoln. That was the sum of his
offence. The mistake had occurred in the Northern fac-
tory. Of course, if he did not intend to sell Lincoln medals,
there was no crime.

"Don't I tell you?" said the Italian to Richling, as
they were walking away together. "Bound to have war:
is already begin-n."

" It began with me the day I got married," said Richling.

Ristofalo waited some time, and then asked : —

" How?'

" I shouldn't have said so," replied Richling ; " I can't explain."

" Thass all right," said the other. And, a little later: " Smith Izard call' you by name. How he know yo' name?"

" I can't imagine!"

The Italian waved his hand.

" Thass all right, too; nothin' to me." Then, after another pause : " Think you saved my life to-day."

" The honors are easy," said Richling.

He went to bed again for two or three days. He liked it little when Dr. Sevier attributed the illness to a few moments' violent exertion and excitement.

" It was bravely done, at any rate, Richling," said the Doctor.

" *That* it was ! " said Kate Ristofalo, who had happened to call to see the sick man at the same hour. " Doctor, ye'r mighty right ! Ha ! "

Mrs. Reisen expressed a like opinion, and the two kind women met the two men's obvious wish by leaving the room.

" Doctor," said Richling at once, " the last time you said it was love-sickness; this time you say it's excitement ; at the bottom it isn't either. Will you please tell me what it really is? What is this thing that puts me here on my back this way?"

" Richling," replied the Doctor, slowly, " if I tell you the honest truth, it began in that prison."

The patient knit his hands under his head and lay motionless and silent.

" Yes," he said, after a time.   And by and by again :
" Yes ; I feared as much.   And can it be that my *physical*
manhood is going to fail me at such a time as this ? "   He
drew a long breath and turned restively in the bed.

" We'll try to keep it from doing that," replied the
physician.   " I've told you this, Richling, old fellow, to
impress upon you the necessity of keeping out of all this
hubbub, — this night-marching and mass-meeting and
exciting nonsense."

" And am I always — always to be blown back — blown
back this way ? " said Richling, half to himself, half to his
friend.

" There, now," responded the Doctor, " just stop talking entirely.   No, no ; not always blown back.   A sick
man always thinks the present moment is the whole boundless future.   Get well.   And to that end possess your
soul in patience.   No newspapers.   Read your Bible.   It
will calm you.   I've been trying it myself."   His tone was
full of cheer, but it was also so motherly and the touch so
gentle with which he put back the sick man's locks — as
if they had been a lad's — that Richling turned away his
face with chagrin.

" Come ! " said the Doctor, more sturdily, laying his
hand on the patient's shoulder.   " You'll not lie here
more than a day or two.   Before you know it summer
will be gone, and you'll be sending for Mary."

Richling turned again, put out a parting hand, and
smiled with new courage.

CHAPTER XLVII.

NOW I LAY ME —

TIME may drag slowly, but it never drags backward. So the summer wore on, Richling following his physician's directions; keeping to his work only — out of public excitements and all overstrain; and to every day, as he bade it good-by, his eager heart, lightened each time by that much, said, " When you come around again. next year, Mary and I will meet you hand in hand." This was *his* excitement, and he seemed to flourish on it.

But day by day, week by week, the excitements of the times rose. Dr. Sevier was deeply stirred, and ever on the alert, looking out upon every quarter of the political sky, listening to the rising thunder, watching the gathering storm. There could hardly have been any one more completely engrossed by it. If there was, it was his book-keeper. It wasn't so much the Constitution that enlisted Narcisse's concern; nor yet the Union, which seemed to him safe enough; much less did the desire to see the enforcement of the laws consume him. Nor was it altogether the " 'oman candles " and the " 'ockets " ; but the rhetoric.

Ah, the " 'eto'ic" ! He bathed, he paddled, dove, splashed, in a surf of it.

" Doctah," — shaking his finely turned shoulders into his coat and lifting his hat toward his head, — " I had the honah, and at the same time the pleasu', to yeh you make a shawt speech lass evening. I was p'oud to yeh yo' bunning eloquence, Doctah,— if you'll allow. Yesseh. Eve'ybody said 'twas the moze bilious effo't of the o'-ca-sion."

Dr. Sevier actually looked up and smiled, and thanked the happy young man for the compliment.

" Yesseh," continued his admirer, "I nevveh flatteh. I give me'-it where the me'-it lies. Well, seh, we juz make the welkin 'ing faw joy when you finally stop' at the en'. Pehchance you heard my voice among that sea of head' ? But I doubt — in 'such a vas' up'ising — so many imposing pageant', in fact, — and those 'ocket' exploding in the staw-y heaven', as they say. I think I like that exp'ession I saw on the newzpapeh, wheh it says : ' Long biffo the appointed owwa, thousan' of flashing tawches and tas'eful t'anspa'encies with divuz devices whose blazing effulgence turn' day into night.' Thass a ve'y talented style, in fact. Well, *au 'evoi'*, Doctah. I'm going ad the — an' thass anotheh thing I like — 'tis faw the ladies to 'ing bells that way on the balconies. Because Mr. Bell and Eve'et is name *bell*, and so is the *bells* name' juz the same way, and so they 'ing the *bells* to signify. I had to elucidate that to my hant. Well, *au 'evoi'*, Doctah."

The Doctor raised his eyes from his letter-writing. The young man had turned, and was actually going out without another word. What perversity moved the phy-sician no one will ever know ; but he sternly called : —

" Narcisse? "

The Creole wheeled about on the threshold.

" Yesseh? "

The Doctor held him with a firm, grave eye, and slowly said : —

" I suppose before you return you will go to the post office." He said nothing more, — only that, just in his loose way, — and dropped his eyes again upon his pen. Narcisse gave him one long black look, and silently went out.

But a sweet complacency could not stay long away from the young man's breast. The world was too beautiful, the white, hot sky above was in such fine harmony with his puffed lawn shirt-bosom and his white linen pantaloons, bulging at the thighs and tapering at the ankles, and at the corner of Canal and Royal streets he met so many members of the Yancey Guards and Southern Guards and Chalmette Guards and Union Guards and Lane Dragoons and Breckenridge Guards and Douglas Rangers and Everett Knights, and had the pleasant trouble of stepping aside and yielding the pavement to the far-spreading crinoline. Oh, life was one scintillating cluster breast-pin of ecstasies! And there was another thing, — General William Walker's filibusters! Royal street, St. Charles, the rotunda of the St. Charles Hotel, were full of them.

It made Dr. Sevier both sad and fierce to see what hold their lawless enterprise took upon the youth of the city. Not that any great number were drawn into the movement, least of all Narcisse; but it captivated their interest and sympathy, and heightened the general unrest, when calmness was what every thoughtful man saw to be the country's greatest need.

An incident to illustrate the Doctor's state of mind.

It occurred one evening in the St. Charles rotunda. He saw some citizens of high standing preparing to drink at the bar with a group of broad-hatted men, whose bronzed foreheads and general out-of-door mien hinted rather ostentatiously of Honduras and Ruatan Island. As he passed close to them one of the citizens faced him blandly, and unexpectedly took his hand, but quickly let 't go again. The rest only glanced at the Doctor, and drew nearer to the bar.

"I trust you're not unwell, Doctor," said the sociable one, with something of a smile, and something of a frown, at the tall physician's gloomy brow.

"I am well, sir."

"I — didn't know," said the man again, throwing an aggressive resentment into his tone; "you seemed preoccupied."

"I was," replied the Doctor, returning his glance with so keen an eye that the man smiled again, appeasingly. "I was thinking how barely skin-deep civilization is."

The man ha-ha'd artificially, stepping backward as he said, "That's so!" He looked after the departing Doctor an instant and then joined his companions.

Richling had a touch of this contagion. He looked from Garibaldi to Walker and back again, and could not see any enormous difference between them. He said as much to one of the bakery's customers, a restaurateur with a well-oiled tongue, who had praised him for his intrepidity in the rescue of the medal-peddler, which, it seems, he had witnessed. With this praise still upon his lips the caterer walked with Richling to the restaurant door, and detained him there to enlarge upon the subject of Spanish-American misrule, and the golden rewards that must naturally fall to those who should supplant it with stable government. Richling listened and replied and replied again and listened; and presently the restaurateur startled him with an offer to secure him a captain's commission under Walker. He laughed incredulously; but the restaurateur, very much in earnest, talked on; and by littles, but rapidly, Richling admitted the value of the various considerations urged. Two or three months of rapid adventure; complete physical renovation — of course

— natural sequence; the plaudits of a grateful people; maybe fortune also, but at least a certainty of finding the road to it, — all this to meet Mary with next fall.

"I'm in a great hurry just now," said Richling; "but I'll talk about this thing with you again to-morrow or next day," and so left.

The restaurateur turned to his head-waiter, stuck his tongue in his cheek, and pulled down the lower lid of an eye with his forefinger. He meant to say he had been lying for the pure fun of it.

When Dr. Sevier came that afternoon to see Reisen — of whom there was now but little left, and that little unable to leave the bed — Richling took occasion to raise the subject that had entangled his fancy. He was careful to say nothing of himself or the restaurateur, or anything, indeed, but a timid generality or two. But the Doctor responded with a clear, sudden energy that, when he was gone, left Richling feeling painfully blank, and yet unable to find anything to resent except the Doctor's superfluous — as he thought, quite superfluous — mention of the island of Cozumel.

However, and after all, that which for the most part kept the public mind heated was, as we have said, the political campaign. Popular feeling grew tremulous with it as the landscape did under the burning sun. It was a very hot summer. Not a good one for feeble folk; and one early dawn poor Reisen suddenly felt all his reason come back to him, opened his eyes, and lo! he had crossed the river in the night, and was on the other side.

Dr. Sevier's experienced horse halted of his own will to let a procession pass. In the carriage at its head the physician saw the little rector, sitting beside a man of German ecclesiastical appearance. Behind it followed a majestic hearse, drawn by black-plumed and caparisoned

horses, — four of them. Then came a ong line of red-
shirted firemen; for he in the hearse had been an
" exempt." Then a further line of big-handed, white-
gloved men in beavers and regalias; for he had been also
a Freemason and an Odd-fellow. Then another column,
of emotionless-visaged German women, all in bunchy black
gowns, walking out of time to the solemn roll and pulse
of the muffled drums, and the brazen peals of the funeral
march. A few carriages closed the long line. In the
first of them the waiting Doctor marked, with a sudden
understanding of all, the pale face of John Richling, and
by his side the widow who had been forty years a wife,—
weary and red with weeping. The Doctor took off his
hat.

CHAPTER XLVIII.

RISE UP, MY LOVE, MY FAIR ONE !

THE summer at length was past, and the burning heat was over and gone. The days were refreshed with the balm of a waning October. There had been no fever. True, the nights were still aglare with torches, and the street echoes kept awake by trumpet notes and huzzas, by the tramp of feet and the delicate hint of the bell-ringing ; and men on the stump and off it ; in the "wigwams ;" along the sidewalks, as they came forth, wiping their mouths, from the free-lunch counters, and on the curbstones and "flags" of Carondelet street, were saying things to make a patriot's heart ache. But contrariwise, in that same Carondelet street, and hence in all the streets of the big, scattered town, the most prosperous commercial year — they measure from September to September — that had ever risen upon New Orleans had closed its distended record, and no one knew or dreamed that, for nearly a quarter of a century to come, the proud city would never see the equal of that golden year just gone. And so, away yonder among the great lakes on the northern border of the anxious but hopeful country, Mary was calling, calling, like an unseen bird piping across the fields for its mate, to know if she and the one little nestling might not come to hers.

And at length, after two or three unexpected contingencies had caused delays of one week after another, all

in a silent tremor of joy, John wrote the word —
" Come ! "

He was on his way to put it into the post-office, in
Royal street. At the newspaper offices, in Camp street,
he had to go out into the middle of the way to get around
the crowd that surrounded the bulletin-boards, and that
scuffled for copies of the latest issue. The day of days
was passing ; the returns of election were coming in. In
front of the " Picayune " office he ran square against a
small man, who had just pulled himself and the most of
his clothing out of the press with the last news crumpled
in the hand that he still held above his head.

" Hello, Richling, this is pretty exciting, isn't it ? " It
was the little clergyman. " Come on, I'll go your way ;
let's get out of this."

He took Richling's arm, and they went on down the
street, the rector reading aloud as they walked, and shop-
keepers and salesmen at their doors catching what they
could of his words as the two passed.

" It's dreadful ! dreadful ! " said the little man, thrusting the paper into his pocket in a wad.

" Hi ! Mistoo Itchlin," quoth Narcisse, passing them
like an arrow, on his way to the paper offices.

" He's happy," said Richling.

" Well, then, he's the only happy man I know of in
New Orleans to-day," said the little rector, jerking his
head and drawing a sigh through his teeth.

" No," said Richling, " I'm another. You see this
letter." He showed it with the direction turned down.
" I'm going now to mail it. When my wife gets it she
starts."

The preacher glanced quickly into his face. Richling
met his gaze with eyes that danced with suppressed joy.
The two friends attracted no attention from those whom

they passed or who passed them; the newsboys were scampering here and there, everybody buying from them, and the walls of Common street ringing with their shouted proffers of the "full account" of the election.

"Richling, don't do it."

"Why not?" Richling showed only amusement.

"For several reasons," replied the other. "In the first place, look at your business!"

"Never so good as to-day."

"True. And it entirely absorbs you. What time would you have at your fireside, or even at your family table? None. It's — well you know what it is — it's a bakery, you know. You couldn't expect to lodge *your* wife and little girl in a bakery in Benjamin street; you know you couldn't. Now, *you* — you don't mind it — or, I mean, you can stand it. Those things never need damage a gentleman. But with your wife it would be different. You smile, but — why, you know she couldn't go there. And if you put her anywhere where a lady ought to be, in New Orleans, she would be — well, don't you see she would be about as far away as if she were in Milwaukee? Richling, I don't know how it looks to you for me to be so meddlesome, and I believe you think I'm making a very poor argument; but you see this is only one point and the smallest. Now" —

Richling raised his thin hand, and said pleasantly : —

"It's no use. You can't understand; it wouldn't be possible to explain; for you simply don't know Mary."

"But there are some things I do know. Just think; she's with her mother where she is. Imagine her falling ill here, — as you've told me she used to do, — and you with that bakery on your hands."

Richling looked grave.

"Oh no," continued the little man. "You've been so

brave and patient, you and your wife, both, — do be so a little bit longer! Live close; save your money; go on rising in value in your business; and after a little you'll rise clear out of the sphere you're now in. You'll command your own time; you'll build your own little home; and life and happiness and usefulness will be fairly and broadly open before you." Richling gave heed with a troubled face, and let his companion draw him into the shadow of that "St. Charles" from the foot of whose stair-way he had once been dragged away as a vagrant.

"See, Richling! Every few weeks you may read in some paper of how a man on some ferry-boat jumps for the wharf before the boat has touched it, falls into the water, and — Make sure! Be brave a little longer — only a little longer! Wait till you're sure!"

"I'm sure enough!"

"Oh, no, you're not! Wait till this political broil is over. They say Lincoln is elected. If so, the South is not going to submit to it. Nobody can tell what the consequences are to be. Suppose we should have war? I don't think we shall, but suppose we should? There would be a general upheaval, commercial stagnation, industrial collapse, shrinkage everywhere! Wait till it's over. It may not be two weeks hence; it can hardly be more than ninety days at the outside. If it should the North would be ruined, and you may be sure they are not going to allow *that*. Then, when all starts fair again, bring your wife and baby. I'll tell you what to do, Richling!"

"Will you?" responded the listener, with an amiable laugh, that the little man tried to echo.

"Yes. Ask Dr. Sevier! He's right here in the next

street. He was on your side last time; maybe he'll be so now."

"Done!" said Richling. They went. The rector said he would do an errand in Canal street, while Richling should go up and see the physician.

Dr. Sevier was in.

"Why, Richling!" He rose to receive him. "How are you?" He cast his eye over his visitor with professional scrutiny. "What brings *you* here?"

"To tell you that I've written for Mary," said Richling, sinking wearily into a chair.

"Have you mailed the letter?"

"I'm taking it to the post-office now."

The Doctor threw one leg energetically over the other, and picked up the same paper-knife that he had handled when, two years and a half before, he had sat thus, talking to Mary and John on the eve of their separation.

"Richling, I'll tell you. I've been thinking about this thing for some time, and I've decided to make you a proposal. I look at you and at Mary and at the times — the condition of the country — the probable future — everything. I know you, physically and mentally, better than anybody else does. I can say the same of Mary. So, of course, I don't make this proposal impulsively, and I don't want it rejected.

"Richling, I'll lend you two thousand to twenty-five hundred dollars, payable at your convenience, if you will just go to your room, pack up, go home, and take from six to twelve months' holiday with your wife and child."

The listener opened his mouth in blank astonishment.

"Why, Doctor, you're jesting! You can't suppose" —

"I don't suppose anything. I simply want you to do it."

"Well, I simply can't!"

" Did you ever regret taking my advice, Richling ? "

" No, never. But this — why, it's utterly impossible ! Me leave the results of four years' struggle to go holidaying? I can't understand you, Doctor."

" 'Twould take weeks to explain."

" It's idle to think of it," said Richling, half to himself.

" Go home and think of it twenty-four hours," said the Doctor.

" It is useless, Doctor."

" Very good, then ; send for Mary. Mail your letter."

" You don't mean it ! " said Richling.

" Yes, I do. Send for Mary ; and tell her I advised it." He turned quickly away to his desk, for Richling's eyes had filled with tears ; but turned again and rose as Richling rose. They joined hands.

" Yes, Richling, send for her. It's the right thing to do — if you will not do the other. You know I want you to be happy."

" Doctor, one word. In your opinion is there going to be war ? "

" I don't know. But if there is it's time for husband and wife and child to draw close together. Good-day."

And so the letter went

CHAPTER XLIX.

A BUNDLE OF HOPES.

RICHLING insisted, in the face of much scepticism on the part of the baker's widow, that he felt better, was better, and would go on getting better, now that the weather was cool once more.

"Well, I hope you vill, Mr. Richlin', dtat's a fect. 'Specially ven yo' vife comin'. Dough I could a-tooken care ye choost tso koot as vot she couldt."

"But maybe you couldn't take care of her as well as I tan," said the happy Richling.

"Oh, tdat's a tdifferendt. A voman kin tek care terself."

Visiting the French market on one of these glad mornngs, as his business often required him to do, he fell in with Narcisse, just withdrawing from the celebrated coffee-stand of Rose Nicaud. Richling stopped in the moving crowd and exchanged salutations very willingly; for here was one more chance to hear himself tell the fact of Mary's expected coming.

"So'y, Mistoo Itchlin," said Narcisse, whipping away the pastry crumbs from his lap with a handkerchief and wiping his mouth, "not to encounteh you a lill biffo', to join in pahtaking the cup what cheeahs at the same time whilce it invigo'ates; to-wit, the coffee-cup — as the maxim say. I dunno by what fawmule she makes that coffee, but 'tis astonishin' how 'tis good, in fact. I dunne if you'll billieve me, but I feel almost I could pahtake anotheh cup — ? 'Tis the tooth." He gave Richling time to make any handsome offer that might spontaneously suggest itself, but seeing that the response was only an over-gay expression of face, he added, " But I conclude no. In fact, Mistoo Itchlin, thass a thing I have dis- covud, — that too much coffee millytates ag'inst the chi'og'aphy ; and thus I abstain. Well, seh, ole Abe is elected."

" Yes," rejoined Richling, " and there's no telling what the result will be."

" You co'ect, Mistoo Itchlin." Narcisse tried to look troubled.

" I've got a bit of private news that I don't think you've heard," said Richling. And the Creole rejoined promptly : —

" Well, I *thought* I saw something on yo' thoughts — if you'll excuse my tautology. Thass a ve'y diffycult to p'event sometime'. But, Mistoo Itchlin, I trus' 'tis not you 'ave allowed somebody to swin'le you ? — confiding them too indiscweetly, in fact ? " He took a pretty attitude, his eyes reposing in Richling's.

Richling laughed outright.

" No, nothing of that kind. No, I " —

" Well, I'm ve'y glad," interrupted Narcisse.

" Oh, no, 'tisn't trouble at all ! I've sent for Mrs. Richling. We're going to resume housekeeping."

Narcisse gave a glad start, took his hat off, passed it to his left hand, extended his right, bowed from the middle with princely grace, and, with joy breaking all over his face, said : —

" Mistoo Itchlin, in fact, — shake ! "

They shook.

" Yesseh — an' many 'appy 'eturn ! I dunno if you kin billieve that, M'stoo Itchlin ; but I was juz about to 'ead that in yo' physio'nomie! Yesseh. But, Mistoo Itchlin, when shall the happy o'casion take effect?"

"Pretty soon. Not as soon as I thought, for I got a despatch yesterday, saying her mother is very ill, and of course I telegraphed her to stay till her mother is at least convalescent. But I think that will be soon. Her mother has had these attacks before. I have good hopes that before long Mrs. Richling will actually be here."

Richling began to move away down the crowded market-house, but Narcisse said: —

"Thass yo' di'ection? 'Tis the same, mine. We may accompany togetheh — if you'll allow yo' 'umble suvvant?"

"Come along! You do me honor!" Richling laid his hand on Narcisse's shoulder and they went at a gait quickened by the happy husband's elation. Narcisse was very proud of the touch, and, as they began to traverse the vegetable market, took the most populous arcade.

"Mistoo Itchlin," he began again, "I muz congwatu*late* you! You know I always admiah yo' lady to excess. But appopo of that news, I might infawm you some intelligens consunning myseff."

"Good!" exclaimed Richling. "For it's good news, isn't it?"

"Yesseh, — as you may say, — yes. Faw in fact, Mistoo Itchlin, I 'ave ass Dr. Seveeah to haugment me."

"Hurrah!" cried Richling. He coughed and laughed and moved aside to a pillar and coughed, until people looked at him, and lifted his eyes, tired but smiling, and, paying his compliments to the paroxysm in or e or two illwishes, wiped his eyes at last, and said: —

"And the Doctor augmented you?"

"Well, no, I can't say that — not p'ecisely "

"Why, what did he do?"

" Well, he 'efuse' me, in fact."

" Why — but that isn't good news, then. '

Narcisse gave his head a bright, argumentative twitch.

" Yesseh. 'Tis t'ue he 'efuse'; but ad the same time — I dunno — I thing he wasn' so mad about it as he make out. An' you know thass one thing, Mistoo Itchlin, whilce they got life they got hope; and hence I ente'tain the same."

They had reached that flagged area without covering or inclosure, before the third of the three old market-houses, where those dealers in the entire miscellanies of a house-wife's equipment, excepting only stoves and furniture, spread their wares and fabrics in the open weather before the Bazar market rose to give them refuge. He grew suddenly fierce.

" But any'ow I don't care! I had the spunk to ass 'im, an' he din 'ave the spunk to dischawge me! All he can do, 'tis to shake the fis' of impatience." He was looking into his companion's face, as they walked, with an eye distended with defiance.

" Look out!" exclaimed Richling, reaching a hurried hand to draw him aside. Narcisse swerved just in time to avoid stepping into a pile of crockery, but in so doing went full into the arms of a stately female figure dressed in the crispest French calico and embarrassed with num-erous small packages of dry goods. The bundles flew hither and yon. Narcisse tried to catch the largest as he saw it going, but only sent it farther than it would have gone, and as it struck the ground it burst like a pome-granate. But the contents were white: little thin, square-folded fractions of barred jaconet and white flannel; rolls of slender white lutestring ribbon; very narrow papers of tiny white pearl buttons, minute white worsted socks.

spools of white floss, cards of safety-pins, pieces of white castile soap, etc.

" *Mille pardons, madame!* " exclaimed Narcisse; " I make you a thousan' poddons, madam! "

He was ill-prepared for the majestic wrath that flashed from the eyes and radiated from the whole dilating, and subsiding, and reëxpanding, and rising, and stiffening form of Kate Ristofalo!

"Officerr," she panted,— for instantly there was a crowd, and a man with the silver-crescent badge was switching the assemblage on the legs with his cane to make room,— " Officerr," she gasped, levelling her tremulous finger at Narcisse, " arrist that man! "

"Mrs. Ristofalo!" exclaimed Richling, "don't do that! It was all an accident! Why, don't you see it's Narcisse, —- my friend?"

" Yer frind rised his hand to sthrike me, sur, he did! Yer frind rised his hand to sthrike me, he did!" And up she went and down she went, shortening and lengthening, swelling and decreasing. " Yes, yes, I know yer frind; indeed I do! I paid two dollars and a half fur his acquaintans nigh upon three years agone, sur. Yer frind!" And still she went up and down, enlarging, diminishing, heaving her breath and waving her chin around, and saying, in broken utterances,— while a hackman on her right held his whip in her auditor's face, crying, " Carriage, sir? Carriage, sir?"—

" Why didn'— he rin agin— a man, sur! I— I— oh! I wish Mr. Ristofalah war heer!— to teach um how— to walk!— Yer frind, sur— ixposing me!" She pointed to Narcisse and the policeman gathering up the scattered lot of tiny things. Her eyes filled with tears, but still shot lightning. "If he's hurrted me, he's got 'o suffer fur ud, Mr. Richlin'!" And she expanded again,

"Carriage, sir, carriage?" continued the man with the whip.

"Yes!" said Richling and Mrs. Ristofalo in a breath. She took his arm, the hackman seized the bundles from the policeman, threw open his hack door, laid the bundles on the front seat, and let down the folding steps. The crowd dwindled away to a few urchins.

"Officerr," said Mrs. Ristofalo, her foot on the step and composure once more in her voice, "ye needn't arrist um. I could of done ud, sur," she added to Narcisse himself, "but I'm too much of a laydy, sur!" And she sank together and stretched herself up once more, entered the vehicle, and sat with a perpendicular back, her arms folded on her still heaving bosom, and her head high.

As to her ability to have that arrest made, Kate Ris tofalo was in error. Narcisse smiled to himself; for he was conscious of one advantage that overtopped all the sacredness of female helplessness, public right, or any other thing whatsoever. It lay in the simple fact that he was acquainted with the policeman. He bowed blandly to the officer, stepped backward, touching his hat, and walked away, the policeman imitating each movement with the promptness and faithfulness of a mirror.

"Aren't ye goin' to get in, Mr. Richlin'?" asked Mrs. Ristofalo. She smiled first and then looked alarmed.

"I — I can't very well — if you'll excuse me, ma'am."

"Ah, Mr. Richlin'!" — she pouted girlishly. "Gettin' proud!" She gave her head a series of movements, as to say she might be angry if she would, but she wouldn't. "Ye won't know uz when Mrs. Richlin' comes."

Richling laughed, but she gave a smiling toss to indicate that it was a serious matter.

"Come," she insisted, patting the seat beside her with honeyed persuasiveness, "come and tell me all about ud.

Mr. Ristofalah nivver goes into peticklers, an' so I har'ly know anny more than jist she's a-comin'. Come, git in an' tell me about Mrs. Richlin' — that is, if ye like the subject — and I don't believe ye do." She lifted her finger, shook it roguishly close to her own face, and looked at him sidewise. " Ah, nivver mind, sur! that's rright! Furgit yer old frinds — maybe ye wudden't do ud if ye knewn everythin'. But that's rright; that's the way with min." She suddenly changed to subdued earnestness, turne.l the catch of the door, and, as the door swung open, said : " Come, if ud's only fur a bit o' the way — if ud's only fur a ming-ute. I've got somethin' to tell ye.'

" I must get out at Washington Market," said Richling, as he got in. The hack hurried down Old Levee street.

" And now," said she, merriment dancing in her eyes, her folded arms tightening upon her bosom, and her lips struggling against their own smile, " I'm just a good mind not to tell ye at ahll! "

Her humor was contagious and Richling was ready to catch it. His own eye twinkled.

" W∧ll, Mrs. Ristofalo, of course, if you feel any embarrassment " —

" Ye villain! " she cried, with delighted indignation, " I didn't mean nawthing about *that*, an' ye knew ud! Here, git out o' this carridge! " But she made no effort to eject him.

" Mary and I are interested in all your hopes," said Richling, smiling softly upon the damaged bundle which he was making into a tight package again on his knee. " You'll tell me your good news if it's only that I may tell her, will you not? "

" *I* will. And it's joost this, — Mr. Richlin',— that if there be's a war Mr. Ristofalah's to be lit out o' prison."

" I'm very glad! " cried Richling, but stopped short,

for Mrs. Ristofalo's growing dignity indicated that there was more to be told.

"I'm sure ye air, Mr. Richlin'; and I'm sure ye'll be glad — a heap gladder nor I am — that in that case he's to be Captain Ristofalah."

"Indeed!"

'Yes, sur." The wife laid her palm against her floating ribs and breathed a sigh. "I don't like ud, Mr. Richlin'. No, sur. I don't like tytles." She got her fan from under her handkerchief and set it a-going. "I nivver liked the idee of bein' a tytled man's wife. No, sur." She shook her head, elevating it as she shook it. "It creates too much invy, Mr. Richlin'. Well, good-by." The carriage was stopping at the Washington Market. "Now, don't ye mintion it to a livin' soul, Mr. Richlin'!"

Richling said "No."

"No, sur; fur there be's manny a slip 'tuxt the cup an' the lip, ye know; an' there may be no war, after all, and we may all be disapp'inted. But he's bound to be tleared if he's tried, and don't ye see — I — I don't want um to be a captain, anyhow, don't ye see?"

Richling saw, and they parted.

.Thus everybody hoped. Dr. Sevier, wifeless, childless, had his hopes too, nevertheless. Hopes for the hospital and his many patients in it and out of it; hopes for his town and his State; hopes for Richling and Mary; and hopes with fears, and fears with hopes, for the great sisterhood of States. Richling had one hope more. After some weeks had passed Dr. Sevier ventured once more to say: —

"Richling, go home. Go to your wife. I must tell you you're no ordinary sick man. Your life is in danger."

" Will I be out of danger if I go home?" asked Richling.
Dr. Sevier made no answer.

" Do you still think we may have war?" asked Richling again.

" I know we shall."

" And will the soldiers come back," asked the young
man, smilingly, " when they find their lives in danger?"

" Now, Richling, that's another thing entirely; that's
the battle-field."

" Isn't it all the *same* thing, Doctor? Isn't it all a battle-field?"

The Doctor turned impatiently, disdaining to reply.
But in a moment he retorted: —

" We take wounded men off the field."

" They don't take themselves off," said Richling,
smiling.

" Well," rejoined the Doctor, rising and striding toward a window, " a good general may order a retreat."

" Yes, but — maybe I oughtn't to say what I was
thinking " —

" Oh, say it."

" Well, then, he don't let his surgeon order it. Doctor," continued Richling, smiling apologetically as his
friend confronted him, " you know, as you say, better
than any one else, all that Mary and I have gone through
— nearly all — and how we've gone through it. Now,
if my life should end here shortly, what would the whole
thing mean? It would mean nothing, Doctor;. it would
be meaningless. No, sir; this isn't the end. Mary and
I " — his voice trembled an instant and then was firm
again — " are designed for a long life. I argue from the
simple fitness of things, — this is not the end."

Dr Sevier turned his face quickly toward the window,
and so remained.

CHAPTER L.

FALL IN!

THERE came a sound of drums. Twice on such a day, once the day before, thrice the next day, till by and by it was the common thing. High-stepping childhood, with laths and broom-handles at shoulder, was not fated, as in the insipid days of peace, to find, on running to the corner, its high hopes mocked by a wagon of empty barrels rumbling over the cobble-stones. No; it was the Washington Artillery, or the Crescent Rifles, or the Orleans Battalion, or, best of all, the blue-jacketed, white-leggined, red-breeched, and red-fezzed Zouaves; or, better than the best, it was all of them together, their captains stepping backward, sword in both hands, calling "*Gauche! gauche!*" ("Left! left!") "Guide right!" —"*Portez armes!*" and facing around again, throwing their shining blades stiffly to belt and epaulette, and glancing askance from under their abundant plumes to the crowded balconies above. Yea, and the drum-majors before, and the brilliant-petticoated *vivandières* behind!

What pomp! what giddy rounds! Pennons, cock-feathers, clattering steeds, pealing salvos, banners, columns, ladies' favors, balls, concerts, toasts, the Free Gift Lottery — don't you recollect? — and this uniform and that uniform, brother a captain, father a colonel, uncle a major, the little rector a chaplain, Captain Risto-falo of the Tiger Rifles; the levee covered with munitions of war, steamboats unloading troops, troops, troops,

from Opelousas, Attakapas, Texas ; and a supper to this
company, a flag to that battalion, farewell sermon to the
Washington Artillery, tears and a kiss to a spurred and
sashed lover, hurried weddings, — no end of them, — a
sword to such a one, addresses by such and such, sere-
nades to Miss and to Mademoiselle.

Soon it will have been a quarter of a century ago!

And yet — do you not hear them now, coming down
the broad, granite-paved, moon-lit street, the light that
was made for lovers glancing on bayonet and sword soon
to be red with brothers' blood, their brave young hearts
already lifted up with the triumph of battles to come, and
the trumpets waking the midnight stillness with the gay
notes of the Cracovienne? —

> " Again, again, the pealing drum,
> The clashing horn, they come, they come,
> And lofty deeds and daring high
> Blend with their notes of victory."

Ah! the laughter; the music; the bravado; the dancing; the songs! "*Voilà l'Zouzou!*" "Dixie!" "*Aux
armes, vos citoyens!*" The Bonnie Blue Flag!" — it
wasn't bonnie very long. Later the maidens at home
learned to sing a little song, — it is among the missing
now, — a part of it ran: —

> " Sleeping on grassy couches ;
> Pillowed on hillocks damp ;
> Of martial fame how little we know
> Till brothers are in the camp."

By and by they began to depart. How many they
were! How many, many! We had too lightly let them
go. And when all were gone, and they of Carondelet
street and its tributaries, massed in that old gray, brittl ⤭

shanked regiment, the Confederate Guards, were having
their daily dress parade in Coliseum place, and only they
and the Foreign Legion remained; when sister Jane made
lint, and flour was high, and the sounds of commerce
were quite hushed, and in the custom-house gun-carriages
were a-making, and in the foundries big guns were being
cast, and the cotton gun-boats and the rams were building, and at the rotting wharves the masts of a few empty
ships stood like dead trees in a blasted wilderness, and
poor soldiers' wives crowded around the " Free Market,"
and grass began to spring up in the streets, — they were
many still, while far away; but some marched no more,
and others marched on bleeding feet, in rags; and it was
very, very hard for some of us to hold the voice steady
and sing on through the chorus of the little song: —

> " Brave boys are they!
>   Gone at their country's call.
> And yet — and yet — we cannot forget
>   That many brave boys must fall."

Oh! Shiloh, Shiloh!

But before the gloom had settled down upon us it was
a gay dream.

" Mistoo Itchlin, in fact 'ow you ligue my uniefawm?
You think it suit my style? They got about two poun'
of gole lace on that uniefawm. Yesseh. Me, the h-only
thing — I don' ligue those epaulette'. So soon ev'ybody
see that on me, 'tis ' Lieut'nan'!' in thiz place, an' ' Lieut-
'nan'!' in that place. My de'seh, you'd thing I'm a
majo'-gen'l, in fact. Well, of co'se, I don' ligue that."

" And so you're a lieutenant?"

" Third! Of the Chasseurs-á-Pied! Coon he'p 't, in
fact; the fellehs elected me. Goin' at Pensacola tomaw. Dr. Seveeah continue my sala'y whilce I'm gone,

no matteh the len'th. Me, I don' care, so long the sala'y
continue, if that waugh las' ten yeah! You ah pe'haps
goin' ad the ball to-nighd, Mistoo Itchlin? I dunno 'ow
'tis — I suppose you'll be aztonizh' w'en I infawm you —
that ball wemine me of that battle of Wattaloo! Did
you evva yeh those line' of Lawd By'on, —

> 'Theh was a soun' of wibalwy by night,
> W'en — 'Ush-'ark! — A deep saun' stwike' —?

Thaz by Lawd By'on. Yesseh. Well " —

The Creole lifted his right hand energetically, laid its
inner edge against the brass buttons of his *képi*, and
then waved it gracefully abroad : —

" *Au 'evoi*, Mistoo Itchlin. I leave you to defen' the
city."

" To-morrow," in those days of unreadiness and dis-
connection, glided just beyond reach continually. When
at times its realization was at length grasped, it was
away over on the far side of a fortnight or farther.
However, the to-morrow for Narcisse came at last.

A quiet order for attention runs down the column.
Attention it is. Another order follows, higher-keyed,
longer drawn out, and with one sharp " clack ! " the
sword-bayoneted rifles go to the shoulders of as fine a
battalion as any in the land of Dixie.

" *En avant !* " — Narcisse's heart stands still for joy —
" *Marche !* "

The bugle rings, the drums beat ; " tramp, tramp," in
quick succession, go the short-stepping, nimble Creole
feet, and the old walls of the Rue Chartres ring again
with the pealing huzza, as they rang in the days of Vil
leré and Lafrénière, and in the days of the young Galvez,
and in the days of Jackson.

The old Ponchartrain cars move off, packed. Down at the "Old Lake End" the steamer for Mobile receives the burden. The gong clangs in her engineroom, the walking-beam silently stirs, there is a hiss of water underneath, the gang-plank is in, the wet hawserends whip through the hawse-holes, — she moves ; clang goes the gong again — she glides — or is it the crowded wharf that is gliding? — No. — Snatch the kisses ! snatch them ! Adieu ! Adieu ! She's off, huzza — she's off !

Now she stands away. See the mass of gay colors — red, gold, blue, yellow, with glitter of steel and flutter of flags, a black veil of smoke sweeping over. Wave, mothers and daughters, wives, sisters, sweethearts — wave, wave ; you little know the future !

And now she is a little thing, her white wake following her afar across the green waters, the call of the bugle floating softly back. And now she is a speck. And now a little smoky stain against the eastern blue is all, — and now she is gone. Gone ! Gone !

Farewell, soldier boys ! Light-hearted, little-forecasting, brave, merry boys ! God accept you, our offering of first fruits ! See that mother — that wife — take them away ; it is too much. Comfort them, father, brother ; tell them their tears may be for naught.

> "And yet — and yet — we cannot forget
> That many brave boys must fall."

Never so glad a day had risen upon the head of Narcisse. For the first time in his life he moved beyond the corporate limits of his native town.

" ' Ezcape fum the aunt, thou sluggud !' "   " *Au 'evoï* " to his aunt and the uncle of his aunt. " *Au evoï* ! *Au 'evoï* !" — desk, pen, book — work, ca--

thought, restraint — all sinking, sinking beneath the receding horizon of Lake Ponchartrain, and the wide world and a soldier's life before him.

Farewell, Byronic youth! You are not of so frail a stuff as you have seemed. You shall thirst by day and hunger by night. You shall keep vigil on the sands of the Gulf and on the banks of the Potomac. You shall grow brown, but prettier. You shall shiver in loathsome tatters, yet keep your grace, your courtesy, your joyousness. You shall ditch and lie down in ditches, and shall sing your saucy songs of defiance in the face of the foe, so blackened with powder and dust and smoke that your mother in heaven would not know her child. And you shall borrow to your heart's content chickens, hogs, rails, milk, buttermilk, sweet potatoes, what not; and shall learn the American songs, and by the camp-fire of Shenandoah valley sing "The years creep slowly by, Lorena" to messmates with shaded eyes, and "Her bright smile haunts me still." Ah, boy! there's an old woman still living in the Rue Casa Calvo — your bright smile haunts her still. And there shall be blood on your sword, and blood — twice — thrice — on your brow. Your captain shall die in your arms; and you shall lead charge after charge, and shall step up from rank to rank; and all at once, one day, just in the final onset, with the cheer on your lips, and your red sword waving high, with but one lightning stroke of agony, down, down you shall go in the death of your dearest choice.

CHAPTER LI.

BLUE BONNETS OVER THE BORDER.

ONE morning, about the 1st of June, 1861, in the city of New York, two men of the mercantile class came from a cross street into Broadway, near what was then the upper region of its wholesale stores. They paused on the corner, near the edge of the sidewalk.

"Even when the States were seceding," said one of them, "I couldn't make up my mind that they really meant to break up the Union."

He had rosy cheeks, a retreating chin, and amiable, inquiring eyes. The other had a narrower face, alert eyes, thin nostrils, and a generally aggressive look. He did not reply at once, but, after a quick glance down the great thoroughfare and another one up it, said, while his eyes still ran here and there : —

"Wonderful street, this Broadway!"

He straightened up to his fullest height and looked again, now down the way, now up, his eye kindling with the electric contagion of the scene. His senses were all awake. They took in, with a spirit of welcome, all the vast movement : the uproar, the feeling of unbounded multitude, the commercial splendor, the miles of towering buildings ; the long, writhing, grinding mass of coming and going vehicles, the rush of innumerable feet, and the countless forms and faces hurrying, dancing, gliding by, as though all the world's mankind, and womankind and childhood must pass that way before night.

" How many people, do you suppose, go by this corner in a single hour?" asked the man with the retreating chin. But again he got no answer. He might as well not have yielded the topic of conversation as he had done; so he resumed it. " No, I didn't believe it," he said. " Why, look at the Southern vote of last November — look at New Orleans. The way it went there, I shouldn't have supposed twenty-five per cent. of the people would be in favor of secession. Would you?"

But his companion, instead of looking at New Orleans, took note of two women who had come to a halt within a yard of them and seemed to be waiting, as he and his companion were, for an opportunity to cross the street. The two new-comers were very different in appearance, the one from the other. The older and larger was much beyond middle life, red, fat, and dressed in black stuff, good as to fabric, but uncommonly bad as to fit. The other was young and pretty, refined, tastefully dressed, and only the more interesting for the look of permanent anxiety that asserted itself with distinctness about the corners of her eyes and mouth. She held by the hand a rosy, chubby little child, that seemed about three years old, and might be a girl or might be a boy, so far as could be discerned by masculine eyes. The man did not see this fifth member of their group until the elder woman caught it under the arms in her large hands, and, lifting it above her shoulder, said, looking far up the street: —

" O paypy, paypy, choost look de fla-ags! One, two, dtree, — a tuzzent, a hundut, a dtowsant fla-ags!"

Evidently the child did not know her well. The little face remained without a smile, the lips sealed, the shoulders drawn up, and the legs pointing straight to the spot whence they had been lifted. She set it down again.

" We're not going to get by here," said the less talkative man. "They must be expecting some troops to pass here. Don't you see the windows full of women and children?"

"Let's wait and look at them," responded the other, and his companion did not dissent.

"Well, sir," said the more communicative one, after a moment's contemplation, "I never expected to see this!" He indicated by a gesture the stupendous life of Broadway beginning slowly to roll back upon itself like an obstructed river. It was obviously gathering in a general pause to concentrate its attention upon something of leading interest about to appear to view. "We're in earnest at last, and we can see, now, that the South was in the deadest kind of earnest from the word go."

"They can't be any more in earnest than we are, now," said the more decided speaker.

"I had great hopes of the peace convention," said the rosier man.

"I never had a bit," responded the other.

"The suspense was awful — waiting to know what Lincoln would do when he came in," said he of the poor chin. "My wife was in the South visiting her relatives; and we kept putting off her return, hoping for a quieter state of affairs — hoping and putting off — till first thing you knew the lines closed down and she had the hardest kind of a job to get through."

"I never had a doubt as to what Lincoln would do," said the man with sharp eyes; but while he spoke he covertly rubbed his companion's elbow with his own, and by his glance toward the younger of the two women gave him to understand that, though her face was partly turned away, the very pretty ear, with no ear-ring in the hole pierced for it, was listening. And the readier speaker rejoined in a suppressed voice: —

"That's the little lady I travelled in the same car with all the way from Chicago."

"No times for ladies to be travelling alone," muttered the other.

"She hoped to take a steam-ship for New Orleans, to join her husband there."

"Some rebel fellow, I suppose."

"No, a Union man, she says."

"Oh, of course!" said the sharp-eyed one, sceptically. "Well, she's missed it. The last steamer's gone and may get back or may not." He looked at her again, narrowly, from behind his companion's shoulder. She was stooping slightly toward the child, rearranging some tie under its lifted chin and answering its questions in what seemed a chastened voice. He murmured to his fellow, "How do you know she isn't a spy?"

The other one turned upon him a look of pure amusement, but, seeing the set lips and earnest eye of his companion, said softly, with a faint, scouting hiss and smile: —

"She's a perfect lady — a perfect one."

"Her friend isn't," said the aggressive man.

"Here they come," observed the other aloud, looking up the street. There was a general turning of attention and concentration of the street's population toward the edge of either sidewalk. A force of police was clearing back into the by-streets a dense tangle of drays, wagons, carriages, and white-topped omnibuses, and far up the way could be seen the fluttering and tossing of handkerchiefs, and in the midst a solid mass of blue with a sheen of bayonets above, and every now and then a brazen reflection from in front, where the martial band marched before. It was not playing. The ear caught distantly, instead of its notes, the warlike thunder of the drum corps.

The sharper man nudged his companion mysteriously.

"Listen," he whispered. Neither they nor the other pair had materially changed their relative positions. The older woman was speaking.

"Twas te fun'est dting! You pe lookin' for te Noo 'Leants shteamer, undt me lookin' for te Hambourg shteamer, undt coompt right so togeder undt never vouldn't 'a' knowedt udt yet, ovver te mayne exdt me, 'Misses Reisen, vot iss your name?' undt you headt udt. Undt te minudt you shpeak, udt choost come to me like a flash o' lightenin'—'Udt iss Misses Richlin'!'" The speaker's companion gave her such attention as one may give in a crowd to words that have been heard two or three times already within the hour.

"Yes, Alice," she said, once or twice to the little one, who pulled softly at her skirt asking confidential questions. But the baker's widow went on with her story, enjoying it for its own sake.

"You know, Mr. Richlin' he told me finfty dtimes, 'Misses Reisen, doant kif up te pissness!' Ovver I see te mutcheenery proke undt te foundtries all makin' guns undt kennons, undt I choost says, 'I kot plenteh moneh—I tdtink I kfit undt go home.' Ovver I sayss to de Doctor, 'Dte oneh dting—vot Mr. Richlin' ko-in to tdo?'" Undt Dr. Tseweer he sayss, 'How menneh pa'ls flour you kot shtowed away?' Undt I sayss, 'Tsoo hundut finfty. Undt he sayss, 'Misses Reisen, Mr. Richlin' done made you rich; you choost kif um dtat flour; udt be wort' tweny-fife tollahs te pa'l, yet.' Undt sayss I, 'Doctor, you' right, undt I dtank you for te goodt idea; I kif Mr. Richlin' innahow one pa'l.' Undt I done-d it. Ovver I sayss, 'Doctor, dtat's not like a rigler sellery, yet.' Undt dten he sayss, 'You know, mine pookkeeper he gone to te vor, undt I need'"—

A crash of brazen music burst upon the ear and drowned the voice. The throng of the sidewalk pushed hard upon its edge.

"Let me hold the little girl up," ventured the milder man, and set her gently upon his shoulder, as amidst a confusion of outcries and flutter of hats and handkerchiefs the broad, dense column came on with measured tread, its stars and stripes waving in the breeze and its backward-slanting thicket of bayoneted arms glittering in the morning sun. All at once there arose from the great column, in harmony with the pealing music, the hoarse roar of the soldiers' own voices singing in time to the rhythm of their tread. And a thrill runs through the people, and they answer with mad huzzas and frantic wavings and smiles, half of wild ardor and half of wild pain; and the keen-eyed man here by Mary lets the tears roll down his cheeks unhindered as he swings his hat and cries "Hurrah! hurrah!" while on tramps the mighty column, singing from its thousand thirsty throats the song of John Brown's Body.

Yea, so, soldiers of the Union, — though that little mother there weeps but does not wave, as the sharp-eyed man notes well through his tears, — yet even so, yea, all the more, go — "go marching on," saviors of the Union; your cause is just. Lo, now, since nigh twenty-five years have passed, we of the South can say it!

"And yet — and yet, we cannot forget" —

and we would not.

CHAPTER LII.

A PASS THROUGH THE LINES.

ABOUT the middle of September following the date of the foregoing incident, there occurred in a farm-house head-quarters on the Indiana shore of the Ohio river the following conversation : —

"You say you wish me to give you a pass through the lines, ma'am. Why do you wish to go through?"

"I want to join my husband in New Orleans."

"Why, ma'am, you'd much better let New Orleans come through the lines. We shall have possession of it, most likely, within a month." The speaker smiled very pleasantly, for very pleasant and sweet was the young face before him, despite its lines of mental distress, and very soft and melodious the voice that proceeded from it.

"Do you think so?" replied the applicant, with an unhopeful smile. "My friends have been keeping me at home for months on that idea, but the fact seems as far off now as ever. I should go straight through without stopping, if I had a pass."

"Ho!" exclaimed the man, softly, with pitying amusement. "Certainly, I understand you would try to do so. But, my dear madam, you would find yourself very much mistaken. Suppose, now, we should let you through our lines. You'd be between two fires. You'd still have to get into the rebel lines. You don't know what you're undertaking."

She smiled wistfully.

"I'm undertaking to get to my husband."

"Yes, yes," said the officer, pulling his handkerchief from between two brass buttons of his double-breasted coat and wiping his brow. She did not notice that he made this motion purely as a cover for the searching glance which he suddenly gave her from head to foot. "Yes," he continued, "but you don't know what it is, ma'am. After you get through the *other* lines, what are you going to do *then?* There's a perfect reign of terror over there. I wouldn't let a lady relative of mine take such risks for thousands of dollars. I don't think your husband ought to thank me for giving you a pass. You say he's a Union man; why don't he come to you?"

Tears leaped into the applicant's eyes.

"He's become too sick to travel," she said.

"Lately?"

"Yes, sir."

"I thought you said you hadn't heard from him for months." The officer looked at her with narrowed eyes.

"I said I hadn't had a letter from him." The speaker blushed to find her veracity on trial. She bit her lip, and added, with perceptible tremor: "I got one lately from his physician."

"How did you get it?"

"What, sir?"

"Now, madam, you know what I asked you, don't you?"

"Yes, sir."

"Yes. Well, I'd like you to answer."

"I found it, three mornings ago, under the front door of the house where I live with my mother and my little girl."

"Who put it there?"

" I do not know."

The officer looked her steadily in the eyes. They were blue. His own dropped.

" You ought to have brought that letter with you, ma'am," he said, looking up again ; " don't you see how valuable it would be to you? "

" I did bring it," she replied, with alacrity, rummaged a moment in a skirt-pocket, and brought it out. The officer received it and read the superscription audibly.

" ' Mrs. John H——.' Are you Mrs. John H—— ? "

" That is not the envelope it was in," she replied. " It was not directed at all. I put it into that envelope merely to preserve it. That's the envelope of a different letter, — a letter from my mother."

" Are you Mrs. John H—— ? " asked her questioner again. She had turned partly aside and was looking across the apartment and out through a window. He spoke once more. " Is this your name? "

" What, sir ? "

He smiled cynically.

" Please don't do that again, madam."

She blushed down into the collar of her dress.

" That is my name, sir."

The man put the missive to his nose, snuffed it softly, and looked amused, yet displeased.

" Mrs. H——, did you notice just a faint smell of — garlic — about this — ? "

" Yes, sir."

" Well, I have no less than three or four others with the very same odor." He smiled on. " And so, no doubt, we are both of the same private opinion that the bearer of this letter was — who, Mrs. H—— ? "

Mrs. H—— frequently by turns raised her eyes honestly to her questioner's and dropped them to where, in her lap, the fingers of one hand fumbled with a lone wedding-ring on the other, while she said: —

"Do you think, sir, if you were in my place you would like to give the name of the person you thought had risked his life to bring you word that your husband — your wife — was very ill, and needed your presence? Would you like to do it?"

The officer looked severe.

"Don't you know perfectly well that wasn't his principal errand inside our lines?"

"No."

"No!" echoed the man; "and you don't know perfectly well, I suppose, that he's been shot at along this line times enough to have turned his hair white? Or that he crossed the river for the third time last night, loaded down with musket-caps for the rebels?"

"No."

"But you must admit you know a certain person, wherever he may be, or whatever he may be doing, named Raphael Ristofalo?"

"I do not."

The officer smiled again.

"Yes, I see. That is to say, you don't *admit* it. And you don't deny it."

The reply came more slowly: —

"I do not."

"Well, now, Mrs. H——, I've given you a pretty long audience. I'll tell you what I'll do. But do you please tell me, first, you affirm on your word of honor that your name is really Mrs. H—— ; that you are no spy, and have had no voluntary communication with any, and that you are a true and sincere Union woman."

"I affirm it all."

"Well, then, come in to-morrow at this hour, and if I

am going to give you a pass at all I'll give it to you then Here, here's your letter."

As she received the missive she lifted her eyes, suffused, but full of hope, to his, and said : —

"God grant you the heart to do it, sir, and bless you."

The man laughed. Her eyes fell, she blushed, and, saying not a word, turned toward the door and had reached the threshold when the officer called, with a certain ringing energy : —

"Mrs. Richling!"

She wheeled as if he had struck her, and answered : —

"What, sir!" Then, turning as red as a rose, she said, "O sir, that was cruel!" covered her face with her hands, and sobbed aloud. It was only as she was in the midst of these last words that she recognized in the officer before her the sharper-visaged of those two men who had stood by her in Broadway.

"Step back here, Mrs. Richling."

She came.

"Well, madam! I should like to know what we are coming to, when a lady like you — a palpable, undoubted lady — can stoop to such deceptions!"

"Sir," said Mary, looking at him steadfastly and then shaking her head in solemn asseveration, "all that I have said to you is the truth."

"Then will you explain how it is that you go by one name in one part of the country, and by another in another part?"

"No," she said. It was very hard to speak. The twitching of her mouth would hardly let her form a word. "No — no — I can't — tell you."

"Very well, ma'am. If you don't start back to Milwaukee by the next train, and stay there, I shall!" —

"Oh, don't say that, sir! I must go to my husband! Indeed, sir, it's nothing but a foolish mistake, made years ago, that's never harmed any one but us. I'll take all the blame of it if you'll only give me a pass!"

The officer motioned her to be silent.

"You'll have to do as I tell you, ma'am. If not, I shall know it; you will be arrested, and I shall give you a sort of pass that you'd be a long time asking for." He looked at the face mutely confronting him and felt himself relenting. "I dare say this does sound very cruel to you, ma'am; but remember, this is a cruel war. I don't judge you. If I did, and could harden my heart as I ought to, I'd have you arrested now. But, I say, you'd better take my advice. Good-morning! *No, ma'am, I can't hear you!* So, now, that's enough! Good-morning, madam!"

CHAPTER LIII.

TRY AGAIN.

ONE afternoon in the month of February, 1862, a
locomotive engine and a single weather-beaten pas-
senger-coach, moving southward at a very moderate speed
through the middle of Kentucky, stopped in response to a
handkerchief signal at the southern end of a deep, rocky
valley, and, in a patch of gray, snow-flecked woods, took
on board Mary Richling, dressed in deep mourning, and
her little Alice. The three or four passengers already in
the coach saw no sign of human life through the closed
panes save the roof of one small cabin that sent up its
slender thread of blue smoke at one corner of a little
badly cleared field a quarter of a mile away on a huge
hill-side. As the scant train crawled off again into a
deep, ice-hung defile, it passed the silent figure of a man
in butternut homespun, spattered with dry mud, standing
close beside the track on a heap of cross-tie cinders and
fire-bent railroad iron, a gray goat-beard under his chin,
and a quilted homespun hat on his head. From beneath
the limp brim of this covering, as the train moved by him,
a tender, silly smile beamed upward toward cne hastily
raised window, whence the smile of Mary and the grave,
unemotional gaze of the child met it for a moment before
the train swung round a curve in the narrow way, and
quickened speed on down grade.

The conductor came and collected her fare. He smelt
o: tobacco above the smell of the coach in general.

"Do you charge anything for the little girl?"

The purse in which the inquirer's finger and thumb tarried was limber and flat.

"No, ma'am."

It was not the customary official negative; a tawdry benevolence of face went with it, as if to say he did not charge because he would not; and when Mary returned a faint beam of appreciation he went out upon the rear platform and wiped the plenteous dust from his shoulders and cap. Then he returned to his seat at the stove and renewed his conversation with a lieutenant in hard-used blue, who said "the rebel lines ought never to have been allowed to fall back to Nashville," and who knew "how Grant could have taken Fort Donelson a week ago if he had had any sense."

There were but few persons, as we have said, in the car. A rough man in one corner had a little captive, a tiny, dappled fawn, tied by a short, rough bit of rope to the foot of the car-seat. When the conductor by and by lifted the little Alice up from the cushion, where she sat with her bootees straight in front of her at its edge, and carried her, speechless and drawn together like a kitten, and stood her beside the captive orphan, she simply turned about and pattered back to her mother's side.

"I don't believe she even saw it," said the conductor, standing again by Mary.

"Yes, she did," replied Mary, smiling upon the child's head as she smoothed its golden curls; "she'll talk about it to-morrow."

The conductor lingered a moment, wanting to put his own hand there, but did not venture, perhaps because of the person sitting on the next seat behind, who looked at him rather steadily until he began to move away.

This was a man of slender, commanding figure and

advanced years. Beside him, next the window, sat a decidedly aristocratic woman, evidently his wife. She, too, was of fine stature, and so, without leaning forward from the back of her seat, or unfolding her arms, she could make kind eyes to Alice, as the child with growing frequency stole glances, at first over her own little shoulder, and later over her mother's, facing backward and kneeling on the cushion. At length a cooky passed between them in dead silence, and the child turned and gazed mutely in her mother's face, with the cooky just in sight.

" It can't hurt her," said the lady, in a sweet voice, to Mary, leaning forward with her hands in her lap. By the time the sun began to set in a cool, golden haze across some wide stretches of rolling fallow, a conversation had sprung up, and the child was in the lady's lap, her little hand against the silken bosom, playing with a costly watch.

The talk began about the care of Alice, passed to the diet, and then to the government, of children, all in a light way, a similarity of convictions pleasing the two ladies more and more as they found it run further and further. Both talked, but the strange lady sustained the conversation, although it was plainly both a pastime and a comfort to Mary. Whenever it threatened to flag the handsome stranger persisted in reviving it.

Her husband only listened and smiled, and with one finger made every now and then a soft, slow pass at Alice, who each time shrank as slowly and softly back into his wife's fine arm. Presently, however, Mary raised her eyebrows a little and smiled, to see her sitting quietly in the gentleman's lap ; and as she turned away and rested her elbow on the window-sill and her cheek on her hand in a manner that betrayed weariness, and looked out upon the ever-turning landscape, he murmured to his wife, "I haven't a doubt in my mind," and nodded significantly at the preoccupied little shape in his arms. His manner with the child was imperceptibly adroit, and very soon her prattle began to be heard. Mary was just turning to offer a gentle check to this rising volubility, when up jumped the little one to a standing posture on the gentleman's knee, and, all unsolicited and with silent clapping of hands, plumped out her full name : —

"Alice Sevier Witchlin' ! "

The husband threw a quick glance toward his wife ; but she avoided it and called Mary's attention to the sunset as seen through the opposite windows. Mary looked and responded with expressions of admiration, but was visibly disquieted, and the next moment called her child to her.

"My little girl mustn't talk so loud and fast in the cars," she said, with tender pleasantness, standing her upon the seat and brushing back the stray golden waves from the baby's temples, and the brown ones, so like them, from her own. She turned a look of amused apology to the gentleman, and added, "She gets almost boisterous sometimes," then gave her regard once more to her offspring, seating the little one beside her as in the beginning, and answering her musical small questions with composing yeas and nays.

"I suppose," she said, after a pause and a look out through the window, — "I suppose we ought soon to be reaching M—— station, now, should we not?"

"What, in Tennessee? Oh! no," replied the gentleman. "In ordinary times we should; but at this slow rate we cannot nearly do it. We're on a road, you see, that was destroyed by the retreating army and made over by the Union forces. Besides, there are three trains of troops ahead of us, that must stop and unload between here and there, and keep you waiting, there's no telling how long."

"Then I'll get there in the night!" exclaimed Mary.

"Yes, probably after midnight."

"Oh, I shouldn't have *thought* of coming before to-morrow if I had known that!" In the extremity of her dismay she rose half from her seat and looked around with alarm.

"Have you no friends expecting to receive you there?" asked the lady.

"Not a soul! And the conductor says there's no lodging-place nearer than three miles" —

"And that's gone now," said the gentleman.

"You'll have to get out at the same station with us," said the lady, her manner kindness itself and at the same time absolute.

"I think you have claims on us, anyhow, that we'd like to pay."

"Oh! impossible," said Mary. "You're certainly mistaking me."

"I think you have," insisted the lady; "that is, if your name is Richling."

Mary blushed.

"I don't think you know my husband," she said; "he lives a long way from here."

"In New Orleans?" asked the gentleman.

"Yes, sir," said Mary, boldly. She couldn't fear such good faces.

"His first name is John, isn't it?"

"Yes, sir. Do you really know John, sir?" The lines of pleasure and distress mingled strangely in Mary's face. The gentleman smiled. He tapped little Alice's head with the tips of his fingers.

"I used to hold him on my knee when he was no bigger than this little image of him here."

The tears leaped into Mary's eyes.

"Mr. Thornton," she whispered, huskily, and could say no more.

"You must come home with us," said the lady, touching her tenderly on the shoulder. "It's a wonder of good fortune that we've met. Mr. Thornton has something to say to you, — a matter of business. He's the family's lawyer, you know."

"I must get to my husband without delay," said Mary.

"Get to your husband?" asked the lawyer, in astonishment.

"Yes, sir."

"Through the lines?"

"Yes, sir."

"I told him so," said the lady.

"I don't know how to credit it," said he. "Why, my child, I don't think you can possibly know what you are attempting. Your friends ought never to have allowed you to conceive such a thing. You must let us dissuade you. It will not be taking too much liberty, will it? Has your husband never told you what good friends we were?"

Mary nodded and tried to speak.

"Often," said Mrs. Thornton to her husband, interpreting the half-articulated reply.

They sat and talked in low tones, under the dismal lamp of the railroad coach, for two or three hours. Mr. Thornton came around and took the seat in front of Mary, and sat with one leg under him, facing back toward her. Mrs. Thornton sat beside her, and Alice slumbered on the seat behind, vacated by the lawyer and his wife.

" You needn't tell me John's story," said the gentleman ;
" I know it. What I didn't know before, I got from a
man with whom I corresponded in New Orleans."

" Dr. Sevier ? "

" No, a man who got it from the Doctor."

So they had Mary tell her own story.

" I thought I should start just as soon as my mother's
health would permit. John wouldn't have me start
before that, and, after all, I don't see how I could have
done it — rightly. But by the time she was well — or
partly well — every one was in the greatest anxiety
and doubt everywhere. You know how it was."

" Yes," said Mrs. Thornton.

" And everybody thinking everything would soon be
settled," continued Mary.

" Yes," said the sympathetic lady, and her husband
touched her quietly, meaning for her not to interrupt.

" We didn't think the Union *could* be broken so easily,"
pursued Mary. " And then all at once it was unsafe and
improper to travel alone. Still I went to New York, to
take steamer around by sea. But the last steamer had
sailed, and I had to go back home ; for — the fact is," —
she smiled, — " my money was all gone. It was September before I could raise enough to start again ; but
one morning I got a letter from New Orleans, telling me
that John was very ill, and enclosing money for me to
travel with."

She went on to tell the story of her efforts to get a pass
on the bank of the Ohio river, and how she had gone
home once more, knowing she was watched, not daring
for a long time to stir abroad, and feeding on the frequent
hope that New Orleans was soon to be taken by one or
another of the many naval expeditions that from time to
time were, or were said to be, sailing.

" And then suddenly — my mother died."

Mrs. Thornton gave a deep sigh.

" And then," said Mary, with a sudden brightening, but in a low voice, " I determined to make one last effort. I sold everything in the world I had and took Alice and started. I've come very slowly, a little way at a time, feeling along, for I was resolved not to be turned back. I've been weeks getting this far, and the lines keep moving south ahead of me. But I haven't been turned back," she went on to say, with a smile, " and everybody, white and black, everywhere, has been just as kind as kind can be." Tears stopped her again.

" Well, never mind, Mrs. Richling," said Mrs. Thornton ; then turned to her husband, and asked, " May I tell her ? "

" Yes."

" Well, Mrs. Richling, — but do you wish to be called Mrs. Richling ? "

" Yes," said Mary, and " Certainly," said Mr. Thornton.

" Well, Mrs. Richling, Mr. Thornton has some money for your husband. Not a great deal, but still — some. The younger of the two sisters died a few weeks ago. She was married, but she was rich in her own right. She left almost everything to her sister ; but Mr. Thornton persuaded her to leave some money — well, two thousand — 'tisn't much, but it's something, you know — to — ah to Mr. Richling. Husband has it now at home and will give it to you, — at the breakfast-table to-morrow morning ; can't you, dear ? "

" Yes."

" Yes, and we'll not try to persuade you to give up your idea of going to New Orleans. I know we couldn't do it. We'll watch our chance, — eh, husband ? — and

put you through the lines; and not only that, but give
you letters to — why, dear," said the lady, turning to her
partner in good works, "you can give Mrs. Richling a
letter to Governor Blank; and another to General Um-hm,
can't you? and — yes, and one to Judge Youknow.
Oh, they will take you anywhere! But first you'll stop
with us till you get well rested — a week or two, or as
much longer as you will."

Mary pressed the speaker's hand.

"I can't stay."

"Oh, you know you needn't have the least fear of
seeing any of John's relatives. They don't live in this
part of the State at all; and, even if they did, husband
has no business with them just now, and being a Union
man, you know"—

"I want to see my husband," said Mary, not waiting
to hear what Union sympathies had to do with the
matter.

"Yes," said the lady, in a suddenly subdued tone.
"Well, we'll get you through just as quickly as we can."
And soon they all began to put on wraps and gather their
luggage. Mary went with them to their home, laid her
tired head beside her child's in sleep, and late next morning rose to hear that Fort Donelson was taken, and the
Southern forces were falling back. A day or two later
came word that Columbus, on the Mississippi, had been
evacuated. It was idle for a woman to try just then to
perform the task she had set for herself. The Federal
lines!

"Why, my dear child, they're trying to find the Confederate lines and strike them. You can't lose anything
— you may gain much — by remaining quiet here awhile.
The Mississippi, I don't doubt, will soon be open from
end to end."

A fortnight seemed scarcely more than a day when it was past, and presently two of them had gone. One day comes Mr. Thornton, saying : —

"My dear child, I cannot tell you how I have the news, but you may depend upon its correctness. New Orleans is to be attacked by the most powerful naval expedition that ever sailed under the United States flag. If the place is not in our hands by the first of April I will put you through both lines, if I have to go with you myself." When Mary made no answer, he added, "Your delays have all been unavoidable, my child!"

"Oh, I don't know; I don't know!" exclaimed Mary, with sudden distraction; "it seems to me I *must* be to blame, or I'd have been through long ago. I ought to have *run through* the lines. I ought to have 'run the blockade.'"

"My child," said the lawyer, "you're mad."

"You'll see," replied Mary, almost in soliloquy.

CHAPTER LIV.

" WHO GOES THERE? "

THE scene and incident now to be described are without date. As Mary recalled them, years afterward,
they hung out against the memory a bold, clear picture,
cast upon it as the magic lantern casts its tableaux upon
the darkened canvas. She had lost the day of the month,
the day of the week, all sense of location, and the points
of the compass. The most that she knew was that she
was somewhere near the meeting of the boundaries of
three States. Either she was just within the southern
bound of Tennessee, or the extreme north-eastern corner
of Mississippi, or else the north-western corner of Ala-
bama. She was aware, too, that she had crossed the
Tennessee river; that the sun had risen on her left and
had set on her right, and that by and by this beautiful
day would fade and pass from this unknown land, and
the firelight and lamplight draw around them the home-
groups under the roof-trees, here where she was a homeless
stranger, the same as in the home-lands where she had
once loved and been beloved.

She was seated in a small, light buggy drawn by one
good horse. Beside her the reins were held by a rather
tall man, of middle age, gray, dark, round-shouldered,
and dressed in the loose blue flannel so much worn by
followers of the Federal camp. Under the stiff brim of
his soft-crowned black hat a pair of clear eyes gave a
continuous playful twinkle. Between this person and

Mary protruded, at the edge of the buggy-seat, two small bootees that have already had mention, and from his elbow to hers, and back to his, continually swayed drowsily the little golden head to which the bootees bore a certain close relation. The dust of the highway was on the buggy and the blue flannel and the bootees. It showed with special boldness on a black sun-bonnet that covered Mary's head, and that somehow lost all its homeliness whenever it rose sufficiently in front to show the face within. But the highway itself was not there; it had been left behind some hours earlier. The buggy was moving at a quiet jog along a "neighborhood road," with unploughed fields on the right and a darkling woods pasture on the left. By the feathery softness and pale-ness of the sweet-smelling foliage you might have guessed it was not far from the middle of April, one way or another; and, by certain allusions to Pittsburg Landing as a place of conspicuous note, you might have known that Shiloh had been fought. There was that feeling of desolation in the land that remains after armies have passed over, let them tread never so lightly.

" D'you know what them rails is put that way fur?" asked the man. He pointed down with his buggy-whip just off the roadside, first on one hand and then on the other.

" No," said Mary, turning the sun-bonnet's limp front toward the questioner and then to the disjointed fence on her nearer side; " that's what I've been wondering for days. They've been ordinary worm fences, haven't they?"

" Jess so," responded the man, with his accustomed twinkle. " But I think I see you oncet or twicet lookin' at 'em and sort o' tryin' to make out how come they got into that shape." The long-reiterated W's of the rail-fence

had been pulled apart into separate V's, and the two
sides of each of these had been drawn narrowly together, so that what had been two parallel lines of fence,
with the lane between, was now a long double row of
wedge-shaped piles of rails, all pointing into the woods
on the left.

"How did it happen?" asked Mary, with a smile of
curiosity.

"Didn't happen at all, 'twas jess *done* by live men,
and in a powerful few minutes at that. Sort o' shows
what we're approachin' unto, as it were, eh? Not but
they's plenty behind us done the same way, all the way
back into Kentuck', as you already done see; but this's
been done sence the last rain, and it rained night afore
last."

"Still I'm not sure what it means," said Mary; "has
there been fighting here?"

"Go up head," said the man, with a facetious gesture.
"See? The fight came through these here woods,
here. 'Taint been much over twenty-four hours, I
reckon, since every one o' them-ah sort o' shut-up-fan-
shape sort o' fish-traps had a gray-jacket in it layin' flat
down an' firin' through the rails, sort o' random-like,
only not much so." His manner of speech seemed a sort
of harlequin patchwork from the bad English of many
sections, the outcome of a humorous and eclectic fondness
for verbal deformities. But his lightness received a
sudden check.

"Heigh-h-h!" he gravely and softly exclaimed, gathering the reins closer, as the horse swerved and dashed
ahead. Two or three buzzards started up from the roadside, with their horrid flapping and whiff of quills, and
circled low overhead. "Heigh-h-h!" he continued soothingly. "Ho-o-o-o! somebody lost a good nag there, — a

six-pound shot right through his head and neck. Whoever made that shot killed two birds with one stone,
sho !" He was half risen from his seat, looking back.
As he turned again, and sat down, the drooping black
sun-bonnet quite concealed the face within. He looked
at it a moment. "If you think you don't like the risks
we can still turn back."

"No," said the voice from out the sun-bonnet ; "go on."

"If we don't turn back now we can't turn back at all."

"Go on," said Mary ; "I can't turn back."

"You're a good· soldier," said the man, playfully
again. "You're a better one than me, I reckon ; I kin
turn back frequently, as it were. I've done it 'many a
time and oft,' as the felleh says."

Mary looked up with feminine surprise. He made a
pretence of silent laughter, that showed a hundred crows'
feet in his twinkling eyes.

"Oh, don't you fret ; I'm not goin' to run the wrong
way with you in charge. Didn't you hear me promise
Mr. Thornton? Well, you see, I've got a sort o' bad
memory, that kind o' won't let me forgit when I make a
promise ; — bothers me that way a heap sometimes."
He smirked in a self-deprecating way, and pulled his
hat-brim down in front. Presently he spoke again,
looking straight ahead over the horse's ears :—

"Now, that's the mischief about comin' with me — got
to run both blockades at oncet. Now, if you'd been a
good Secesh and could somehow or 'nother of got a pass
through the Union lines you'd of been all gay. But bein'
Union, the fu'ther you git along the wuss off you air,
'less-n I kin take you and carry you 'way 'long yonder to
where you kin jess jump onto a southbound Rebel rail
road and light down amongst folks that'll never think o'
you havin' run through the lines."

" But you can't do that," said Mary, not in the form
of a request. " You know you agreed with Mr. Thornton
that you would simply " —

" Put you down in a safe place," said the man,
jocosely ; " that's what it meant, and don't you get
nervous ". — His face suddenly changed ; he raised his
whip and held it up for attention and silence, looking at
Mary, and smiling while he listened. " Do you hear anything ? "

" Yes," said Mary, in a hushed tone. There were
some old fields on the right-hand now, and a wood on
the left. Just within the wood a turtle-dove was cooing.

" I don't mean that," said the man, softly.

" No," said Mary, " you mean this, away over here."
She pointed across the fields, almost straight away in
front.

" 'Taint so scandalous far ' awa-a-ay ' as you talk like,"
murmured the man, jestingly ; and just then a fresh
breath of the evening breeze brought plainer and nearer
the soft boom of a bass-drum.

" Are they coming this way ? " asked Mary.

" No ; they're sort o' dress-paradin' in camp, I reckon."
He began to draw rein. " We turn off here, anyway,"
he said, and drove slowly, but point blank into the
forest.

" I don't see any road," said Mary. It was so dark in
the wood that even her child, muffled in a shawl and
asleep in her arms, was a dim shape.

" Yes,' was the reply ; " we have to sort o' smell out
the way here ; but my smellers is good, at times, and
pretty soon we'll strike a little sort o' somepnuther like a
road, about a quarter from here."

Pretty soon they did so. It started suddenly from the
edge of an old field in the forest, and ran gradually down,

winding among the trees, into a densely wooded bottom, where even Mary's short form often had to bend low to avoid the boughs of beech-trees and festoons of grape-vine. Under one beech the buggy stood still a moment. The man drew and opened a large clasp-knife and cut one of the long, tough withes. He handed it to Mary, as they started on again.

" With compliments," he said, " and hoping you won't find no use for it."

" What is it for? "

" Why, you see, later on we'll be in the saddle; and if such a thing should jess accidentally happen to happen, which I hope it won't, to be sho', that I should happen to sort o' absent-mindedly yell out ' Go!' like as if a hornet had stabbed me, you jess come down with that switch, and make the critter under you run like a scared dog, as it were."

" Must I? "

" No, I don't say you *must*, but you'd better, I bet you You needn't if you don't want to."

Presently the dim path led them into a clear, rippling creek, and seemed to Mary to end; but when the buggy wheels had crunched softly along down stream over some fifty or sixty yards of gravelly shallow, the road showed itself faintly again on the other bank, and the horse, with a plunge or two and a scramble, jerked them safely over the top, and moved forward in the direction of the rising moon. They skirted a small field full of ghostly dead trees, where corn was beginning to make a show, turned its angle, and saw the path under their feet plain to view, smooth and hard.

" See that? " said the man, in a tone of playful triumph, as the animal started off at a brisk trot, lifted his head and neighed. " ' My day's work's done,' sezee;

' I done hoed my row.' " A responsive neigh came out of the darkness ahead. " That's the trick ! " said the man. " Thanks, as the felleh says." He looked to Mary for her appreciation of his humor.

" I suppose that means a good deal ; does it? " asked she, with a smile.

" Jess so ! It means, first of all, fresh hosses. And then it means a house what aint been burnt by jayhawkers yit, and a man and woman a-waitin' in it, and some bacon and cornpone, and maybe a little coffee ; and milk, anyhow, till you can't rest, and buttermilk to fare-you-well. Now, have you ever learned the trick o' jess sort o' qui'lin'[1] up, cloze an' all, dry so, and puttin' half a night's rest into an hour's sleep? 'Caze why, in one hour we must be in the saddle. No mo' buggy, and powerful few roads. Comes as nigh coonin' it as I reckon you ever 'lowed you'd like to do, don't it? "

He smiled, pretending to hold back much laughter, and Mary smiled too. At mention of a woman she had removed her bonnet and was smoothing her hair with her hand.

" I don't care," she said, " if only you'll bring us through."

The man made a ludicrous gesture of self-abasement.

" Not knowin', can't say, as the felleh says ; but what I can tell you — I always start out to make a spoon or spoil a horn, and which one I'll do I seldom ever promise till it's done. But I have a sneakin' notion, as it were, that I'm the clean sand, and no discount, as Mr. Lincoln says, and I do my best. Angels can do no more, as the felleh says."

He drew rein. " Whoa ! " Mary saw a small log

---

[1] Coiling.

cabin, and a fire-light shining under the bottom of the door.

"The woods seem to be on fire just over there in three or four places, are they not?" she asked, as she passed the sleeping Alice down to the man, who had got out of the buggy.

"Them's the camps," said another man, who had come out of the house and was letting the horse out of the shafts.

"If we was on the rise o' the hill yonder we could see the Confedick camps, couldn't we, Isaiah?" asked Mary's guide.

"Easy," said that prophet. "I heer 'em to-day two, three times, plain, cheerin' at somethin'."

About the middle of that night Mary Richling was sitting very still and upright on a large dark horse that stood champing his Mexican bit in the black shadow of a great oak. Alice rested before her, fast asleep against her bosom. Mary held by the bridle another horse, whose naked saddle-tree was empty. A few steps in front of her the light of the full moon shone almost straight down upon a narrow road that just there emerged from the shadow of woods on either side, and divided into a main right fork and a much smaller one that curved around to Mary's left. Off in the direction of the main fork the sky was all aglow with camp-fires. Only just here on the left there was a cool and grateful darkness.

She lifted her head alertly. A twig crackled under a tread, and the next moment a man came out of the bushes at the left, and without a word took the bridle of the led horse from her fingers and vaulted into the saddle. The hand that rested a moment on the cantle as he rose grasped a "navy-six." He was dressed in dull home-

spun but he was the same who had been dressed in blue.
He turned his horse and led the way down the lesser road.

" If we'd of gone three hundred yards further," he
whispered, falling back and smiling broadly, " we'd 'a'
run into the pickets. I went nigh enough to see the
videttes settin' on their hosses in the main road. This
here aint no road; it just goes up to a nigger quarters.
I've got one o' the niggers to show us the way."

" Where is he?" whispered Mary; but, before her companion could answer, a tattered form moved from behind
a bush a little in advance and started ahead in the path,
walking and beckoning. Presently they turned into a
clear, open forest and followed the long, rapid, swinging
stride of the negro for nearly an hour. Then they halted
on the bank of a deep, narrow stream. The negro made
a motion for them to keep well to the right when they
should enter the water. The white man softly lifted Alice
to his arms, directed and assisted Mary to kneel in her
saddle, with her skirts gathered carefully under her, and
so they went down into the cold stream, the negro first,
with arms outstretched above the flood; then Mary, and
then the white man, — or, let us say plainly the spy, —
with the unawakened child on his breast. And so they
rose out of it on the farther side without a shoe or garment
wet save the rags of their dark guide.

Again they followed him, along a line of stake-and-
rider fence, with the woods on one side and the bright
moonlight flooding a field of young cotton on the other.
Now they heard the distant baying of house-dogs, now
the doleful call of the chuck-will's-widow; and once Mary's
blood turned, for an instant, to ice, at the unearthly shriek
of the hoot-owl just above her head. At length they
found themselves in a dim, narrow road, and the negro
stopped.

" Dess keep dish yeh road fo' 'bout half mile an' you strak 'pon the broad, main road. Tek de right, an' you go whah yo' fancy tek you."

" Good-by," whispered Mary.

" Good-by, miss," said the negro, in the same low voice ; " good-by, boss ; don't you fo'git you promise tek me thoo to de Yankee' when you come back. I 'feered you gwine fo'git it, boss."

The spy said he would not, and they left him. The half-mile was soon passed, though it turned out to be a mile and a half, and at length Mary's companion looked back, as they rode single file, with Mary in the rear, and said softly, " There's the road," pointing at its broad, pale line with his six-shooter.

As they entered it and turned to the right, Mary, with Alice again in her arms, moved somewhat ahead of her companion, her indifferent horsemanship having compelled him to drop back to avoid a prickly bush. His horse was just quickening his pace to regain the lost position when a man sprang up from the ground on the farther side of the highway, snatched a carbine from the earth and cried, " Halt ! "

The dark, recumbent forms of six or eight others could be seen, enveloped in their blankets, lying about a few red coals. Mary turned a frightened look backward and met tbe eyes of her companion.

" Move a little faster," said he, in a low, clear voice. As she promptly did so she heard him answer the challenge. His horse trotted softly after hers.

" Don't stop us, my friend ; we're taking a sick child to the doctor."

" Halt, you hound ! " the cry rang out ; and as Mary glanced back three or four men were just leaping into the road. But she saw, also, her companion, his face suffused

with an earnestness that was almost an agony, rise in his
stirrups, with the stoop of his shoulders all gone, and
wildly cry : —

"Go!"

She smote the horse and flew.   Alice awoke and
screamed.

"Hush, my darling!" said the mother, laying on the
withe ; "mamma's here.   Hush, darling! — mamma's here
Don't be frightened, darling baby!   O God, spare m,
child!" and away she sped.

The report of a carbine rang out and went rolling away
in a thousand echoes through the wood.   Two others
followed in sharp succession, and there went close by
Mary's ear the waspish whine of a minie-ball.   At the
same moment she recognized, once, — twice, — thrice, —
just at her back where the hoofs of her companion's horse
were clattering, — the tart rejoinders of his navy-six.

"Go!" he cried again.   "Lay low! lay low! cover the
child!"   But his words were needless.   With head
bowed forward and form crouched over the crying, clinging child, with slackened rein and fluttering dress, and
sun-bonnet and loosened hair blown back upon her
shoulders, with lips compressed and silent prayers, Mary
was riding for life and liberty and her husband's bedside.

"O mamma! mamma!" wailed the terrified little one.

"Go on! Go on!" cried the voice behind ; "they're
saddling — up! Go! go! We're goin' to make it. We're
goin' to *make* it! Go-o-o!"

Half an hour later they were again riding abreast, at a
moderate gallop.   Alice's cries had been quieted, but she
still clung to her mother in a great tremor.   Mary and
her companion conversed earnestly in the subdued tone
that had become their habit.

" No, I don't think they followed us fur," said the spy.
" Seem like they's jess some scouts, most likely a-comin'
in to report, feelin' pooty safe and sort o' takin' it easy
and careless; ' dreamin' the happy hours away,' as the
felleh says. I reckon they sort o' believed my story, too,
the little gal yelled so sort o' skilful. We kin slack up
some more now; we want to get our critters lookin' cool
and quiet ag'in as quick as we kin, befo' we meet up with
somebody." They reined into a gentle trot. He drew
his revolver, whose emptied chambers he had already re-
filled. " D'd you hear this little felleh sing, ' Listen to
the mockin'-bird'? "

" Yes," said Mary; " but I hope it didn't hit any of
them."

He made no reply.

" Don't you?" she asked.

He grinned.

" D'you want a felleh to wish he was a bad shot?"

" Yes," said Mary, smiling.

" Well, seein' as you're along, I do. For they wouldn't
give us up so easy if I'd a hit one. Oh, — mine was only
sort o' complimentary shots, — much as to say, ' Same to
you, gents,' as the felleh says."

Mary gave him a pleasant glance by way of courtesy,
but was busy calming the child. The man let his weapon
into its holster under his homespun coat and lapsed into
silence. He looked long and steadily at the small feminine figure of his companion. His eyes passed slowly
from the knee thrown over the saddle's horn to the gentle
forehead slightly bowed, as her face sank to meet the uplifted kisses of the trembling child, then over the crown
and down the heavy, loosened tresses that hid the sun-
bonnet hanging back from her throat by its strings and
flowed on down to the saddle-bow. His admiring eyes,

grave for once, had made the journey twice before he noticed that the child was trying to comfort the mother, and that the light of the sinking moon was glistening back from Mary's falling tears.

"Better let me have the little one," he said, "and you sort o' fix up a little, befo' we happen to meet up with somebody, as I said. It's lucky we haven't done it already."

A little coaxing prevailed with Alice, and the transfer was made. Mary turned away her wet eyes, smiling for shame of them, and began to coil her hair, her companion's eye following.

"Oh, you aint got no business to be ashamed of a few tears. I knowed you was a good soldier, befo' ever we started; I see' it in yo' eye. Not as I want to be complimentin' of you jess now. 'I come not here to talk,' as they used to say in school. D'd you ever hear that piece?"

"Yes," said Mary.

"That's taken from Romans, aint it?"

"No," said Mary again, with a broad smile.

"I didn't know," said the man; "I aint no brag Bible scholar." He put on a look of droll modesty. "I used to could say the ten commandments of the decalogue oncet, and I still tries to keep 'em, in ginerally. There's another burnt house. That's the third one we done passed inside a mile. Raiders was along here about two weeks back. Hear that rooster crowin'? When we pass the plantation whar he is and rise the next hill, we'll be in sight o' the little town whar we stop for refresh*ments*, as the railroad man says. You must begin to feel jess about everlastin'ly wore out, don't you?"

"No," said Mary; but he made a movement of the head to indicate that he had his belief to the contrary.

At an abrupt angle of the road Mary's heart leaped

into her throat to find herself and her companion suddenly face to face with two horsemen in gray, journeying leisurely toward them on particularly good horses. One wore a slouched hat, the other a Federal officer's cap. They were the first Confederates she had ever seen eye to eye.

"Ride on a little piece and stop," murmured the spy The strangers lifted their hats respectfully as she passed them.

"Gents," said the spy, "good-morning!" He threw a leg over the pommel of his saddle and the three men halted in a group. One of them copied the spy's attitude. They returned the greeting in kind.

"What command do you belong to?" asked the lone stranger.

"Simmons's battery," said one. "Whoa!" — to his horse.

"Mississippi?" asked Mary's guardian.

"Rackensack," said the man in the blue cap.

"Arkansas," said the other in the same breath. "What is your command?"

"Signal service," replied the spy. "Reckon I look mighty like a citizen jess about now, don't I?" He gave them his little laugh of self-depreciation and looked toward Mary, where she had halted and was letting her horse nip the new grass of the roadside.

"See any troops along the way you come?" asked the man in the hat.

"No; on'y a squad o' fellehs back yonder who was all unsaddled and fast asleep, and jumped up worse scared'n a drove o' wile hogs. We both sort o' got a little mad and jess swapped a few shots, you know, kind o' tit for tat, as it were. Enemy's loss unknown." He stooped more than ever in the shoulders, and laughed. The men were amused "If you see 'em, I'd like you to mention me " — He paused to exchange smiles again. "And tell 'em the next time they see a man hurryin' along with a lady and sick child to see the doctor, they better hold their fire till they sho he's on'y a citizen." He let his foot down into the stirrup again and they all smiled broadly. "Good-morning!" The two parties went their ways.

"Jess as leave not of met up with them two butter-milk rangers," said the spy, once more at Mary's side; "but seein' as thah we was the oniest thing was to put on all the brass I had."

From the top of the next hill the travellers descended into a village lying fast asleep, with the morning star blazing over it, the cocks calling to each other from their roosts, and here and there a light twinkling from a kitchen window, or a lazy axe-stroke smiting the logs at a wood-pile. In the middle of the village one lone old man, half-dressed, was lazily opening the little wooden " store" that monopolized its commerce. The travellers responded to his silent bow, rode on through the place, passed over and down another hill, met an aged negro, who passed on the roadside, lifting his forlorn hat and bowing low; and, as soon as they could be sure they had gone beyond his sight and hearing, turned abruptly into a dark wood on the left. Twice again they turned to the left, going very warily through the deep shadows of the forest, and so returned half around the village, seeing no one. Then they stopped and dismounted at a stable-door, on the outskirts of the place. The spy opened it with a key from his own pocket, went in and came out again with a great armful of hay, which he spread for the horses' feet to muffle their tread, led them into the stable, removed the hay again, and closed and locked the door.

"Make yourself small," he whispered, "and walk

fast." They passed by a garden path up to the back
porch and door of a small unpainted cottage. He
knocked, three soft, measured taps.

"Day's breakin'," he whispered again, as he stood
with Alice asleep in his arms, while somebody was heard
stirring within.

"Sam?" said a low, wary voice just within the un-
opened door.

"Sister," softly responded the spy, and the door swung
inward, and revealed a tall woman, with an austere but
good face, that could just be made out by the dim light
of a tallow candle shining from the next room. The
travellers entered and the door was shut.

"Well," said the spy, standing and smiling foolishly,
and bending playfully in the shoulders, "well, Mrs.
Richlin',"— he gave his hand a limp wave abroad and
smirked, — "' In Dixie's land you take yo' stand.' This
is it. You're in it! — Mrs. Richlin', my sister; sister,
Mrs. Richlin'."

"Pleased to know ye," said the woman, without the
faintest ray of emotion. "Take a seat and sit down."
She produced a chair bottomed with raw-hide.

"Thank you," was all Mary could think of to reply as
she accepted the seat, and "Thank you" again when the
woman brought a glass of water. The spy laid Alice on
a bed in sight of Mary in another chamber. He came
back on tiptoe.

"Now, the next thing is to git you furder south.
Wust of it is that, seein' as you got sich a weakness fur
tellin' the truth, we'll jess have to sort o' slide you along
fum one Union man to another; sort o' hole fass what I
give ye, as you used to say yourself, I reckon. But
you've got one strong holt." His eye went to his sister's,
and he started away without a word, and was presently

heard making a fire, while the woman went about spreading a small table with cold meats and corn-bread, milk
and butter. Her brother came back once more.

" Yes," he said to Mary, " you've got one mighty good
card, and that's it in yonder on the bed. 'Humph!'
folks'll say; 'didn't come fur with that there baby,
sno!'"

" I wouldn't go far without her," said Mary, brightly.

" *I* say," responded the hostess, with her back turned,
and said no more.

" Sister," said the spy, " we'll want the buggy."

" All right," responded the sister.

" I'll go feed the hosses," said he, and went out. In
a few minutes he returned. " Joe must give 'em a good
rubbin' when he comes, sister," he said.

" All right," replied the woman, and then turning to
Mary, " Come."

" What, ma'm?"

" Eat." She touched the back of a chair. " Sam,
bring the baby." She stood and waited on the table.

Mary was still eating, when suddenly she rose up, saying: —

" Why, where is Mr. ——, your brother?"

" He's gone to take a sleep outside," said his sister.
" It's too resky for him to sleep in a house."

She faintly smiled, for the first time, at the end of this
long speech.

" But," said Mary, " oh, I haven't uttered a word of
thanks. What will he think of me?"

She sank into her chair again with an elbow on the
table, and looked up at the tall standing figure on the
other side, with a little laugh of mortification.

" You kin thank God," replied the figure. " *He* aint
gone." Another ghost of a smile was seen for a moment

on the grave face. "Sam aint thinkin' about that. You hurry and finish and lay down and sleep, and when you wake up he'll be back here ready, to take you along furder. That's a healthy little one. She wants some more buttermilk. Give it to her. If she don't drink it the pigs'll git it, as the ole woman says. . . . Now you better lay down on the bed in yonder and go to sleep. Jess sort o' loosen yo' cloze; don't take off noth'n' but dress and shoes. You needn't be afeard to sleep sound; I'm goin' to keep a lookout."

CHAPTER LV.

DIXIE.

IN her sleep Mary dreamed over again the late rencon-
tre. Again she heard the challenging outcry, and
again was lashing her horse to his utmost speed; but
this time her enemy seemed too fleet for her. He overtook — he laid his hand upon her. A scream was just at
her lips, when she awoke with a wild start, to find the tall
woman standing over her, and bidding her in a whisper
rise with all stealth and dress with all speed.

"Where's Alice?" asked Mary. "Where's my little
girl?"

"She's there. Never mind her yit, till you're dressed
Here; not them cloze; these here homespun things.
Make haste, but don't get excited."

"How long have I slept?" asked Mary, hurriedly obey-
ing.

"You couldn't 'a' more'n got to sleep. Sam oughtn't
to have shot back at 'em. They're after 'im, hot; four of
'em jess now passed through on the road, right here past
my front gate."

"What kept them back so long?" asked Mary, trom-
blingly attempting to button her dress in the back.

"Let me do that," said the woman. "They couldn't
come very fast; had to kind o' beat the bushes every
hundred yards or so. If they'd of been more of 'em
they'd a-come faster, 'cause they'd a-left one or two
behind at each turn-out, and come along with the rest.

There; now that there hat, there, on the table." As
Mary took the hat the speaker stepped to a window and
peeped into the early day. A suppressed exclamation
escaped her. " O you poor boy ! " she murmured. Mary
sprang toward her, but the stronger woman hurried her
away from the spot.

"Come; take up the little one 'thout wakin' her.
Three more of 'em's a-passin'. The little young feller in
the middle reelin' and swayin' in his saddle, and t'others
givin' him water from his canteen."

" Wounded ? " asked Mary, with a terrified look, bringing the sleeping child.

" Yes, the last wound he'll ever git, I reckon. Jess
take the baby, so. Sam's already took her cloze. He's
waitin' out in the woods here behind the house. He's got
the critters down in the hollow. Now, here ! This here
bundle's a ridin'-skirt. It's not mournin', but you mustn't
mind. It's mighty green and cottony-lookin', but — anyhow, you jess put it on when you git into the woods.
Now it's good sun-up outside. The way you must do —
you jess keep on the lef' side o' me, close, so as when I
jess santer out e-easy todex the back gate you'll be hid
from all the other houses. Then when we git to the back
gate I'll kind o' stand like I was lookin' into the pig-pen,
and you jess slide away on a line with me into the woods,
and there'll be Sam. No, no; take your hat off and sort
o' hide it. Now; you ready ? "

Mary threw her arms around the woman's neck and
kissed her passionately.

"Oh, don't stop for that !" said the woman, smiling
with an awkward diffidence. " Come !"

" What is the day of the month ? " asked Mary of the
spy.

They had been riding briskly along a mere cattle-path in the woods for half an hour, and had just struck into an old, unused road that promised to lead them presently into and through some fields of cotton. Alice, slumbering heavily, had been, little by little, dressed, and was now in the man's arms. As Mary spoke they slackened pace to a quiet trot, and crossed a broad highway nearly at right angles.

"That would 'a' been our road with the buggy," said the man, " if we could of took things easy." They were riding almost straight away from the sun. His dress had been changed again, and in a suit of new, dark brown homespun wool, over a pink calico shirt and white cuffs and collar, he presented the best possible picture of spruce gentility that the times would justify. " ' What day of the month,' did you ask? *I'*ll never tell you, but I know it's Friday."

"Then it's the eighteenth," said Mary.

They met an old negro driving three yoke of oxen attached to a single empty cart.

"Uncle," said the spy, " I don't reckon the boss will mind our sort o' ridin' straight thoo his grove, will he?"

"Not 'tall, boss; on'y dess be so kyine an' shet de gates behine you, sah."

They passed those gates and many another, shutting them faithfully, and journeying on through miles of fragrant lane and fields of young cotton and corn, and stretches of wood where the squirrel scampered before them and reaches of fallow grounds still wet with dew, and patches of sedge, and old fields grown up with thickets of young trees ; now pushing their horses to a rapid gallop, where they were confident of escaping notice, and now ambling leisurely, where the eyes of men afield, or of women at home, followed them with nr io scrutiny; or some straggling Confederate soldier on foot or in the saddle met them in the way.

"How far must we go before we can stop?" asked Mary.

"Jess as far's the critters'll take us without showin' distress."

"South is out that way, isn't it?" she asked again, pointing off to the left.

"Look here," said the spy, with a look that was humorous, but not only humorous.

"What?"

"Two or three times last night, and now ag'in, you gimme a sort o' sneakin' notion you don't trust me," said he.

"Oh!" exclaimed she, "I do! Only I'm so anxious to be going south."

"Jess so," said the man. "Well, we're goin' sort o' due west right now. You see we dassent take this railroad anywheres about here," — they were even then crossing the track of the Mobile and Ohio Railway — "because that's jess where they *sho* to be on the lookout fur us. And I can't take you straight south on the dirt roads, because I don't know the country down that way. But this way I know it like your hand knows the way to your mouth, as the felleh says. Learned it most all sence the war broke out, too. And so the whole thing is we got to jess keep straight across the country here till we strike the Mississippi Central."

"What time will that be?"

"Time! You don't mean time o' day, do you?" he asked.

"Yes," said Mary, smiling.

"Why, we'll be lucky to make it in two whole days. Won't we, Alice!" The child had waked, and was staring into her mother's face. Mary caressed her. The spy looked at them silently. The mother looked up, as if to speak, but was silent.

"Hello!" said the man, softly; for a tear shone through her smile. Whereat she laughed.

"I ought to be ashamed to be so unreasonable," she said.

"Well, now, I'd like to contradict you for once," responds the spy; "but the fact is, how kin I, when Noo Orleens is jest about south-west frum here, anyhow?"

"Yes," said Mary, pleasantly, "it's between south and south-west."

The spy made a gesture of mock amazement.

"Well, you air partickly what you say. I never hear o' but one party that was more partickly than you. I reckon you never hear' tell o' him, did you?"

"Who was he?" asked Mary.

"Well, I never got his name, nor his habitation, as the felleh says; but he was so conscientious that when a highwayman attackted him onct, he wouldn't holla murder nor he wouldn't holla thief, 'cause he wasn't certain whether the highwayman wanted to kill him or rob him. He was something like George Washington, who couldn't tell a lie. Did you ever hear that story about George Washington?"

"About his chopping the cherry-tree with his hatchet?" asked Mary.

"Oh, I see you done heard the story!" said the spy, and left it untold; but whether he was making game of his auditor or not she did not know, and never found out. But on they went, by many a home; through miles of growing crops, and now through miles of lofty pine forests, and by log-cabins and unpainted cottages, from within whose open doors came often the loud feline growl of the spinning-wheel. So on and on, Mary spending the first night in a lone forest cabin of pine poles, whose master, a Confederate deserter, fed his ague-shaken wife and cotton-headed children oftener with the spoils of his rifle than with the products of the field. The spy and the deserter lay down together, and together rose again with the dawn, in a deep thicket, a few hundred yards away.

The travellers had almost reached the end of this toilsome horseback journey, when rains set in, and, for forty-eight hours more, swollen floods and broken bridges held them back, though within hearing of the locomotive's whistle.

But at length, one morning, Mary stepped aboard the train that had not long before started south from the town of Holly Springs, Mississippi, assisted with decorous alacrity by the conductor, and followed by the station-agent with Alice in his arms, and by the telegraph-operator with a home-made satchel or two of luggage and luncheon. It was disgusting, — to two thin, tough-necked women, who climbed aboard, unassisted, at the other end of the same coach.

"You kin just bet she's a widder, and them fellers knows it," said one to the other, taking a seat and spitting expertly through the window.

"If she aint," responded the other, putting a peeled snuff-stick into her cheek, "then her husband's got the brass buttons, and they knows that. Look at 'er a-smi-i-ilin' ! "

"What you reckon makes her look so wore out?" asked the first. And the other replied promptly, with unbounded loathing, "Dayncin'," and sent her emphasis out of the window in liquid form without disturbing her intervening companion.

During the delay caused by the rain Mary had found

time to refit her borrowed costume. Her dress was a stout, close-fitting homespun of mixed cotton and wool, woven in a neat plaid of walnut-brown, oak-red, and the pale olive dye of the hickory. Her hat was a simple round thing of woven pine straw, with a slightly drooping brim, its native brown gloss undisturbed, and the low crown wrapped about with a wreath of wild grasses plaited together with a bit of yellow cord. Alice wore a much-washed pink calico frock and a hood of the same stuff.

" Some officer's wife," said two very sweet and lady-like persons, of unequal age and equal good taste in dress, as their eyes took an inventory of her apparel. They wore bonnets that were quite handsome, and had real false flowers and silk ribbons on them.

" Yes, she's been to camp somewhere to see him."

" Beautiful child she's got," said one, as Alice began softly to smite her mother's shoulder for private attention, and to whisper gravely as Mary bent down.

Two or three soldiers took their feet off the seats, and one of them, at the amiably murmured request of the conductor, put his shoes on.

" The car in front is your car," said the conductor to another man, in especially dirty gray uniform.

" You kin hev it," said the soldier, throwing his palm open with an air of happy extravagance, and a group of gray-headed " citizens," just behind, exploded a loud country laugh.

" D' I onderstaynd you to lafe at me, saw?" drawled the soldier, turning back with a pretence of heavy gloom on his uncombed brow.

" Laughin' at yo' friend yondeh," said one of the citizens, grinning and waving his hand after the departing conductor.

"'Caze if you lafe at me again, saw," — the frown deepened, — " I'll thess go 'ight straight out iss caw." '

The laugh that followed this dreadful threat was loud and general, the victims laughing loudest of all, and the soldier smiling about benignly, and slowly scratching his elbows. Even the two ladies smiled. Alice's face remained impassive. She looked twice into her mother's to see if there was no smile there. But the mother smiled at her, took off her hood and smoothed back the fine gold, then put the hood on again, and tied its strings under the upstretched chin.

Presently Alice pulled softly at the hollow of her mother's elbow.

" Mamma — mamma ! " she whispered. Mary bowed her ear. The child gazed solemnly across the car at another stranger, then pulled the mother's arm again, " That man over there — winked at me."

And thereupon another man, sitting sidewise on the seat in front, and looking back at Alice, tittered softly, and said to Mary, with a raw drawl : —

" She's a-beginnin' young."

" She means some one on the other side," said Mary, quite pleasantly, and the man had sense enough to hush.

The jest and the laugh ran to and fro everywhere. It seemed very strange to Mary to find it so. There were two or three convalescent wounded men in the car, going home on leave, and they appeared never to weary of the threadbare joke of calling their wounds " furloughs." There was one little slip of a fellow — he could hardly have been seventeen — wounded in the hand, whom they kept teazed to the point of exasperation by urging him to confess that he had shot himself for a furlough, and of

---

¹ Out of this car.

whom they said, later, when he had got off at a flag station, that he was the bravest soldier in his company. No one on the train seemed to feel that he had got all that was coming to him until the conductor had exchanged a jest with him. The land laughed. On the right hand and on the left it dimpled and wrinkled in gentle depressions and ridges, and rolled away in fields of young corn and cotton. The train skipped and clattered along at a happy-go-lucky, twelve-miles-an-hour gait, over trestles and stock-pits, through flowery cuts and along slender, rain-washed embankments where dewberries were ripening, and whence cattle ran down and galloped off across the meadows on this side and that, tails up and heads down, throwing their horns about, making light of the screaming destruction, in their dumb way, as the people made light of the war. At stations where the train stopped — and it stopped on the faintest excuse — a long line of heads and gray shoulders was thrust out of the windows of the soldiers' car, in front, with all manner of masculine head-coverings, even bloody handkerchiefs; and woe to the negro or negress or "citizen" who, by any conspicuous demerit or excellence of dress, form, stature, speech, or bearing, drew the fire of that line! No human power of face or tongue could stand the incessant volley of stale quips and mouldy jokes, affirmative, interrogative, and exclamatory, that fell about their victim.

At one spot, in a lovely natural grove, where the air was spiced with the gentle pungency of the young hickory foliage, the train paused a moment to let off a man in fine gray cloth, whose yellow stripes and one golden star on the coat-collar indicated a major of cavalry. It seemed as though pandemonium had opened. Mules braying, negroes yodling, axes ringing, teamsters singing, men shouting and howling, and all at nothing; mess-fires

smoking all about in the same hap-hazard, but roomy, disorder in which the trees of the grove had grown; the
railroad side lined with a motley crowd of jolly fellows
in spurs, and the atmosphere between them and the line
of heads in the car-windows murky with the interchange
of compliments that flew back and forth from the " web-
foots "[1] to the " critter company," and from the " critter
company" to the " web-foots." As the train moved off,
" I say, boys," drawled a lank, coatless giant on the
roadside, with but one suspender and one spur, " tha-at's
right! Gen'l Beerygyard told you to strike fo' yo' homes,
an' I see you' a-doin' it ez fass as you kin git thah."
And the " citizens " in the rear car-windows giggled even
at that; while the " web-foots " he-hawed their derision,
and the train went on, as one might say, with its hands
in its pockets, whooping and whistling over the fields —
after the cows; for the day was declining.

Mary was awed. As she had been forewarned to do,
she tried not to seem unaccustomed to, or out of harmony
with, all this exuberance. But there was something so
brave in it, coming from a people who were playing a losing game with their lives and fortunes for their stakes;
something so gallant in it, laughing and gibing in the
sight of blood, and smell of fire, and shortness of food and
raiment, that she feared she had betrayed a stranger's
wonder and admiration every time the train stopped, and
the idlers of the station platform lingered about her window and silently paid their ungraceful but complimentary
tribute of simulated casual glances.

For, with all this jest, it was very plain there was but
little joy. It was not gladness; it was bravery. It was
the humor of an invincible spirit — the gayety of defi-

[1] Infantry.

ance. She could easily see the grim earnestness beneath
the jocund temper, and beneath the unrepining smile the
privation and the apprehension. What joy there was, was
a martial joy. The people were confident of victory at
last, — a victorious end, whatever might lie between ·
and of even what lay between they would confess no
fear. Richmond was safe, Memphis safer, New Orleans
safest. Yea, notwithstanding Porter and Farragut were
pelting away at Forts Jackson and St. Philip. Indeed,
if the rumor be true, if Farragut's ships had passed those
forts, leaving Porter behind, then the Yankee sea-serpent
was cut in two, and there was an end of him in that direction. Ha! ha!

"Is to-day the twenty-sixth?" asked Mary, at last, of
one of the ladies in real ribbons, leaning over toward
her.

"Yes, ma'am."

It was the younger one who replied. As she did so she
came over and sat by Mary.

"I judge, from what I heard your little girl asking you,
that you are going beyond Jackson."

"I'm going to New Orleans."

"Do you live there?" The lady's interest seemed
genuine and kind.

"Yes. I am going to join my husband there."

Mary saw by the reflection in the lady's face that a
sudden gladness must have overspread her own.

"He'll be mighty glad, I'm sure," said the pleasant
stranger, patting Alice's cheek, and looking, with a pretty
fellow-feeling, first into the child's face and then into
Mary's.

"Yes, he will," said Mary, looking down upon the
curling locks at her elbow with a mother's happiness.

"Is he in the army?" asked the lady.

Mary's face fell.

" His health is bad," she replied.

" I know some nice people down in New Orleans," said the lady again.

" We haven't many acquaintances," rejoined Mary, with a timidity that was almost trepidation. Her eyes dropped, and she began softly to smooth Alice's collar and hair.

" I didn't know," said the lady, " but you might know some of them. For instance, there's Dr. Sevier."

Mary gave a start and smiled.

" Why, is he your friend too?" she asked. She looked up into the lady's quiet, brown eyes and down again into her own lap, where her hands had suddenly knit together, and then again into the lady's face. " We have no friend like Dr. Sevier."

" Mother," called the lady softly, and beckoned. The senior lady leaned toward her. " Mother, this lady is from New Orleans and is an intimate friend of Dr. Sevier.'

The mother was pleased.

" What might one call your name?" she asked, taking a seat behind Mary and continuing to show her pleasure.

" Richling."

The mother and daughter looked at each other. They had never heard the name before.

Yet only a little while later the mother was saying to Mary, — they were expecting at any moment to hear the whistle for the terminus of the route, the central Mississippi town of Canton: —

"My dear child, no! I couldn't sleep to-night if I thought you was all alone in one o' them old hotels in Canton. No, you must come home with us. We're barely two mile' from town, and we'll have the carriage ready for you bright and early in the morning, and our

coachman will put you on the cars just as nice —
Trouble?" She laughed at the idea. "No; I tell you
what would trouble me,— that is, if we'd allow it; that'd
be for you to stop in one o' them hotels all alone, child,
and like' as not some careless servant not wake you in
time for the cars to-morrow." At this word she saw
capitulation in Mary's eyes. "Come, now, my child,
we're not going to take no for an answer."

Nor did they.

But what was the result? The next morning, when
Mary and Alice stood ready for the carriage, and it was
high time they were gone, the carriage was not ready;
the horses had got astray in the night. And while the
black coachman was on one horse, which he had found
and caught, and was scouring the neighboring fields and
lanes and meadows in search of the other, there came out
from townward upon the still, country air the long whistle
of the departing train; and then the distant rattle and roar
of its far southern journey began, and then its warning
notes to the scattering colts and cattle.

"Look away!" — it seemed to sing — "Look away!"
— the notes fading, failing, on the ear,— "away — away
— away down south in Dixie," — the last train that left
for New Orleans until the war was over.

CHAPTER LVI.

FIRE AND SWORD.

THE year the war began dates also, for New Orleans, the advent of two better things: street-cars and the fire-alarm telegraph. The frantic incoherence of the old alarum gave way to the few solemn, numbered strokes that called to duty in the face of hot danger, like the electric voice of a calm commander. The same new system also silenced, once for all, the old nine-o'clock gun. For there were not only taps to signify each new fire-district, — one for the first, two for the second, three, four, five, six seven, eight, and nine, — but there was also one lone toll at mid-day for the hungry mechanic, and nine at the evening hour when the tired workman called his children in from the street and turned to his couch, and the slave must show cause in a master's handwriting why he or she was not under that master's roof.

And then there was one signal more. Fire is a dreadful thing, and all the alarm signals were for fire except this one. Yet the profoundest wish of every good man and tender women in New Orleans, when this pleasing novelty of electro-magnetic warnings was first published for the common edification, was that mid-day or midnight, midsummer or midwinter, let come what might of danger or loss or distress, that one particular signal might not sound. Twelve taps. Anything but that.

Dr. Sevier and Richling had that wish together. They had many wishes that were greatly at variance the one's from the other's. The Doctor had struggled for the Union until the very smoke of war began to rise into the sky; but then he "went with the South." He was the only one in New Orleans who knew — whatever some others may have suspected — that Richling's heart was on the other side. Had Richling's bodily strength remained, so that he could have been a possible factor, however small, in the strife, it is hard to say whether they could have been together day by day and night by night, as they came to be when the Doctor took the failing man into his own home, and have lived in amity, as they did. But there is this to be counted; they were both, though from different directions, for peace, and their gentle forbearance toward each other taught them a moderation of sentiment concerning the whole great issue. And, as I say, they both together held the one .onging hope that, whatever war should bring of final gladness or lamentation, the steeples of New Orleans might never toll — twelve.

But one bright Thursday April morning, as Richling was sitting, half dressed, by an open window of his room in Dr. Sevier's house, leaning on the arm of his soft chair and looking out at the passers on the street, among whom he had begun to notice some singular evidences of excitement, there came from a slender Gothic church-spire that was highest of all in the city, just beyond a few roofs in front of him, the clear, sudden, brazen peal of its one great bell.

"Fire," thought Richling; and yet, he knew not why, wondered where Dr. Sevier might be. He had not seen him that morning. A high official had sent for him at sunrise and he had not returned.

"Clang," went the bell again, and the softer ding — dang — dong of others, struck at the same instant, came floating in from various distances. And then it clanged again — and again — and again — the loud one near, the soft ones, one by one, after it — six, seven, eight, nine — ah! stop there! stop there! But still the alarm pealed on; ten — alas! alas! — eleven — oh, oh, the women and children! — twelve! And then the fainter, final asseverations of the more distant bells — twelve! twelve! twelve! — and a hundred and seventy thousand souls knew by that sign that the foe had passed the forts. New Orleans had fallen.

Richling dressed himself hurriedly and went out. Everywhere drums were beating to arms. Couriers and aides-de-camp were galloping here and there. Men in uniform were hurrying on foot to this and that rendezvous. Crowds of the idle and poor were streaming out toward the levee. Carriages and cabs rattled frantically from place to place; men ran out-of-doors and leaped into them and leaped out of them and sprang up stairways; hundreds of all manner of vehicles, fit and unfit to carry passengers and goods, crowded toward the railroad depots and steam-boat landings; women ran into the streets wringing their hands and holding their brows; and children stood in the door-ways and gate-ways and trembled and called and cried.

Richling took the new Dauphine street-car. Far down in the Third district, where there was a silence like that of a village lane, he approached a little cottage painted with Venetian red, setting in its garden of oranges, pomegranates, and bananas, and marigolds, and coxcombs behind its white paling fence and green gate.

The gate was open. In it stood a tall, strong woman, good-looking, rosy, and neatly dressed. That she was tall you could prove by the gate, and that she was strong, by the graceful muscularity with which she held two infants, — pretty, swarthy little fellows, with joyous black eyes, and evidently of one age and parentage, — each in the hollow of a fine, round arm. There was just a hint of emotional disorder in her shining hair and a trace of tears about her eyes. As the visitor drew near, a fresh show of distressed exaltation was visible in the slight play of her form.

"Ah! Mr. Richlin'," she cried, the moment he came within hearing, "'the dispot's heels is on our shores!'" Tears filled her eyes again. Mike, the bruiser, in his sixth year, who had been leaning backward against her knees and covering his legs with her skirts, ran forward and clasped the visitor's lower limbs with the nerve and intention of a wrestler. Kate followed with the cherubs. They were Raphael's.

"Yes, it's terrible," said Richling.

"Ah! no, Mr. Richlin'," replied Kate, lifting her head proudly as she returned with him toward the gate, "it's outrageouz; but it's not terrible. At least it's not for me, Mr. Richlin'. I'm only Mrs. Captain Ristofalah; and whin I see the collonels' and gin'r'ls' ladies a-prancin' around in their carridges I feel my *humility;* but it's my djuty to be *brave,* sur! An' I'll help to *fight* thim, sur, if the min can't do ud. Mr. Richlin', my husband is the intimit frind of Gin'r'l Garrybaldy, sur! I'll help to burrin the cittee, sur! — rather nor give ud up to thim vandjals! Come in, Mr. Richlin'; come in." She led the way up the narrow shell-walk. "Come in, sur, it may be the last time ye' do ud before the flames is leppin' from the roof! Ah! I knowed ye'd come. I was a-lookin' for ye. I knowed *ye'd* prcve yerself tnat frind in need that he's the frind indeed! Take a seat an' sit down." She faced about on the vine-covered porch, and dropped into a rocking-chair, her eyes still at the point of over flow "But ah! Mr. Richlin', where's all thim flatterers that fawned around uz in the days of tytled prosperity?"

Richling said nothing; he had not seen any throngs of that sort.

"Gone, sur! and it's a relief; it's a relief, Mr. Richlin'!" She marshalled the twins on her lap, Carlo commanding the right, Francisco the left.

"You mustn't expect too much of them," said Richling, drawing Mike between his knees, "in such a time of alarm and confusion as this." And Kate responded generously: —

"Well, I suppose you're right, sur."

"I've come down," resumed the visitor, letting Mike count off "Rich man, poor man, beggar man, thief," on the buttons of his coat, "to give you any help I can in getting ready to leave town. For you mustn't think of staying. It isn't possible to be anything short of dreadful to stay in a city occupied by hostile troops. It's almost certain the Confederates will try to hold the city, and there may be a bombardment. The city may be taken and retaken half-a-dozen times before the war is over."

"Mr. Richlin'," said Kate, with a majestic lifting of the hand, "I'll niver rin away from the Yanks."

"No, but you must *go* away from them. You mustn't put yourself in such a position that you can't go to your husband if he needs you, Mrs. Ristofalo; don't get separated from him."

"Ah! Mr. Richlin', it's you as has the right to say so; and I'll do as you say. Mr. Richlin', my husband"—her voice trembled—"may be wounded this hour. I'll go, sur, indeed I will; but, sur, if Captain Raphael Ristofalah wor *here*, sur, he'd be ad the *front*, sur, and Kate Ristofalah would be at his galliant side!"

"Well, then, I'm glad he's not here," rejoined Richling, "for I'd have to take care of the children."

"Ha! ha! ha!" laughed Kate. "No, sur! I'd take
the lion's whelps with me, sur! Why, that little Mike
theyre can han'le the dthrum-sticks to beat the felley in
the big hat!" And she laughed again.

They made arrangements for her and the three children
to go "out into the confederacy" within two or three
days at furthest; as soon as she and her feeble helper
could hurry a few matters of business to completion at and
about the Picayune Tier. Richling did not get back to
the Doctor's house until night had fallen and the sky was
set aglare by seven miles' length of tortuous harbor front
covered with millions' worth of burning merchandise.
The city was being evacuated.

Dr. Sevier and he had but few words. Richling was
dejected from weariness, and his friend weary with de-
jections.

"Where have you been all day?" asked the Doctor,
with a touch of irritation.

"Getting Kate Ristofalo ready to leave the city."

"You shouldn't have left the house; but it's no use to
tell you anything. Has she gone?"

"No."

"Well, in the name of common-sense, then, when is
she going?"

"In two or three days," replied Richling, almost in
retort.

The Doctor laughed with impatience.

"If you feel responsible for her going get her off by
to-morrow afternoon at the furthest." He dropped his
tired head against the back of his chair.

"Why," said Richling, "I don't suppose the fleet can

fight its way through all opposition and get here short of a week."

The Doctor laid his long fingers upon his brow and rolled his head from side to side. Then, slowly raising it : —

"Well, Richling!" he said, "there must have been some mistake made when you was put upon the earth."

Richling's thin cheek flushed. The Doctor's face confessed the bitterest resentment.

"Why, the fleet is only eighteen miles from here now." He ceased, and then added, with sudden kindness of tone, "I want you to do something for me, will you?"

"Yes."

"Well, then, go to bed ; I'm going. You'll need every grain of strength you've got for to-morrow. I'm afraid then it will not be enough. This is an awful business, Richling."

They went upstairs together. As they were parting at its top Richling said : —

"You told me a few days ago that if the city should fall, which we didn't expect" —

"That I'd not leave," said the Doctor. "No; I shall stay. I haven't the stamina to take the field, and I can't be a runaway. Anyhow, I couldn't take you along. You couldn't bear the travel, and I wouldn't go and leave you here, Richling — old fellow!"

He laid his hand gently on the sick man's shoulder, who made no response, so afraid was he that another word would mar the perfection of the last.

When Richling went out the next morning the whole city was in an ecstasy of rage and terror. Thousands had gathered what they could in their hands, and were flying by every avenue of escape. Thousands ran hither and thither, not knowing where or how to fly. He saw the wife and son of the silver-haired banker rattling and bouncing away toward one of the railway depots in a butcher's cart. A messenger from Kate by good chance met him with word that she would be ready for the afternoon train of the Jackson Railroad, and asking anew his earliest attention to her interests about the lugger landing.

He hastened to the levee. The huge, writhing river, risen up above the town, was full to the levee's top, and, as though the enemy's fleet was that much more than it could bear, was silently running over by a hundred rills into the streets of the stricken city.

As far as the eye could reach, black smoke, white smoke, brown smoke, and red flames rolled and spread, and licked and leaped, from unnumbered piles of cotton bales, and wooden wharves, and ships cut adrift, and steam-boats that blazed like shavings, floating down the harbor as they blazed. He stood for a moment to see a little revenue cutter, — a pretty topsail schooner, — lying at the foot of Canal street, sink before his eyes into the turbid yellow depths of the river, scuttled. Then he hurried on. Huge mobs ran to and fro in the fire and smoke, howling, breaking, and stealing. Women and children hurried back and forth like swarms of giant ants, with buckets and baskets, and dippers and bags, and bonnets, hats, petticoats, anything, — now empty, and now full of rice and sugar and meal and corn and syrup, — and robbed each other, and cursed and fought, and slipped down in pools of molasses, and threw live pigs and coops of chickens into the river, and with one voiceless rush left the broad levee a smoking, crackling desert, when some shells exploded on a burning gunboat, and presently were back again like a flock of evil birds.

It began to rain, but Richling sought no shelter. The

CHAPTER LVII.

ALMOST IN SIGHT.

IN St. Tammany Parish, on the northern border of Lake Ponchartrain, about thirty miles from New Orleans, in a straight line across the waters of the lake, stood in time of the war, and may stand yet, an old house, of the Creole colonial fashion, all of cypress from sills to shingles, standing on brick pillars ten feet from the ground, a wide veranda in front, and a double flight of front steps running up to it sidewise and meeting in a balustraded landing at its edge. Scarcely anything short of a steamer's roof or a light-house window could have offered a finer stand-point from which to sweep a glass round the southern semi-circle of water and sky than did this stair-landing; and here, a long ship's-glass in her hands, and the accustomed look of care on her face, faintly frowning against the glare of noonday, stood Mary Richling. She still had on the pine-straw hat, and the skirt — stirring softly in a breeze that had to come around from the north side of the house before it reached her — was the brown and olive homespun.

"No use," said an old, fat, and sun-tanned man from his willow chair on the veranda behind her. There was a slight palsied oscillation in his head. He leaned forward somewhat on a staff, and as he spoke his entire shapeless and nearly helpless form quaked with the effort. But Mary, for all his advice, raised the glass and swung it slowly from east to west.

The house was near the edge of a slightly rising ground, close to the margin of a bayou that glided around toward the left from the woods at its back, and ran, deep and silent, under the shadows of a few huge, wide-spreading, moss-hung live-oaks that stood along its hither shore, laving their roots in its waters, and throwing their vast green images upon its glassy surface. As the dark stream slipped away from these it flashed a little while in the bright open space of a marsh, and, just entering the shade of a spectral cypress wood, turned as if to avoid it, swung more than half about, and shone sky-blue, silver, and green as it swept out into the unbroken sunshine of the prairie.

It was over this flowery savanna, broadening out on either hand, and spreading far away until its bright green margin joined, with the perfection of a mosaic, the distant blue of the lake, that Mary, dallying a moment with hope, passed her long glass. She spoke with it still raised and her gaze bent through it: —

"There's a big alligator crossing the bayou down in the bend."

"Yes," said the aged man, moving his flat, carpet-slippered feet a laborious inch; "alligator. Alligator not goin' take you 'cross lake. No use lookin'. 'Ow Peter goin' come when win' dead ahead? Can't do it."

Yet Mary lifted the glass a little higher, beyond the green, beyond the crimpling wavelets of the nearer distance that seemed drawn by the magical lens almost into her hand, out to the fine, straight line that cut the cool blue below from the boundless blue above. Round swung the glass, slowly, waveringly, in her unpractised hand, from the low cypress forests of Manchac on the west, to the skies that glittered over the unseen marshes of the Rigolets on the farthest east.

" You see sail yondeh?" came the slow inquiry from behind.

" No," said Mary, letting the instrument down, and resting it on the balustrade.

" Humph! No! Dawn't I tell you is no use look? "

" He was to have got here three days ago," said Mary, shutting the glass and gazing in anxious abstraction across the prairie.

The Spanish Creole grunted.

"When win' change, he goin' start. He dawn't start till win' change. Win' keep ligue dat, he dawn't start 't all." He moved his orange-wood staff an inch, to suit the previous movement of his feet, and Mary came and laid the glass on its brackets in the veranda, near the open door of a hall that ran through the dwelling to another veranda in the rear.

In the middle of the hall a small woman, as dry as the peppers that hung in strings on the wall behind her, sat in a rush-bottomed rocking-chair plaiting a palmetto hat, and with her elbow swinging a tattered manilla hammock, in whose bulging middle lay Alice, taking her compulsory noonday nap. Mary came, expressed her thanks in sprightly whispers, lifted the child out, and carried her to a room. How had Mary got here?

The morning after that on which she had missed the cars at Canton she had taken a south-bound train for Camp Moore, the camp of the forces that had evacuated New Orleans, situated near the railway station of Tangipahoa, some eighty miles north of the captured city. Thence, after a day or two of unavoidable delay, and of careful effort to know the wisest step, she had taken stage, — a crazy ambulance, — with some others, two women, three children, and an old man, and for two days had travelled through a beautiful country of red and yellow clays

and sands below and murmuring pines above, — vast col-
onnades of towering, branchless brown columns holding
high their green, translucent roof, and opening up their
wide, bright, sunshot vistas of gentle, grassy hills that
undulated far away under the balsamic forest, and melted
at length into luminous green unity and deer-haunted
solitudes.   Now she went down into richer bottom-lands,
where the cotton and corn were growing tall and pretty
to look upon, like suddenly grown ·girls, and the sun
was beginning to shine hot.   Now she passed over rustic
bridges, under posted warnings to drive slow or pay a fine,
or through sandy fords across purling streams, hearing
the monotone of some unseen mill-dam, or scaring the
tall gray crane from his fishing, or the otter from his
pranks.   Again she went up into leagues of clear pine
forest, with stems as straight as lances ; meeting now a
farmer, and now a school-girl or two, and once a squad
of scouts, ill-mounted, worse clad, and yet more sorrily
armed ; bivouacking with the jolly, tattered fellows, Mary
and one of the other women singing for them, and the
" boys " singing for Mary, and each applauding each
about the pine-knot fire, and the women and children by
and by lying down to slumber, in soldier fashion, with
their feet to the brands, under the pines and the stars,
while the gray-coats stood guard in the wavering fire-
light ; but Mary lying broad awake staring at the great
constellation of the Scorpion, and thinking now of him
she sought, and now remorsefully of that other scout, that
poor boy whom the spy had shot far away yonder to the
north and eastward.   Now she rose and journeyed again.
Rare hours were those for Alice.   They came at length
into a low, barren land, of dwarfed and scrawny pines,
with here and there a marshy flat ; thence through a
narrow strip of hickories, oaks, cypresses, and dwarf

palmetto, and so on into beds of white sand and oyster-shells, and then into one of the villages on the north shore of Lake Pontchartrain.

Her many little adventures by the way, the sayings and doings and seeings of Alice, and all those little adroitnesses by which Mary from time to time succeeded in avoiding or turning aside the suspicions that hovered about her, and the hundred times in which Alice was her strongest and most perfect protection, we cannot pause to tell. But we give a few lines to one matter.

Mary had not yet descended from the ambulance at her journey's end; she and Alice only were in it; its tired mules were dragging it slowly through the sandy street of the village, and the driver was praising the milk, eggs, chickens, and genteel seclusion of Mrs.——'s "hotel," at that end of the village toward which he was driving, when a man on horseback met them, and, in passing, raised his hat to Mary. The act was only the usual courtesy of the highway; yet Mary was startled, disconcerted, and had to ask the unobservant, loquacious driver to repeat what he had said. Two days afterward Mary was walking at the twilight hour, in a narrow, sandy road, that ran from the village out into the country to the eastward. Alice walked beside her, plying her with questions. At a turn of the path, without warning, she confronted this horseman again. He reined up and lifted his hat. An elated look brightened his face.

"It's all fixed," he said. But Mary looked distressed, even alarmed.

"You shouldn't have done this," she replied.

The man waved his hand downward repressively, but with a countenance full of humor.

"Hold on. It's *still* my deal. This is the last time, and then I'm done. Make a spoon or spoil a horn, you know. When you commence to do a thing, do it. Them's the words that's inscribed on my banner, as the felleh says; only I, Sam, aint got much banner. And if I sort o' use about this low country a little while for my health, as it were, and nibble around sort o' *pro bono publico* takin' notes, why you aint a-carin', is you? For wherefore shouldest thou?" He put on a yet more ludicrous look, and spread his hand off at one side, working his outstretched fingers.

"Yes," responded Mary, with severe gravity; "I must care. You did finish at Holly Springs. I was to find the rest of the way as best I could. That was the understanding. Go away!" She made a commanding gesture, though she wore a pleading look. He looked grave; but his habitual grimace stole through his gravity and invited her smile. But she remained fixed. He gathered the rein and straightened up in the saddle.

"Yes," she insisted, answering his inquiring attitude; "go! I shall be grateful to you as long as I live. It wasn't because I mistrusted you that I refused your aid at Camp Moore or at —— that other place on this side. I don't mistrust you. But don't you see — you must see — it's your duty to see — that this staying and — and — foll — following — is — is — wrong." She stood, holding her skirt in one hand, and Alice's hand in the other, not upright, but in a slightly shrinking attitude, and as she added once more, "Go! I implore you — go!" her eyes filled.

"I will; I'll go," said the man, with a soft chuckle, intended for self-abasement. "I go, thou goest, he goes. 'I'll skedaddle,' as the felleh says. And yit it do seem to me sorter like, — if my moral sense is worthy of any consideration, which is doubtful, may be, — seems to me like it's sort o' jumpin' the bounty for you to go and go back on an arrangement that's been all fixed up nice and tight, and when it's on'y jess to sort o' ' jump into the wagon' that's to call for you to-morrow, sun-up, drove by a nigger boy, and ride a few mile' to a house on the bayou, and wait there till a man comes with a nice little schooner, and take you on bode and sail off, and ' good-by, Sally,' and me never in sight from fust to last, ' and no questions axed.' "

" I don't reject the arrangement," replied Mary, with tearful pleasantness. " If you'll do as I say, I'll do as you say ; and that will be final proof to you that I believe you're "— she fell back a step, laughingly — " ' the clean sand ! '" She thought the man would have perpetrated some small antic ; but he did not. He did not even smile, but lifted the rein a little till the horse stepped forward, and, putting out his hand, said : —

" Good-by. You don't need no directions. Jess tell the lady where you' boardin' that you've sort o' consented to spend a day or two with old Adrien Sanchez, and get into the wagon when it comes for you." He let go her hand. " Good-by, Alice." The child looked up in silence and pressed herself against her mother. " Good-by," said he once more.

" Good-by," replied Mary.

His eyes lingered as she dropped her own.

" Come, Alice," she said, resisting the little one's effort to stoop and pick a wild-pea blossom, and the mother and child started slowly back the way they had come. The spy turned his horse, and moved still more slowly in the opposite direction. But before he had gone many rods he turned the animal's head again, rode as slowly back, and, beside the spot where Mary had stood, got down, and from the small imprint of her shoe in the damp sand took the pea-blossom, which, in turning to

depart, she had unawares trodden under foot.   He looked
at the small, crushed thing for a moment, and then thrust
it into his bosom; but in a moment, as if by a counter
impulse, drew it forth again, let it flutter to the ground,
following it with his eyes, shook his head with an amused
air, half of defiance and half of discomfiture, turned, drew
himself into the saddle, and with one hand laid upon
another on the saddle-bow and his eyes resting on them
in meditation, passed finally out of sight.

Here, then, in this lone old Creole cottage, Mary was
tarrying, prisoner of hope, coming out all hours of the
day, and scanning the wide view, first, only her hand to
shade her brow, and then with the old ship's-glass, Alice
often standing by and looking up at this extraordinary
toy with unspoken wonder.   All that Mary could tell her
of things seeable through it could never persuade the
child to risk her own eye at either end of it.   So Mary
would look again and see, out in the prairie, in the morning, the reed birds, the marsh hen, the blackbirds, the
sparrows, the starlings, with their red and yellow epaulets,
rising and fluttering and sinking again among the lilies
and mallows, and the white crane, paler than a ghost,
wading in the grassy shallows.   She saw the ravening
garfish leap from the bayou, and the mullet in shining
hundreds spatter away to left and right; and the fisherman and the shrimp-catcher in their canoes come gliding
up the glassy stream, riding down the water-lilies, that
rose again behind and shook the drops from their crowns,
like water-sprites.   Here and there, farther out, she saw
the little cat-boats of the neighboring village crawling along
the edge of the lake, taking their timid morning cruises.
And far away she saw the titanic clouds; but on the hori
zon, no sail.

In the evening she would see mocking-birds coming out of the savanna and flying into the live-oaks. A summer duck might dart from the cypresses, speed across the wide green level, and become a swerving, vanishing speck on the sky. The heron might come round the bayou's bend, and suddenly take fright and fly back again. The rattling kingfisher might come up the stream, and the blue crane sail silently through the purple haze that hung between the swamp and the bayou. She would see the gulls, gray and white, on the margin of the lake, the sun setting beyond its western end, and the sky and water turning all beautiful tints; and every now and then, low down along the cool, wrinkling waters, passed across the round eye of the glass the broad, downward-curved wing of the pelican. But when she ventured to lift the glass to the horizon, she swept it from east to west in vain No sail.

" Dawn't I tell you no use look? Peter dawn't comin in day-time, nohow."

But on the fifth morning Mary had hardly made her appearance on the veranda, and had not ventured near the spy-glass yet, when the old man said : —

" She rain back in swamp las' night; can smell."

" How do you feel this morning?" asked Mary, facing around from her first glance across the waters. He did not heed.

" See dat win'?" he asked, lifting one hand a little from the top of his staff.

" Yes," responded Mary, eagerly ; " why, it's — hasn't it — changed?"

" Yes, change' las' night 'fo' went to bed."

The old man's manner betrayed his contempt for one who could be interested in such a change, and yet not know when it took place.

" Why, then," began Mary, and started as if to take down the glass.

" What you doin'? " demanded its owner.   " Better let glass 'lone ; fool' wid him enough."

Mary flushed, and, with a smile of resentful apology, was about to reply, when he continued : —

" What you want glass for?   Dare Peter' schooner — right dare in bayou.   What want glass for?   Can't see schooner hundred yard' off 'dout glass? "   And he turned away his poor wabbling head in disgust.

Mary looked an instant at two bare, rakish, yellow poles showing out against the clump of cypresses, and the trim little white hull and apple-green deck from which they sprang, then clasped her hands and ran into the house.

CHAPTER LVIII.

A GOLDEN SUNSET.

DR. SEVIER came to Richling's room one afternoon, and handed him a sealed letter. The postmark was blurred, but it was easy still to read the abbreviation of the State's name, — Kentucky. It had come by way of New York and the sea. The sick man reached out for it with avidity from the large bed in which he sat bolstered up. He tore it open with unsteady fingers, and sought the signature.

"It's from a lawyer."

"An old acquaintance?" asked the doctor.

"Yes,' responded Richling, his eyes glancing eagerly along the lines. "Mary's in the Confederate lines! — Mary and Alice!" The hand that held the letter dropped to his lap. "It doesn't say a word about how she got through!"

"But *where* did she get through?" asked the physician. "Whereabouts is she now?"

"She got through away up to the eastward of Corinth, Mississippi. Doctor, she may be within fifty miles of us this very minute! Do you think they'll give her a pass to come in?"

"They may, Richling; I hope they will."

"I think I'd get well if she'd come," said the invalid. But his friend made no answer.

A day or two afterward — it was drawing to the close of a beautiful afternoon in early May — Dr. Sevier came into the room and stood at a window looking out. Madame Zénobie sat by the bedside softly fanning the patient. Richling, with his eyes, motioned her to retire. She smiled and nodded approvingly, as if to say that that was just what she was about to propose, and went out, shutting the door with just sound enough to announce her departure to Dr. Sevier.

He came from the window to the bedside and sat down. The sick man looked at him, with a feeble eye, and said, in little more than a whisper : —

" Mary and Alice " —

" Yes," said the Doctor.

" If they don't come to-night they'll be too late."

" God knows, my dear boy ! "

" Doctor " —

" What, Richling ? "

" Did you ever try to guess " —

" Guess what, Richling ? "

" *His* use of my life."

" Why, yes, my poor boy, I have tried. But I only make out its use to me."

The sick man's eye brightened.

" Has it been ? "

The Doctor nodded. He reached out and took the wasted hand in his. It tried to answer his pressure. The invalid spoke.

" I'm glad you told me that before — before it was too late."

" Are you, my dear boy ? Shall I tell you more ? "

" Yes," the sick man huskily replied ; " oh, yes."

" Well, Richling, — you know we're great cowards about saying such things ; it's a part of our poor human weakness and distrust of each other, and the emptiness of words, — but — lately — only just here, very lately, I've learned to call the meekest, lovingest One that ever trod our earth, Master ; and it's been your life, my dear fellow, that has taught me." He pressed the sick man's hand slowly and tremulously, then let it go, but continued to caress it in a tender, absent way, looking on the floor as he spoke on.

"Richling, Nature herself appoints some men to poverty and some to riches. God throws the poor upon our charge — in mercy to *us*. Couldn't he take care of them without us if he wished? Are they not his? It's easy for the poor to feel, when they are helped by us, that the rich are a godsend to them ; but they don't see, and many of their helpers don't see, that the poor are a godsend to the rich. They're set over against each other to keep pity and mercy and charity in the human heart. If every one were entirely able to take care of himself we'd turn to stone." The speaker ceased.

"Go on," whispered the listener.

"That will never be," continued the Doctor. "God Almighty will never let us find a way to quite abolish poverty. Riches don't always bless the man they come to, but they bless the world. And so with poverty ; and it's no contemptible commission, Richling, to be appointed by God to bear that blessing to mankind which keeps its brotherhood universal. See, now," — he looked up with a gentle smile, — "from what a distance he brought our two hearts together. Why, Richling, the man that can make the rich and poor love each other will make the world happier than it has ever been since man fell !'

"Go on," whispered Richling.

"No," said the Doctor.

"Well, now, Doctor — *I* want to say — something." The invalid spoke with a weak and broken utterance, with many breaks and starts that we may set aside.

" For a long time," he said, beginning as if half in soliloquy, " I couldn't believe I was coming to this early end, simply because I didn't see why I should. I know that was foolish. I thought my hardships " — He ceased entirely, and, when his strength would allow, resumed : —

" I thought they were sent in order that when I should come to fortune I might take part in correcting some evils that are strangely overlooked."

The Doctor nodded, and, after a moment of rest, Richling said again : —

" But now I see — that is not my work. May be it is Mary's. May be it's my little girl's."

" Or mine," murmured the Doctor.

" Yes, Doctor, I've been lying here to-day thinking of something I never thought of before, though I dare say you have, often. There could be no art of healing till the earth was full of graves. It is by shipwreck that we learn to build ships. All our safety — all our betterment — is secured by our knowledge of others' disasters that need not have happened had they only *known*. Will you — finish my mission?" The sick man's hand softly grasped the hand that lay upon it. And the Doctor responded : —

" How shall I do that, Richling?"

" Tell my story."

" But I don't know it all, Richling."

" I'll tell you all that's behind. You know I'm a native of Kentucky. My name is not Richling. I belong to one of the proudest, most distinguished families in that State or in all the land. Until I married I never knew an ungratified wish. I think my bringing-up, not to be wicked, was as bad as could be. It was based upon the idea that I was always to be master, and never servant. I was to go through life with soft hands. I

was educated to know, but not to do. When I left
school my parents let me travel. They would have let
me do anything except work. In the West — in Milwaukee — I met Mary. It was by mere chance. She
was poor, but cultivated and refined; trained — you know
— for knowing, not doing. I loved her and courted her,
and she encouraged my suit, under the idea, you know,
again," — he smiled faintly and sadly, — " that it was
nobody's business but ours. I offered my hand and was
accepted. But, when I came to announce our engage-
ment to my family, they warned me that if I married her
they would disinherit and disown me."

" What was their reason, Richling?"

" Nothing."

" But, Richling, they had a reason of some sort."

" Nothing in the world but that Mary was a Northern
girl. Simple sectional prejudice. I didn't tell Mary.
I didn't think they would do it; but I knew Mary would
refuse to put me to the risk. We married, and they
carried out their threat."

The Doctor uttered a low exclamation, and both were
silent.

" Doctor," began the sick man once more.

" Yes, Richling."

" I suppose you never looked into the case of a man
who needed help, but you were sure to find that some one
thing was the key to all his troubles; did you?"

The Doctor was silent again.

" I'll give you the key to mine, Doctor: I took up the
gage thrown down by my family as though it were
thrown down by society at large. I said I would match
pride with pride. I said I would go among strangers,
take a new name, and make it as honorable as the old.
I saw Mary didn't think it wise; but she believed what

ever I did was best, and " — he smiled and whispered
— " I thought so too.   I suppose my troubles have more
than one key ; but that's the outside one.   Let me rest a
little.

" Doctor, I die nameless.   I had a name, a good name,
and only too proud a one.   It's mine still.   I've never
tarnished it — not even in prison.   I will not stain it now
by disclosing it.   I carry it with me to God's throne."

The whisperer ceased, exhausted.   The Doctor rested an
elbow on a knee and laid his face in his hand.   Presently
Richling moved, and he raised a look of sad inquiry.

" Bury me here in New Orleans, Doctor, will you?"

" Why, Richling?"

" Well — this has been — my — battle-ground.   I'd
like to be buried on the field, — like the other soldiers.
Not that I've been a good one ; but — I want to lie where
you can point to me as you tell my story.   If it could be
so, I should like to lie in sight — of that old prison."

The Doctor brushed his eyes with his handkerchief and
wiped his brow.

" Doctor," said the invalid again, " will you read me
just four verses in the Bible ? "

" Why, yes, my boy, as many as you wish to hear."

" No, only four."   His free hand moved for the book
that lay on the bed, and presently the Doctor read : —

" ' My brethren, count it all joy when ye fall into divers temp
tations ;

" ' Knowing this, that the trying of your faith worketh patience.

" ' But let patience have her perfect work, that ye may be perfect and entire, wanting nothing.

" ' If any of you lack wisdom, let him ask of God, that giveth to
all men liberally, and upbraideth not; and it shall be given him.' "

" There," whispered the sick man, and rested with a

peaceful look in all his face. " It — doesn't mean wisdom in general, Doctor, — such as Solomon asked for."

" Doesn't it ? " said the other, meekly.

" No. It means the wisdom necessary to let — patience — have her perf — I was a long time — getting anywhere near that.

" Doctor — do you remember how fond — Mary was of singing — all kinds of — little old songs ? "

" Of course I do, my dear boy."

" Did you ever sing — Doctor ? "

" O my dear fellow ! I never did really sing, and I haven't uttered a note since — for twenty years."

" Can't you sing — ever so softly — just a verse — of — ' I'm a Pilgrim ' ? "

" I — I — it's impossible, Richling, old fellow. I don't know either the words or the tune. I never sing." He smiled at himself through his tears.

" Well, all right," whispered Richling. He lay with closed eyes for a moment, and then, as he opened them, breathed faintly through his parted lips the words, spoken, not sung, while his hand feebly beat the imagined cadence : —

> " ' The sun shines bright in my old Kentucky home ;
>   'Tis summer, the darkies are gay ;
>   The corn-tops are ripe, and the meadows are in bloom,
>   And the birds make music all the day.' "

The Doctor hid his face in his hands, and all was still. By and by there came a whisper again. The Doctor raised his head.

" Doctor, there's one thing " —

" Yes, I know there is, Richling."

" Doctor, — I've been a poor stick of a husband."

" I never knew a good one, Richling."

"Doctor, you'll be a friend to Mary?"

The Doctor nodded; his eyes were full.

The sick man drew from his breast a small ambrotype, pressed it to his lips, and poised it in his trembling fingers. It was the likeness of the little Alice. He turned his eyes to his friend.

"I didn't need Mary's. But this is all I've ever seen of my little girl. To-morrow, at daybreak, — it will be just at daybreak, — when you see that I've passed, I want you to lay this here on my breast. Then fold my hands upon it" —

His speech was arrested. He seemed to hearken an instant.

"Doctor," he said, with excitement in his eye and sudden strength of voice, "what is that I hear?"

"I don't know," replied his friend; "one of the servants probably down in the hall." But he, too, seemed to have been startled. He lifted his head. There was a sound of some one coming up the stairs in haste.

"Doctor." The Doctor was rising from his chair.

"Lie still, Richling."

But the sick man suddenly sat erect.

"Doctor — it's — O Doctor, I" —

The door flew open; there was a low outcry from the threshold, a moan of joy from the sick man, a throwing wide of arms, and a rush to the bedside, and John and Mary Richling — and the little Alice, too —

Come, Doctor Sevier; come out and close the door.

"Strangest thing on earth!" I once heard a physician say,— "the mysterious power that the dying so often have to fix the very hour of their approaching end!" It was so in John Richling's case. It was as he said. Had Mary and Alice not come when they did, they would have been too late. He "tarried but a night;" and at the dawn Mary uttered the bitter cry of the widow, and Doctor Sevier closed the eyes of the one who had committed no fault, — against this world, at least, — save that he had been by nature a pilgrim and a stranger in it.

CHAPTER LIX.

AFTERGLOW.

MARY, with Alice holding one hand, flowers in the other, was walking one day down the central avenue of the old Girod Cemetery, breaking the silence of the place only by the soft grinding of her footsteps on the shell walk, and was just entering a transverse alley, when she stopped.

Just at hand a large, broad woman, very plainly dressed, was drawing back a single step from the front of a tomb, and dropping her hands from a coarse vase of flowers that she had that moment placed on the narrow stone shelf under the tablet. The blossoms touched, without hiding, the newly cut name. She had hung a little plaster crucifix against it from above. She must have heard the footfall so near by, and marked its stoppage; but, with the oblivion common to the practisers of her religion, she took no outward notice. She crossed herself, sank upon her knees, and with her eyes upon the shrine she had made remained thus. The tears ran down Mary's face. It was Madame Zénobie. They went and lived together.

The name of the street where their house stood has slipped me, as has that of the clean, unfrequented, round-stoned way up which one looked from the small cottage's veranda, and which, running down to their old arched gate, came there to an end, as if that were a pretty place to stop at in the shade until evening. Grass grows now, as it did then, between the round stones; and in the towering sycamores of the reddened brick sidewalk the long, quavering note of the cicada parts the wide summer noonday silence. The stillness yields to little else, save now and then the tinkle of a mule-bell, where in the distance the softly rumbling street-car invites one to the centre of the town's activities, or the voice of some fowl that, having laid an egg, is asserting her right to the credit of it. Some forty feet back, within a mossy brick wall that stands waist-high, surmounted by a white, open fence, the green wooden balls on top of whose posts are full eight feet above the sidewalk, the cottage stands high up among a sweet confusion of pale purple and pink crape myrtles, oleanders white and red, and the bristling leaves and plumes of white bells of the Spanish bayonet, all in the shade of lofty magnolias, and one great pecan.

"And this is little Alice," said Doctor Sevier with gentle gravity, as, on his first visit to the place, he shook hands with Mary at the top of the veranda stairs, and laid his fingers upon the child's forehead. He smiled into her uplifted face as her eyes examined his, and stroked the little crown as she turned her glance silently upon her mother, as if to inquire if this were a trustworthy person. Mary led the way to chairs at the veranda's end where the south breeze fanned them, and Alice retreated to her mother's side until her silent question should be settled.

It was still May. They spoke the praises of the day whose sun was just setting. And Mary commended the house, the convenience of its construction, its salubrity; and also, and especially, the excellence and goodness of Madame Zénobie. What a complete and satisfactory arrangement! Was it not? Did not the Doctor think so?

But the Doctor's affirmative responses were unfrequent.

and quite without enthusiasm; and Mary's face, wearing more cheer than was felt within, betrayed, moreover, the feeling of one who, having done the best she knew, falls short of commendation.

She was once more in deep black. Her face was pale, and some of its lines had yielded up a part of their excellence. The outward curves of the rose had given place to the inward curves of the lily — nay, hardly all that; for as she had never had the full red queenliness of the one, neither had she now the severe sanctitude of the other, that soft glow of inquiry, at once so blithe and so self-contained, so modest and so courageous, humble, yet free, still played about her saddened eyes and in her tones. Through the glistening sadness of those eyes smiled resignation; and although the Doctor plainly read care about them and about the mouth, it was a care that was forbearing to feed upon itself, or to take its seat on her brow. The brow was the old one; that is, the young. The joy of life's morning was gone from it forever; but a chastened hope was there, and one could see peace hovering just above it, as though it might in time alight. Such were the things that divided her austere friend's attention as she sat before him, seeking, with timid smiles and interrogative argument, for this new beginning of life some heartiness of approval from him.

"Doctor," she plucked up courage to say at last, with a geniality that scantily hid the inner distress, "you don't seem pleased."

"I can't say I am, Mary. You've provided for things in sight; but I see no provision for unseen contingencies. They're sure to come, you know. How are you going to meet them?"

"Well," said Mary, with slow, smiling caution, "there's my two thousand dollars that you've put at interest for me.'

"Why, no; you've already counted the interest on that as part of your necessary income."

"Doctor, 'the Lord will provide,' will he not?"

"No."

"Why, Doctor!" —

"No, Mary; you've got to provide. He's not going to set aside the laws of nature to cover our improvidence. That would be to break faith with all creation for the sake of one or two creatures."

"No; but still, Doctor, without breaking the laws of nature, he will provide. It's in his word."

"Yes, and it ought to be in his word — not in ours. It's for him to say to us, not for us to say to him. But there's another thing, Mary."

"Yes, sir."

"It's this. But first I'll say plainly you've passed through the fires of poverty, and they haven't hurt you. You have one of those imperishable natures that fire can't stain or warp."

"O Doctor, how absurd!" said Mary, with bright genuineness, and a tear in either eye. She drew Alice closer.

"Well, then, I do see two ill effects," replied the Doctor. "In the first place, as I've just tried to show you, you have caught a little of the *recklessness* of the poor."

"I was born with it," exclaimed Mary, with amusement.

"Maybe so," replied her friend; "at any rate you show it." He was silent.

"But what is the other?" asked Mary.

"Why, as to that, I may mistake; but — you seem inclined to settle down and be satisfied with poverty."

"Having food and raiment," said Mary, smiling with some archness, "to be therewith content."

"Yes, but" — the physician shook his head — "that doesn't mean to be satisfied. It's one thing to be content with God's providence, and it's another to be satisfied with poverty. There's not one in a thousand that I'd venture to say it to. He wouldn't understand the fine difference. But you will. I'm sure you do."

"Yes, I do."

"I know you do. You know poverty has its temptations, and warping influences, and debasing effects, just as truly as riches have. See how it narrows our usefulness. Not always, it is true. Sometimes our best usefulness keeps us poor. That's poverty with a good excuse. But that's not poverty satisfying, Mary" —

"No, of course not," said Mary, exhibiting a degree of distress that the Doctor somehow overlooked.

"It's merely," said he, half-extending his open palm, — "it's merely poverty accepted, as a good soldier accepts the dust and smut that are a necessary part of the battle. Now, here's this little girl." — As his open white hand pointed toward Alice she shrank back; but the Doctor seemed blind this afternoon and drove on. — "In a few years — it will not seem like any time at all — she'll be half grown up; she'll have wants that ought to be supplied."

"Oh! don't," exclaimed Mary, and burst into a flood of tears; and the Doctor, while she hid them from her child, sat silently loathing his own stupidity.

"Please, don't mind it," said Mary, stanching the flow. "You were not so badly mistaken. I wasn't satisfied, but I was about to surrender." She smiled at herself and her warlike figure of speech.

He looked away, passed his hand across his forehead and must have muttered audibly his self-reproach; for

Mary looked up again with a faint gleam of the old radiance in her face, saying : —

" I'm glad you didn't let me do it. I'll not do it. I'll take up the struggle again. Indeed, I had already thought of one thing I could do, but I — I — in fact, Doctor, I thought you might not like it."

" What was it ? "

" It was teaching in the public schools. They're in the hands of the military government, I am told. Are they not ? "

" Yes."

" Still," said Mary, speaking rapidly, " I say I'll keep up the " —

But the Doctor lifted his hand.

" No, no. There's to be no more struggle."

" No ? " Mary tried to look pleasantly incredulous.

" No ; and you're not going to be put upon anybody's bounty, either. No. What I was going to say about this little girl here was this, — her name is Alice, is it ? "

" Yes."

The mother dropped an arm around the child, and both she and Alice looked timidly at the questioner.

" Well, by that name, Mary, I claim the care of her."

The color mounted to Mary's brows, but the Doctor raised a finger.

" I mean, of course, Mary, only in so far as such care can go without molesting your perfect motherhood, and all its offices and pleasures."

Her eyes filled again, and her lips parted ; but the Doctor was not going to let her reply.

" Don't try to debate it, Mary. You must see you have no case. Nobody's going to take her from you, nor do any other of the foolish things, I hope, that are so often done in such cases. But you've called her

Alice, and Alice she must be. I don't propose to take care of her for you" —

"Oh, no; of course not," interjected Mary.

"No," said the Doctor; "you'll take care of her for me. I intended it from the first. And that brings up another point. You mustn't teach school. No. I have something else — something better — to suggest. Mary, you and John have been a kind of blessing to me" —

She would have interrupted with expressions of astonishment and dissent, but he would not hear them.

"I think I ought to know best about that," he said. "Your husband taught me a great deal, I think. I want to put some of it into practice. We had a — an understanding, you might say — one day toward the — end — that I should do for him some of the things he had so longed and hoped to do — for the poor and the unfortunate."

"I know," said Mary, the tears dropping down her face.

"He told you?" asked the Doctor.

She nodded.

"Well," resumed the Doctor, "those may not be his words precisely, but it's what they meant to me. And I said I'd do it. But I shall need assistance. I'm a medical practitioner. I attend the sick. But I see a great deal of other sorts of sufferers; and I can't stop for them."

"Certainly not," said Mary, softly.

"No," said he; "I can't make the inquiries and investigations about them and study them, and all that kind of thing, as one should if one's help is going to be help. I can't turn aside for all that. A man must have one direction, you know. But you could look after those things" —

"I?"

"Certainly. You could do it just as I — just as

John — would wish to see it done. You're just the kind of person to do it right."

"O Doctor, don't say so! I'm not fitted for it at all."

"I'm sure you are, Mary. You're fitted by character and outward disposition, and by experience. You're full of cheer" —

She tearfully shook her head. But he insisted.

"You will be — for *his* sake, as you once said to me. Don't you remember?"

She remembered. She recalled all he wished her to: the prayer she had made that, whenever death should part her husband and her, he might not be the one left behind. Yes, she remembered; and the Doctor spoke again : —

"Now, I invite you to make this your principal business. I'll pay you for it, regularly and well, what I think it's worth; and it's worth no trifle. There's not one in a thousand that I'd trust to do it, woman or man ; but I know you will do it all, and do it well, without any nonsense. And if you want to look at it so, Mary, you can just consider that it's John doing it, all the time ; for, in fact, that's just what it is. It beats sewing, Mary, or teaching school, or making preserves, I think."

"Yes," said Mary, looking down on Alice, and stroking her head.

"You can stay right here where you are, with Madame Zénobie, as you had planned ; but you'll give yourself to this better work. I'll give you a *carte blanche*. Only one mistake I charge you not to make ; don't go and come from day to day on the assumption that only the poor are poor, and need counsel and attention."

"I know that would be a mistake," said Mary.

"But I mean more than that," continued the Doctor.

" You must keep a hold on the rich and comfortable and happy. You want to be a medium between the two, identified with both as completely as possible. It's a hard task, Mary. It will take all your cunning."

" And more, too," replied she, half-musing.

" You know," said the Doctor, " I'm not to appear in the matter, of course ; I'm not to be mentioned : that must be one of the conditions."

Mary smiled at him through her welling eyes.

" I'm not fit to do it," she said, folding the wet spots of her handkerchief under. "But still, I'd rather not refuse. If I might try it, I'd like to do so. If I could do it well, it would be a finer monument — to *him* " —

" Than brass or marble," said Dr. Sevier. " Yes, more to his liking."

" Well," said Mary again, " if you think I can do it I'll try it."

" Very well. There's one place you can go to, to begin with, to-morrow morning, if you choose. I'll give you the number. It's just across here in Casa Calvo street."

" Narcisse's aunt ? " asked Mary, with a soft gleam of amusement.

" Yes. Have you been there already ?

She had ; but she only said : —

" There's one thing that I'm afraid will go against me, Doctor, almost everywhere." She lifted a timid look.

The Doctor looked at her inquiringly, and in his private thought said that it was certainly not her face or voice.

" Ah ! " he said, as he suddenly recollected. " Yes ; I had forgotten. You mean your being a Union woman."

" Yes. It seems to me they'll be sure to find it out Don't you think it will interfere ? "

The Doctor mused

" I forgot that," he repeated, and mused again. " You can't blame us, Mary; we're at white heat "—

" Indeed I don't ! " said Mary, with eager earnestness. He reflected yet again.

" But — I don't know, either. It may be not as great a drawback as you think. Here's Madame Zénobie, for instance " —

Madame Zénobie was just coming up the front steps from the garden, pulling herself up upon the veranda wearily by the balustrade. She came forward, and, with graceful acknowledgment, accepted the physician's out-stretched hand and courtesied.

" Here's Madame Zénobie, I say; you seem to get along with her."

Mary smiled again, looked up at the standing quadroon, and replied in a low voice : —

" Madame Zénobie is for the Union herself."

" Ah! no-o-o ! " exclaimed the good woman, with an alarmed face. She lifted her shoulders and ex-tended what Narcisse would have called the han' of rep-u-diation ; then turned away her face, lifted up her underlip with disrelish, and asked the surrounding atmosphere, — " What I got to do wid Union? Nuttin' do wid Union — nuttin' do wid Confédéracie ! " She moved away, addressing the garden and the house by turns. " Ah! no ! " She went in by the front door, talking Creole French, until she was beyond hearing.

Dr. Sevier reached out toward the child at Mary's knee. Here was one who was neither for nor against, nor yet a fear-constrained neutral. Mary pushed her persuasively toward the Doctor, and Alice let herself be lifted to his lap.

" I used to be for it myself," he said, little dreaming he would one day be for it again. As the child sank back into his arm, he noticed a miniature of her father hanging from her neck. He took it into his fingers, and all were silent while he looked long upon the face.

By and by he asked Mary for an account of her wanderings. She gave it. Many of the experiences, that had been hard and dangerous enough when she was passing through them, were full of drollery when they came to be told, and there was much quiet amusement over them. The sunlight faded out, the cicadas hushed their long-drawn, ear-splitting strains, and the moon had begun to shine in the shadowy garden when Dr. Sevier at length let Alice down and rose to take his lonely homeward way, leaving Mary to Alice's prattle, and, when that was hushed in slumber, to gentle tears and whispered thanksgivings above the little head.

CHAPTER LX.

" YET SHALL HE LIVE."

WE need not follow Mary through her ministrations. Her office was no sinecure. It took not only much labor, but, as the Doctor had expected, it took all her cunning. True, nature and experience had equipped her for such work; but for all that there was an art to be learned, and time and again there were cases of mental and moral decrepitude or deformity that baffled all her skill until her skill grew up to them, which in some cases it never did. The greatest tax of all was to seem, and to be, unprofessional; to avoid regarding her work in quantity, and to be simply, merely, in every case, a personal friend; not to become known as a benevolent itinerary, but only a kind and thoughtful neighbor. Blessed word! not benefactor — neighbor!

She had no schemes for helping the unfortunate by multitude. Possibly on that account her usefulness was less than it might have been. But I am not sure; for they say her actual words and deeds were but the seed of ultimate harvests; and that others, moreover, seeing her light shine so brightly along this seemingly narrow path, and moved to imitate her, took that other and broader way, and so both fields were reaped.

But, I say, we need not follow her steps. They would lead deviously through ill-smelling military hospitals, and into buildings that had once been the counting-rooms of Carondelet-street cotton merchants, but were now De-come the prisons of soldiers in gray. One of these places, restored after the war as a cotton factor's counting-room again, had, until a few years ago, a queer, clumsy patch in the plastering of one wall, near the base-board. Some one had made a rough inscription on it with a cotton sampler's marking-brush. It commemorates an incident. Mary by some means became aware beforehand that this incident was going to occur; and one of the most trying struggles of conscience she ever had in her life was that in which she debated with herself one whole night whether she ought to give her knowledge to others or keep it to herself. She kept it. In fact, she said nothing until the war was all over and done, and she never was quite sure whether her silence was right or wrong. And when she asked Dr. Sevier if he thought she had done wrong, he asked : —

"You knew it was going to take place, and kept silence?"

"Yes," said Mary.

"And you want to know whether you did right?"

"Yes. I'd like to know what you think."

He sat very straight, and said not a word, nor changed a line of his face. She got no answer at all.

The inscription was as follows; I used to see it every work-day of the week for years — it may be there yet — 190 Common street, first flight, back office : —

But we move too fast.   Let us go back into the war for
a moment longer.   Mary pursued her calling.   The most
of it she succeeded in doing in a very sunshiny way.
She carried with her, and left behind her, cheer, courage,
hope.   Yet she had a widow's heart, and whenever she
took a widow's hand in hers, and oftentimes, alone or
against her sleeping child's bedside, she had a widow's
tears.   But this work, or these works, — she made each
particular ministration seem as if it were the only one, —
these works, that she might never have had the opportunity to perform had her nest-mate never been taken from
her, seemed to keep John near.   Almost, sometimes, he
seemed to walk at her side in her errands of mercy, or to
spread above her the arms of benediction.   And so even
the bitter was sweet, and she came to believe that never
before had widow such blessed commutation.

One day, a short, slight Confederate prisoner, newly
brought in, and hobbling about the place where he was
confined, with a vile bullet-hole in his foot, came up to
her and said : —

"Allow me, madam, — did that man call you by your
right name, just now?"

Mary looked at him.   She had never seen him before.

"Yes, sir," she said.

She could see the gentleman, under much rags and
dirt.

"Are you Mrs. John Richling?"

A look of dismay came into his face as he asked the
grave question.

"Yes, sir," replied Mary.

His voice dropped, and he asked, with subdued haste : —

"Ith it pothible you're in mourning for him?"

She nodded.

It was the little rector.   He had somehow got it into

his head that preachers ought to fight, and this was one of the results. Mary went away quickly, and told Dr Sevier. The Doctor went to the commanding general. It was a great humiliation to do so, he thought. There was none worse, those days, in the eyes of the people. He craved and got the little man's release on parole. A fortnight later, as Dr. Sevier was sitting at the breakfast table, with the little rector at its opposite end, he all at once rose to his full attenuated height, with a frown and then a smile, and, tumbling the chair backward behind him, exclaimed : —

" Why, Laura!" — for it was that one of his two gay young nieces who stood in the door-way. The banker's wife followed in just behind, and was presently saying, with the prettiest heartiness, that Dr. Sevier looked no older than the day they met the Florida general at dinner years before. She had just come in from the Confederacy, smuggling her son of eighteen back to the city, to save him from the conscript officers, and Laura had come with her. And when the clergyman got his crutches into his armpits and stood on one foot, and he and Laura both blushed as they shook hands, the Doctor knew that she had come to nurse her wounded lover. That she might do this without embarrassment, they got married, and were thereupon as vexed with themselves as they could be under the circumstances that they had not done it four or five years before. Of course there was no parade ; but Dr. Sevier gave a neat little dinner. Mary and Laura were its designers ; Madame Zénobie was the master-builder and made the gumbo. One word about the war, whose smoke was over all the land, would have spoiled the broth. But no such word was spoken.

It happened that the company was almost the same as that which had sat down in brighter days to that other din ner, which the banker's wife recalled with so much pleasure. She and her husband and son were guests; also that Sister Jane, of whom they had talked, a woman of real goodness and rather unrelieved sweetness; also her sister and bankrupted brother-in-law. The brother-in-law mentioned several persons who, he said, once used to be very cordial to him and his wife, but now did not remember them; and his wife chid him, with the air of a fellow-martyr; but they could not spoil the tender gladness of the occasion.

"Well, Doctor," said the banker's wife, looking quite the old lady now, "I suppose your lonely days are over, now that Laura and her husband are to keep house for you."

"Yes," said the Doctor.

But the very thought of it made him more lonely than ever.

"It's a very pleasant and sensible arrangement," said the lady, looking very practical and confidential; "Laura has told me all about it. It's just the thing for them and for you."

"I think so, ma'am," replied Dr. Sevier, and tried to make his statement good.

"I'm sure of it," said the lady, very sweetly and gayly, and made a faint time-to-go beckon with a fan to her husband, to whom, in the farther drawing-room, Laura and Mary stood talking, each with an arm about the other's waist.

CHAPTER LXI.

PEACE.

IT came with tears. But, ah! it lifted such an awful
load from the hearts even of those who loved the lost
cause. Husbands snatched their wives once more to their
bosoms, and the dear, brave, swarthy, rough-bearded,
gray-jacketed boys were caught again in the wild arms of
mothers and sisters. Everywhere there was glad, tearful
kissing. Everywhere? Alas for the silent lips that remained unkissed, and the arms that remained empty!
And alas for those to whom peace came too suddenly
and too soon! Poor Narcisse!

His salary still continues. So does his aunt.

The Ristofalos came back all together. How delighted
Mrs. Colonel Ristofalo — I say Mrs. *Colonel* Ristofalo —
was to see Mary! And how impossible it was, when they
sat down together for a long talk, to avoid every moment
coming back to the one subject of "him."

"Yes, ye see, there bees thim as is *called* col-o-nels,
whin in fact they bees only *liftinent* col-o-nels. Yes.
But it's not so wid him. And he's no different from the
plain Raphael Ristofalah of eight year ago — the same
perfict gintleman that he was when he sold b'iled eggs!"

And the colonel's "lady" smiled a gay triumph that
gave Mary a new affection for her.

Sister Jane bowed to the rod of an inscrutable
Providence. She could not understand how the Confederacy could fail, and justice still be justice; so, without

understanding, she left it all to Heaven, and clung to her faith. Her brother-in-law never recovered his fortunes nor his sweetness. He could not bend his neck to the conqueror's yoke; he went in search of liberty to Brazil —or was it Honduras? Little matter which, now, for he died there, both he and his wife, just as their faces were turning again homeward, and it was dawning upon them once more that there is no land like Dixie in all the wide world over.

The little rector —thanks, he says, to the skill of Dr. Sevier! —recovered perfectly the use of his mangled foot, so that he even loves long walks. I was out walking with him one sunset hour in the autumn of — if I remember aright—1870, when whom should we spy but our good Kate Ristofalo, out driving in her family carriage? The cherubs were beside her,— strong, handsome boys. Mike held the reins; he was but thirteen, but he looked full three years better than that, and had evidently employed the best tailor in St. Charles street to fit his rather noticeable clothes. His mother had changed her mind about his being a bruiser, though there isn't a doubt he had a Derringer in one or another of his pockets. No, she was proposing to make him a doctor — "a surgeon," she said; "and thin, if there bees another war "— She was for making every edge cut.

She did us the honor to stop the carriage, and drive up to the curb-stone for a little chat. Her spirits were up, for Colonel Ristofalo had just been made a city councilman by a rousing majority.

We expressed our regret not to see Raphael himself in the family group enjoying the exquisite air.

"Ha, ha! He ride out for pleasure?"—And then, with sudden gravity,— "Aw, naw, sur! He's too busy. Much use ut is to be married to a public man! Ah! surs,

I'm mighty tired of ut, now I tell ye!" Yet she laughed again, without betraying much fatigue. "And how's Dr. Sevier?"

"He's well," said the clergyman.

"And Mrs. Richling?"

"She's well, too."

Kate looked at the little rector out of the corners of her roguish Irish eyes, a killing look, and said: —

"Ye're sure the both o' thim bees well?"

"Yes, quite well," replied he, ignoring the inane effort at jest. She nodded a blithe good-day, and rolled on toward the lake, happy as the harvest weather, and with a kind heart for all the world. We walked on, and after the walk I dined with the rector. Dr. Sevier's place was vacant, and we talked of him. The prettiest piece of furniture in the dining-room was an extremely handsome child's high chair that remained, unused, against the wall. It was Alice's, and Alice was an almost daily visitor. It had come in almost simultaneously with Laura's marriage, and more and more frequently, as time had passed, the waiter had set it up to the table, at the Doctor's right hand, and lifted Goldenhair into it, until by and by she had totally outgrown it. But she had not grown out of the place of favor at the table. In these later days she had become quite a school-girl, and the Doctor, in his place at the table, would often sit with a faint, continuous smile on his face that no one could bring there but her, to hear her prattle about Madame Locquet, and the various girls at Madame Locquet's school.

"It's actually pathetic," said Laura, as we sat sipping our coffee after the meal, "to see how he idolizes that child." Alice had just left the room.

"Why don't he idolize the child's" — began her husband, in undertone, and did not have to finish to make us understand.

"He does," murmured the smiling wife.

"Then why shouldn't he tell her so?"

"My dear!" objected the wife, very softly and prettily.

"I don't mean to speak lightly," responded the husband, "but — they love each other; they suit each other; they complete each other; they don't feel their disparity of years; they're both so linked to Alice that it would break either heart over again to be separated from her. I don't see why" —

Laura shook her head, smiling in the gentle way that only the happy wives of good men have.

"It will never be."

What changes!

"The years creep slowly by" —

We seem to hear the old song yet. What changes! Laura has put two more leaves into her dining-table. Children fill three seats. Alice has another. It is she, now, not her chair, that is tall — and fair. Mary, too, has a seat at the same board. This is their home now. Her hair is turning all to silver. So early? Yes; but she is — she never was — so beautiful! They all see it — feel it; Dr. Sevier — the gentle, kind, straight old Doctor — most of all. And oh! when they two, who have never joined hands on this earth, go to meet John and Alice, — which God grant may be at one and the same time, — what weeping there will be among God's poor!

THE END.